BEYO
LIGHT

WOODROW MCKANE

To Zoe,
Thankyou for your Support
Kind regards
Woodrow McKane

Beyond the Light
Woodrow McKane

First published in paperback in the UK in 2023.

The right of Woodrow McKane to be identified as the Author of this work has been asserted by him in accordance with the Copyright, Designs and Patents Act 1988.

This novel is a work of fiction. Names and characters are the product of the author's imagination and any resemblance to actual persons, living or dead, is entirely coincidental.

All rights reserved. Apart from any use permitted under UK copyright law no part of this publication may be reproduced, stored in a retrieval system, or transmitted, in any form or by any means, without the prior written permission of the publisher, nor be otherwise circulated in any form of binding or cover other than that in which it is published and without a similar condition being imposed on the subsequent purchaser.

© 2023 Woodrow McKane

Bio

Woodrow McKane.

Martial arts instructor, and an outdoor kinda guy. Convivial company around a campfire, and practising wild camper. Most certainly a pal to all dogs. That's me in a nutshell.

Writing a novel is akin to any other task.
Begin, then continue.

In loving memory of Ronnie and Rita McDowell
my parents, to whom I am eternally grateful.

Enjoy

Prologue

The year 1712 saw a population growth of one in the town of Wick, located in the East Highlands of Scotland, all thanks to the birth of a baby boy. Despite the child's hearing and speech impairment, his parents treated him no differently than any other child. However, the morning of his third birthday was a peculiar occasion, as he inexplicably carved the Latin words Mortis Lux (light of death) into the parish church door, leaving everyone in shock and confusion.

Claims from the locals emerged early the next morning that William had entered their dreams, instilling a sense of the devil's presence. Fuelled by both concern and anger, a mob assembled at the church with the sole purpose of demanding a response from their pastor. After carefully weighing his options, he ultimately agreed to perform an exorcism, providing all violent behaviour ceased. Pact agreed. He began his trek to the croft of the shepherd Gregor Cranson.

Some two hours later, he returned to the church and rung the bell. Once the village folk had gathered, he declared the following.

The Cranson family will now live on the Isle of Scarth. As part of our agreement, they promised that the boy, William, would never step foot on the mainland again. In addition, we have banned any visits to the Isle. Punishment, as set by the church, will be inflicted on those who disobey this rule.

That his actions appeared to placate the majority. The pastor gave a sigh of relief and watched the mumbling crowd disperse. After closing the church doors, he faced a distraught wife, demanding an explanation. The pastor briefly closed his eyes before beginning.

On approaching their croft, the front door opened and out stepped young William. His facial expression showed that he wanted to say something, but then he shut his eyes. When he spoke the words Mortis Lux, a vision appeared that was so intense that it has become etched into my brain. This vision must remain in my mind only, so I implore you never to

discuss this conversation with anyone else. For the next few weeks, I will commit to prayer. Nothing else matters.
One month later, he and his wife would leave the village, never to return.

After moving to the Isle, William began sleeping for close to twenty hours each day. Despite this, the Cranson family remained faithful to their promise and lived on the Isle peacefully.

Upon William's nineteenth birthday, it was found that he was writing while asleep, which led to his family burning all of his written materials. He died mysteriously two weeks before his twenty-first birthday, after being in a sleep that lasted for twenty-six days. According to legend, he hid one book, *The Last Book*, and today its whereabouts are still unknown.

Many centuries would pass until the Latin words Mortis Lux reappeared.

One

Current day, 2 p.m. The Isle of Scarth, home of the Cranson family.

Professor Arlo Norton and Doctor Walter Massam, having converted a bedroom into a provisional operating theatre, peered down on their patient, seventeen-year-old Bran Cranson with apprehension.

In a state of severe anxiety, Arlo addressed the boy's parents, Ross, and Isla.

'Since the commencement of this journey, his brain activity has now reached its pinnacle. No matter how things develop from this moment, we must not interfere!'

One minute later, Bran stopped breathing. In seconds, the heart monitor registered a mind-numbing tone as he flatlined!

With Isla moving to reach her son, Dr Massam instinctively stepped forward to prevent her.

'We strongly advise that you do not intervene as it would endanger his life.'

Isla's voice filled with distress as she screamed out, 'For God's sake, he's flatlined!'

Ross stared intently at Arlo, looking at him with an unwavering gaze. 'Tell me our son will not die!'

'It would be a lie to say, I'm positive, but as it stands, he is trying to confront circumstances that are too complex for us to comprehend. Any interference with his physical form will only result in one end - his death!'

As Isla's tears flowed, Ross, despite his own pain, bit down and provided the best comfort he could for his wife. With the monitor continuing to flatline, Arlo turned pale.

'We must wait...'

Two

One month earlier.

Every parent's dream would be to have a child genius, unless you lived on the Isle of Scarth, and your name was Cranson. Centuries had not changed the stigma attached to the Cranson bloodline since the time of *Devil Will.*

Aged six, Bran sat and passed exams to begin his education at Wick High School. Five years later, he gained a sponsorship, together with admission, into Robert Gordon University. At twelve, National Geographic ran an interview, as his learning capacity had outstripped all records. When aged sixteen, he refused to sit all academic examinations. No matter what repercussions followed, he had no desire to follow a path of learning trodden by many. After heated discussions with his father, he agreed to stay another year, providing the governing bodies did not push the issue of examinations.

However, his life began a new era when, just after his seventeenth birthday on a Monday morning, he marched boldly into the principal's office, towelling down after a 10k run. At six feet, he had forged an athletic physique that many a bully had experienced in the guise of his fists. A career as a pro boxer would certainly have merit.

'Professor Watkins, thank you for my time at the university. However, as of today, I no longer wish to be a student and will return home to continue study. My decision is final.'

Watkins responded tersely. 'I see. Your parents, are they aware?'

'No, but they will agree, of that I'm certain. I've booked a taxi, said my adieux, and would be obliged if you would call my uncle, Jim McTay, so he may meet me at Wick quayside.'

Watkins tutted. 'While I admire your undeniable conviction, the decision rests with your parents. For now, return to your studies, and then I'll call them.'

Bran shrugged, then moved to a seat. 'Unless you intend to force me, I'll wait in your office until you have made contact.'

That Bran had inherited his father's combative readiness, Watkins relented.

'Very well, master Cranson – on one condition.'

‘Aye, if my parents decline my request, I return to my studies?’

Watkins nodded. ‘I think that’s a fair deal. Shake on it?’

‘No need.’

Exhaling, Watkins dialled Ross Cranson’s satellite phone, whose reply revealed a hint of anxiety.

‘Problem with our Bran?’

‘Packed and booked a taxi home, Master Cranson has decided he no longer wishes to be educated at our facility.’

‘Where is he now?’

‘Right next to me.’

‘Put him on.’

A quick but sharp encounter between the two loomed. Watkins passed the phone.

Bran looked rather curtly at Watkins.

‘If I may speak alone?’

Watkins nodded abruptly. ‘I’ll be outside.’

Bran gave no reply, leaving Watkins annoyed as he left the office.

‘Dad?’

‘What’s this about?’

Bran took a breath before speaking.

‘My unwillingness to conform to educational ideals was a low point in our relationship. If you recall, I promised to sit for an additional year. After which, I could make my decision on returning home. Today is that day.’

Ross’s stomach churned over.

‘Trust me, your mother and I have awaited this day from the minute you left. But are you absolutely certain?’

‘Yes, without a doubt.’

‘Okay then, put the principal back on.’

With his parents having lost much of his childhood to education, his father’s words confirmed he belonged on the Isle.

Without fuss or negotiation, Ross approved Bran’s decision. Watkins, although a little concerned, would not create waves, as having such a gifted student was a feather in the university’s cap. Call closed, Watkins turned to Bran.

‘As our brightest student, it has been an honour to have you attend our university. Our doors remain open for your return.’

Bran flushed.

'Professor, Robert Gordon would be my choice if the clocks were to be rolled back.'

With a respectful nod, they shook hands.

After a last goodbye, Bran walked to a library and opened a "Skype call" to his girlfriend and confidant Christie McCall. Christie, a mathematical prodigy and talented artist, held an uncanny similarity to the Harry Potter character, Hermione Granger. Photophobia, a symptom of light intolerance, had forced her to wear sunglasses from an early age, resulting in a regime of bullying during her school life. Within a few days of her arrival at Robert Gordon, the two clicked. Bran's fists proved to be an excellent deterrent for any further bullying.

Three months earlier, Christie had elected to be with her father, who suffered from a terminal illness. Since being apart, the couple had conversed on Skype every day. The current conversation lasted for twenty minutes, to which Bran's parting words of, *"Life or death, whichever is to be my fate, always trust my word forever",* troubled Christie. On asking why, Bran blew a kiss and closed the call.

Thirty minutes later, the university warden became tasked with driving Bran to the moorings in Wick, after which the principal made a lengthy phone call.

Seven hours later, after the family had celebrated their reunion in full Scottish style, Bran was first to bed.

Downstairs Ross, a typical rugged Scotsman, embraced his wife. 'I know what you're thinking, but let's not overreact.'

Nervously running her fingers through her flaming red hair, Isla gazed at an aged oak cupboard situated left of the fireplace.

She sighed. 'I have a bad – bad feeling about this!'

The following morning at 8 a.m., Bran woke to a frenetic greeting from the family's three-year-old, fifty-two kg, Giant Schnauzer, Loki. After hectic play – breakfast.

At the table, Ross began the *interrogation*, using hand signs. A tradition passed down through the generations to soften arguments.

'Plans?'

Bran shrugged. 'I need family time.'

'Then finish brekkie lad and start your day – you have a fortnight before you have to earn your keep.'

'Deal!'

Ten minutes later, Bran, tagged by Loki, bolted from the house to his cherished *den*, an outhouse converted many years ago.

Inside the house, Isla had embraced Ross.

'Something just isn't right.'

'Agreed.'

Their hug tightened just a little.

As Bran stepped into the den, he broke down. Loki nudged in close. With his parent's anguish regarding their ancestral genes, he had concealed the details of his recent experiences.

Over the last few weeks, his dreams had become as real as waking, to the point he was finding it difficult to decipher between the two. More concerning was the fact that whilst falling to sleep, he was experiencing a wave of grey, spectre-like faces that shimmered up to his closed eyes before disappearing. With each passing day, the horrific spectres had increased in number. How or why they appeared was a complete mystery. Only last night he counted fifty-one before he fell into sleep. Their existence terrified him. That William had died during similar sleeping patterns was now all-consuming.

I need sleep to discover why this is happening. But I fear this will raise issues with my parents.

After a few moments, Bran smiled. 'Intelligence is not always a burden.'

That night, over supper, he set his plans.

'I still have the desire to study – can we ask the University to install a satellite feed, with two laptops, one for the house and one for my den? Oh, and don't concern, they'll cover the charges as it's in their interests.'

Ross, relieved that Bran appeared to be acting *normal*, nodded his agreement. 'I'll speak to the principal first thing.'

Bran clapped. 'Excellent... now an early night for me as I'm reading a topic regarding cell and molecular biology.'

Both parents shrugged their acknowledgement of his declaration before laughing. After loving goodnights, Bran moved to his room.

Downstairs, Ross poured two glasses of red wine.

'Mrs C... another day of normality.'

Isla formed a wry smile. Ross's turn to gaze towards the old oak cupboard.

Upstairs, Bran's inner turmoil began. Fear of death during slumber made it problematic when closing his eyes, let alone sleep. It would take over an hour before fatigue kicked in. The grey spectres began their haunting, each expressing a tormented rage before evaporating. Counting helped keep his sanity. For the next few minutes, seventy-two of the most hideous apparitions approached his closed eyes, then faded as he fell into a deep slumber. After being gently nudged by Loki's snout the next morning, Bran felt relieved to still be alive. As the dog bounded onto the bed, he couldn't help but smile at how little space he now had.

'Hell, I've missed you.'

Another nudge from the wet snout led to belly tickles. On recalling last night's dream, he remembered talking to an Amazonian elder whose knowledge of jungle fauna was extraordinary. The fact he could now compile a full dissertation on the subject was exciting. With eyes closed, he visualised his procedure for sleep. The fact he had no memory of passing into slumber agitated him.

Remarkable, but I doubt if anybody can pinpoint the moment sleep occurs. Weird, but why?

A shout of *breakfast* broke his thoughts. Never mind Michelin stars. Mum's cooking is by far the best! His apology to Loki for moving prompted a wagging tail and a dismount from the bed that shook the house.

The installation of two new laptops linked to the internet via a satellite connection boosted morale. Five days later, he emailed a twenty-thousand-word article of the unique flora found along the banks of the Amazon to the University. The principal contacted National Geographic to present one of the most precise papers ever written on the subject.

Bran then turned his attention to building a website promoting the Isle's four holiday cottages, of which three had generators, whilst the fourth he advertised as *natural.* Parents happy, university satisfied, he could now begin a study of his own...

A hand-wound alarm clock ticked to 10 a.m. With supplies of sandwiches and drinks, he would remain undisturbed, to peruse over books that filled every space possible. All were non-fiction.

Ridiculous distortions affect everyone's dreams, unlike mine, which are reality. The only information that is remotely helpful is a piece on lucid dreams. Therefore, I have to uncover my own answers.

A custom-made bed, fitted into one corner, offered a nap. The sequence that followed had become exact. Eyes closed, he gazed into the blackness. The first grey shape appeared. Its hideous face remained for an instant before its agonised demise. Another materialised, then another, dissolving in succession. Detesting the experience, he opened his eyes to gather a little composure, before returning to the morbid spectres. One hundred and three appeared before the entire scenario changed to colour. The scene now depicted a wooden sailing vessel battling against a raging, tempestuous sea. Forcing his eyes to look deeper, he found himself aboard a three-masted Spanish Carrack in the grip of a raging hurricane. He gasped as an enormous wave broke over her bows, drenching him in freezing waters. Another wave, this time much larger, rocked the vessel, almost sweeping Bran overboard. With both hands now gripping the starboard side, he gazed at the brave men fighting to save the vessel. One man, having strapped himself to a mast, screamed desperate commands in a Spanish dialect Bran did not recognise.

The captain?

Another massive wave crashed over the deck, flinging screaming men into the raging sea and smashing Bran against the bow. The impact should have hurt. As the water subsided, the ocean had taken all but the captain. Helpless, Bran watched on as the man loosened his bindings, then forced himself upright. The captain's hopeless cries were his ultimate act of defiance against another wave. As the unforgiving sea began its claim on the stricken ship, Bran felt himself being dragged under and so withdrew from his dream. His last vision was of the vessel's plate on the wheelhouse door – 'El Dorado-1502'. His waking differed from the shock that preceded a nightmare. No jolt, no shout, just a vivid and exact recall of the event. The realism of what had happened questioned his sanity.

I was there? But how could I? Or is this my dream right now?

Jumping out of bed, he ran to the window to look for normality. The chill of the Isle helped.

I am awake..., and that was a dream. I must settle and work this out.

An anxious Google search of "El Dorado 1502" sent a shiver down his spine.

July 11th, 1502, The El Dorado, Spanish Flagship of a fleet of thirty-two, with a contingent of eight-hundred men, left Hispaniola Isle bound for Spain. She carried the former governor of the Isle, Francisco de Bobadillo, who ignored the warning signs of an impending hurricane. The ship sank in the Mona Channel between Puerto Rico and Hispaniola, leaving no survivors. In the same storm, sixteen other ships suffered the exact fate.

Disorientated, Bran closed the laptop.

Have I just witnessed the actual sinking? Or was it just another dream? Is this similar to what William experienced? Is this how he died – killed in a dream? My god, what the hell is happening?

Bran shivered, but not from the icy waters of the Mona Channel, but because there was no difference between being awake or dreaming.

My old dreams, like everyone's, were scatty, never making sense, and the clarity of recall was cloudy – but these are exact?

To confirm the *real* world, he rushed outside to be greeted by the welcoming voice of his father, bringing clarification to his state of mind.

'Long study today, son?'

Bran looked at his watch - 5 p.m..

Five? How is that possible? I was asleep for a few minutes.

'Err – yes dad, I'm shattered.'

'Come on then, let's get ready for our evening meal.'

'Okay – I've data to save to the cloud – a few mins.'

Ross's expression amplified his lack of understanding of the internet.

'The cloud?'

'One day I'll educate you.'

Now grinning, Ross turned and walked to the house whilst Bran returned to study the information regarding the El Dorado. Still confused, he drew a settling breath, then headed for the kitchen where Isla's smile suggested news.

'I've just had a phone call from the university. National Geographic is going to publish your latest work.' Isla looked at Ross. 'Our boy...'

Bran shrugged. 'Put any royalties into dad's boat fund.'

Both parents smiled. Their son's opinion of money? He didn't care for it!

The conversation continued, leaving Bran with a single thought.

My word if they only realised how I discovered the facts...

Three

Professor Arlo Norton, aged sixty-six, of medium build and height, checked his laptop, then made a phone call. Norton, the head of an ancient secret society with the insignia ¥, felt anxious.

In 888AD, following the tragic events surrounding an English mother named Ellenweorc Mendenhall and her mute daughter Adela, the society formed.

At three, Adela exhibited severe autistic traits, with a tendency to sleep for prolonged hours. With the ability to draw perfectly whilst asleep, the church, fearing possession, ordered her to be blessed, resulting in a seizure. Certain the devil was at work, the friar attempted to drown her. With the fury of a protective mother, Ellenweorc attacked. The subsequent struggle resulted in the friar's and her husband's death.

Ellenweorc fled with her remaining family and made their escape to Scotland. From that moment forward, she swore to protect any child showing similar behavioural patterns. The society had laid its seedling roots. Up to the present day, they had connected with ninety-six "gifted" children who became known as "Paragons". The insignia '¥' became the only reference to the secret society. In all cases, the unusual *autistic* traits of the Paragon raised issues within the religious communities. The facts were harrowing. Not one Paragon had survived past their twenty-first birthday. Thirty-five percent had died during a prolonged period of sleep. William Cranson set the longest recorded "death sleep" at twenty-six days. The average was sixteen.

The remaining sixty-five percent were burnt or drowned.

Although Paragons appeared to be gifted, all suffered the loss of at least one of the main five senses. Speech being the most common. In 1003, a blind female child born to a peasant family spoke fluently within a week of its life. The petrified townsfolk drowned the child, fearing she was the devil incarnate. In 1169, a set of twins, born without hearing, played several musical instruments perfectly when aged just two. Priests kidnapped both. Four years later, they died at precisely the same time. Over many centuries, the ¥ continued to locate and assist as best they could. Although they documented each individual, finding a link between loss of senses, and being gifted, proved to be difficult, as many years separated each discovery.

A minor breakthrough happened in 1603 when a French child named Sylvie Caillette penned enchanting novels at the tender age of three. Her parents became puzzled, being she was blind and wrote only during sleep.

The ¥ helped the family through a much-troubled period. The simple rouse of crediting the stories to her elder sister worked fine. Life became normal when she stopped writing aged sixteen.

Time moved on, until Sylvie took up the quill again, aged nineteen. Adamant she required privacy until completion, Sylvie locked herself away for several days. Work finished, the family, together with the local priest, gathered for a fireside reading. After ten minutes, the priest purported it to be the work of the devil.

Within hours, the church hauled the entire family to the local square and demanded Sylvie to be drowned as a witch. Men from the ¥ arrived, resulting in a brutal battle.

From this point onwards, the story becomes cloudy as fear, hearsay, and legend obliterated many of the verifiable facts.

Sylvie's writings had foretold astonishing details regarding life and death, but the church dismissed such talk and would punish anyone who discussed the work. Although the book vanished, its legend became the holy grail to the ¥. Four hundred and fifteen years would pass before another Paragon would write during sleep. Disappointingly, word of William did not reach the ¥ until after his death. As the family rejected any contact with the society, a covert search for his writings began. Their efforts continued until William's father, Gregor, killed a member for trespassing in his barn at nightfall. Concluding that the family had most likely destroyed *The Last Book, they ceased looking.* So, when a flagged search turned up an article about a gifted child on the Isle of Scarth, Professor Norton showed interest. Subsequent inquiries confirmed the boy had no sense defects and that his measured IQ was two hundred and four.

Norton had one thought.

Is this the Paragon we have waited an eternity for?

Four

8 p.m..

Bran watched Isla shut the window on a winters storm. The gentle closing felt like a jackhammer. The moment his mother left; his stomach churned. Sleep and the unnerving spectres would come. As he breathed the chilly air, one thought came to mind.

There will be a transition point from consciousness to sleep.

With trepidation, he peered through closed eyes. As face after face evaporated, Bran kept count. One hundred and seventeen appeared before he fell into slumber. Annoyed, he woke. Three hours had passed, which shocked.

That felt but only a minute.

As frayed nerves calmed, the process began again. However, instead of dissolving, there were now passing to somewhere he could not determine. Frustration set in as he lapsed into another dream. Bran woke himself once more to find almost four hours had elapsed.

Dream timescale differs from normal...? Then what is normal?

With eyes closing, Bran watched on as the morbid grey spectres passed across his view one by one before he drifted into a dream. This time the lure of sleep took over and in moments he began watching a full piece orchestra. Once awake, he compiled a concerto he named *The Garden Symphony*. The impossibility of the achievement subsided quickly, as he had just one question.

Where are the hideous spectres going...?

Five

Next morning, Bran rose early to cook. The normality of the chore helped convince him he was awake. As the aroma of a traditional Scottish breakfast drifted through the house, his parents woke.

Within fifteen minutes, the family were chatting at the table. At 7.30 a.m., an email notification pinged in from the house laptop. Bran smiled as both parents pulled expressions that showed a certain horror at having to interact with technology. Ross looked straight at Bran.

'I suppose you'd better show me how to work this thing.'

Their first email was a booking via the new website.

I am touring Scotland and by chance saw your web pages. With time to spare, I would love to visit the Isle. May I reserve Cliff Cottage for two weeks starting today? Also, because of a heart condition, my "long hike" days are well behind me. Do you have a vehicle/buggy I could rent for the duration?

I would appreciate a prompt reply.

Yours,

Professor Arlo Norton.

The Cranson's were ecstatic. As Ross one-fingered his way around the keyboard, Bran's satisfaction was plain to see.

Dear Professor.

Thank you for your enquiry and yes, "Cliff Cottage" is available. I also have a John Deer Gator. It's as old as the Isle but moves forward – no charge. If you would like to process payment from the links supplied, I will prepare the cottage for your visit. Included in your fee is a boat crossing at 2p.m. from Wick quayside by a Mr Jim McTay. We will meet you at our jetty should this be suitable.

The family waited anxiously for the reply.

Ten minutes later.

Payment processed many thanks; have added £100.00 for the use of the JD. See you at the jetty.

Professor Arlo Norton.

Cheers erupted. Financially, this would be the best March for years.

At 5.20 p.m., having accepted an invitation for an evening meal with the Cranson family, Professor Norton paused before knocking on their door. Nerves were not normally his suit.

Is this to be the boy that answers questions humanity has asked since the dawn of our beginning?

Norton took a deep breath before knocking. In moments, Isla opened the door with a beaming smile, matching her stunning display of red hair.

'Professor, pleased to meet you – Isla and Ross. Welcome to our home.'

'Thank you Isla, please, call me Arlo...'

'Our son, Bran, will be down shortly.' said Ross.

Nodding, Arlo took off his rucksack and produced a bottle of Malbec.

'I hope I have chosen well.'

Ross grinned. 'Red wine is acceptable for two apprentice drunkards.'

Isla tutted; Arlo laughed. 'Make that three.'

The men shook hands.

'Do follow Isla into the lounge. I'll fetch the glasses,' said Ross.

The roaring log fire triggered a serenity in Arlo. 'My word, your home is wonderful – makes you wonder why people choose to live in the city's hustle?'

Isla, beaming at the compliment, replied. 'Thank you, yes, we'd struggle to live amongst others.'

Ross poured. 'A toast to your stay.'

As the three clinked, Bran wandered in with Loki at his side, who gave Arlo a default air-sniff.

Ross placed his hand on Bran's shoulder. 'Arlo, don't concern, Loki won't bother you – this is our son Bran. The two of you should get along just fine being fellow intellects.' Bran elbowed his father.

'Pleased to meet you, professor. Your expertise?'

'History for my troubles – the big lad is a schnauzer?'

'Yes, a Giant, mums' best pal,' laughed Bran.

Isla shook her head. 'Giant pest more like! Too strong willed for me, but he's company for Bran.'

'History – the depth of our ancestry is always fascinating, but for the youth of today, it carries little interest,' said Bran.

'Indeed, and yourself?'

Ross set for the boast of the year. 'Bran is studying at Gordan's. He began aged eleven, not that he takes after his father.'

With a severe disdain for being placed on a pedestal, Bran interrupted. 'Forgive me, but can we forgo education for now? I'm rather hungry.'

With a highland stew flaunting its aroma, no one argued.

One hour later, Arlo beamed as he settled on the opposing side of a chessboard to Bran.

As the lights flickered, Ross stood up. 'I'll need to check on the generator. Err, the one at Cliff Cottage,' he smiled, 'is a tad unpredictable. Oh, and I'll have the JD ready for you in the morning.'

Isla frowned, then moved to a fireside chair and pulled a book – *Slayers of the Dark Web*. Crime was her genre.

With Isla highlighted by the log fire, Arlo recalled the film "The Quiet Man" starring John Wayne and Maureen O'Hara.

The likeness is amazing, but I won't pass comment.

Isla noticed Arlo's micro twitch and, having not commented, she smiled at his courtesy.

'Our Bran has never read a fictional book, says they're a waste of his time.'

Bran rolled his shoulders. 'I crave knowledge and its study; fiction simply cannot fuel my inquisitive nature.'

'I understand your logic, but sometimes fiction can stimulate thoughts to help the inquisitive develop,' said Arlo.

Bran raised an eyebrow. 'Reality is the key to my learning. My emotions exist in black and white, resulting in a curious fact. I've not wept since the age of ten! Anyway, tonight is not for intellectual debate – let's begin on the chequered board?'

Arlo hid his growing excitement.

Such a mindset is paramount to your survival in the world you are soon to experience.

'Young sir, set them up!'

Bran settled. 'Please, you're our guest. I insist you take white.'

Directly looking at Bran, Arlo replied in Latin. 'Tibi gratias ago, tum ut eorum.' (*Thank you, I shall.)*

Bran nodded enthusiastically. 'A frater tuus linguistica, raro aliquis locutus legitur.' (*A fellow linguist).*

Isla peered above her reading glasses. 'Good luck Arlo.'

The game began as Arlo opened with 1.c4.

Bran nodded in respect. 'The English Opening – the classic.'

Twenty moves later, Arlo conceded with a frown.

'My word, young Bran, your mother was not exaggerating.'

'You play well,' replied Bran.

'I'll take that as a compliment, and considering that defeat, I'll make my way back to the cottage to sulk.'

Everyone laughed.

'Then tomorrow, if you wish for a guided tour of our Isle, I'd be more than happy,' suggested Bran.

'That would be excellent. However, I'd have to travel in the buggy if you don't mind?'

'Not at all. If the buggy is ready, I'll drive over... say nine?'

'Agreed.'

Isla placed her book down and moved to shake Arlo's hand.

'It's been a pleasure to have you over.'

'Your fine hosts. I'm thankful to have spotted the advert.'

'Thank you,' flushed Isla.

Turning to leave, Arlo addressed Bran. 'Et quod inceperat griseo obumbratio?' (Have the grey spectres begun?)

Arlo's words shocked Bran to the core, prompting an immediate recall of the ghastly apparitions. Now fighting to control his inner turmoil, he replied. 'Cogitesne?' (*Do you understand?).*

'Ego adsum auxilio.' (*I am here to help).*

The reply had an immediate calming effect on Bran, who took a shallow breath. 'Et ego sincere spem.' (*I hope so.)*

Arlo, smiling, shook Bran's hand before turning to Isla. 'My apologies for the Latin. I hope you don't think I'm being rude.'

'Heaven no. I'm glad our Bran will have someone to match him during your stay.'

'Match him! I doubt that Isla, goodnight to you both.'

Nodding to Bran, he closed the door and looked upward at the night sky.

I had to determine if Bran has control of his emotions. Thankfully, it would appear he's managing his metamorphosis. So far, so good!

Now in bed, Bran conducted a Google search which backed up Arlo's qualifications. Interestingly, he had not boasted of his extreme wealth (twelve billion sterling) and the fact that he owned a twenty-thousand-acre estate near Lincoln, Nebraska, in the U.S.. The tragic death of his wife and only son in a car accident in 2001 was a heartache he would not broch.

Can I trust this man? If he has answers – I must!

His father's return made him feel safe. With a dread of closing his eyes, the following morning seemed a lifetime away.

Six

7.45 a.m.

The spectres had appeared, but Bran welcomed his eventual drift into an uneventful sleep. Upon waking, overwhelmed with unanswered questions, he braved a cold shower.

Isla called from the kitchen.

'If you're spending the day with Arlo, just note the weather forecast is not exactly encouraging.'

Bran, rubbing himself vigorously with the towel, yelled back.

'We'll have a cookout on the south side.'

'You're mad! I'd best pack for you then – oh and dads fixed and fuelled up the John Deer.'

With breakfast consumed and a rucksack full of provisions, Bran set off with Loki on the back of the JD, tail wagging at the pending adventure. As Ross had not fixed the loose driver's seat, Bran grinned as he slid left on the first turn.

Nervously gazing through the kitchen window battered by a pounding rain, Arlo watched on as the JD approached the cottage. With a deep sigh, he swallowed two anti-arrhythmic tablets.

My word, how do I explain to a seventeen-year-old boy that he is one of the most extraordinary humans ever and that he may die before the age of twenty-one?

Bran gave a thumbs-up as Arlo stepped out of the cottage. Both held expressions that concealed an inner turmoil.

'Morning, we have much to discuss,' shouted Arlo above the wind.

Bran nodded coyly and stepped inside. It wasn't often he felt seventeen, but just now he did.

'The JD's fuelled. It can be a sod to start and watch the seat when you turn.' Bran shrugged. 'It's not a comfy ride!'

'Still beats walking – thank you.'

As Bran shook down his poncho, Arlo put the kettle on before moving apprehensively towards the wood burner.

Cliff Cottage, being the original home of William Cranson, had always held a certain charm for Bran, especially the attached stone barn. Family history would say it was the playroom built solely for William. The building now served as a log store.

'Tea or coffee?' asked Arlo.

'Tea is fine, milk, no sugar, please.'

Brew made, Arlo, still feeling the cold, placed a few logs into the wood burner before carrying the mugs to the table.

'Apologies for last night's abrupt introductory. I owe you an explanation.'

Bran spoke directly. 'Do you see the grey spectres?'

Arlo frowned. 'Sadly not.' Now reaching inside a worn briefcase, he passed over several printed documents.

'Records began in 888AD. Ninety-six people, known to us as Paragons, have faced lifelike dreams with just nine encountering the grey spectres.' Arlo's stomach wretched a little as he knew the exact number to be ten!

'Young sir, you belong to a special group of people! These documents will give you a brief historical insight.'

Bran looked puzzled. 'Are any alive now?'

'The Paragon runs through historical blood lines. Currently, you are the only one that we are aware of. Our data base began in the UK before spreading to Europe. As for Asia, Africa, and the rest of the world, sadly, we have little historical information. Fact being, autism spectrum disorder and the Paragon have similarities.'

Bran tilted his head slightly. 'Are you saying that Paragons are autistic?'

'Autism was only first discussed in 1945 by Leo Kanner, an Austrian American psychiatrist and physician. But yes... the Paragon's structure contains a level of autism; however, their trait of long-term sleeping separates them from the normal case study. Many believe that Albert Einstein suffered from Asperger syndrome. One has to say it was an advantage for our greatest scholar.'

Bran leaned back in his chair.

'One of the many altercations I've had during university was to protect a boy who had mild autism. I just flipped and during the scuffle broke the bully's arm. My *academic potential* allowed the incident to be swept under the carpet... but I'll never forget the intensity and rage of my emotional reaction. I have always blamed my father's genes for my violent outbursts – he has a wicked temper.'

Arlo hid a wry smile.

Just one of your eleven "protective" shenanigans, all of which cost me over one hundred and eighty thousand pounds to sweep under the carpet.

'Do you enjoy combat?'

Bran thought for a moment. 'I won't cause an altercation, but I will step in if needed.'

That Bran had revealed an instinct to protect the weak bolstered Arlo. Fact being Bran did not seek the adrenaline of violence as did the natural fighting man. His trigger had always involved injustice.

'Rather chivalrous, one would have to say,' said Arlo.

Concentrating, Bran covered the entire work in eleven minutes, an astonishing display of speed reading. His first question, to the relief of Arlo, was not about death.

'Are all Paragons gifted?'

'I prefer the description of sensory advancement.' Arlo paused. 'Every single Paragon has suffered a loss of one or more primary senses. Why? I cannot explain, as medical records are non-existent. However, it would seem that major senses become superseded by the Paragon trait.'

Bran thought for a moment. 'Given the uniqueness of genius, autistic people possess – I concur.'

Arlo nodded. 'I'm sure you know that many believe that the human brain only uses ten percent of its capacity.'

Bran's brow furrowed. 'A debatable statement...'

'Agreed, but research is based on the conscious, not the sub-conscious mind.'

Not wishing to expand on the unique senses found in the Paragon, Arlo restricted his information.

I must not disclose the Awakening.

'A small percentage of human's touch on what we could class as paranormal sensory perception, the medium or psychic, for instance. Some do provide information that would be impossible to attain given normal thinking. I believe the mind is far superior when using the sub-conscious.'

'But as the human, by default, operates in the conscious state, it then cannot develop the sub-conscious,' said Bran.

'Exactly! In the Paragon's case, sleep is the key aspect of their lives stimulating sub-conscious activity considerably.'

'What senses are unique to the Paragon?'

'Mostly heightened talents similar to the autistic in the conscious world – but it is within the dreamworld is where I believe the Paragon is superior.'

Arlo's concealment of the exact truth regarding sensory advancement pricked his conscience.

Bran must intuitively align with his new senses – therefore I must not interfere at any cost!

'Have any with autism experienced the grey spectres?' said Bran.

'Without records, it is impossible to confirm.'

Once again, Bran remained silent for several minutes.

'As nature generates remarkable athletes, unique talents, and academic genius, then by sheer probability she will also generate individuals with a gifted sub-conscious – the Paragon.'

'Perfectly put,' conceded Arlo with a tilt of his head. 'There is also a sound theory that the pineal gland within the brain links to the Paragon's sensory advancement.'

Bran sifted through his memory bank. 'Ah yes, the pineal gland... our third eye, believed to be the organ through which we dream and imagine. Some claim that, correctly activated, it can transport our mind to other dimensions. However, as there have been no clinical tests, it's purely a general belief.'

'My word, your study has no boundaries.'

'Yes, but right now I'm curious about why I researched the gland...'

'Perhaps you're fated.'

'Humm... Is it possible there are others you have no record of?'

'Most definitely.'

Bran felt uneasy, but the knowledge that he was not unique helped.

'You believe I am a Paragon based on the fact of the grey spectres?'

'And that Paragons pass along a blood line – yes.'

'Yet I have no disabilities?'

Arlo smiled. 'I'm convinced evolution has finally eradicated the imperfections that occur with highlighted senses.'

Bran tapped the papers. 'According to these records, most experienced the dream world before they were ten?'

'Correct, but there is no rule regarding a dream timeline.' Bran showed no response. Arlo continued. 'May I ask a question?'

'Of course.'

‘As each Paragon aged, the grey spectres increased to a peak of around twelve per sleep. How many do you experience at present?’

Bran’s brow furrowed as the figure seemed low. ‘One hundred and forty-six!’

Arlo baulked. ‘One hundred and forty-six – are you certain?’

‘They’re horrifying, something you don’t forget.’

‘Yes, of course, my apologies, but this is unusually high. What was your first count? When did they start?’

‘Around twenty appeared two weeks ago – they have since increased in numbers every night.’

Once again, Arlo’s expression displayed a margin of disbelief.

‘I’m staggered as most took years to arrive at twelve – could you explain an experience?’

A deep sigh preceded Bran’s reply. ‘Upon closing my eyes for sleep, I continue to look through them as though I’m awake. No idea why I tried this, but it’s at that point the spectres materialise. One by one, each dissolving before the next. They cease when I fall to sleep, leading to a dream that matches reality. There is no confusion, no oddities, and the entire scenario logs into my memory base. For instance, I watched the crew of the El Dorado perish as the vessel sank in 1502. And as I can recall every unpleasant detail, this makes it extremely disturbing.’

Arlo frowned. ‘You witnessed a historical event?’

‘Witnessed... I was aboard the bloody vessel! But before she sank, I withdrew, fearing I could have drowned.’

Arlo had studied every written word regarding the Paragon but was now listening to experiences in real-time. He did well to control his excitement.

‘Was the dream in colour?’

‘Yes – it was as real to me as us both chatting now.’

Arlo looked shocked. ‘Coloured *recalls* seldom appear until the Paragon reaches twenty; it would seem your intelligence is advancing your capabilities. The Paragon *dream state* has caused many to lose their minds. Therefore, it is critical to establish your conscious self in order to prevent the onslaught of madness.’

‘That I understand, as it’s an unnerving experience as both the dream and waking world now blend into one.’

Arlo’s expression changed to concern.

'A Paragon's default life becomes sleep. All find the subconscious existence superior to the torment of the conscious world. To maintain connection to the physical world, you will require a powerful mind.'

Bran sat and thought before speaking. 'During the dream, the Paragon would have lost their physical defects and exist without fear of oppression. It's obvious why they would choose sleep. Therefore, since my lifestyle is enjoyable, the challenge should be easier?'

'Trust me, it won't! The harmony sleep appears to provide becomes all-consuming and, as this journey will present many tough challenges, sleep may well become your only option of escapism.'

'I suppose only time will tell...'

Arlo changed the subject. 'When you say the grey spectres dissolve... what happens?'

'Dissolve is perhaps the wrong description as they now pass from my vision and as I always fall into a dream, I don't know where they finish.'

'A recall is different to a dream, being they are based on historical fact.' Arlo's brief pause gave Bran confirmation that an important disclosure was about to be shared. 'It is our belief that a dimension exists between normal consciousness and sleep. A dimension so infinite that the human mind cannot detect it. We named this *the Void...* and only the Paragon can gain access. I must confess this is all theory, nothing factual, but that is our belief.'

Bran paused for a moment's thought. 'A void, interesting. I've often deliberated regarding the separation between *on and off.* There has to be a neutral point between the two, even if it's, as you suggest, infinitesimal!'

'That's an excellent comparison.'

'Problem being my failure to control my passing into the dream world is extremely frustrating. Perhaps this *void* is the key.' Bran switched the topic dramatically. 'How many Paragons have died in their sleep?'

The directness of the question did not shock Arlo. After a deep sigh, he began. 'Your intellect has thrust you well beyond the limitations normal for your age, but what I have to say will disturb you.'

'I require the truth,' said Bran rather grimly.

Arlo stood up.

I must answer with honesty and frankness in order to gain complete trust. I just hope his questions don't push too far.

'Not one Paragon has passed their twenty-first birthday!'

Arlo's words hit hard, causing Bran's stomach to produce a feeling of acute nausea. The seventeen-year-old wanted to scream. The intellect concentrated, allowing his natural ability to remain calculated to override the rush of negative emotions.

'I had already deduced the possibility, but I'm comforted as my concern was of a more immediate death.'

Having expected Bran to break down, Arlo hid his delight.

'The facts are harrowing. Murders account for the death of sixty-five per cent of Paragons. The rest died during what became to be known as the *long sleep.*'

'Long sleep, as Williams?'

'Yes, it is a mystical event in which the Paragon attempts to make *default* their sub-conscience existence. To date, no one has woken once they committed to this act. Williams was the longest ever recorded at twenty-six days!'

Bran frowned. 'This event haunts our family – twenty-six days asleep and then he just... died?'

With his expression oozing empathy, Arlo replied. 'This is the twentieth century. I'm confident your timeline will be different. Already you're exhibiting signs that your sensory perception is beyond all before you.'

'This "long sleep" how is this induced?'

Arlo shifted a little.

I cannot divulge the full explanation just yet, as Bran has to find his own path.

'We don't know! However, every surviving Paragon has taken the sleep.'

Bran bowed his head. 'Can't say I'm excited at the prospect...'

'I'm confident your intelligence will forge a safe path.'

'I sincerely hope so,' shrugged Bran.

Arlo, once again, switched the conversation.

'Over one hundred spectres are extraordinary. As you develop, I dare not estimate the number you will experience.'

'I can't say I hold your enthusiasm over that fact. Have you any data on these spectres?'

'Very little. Whatever you tell me will be an advancement.'

Bran's disappointment showed. With closed eyes, he took a deep breath.

'Their expressions are hideous, depicting various manifestations – evil, sadness and...' he paused just a fraction. 'All portray a manic fear as they dissolve.'

Arlo's utterance became concentrated. 'We are stepping into the unknown. Since the writings of the Paragon Sylvie Caillette, we have discovered very little.'

'William drafted a book?' said Bran.

'Yes, the ¥ spent many years searching without success, as his parents destroyed all copies.'

Concern etched over Bran's face. 'Williams' father, Gregor, killed a trespasser in his barn. Was he of the ¥?'

'Yes.' replied Arlo in a tone of apology.

Bran changed the subject, as his ancestry was not something he wished to dwell on.

'I gleaned my recent paper from talking to an Amazonian tribal elder in a dream. Can you imagine how that feels?'

Again, Arlo felt his level of excitement raise at the disclosure. 'This is your gift developing no question. In fabled stories, Paragons can invade another's sleep. William was one such *sleepwalker*. Others were evil. A boy named Santos López, born in Spain in 1757, caused insanity for monetary gain before he began his sleeping period and eventual death. Apologies for raising that subject.'

A shiver passed over Bran as he nodded his acceptance.

Moving to the window, Arlo remained silent for a few moments. After a steadying breath, he spoke.

'Since time began, humanity has searched for answers concerning their existence...' Hesitating, he then moved to Bran and placed a hand on his shoulder. 'Never allow the words *this is not possible* to dominate. I repeat, whatever transpires, you *will* find the senses to cope.'

Bran sat back in his chair. 'Are you saying I may find the answer to life and... death?'

'We have always believed it is the goal of the Paragon!'

'And the soul, do you believe it exists?'

'As a human being, I hope so. However, everything is conjecture until proven. Bran, the truth behind our existence and our demise is now in your hands! I believe that to be a fact.'

'And if I find these answers?'

'Then conveying the truth will become your most arduous task.'

A knock interrupted their conversation. Arlo quickly shuffled the papers back into his briefcase before answering the door to a storm-swept Ross.

'Mornin all.'

'Morning Ross.'

Ross looked at his son. 'We've received another booking for March, but neither your mother nor I can open the damn thing...'

The jump back into normality relaxed Bran. 'Sure Dad, I can call by home.'

'Great. I'd best tidy up the other cottages, never known a March like this.'

'Technology dad – trust me, it's the future.'

With a jaunty shrug, Ross turned to leave. 'The weather will get worse; I'd forgo the tour today.'

'I reckon that's a good shout,' agreed Arlo.

With a thumbs up, Ross left.

Bran stirred sharply at Arlo, who held his hand up.

'Two people will remain on the Isle from now on.' Arlo's expression of gloom did nothing to bolster Bran's emotional state. 'There is a surreptitious group known as *The Columnae* (the column), formed by various religions centuries ago. Their sole purpose is to oppose the Paragon and the ¥. Initially, it was a fear of the unknown that instigated their initial hatred. Centuries later, this hatred became financially driven in the realisation that the Paragon could become a serious threat to their religious monopoly. Their connection to the Vatican is a guarded secret.'

Bran's face depicted concern.

'Oppose...? Are they responsible for the deaths of Paragons?'

Melancholy clouded Arlo's features. 'Truth... it is their major purpose, but we have lost very few in our care.'

'A few being?' asked Bran, sounding sceptical.

'Around fifteen percent.'

'Not perfect then...'

Arlo blew out his cheeks. 'For a limited period, you can concentrate on your journey as a Paragon. However, outside influences will eventually recognise your potential. Governments will gain knowledge of your capabilities and use you like a lab rat in the guise of scientific or military interest. Of course, religion will oppose your findings. This period will, without question, be the biggest threat to your development. In short, it will make or break you. And as I mentioned, your desire to remain in slumber to evade escalating issues will become difficult to ignore.'

The statement exacted a stark realisation to Bran. 'Am I marked already?'

'For the immediate future, only *the Columnae* will be an irritant – this we can counter. Further down the line, intrusion from the major powers will be a tougher challenge.' Arlo picked up on an uneasiness developing in Bran's expression. 'We are under the radar because you have shown nothing to flag concern. However, we need to be honest with your parents in order that you can concentrate fully on your advancement.'

Bran's reply was more of a statement than an answer. 'My death will not be a consideration and until I have a clear understanding, I won't involve my parents.'

'Of course, I understand your reluctance. Therefore, I will be your guide.'

'To confide is a welcomed comfort,' acknowledged Bran.

Arlo bowed his head. 'It is my life's work; I am honoured.'

Bran thrust his hand forward. Their shake was firm.

'I'll jog back. It helps balance my thoughts.'

'Okay, same time tomorrow, weather permitting?'

'Suits me.' Bran grinned. 'And don't forget the dodgy seat on the JD!' Before working through a light stretch, he looked sternly at Arlo.

'The truth regarding death... are you sure this is possible?'

'For every phenomenon, an explanation exists. However, the human does not possess the sensory capabilities to understand their own existence. The Paragon has that potential.'

Bran's head dropped a little. 'How is this possible, I mean – really?'

Arlo smiled. 'If I may quote the wise words of Kornelius Novak?'

'If it helps,' shrugged Bran.

"Within a mother's womb, rest two babies.'

One asks the other. 'Do you believe in life after birth?'

The other replies. 'Yes, of course. There must be something after birth. Perhaps we are here to prepare for what we will become later.'

'Nonsense.' says the first. 'There is no life after birth. What kind of life would there be?'

'I don't know,' says the second, 'but it will be lighter than here. Perhaps we can walk on our legs and eat with our mouths.'

The first replies. 'That's absurd. Walking is impossible. And eating with our mouths? Ridiculous! The umbilical cord gives us nourishment and everything we need. But the umbilical cord is so short. Therefore, life after birth is logically impossible.'

'Well, there must be something,' insisted the second. 'Perhaps it's different from in here. Maybe we don't need this physical umbilical cord anymore.'

The first replies, 'Nonsense. Besides, if there is something more, why hasn't anyone come back from there? Birth is the end of life and in the afterbirth there is nothing but darkness, silence and oblivion. It leads us nowhere.'

'Well, I don't know,' says the other, 'but we will certainly meet Mother, and she will take care of us.'

The first replied. 'Mother? Do you really believe in Mother? It's ridiculous. If Mother exists, where is she now?'

The other said: 'She is everywhere around us. We are of her. It is inside her we live. Without her, this world neither could, nor would, exist.'

The first said: 'Well, I cannot see her, so it is only logical that she does not exist.'

To this the other replied: 'Sometimes, when you are in silence and focus and really listen, you can perceive her presence and you can hear her loving voice speaking to us from above."

Arlo leaned closer. 'Fiction often stirs the mind.'

'Your point being... I must not doubt the unimaginable,' said Bran.

'Exactly.'

After a deep exhale, Bran set off running. Within five minutes, he crouched down, held his head in his hands, and screamed.

Did I really just have that conversation...? If so, why me?

Back at the cottage, Arlo looked to the heavens.

My stay at Scarth will trigger a domino effect of consequences beyond my control. Until he realises the Paragon's true potential, I am his protector. If successful, evil will face an adversary never experienced before. For the sake of all, I pray he remains stable during this learning period. It is imperative I withhold certain knowledge, especially regarding what we know as the "Awakening of the Initiates".

Moving to his briefcase, he pulled out an ancient leather-bound book containing his entire written knowledge of the Paragon.

I cannot allow Bran to be swayed by those who failed. Every step he takes must be of his own making, especially the mystery of the void. How he discovers this is beyond my knowledge, but then finding it creates a greater problem, as no Paragon has ever survived its lure.

Arlo then wrote memos of their discussions written in a language that only a true Paragon could decipher. Later that evening, he would spend hours on his satellite phone before sleep, where he would then attempt to look through closed eyes – without success. However, he would continue to do the same each night feeling he must.

Seven

Bookings processed; Bran looked out of the front window. As his father had warned, the weather had turned ghastly.

My run has failed to calm. But hey! Uncovering the facts regarding life and death is no gimme...

'Arlo seems like a nice man?' said Isla, calling from the kitchen.

Bran's mind was elsewhere, making Isla prompt him again.

'Sorry Mum, I was miles away. Yes, he's excellent company.' A look of sadness passed over his features. 'Sometimes I wish I could enjoy interaction with kids my age.'

Saddened, Isla replied. 'Well, you can always ask some of your colleagues over, or possess a mobile phone.'

Bran cringed. 'Na, phones create obsessions, as they're laced with social media and odd music. I've a couple of pals, but I've only ever connected with Christie.'

Isla gave him a hug. 'I need to check if she's a prospective daughter-in-law.'

'Mother, just don't!'

Both laughed. Bran excused himself, then left for the den. Once inside, he gathered his thoughts.

The relief in knowing I'm not going mad has certainly helped, but to uncover the reason of our existence, whilst having concerns about my death, really?

Bran shook his head in a way to steel his emotions.

No! I cannot afford to dwell on thoughts of my death. If I am a Paragon, then for now my primary action is to locate this void... But how?

He shivered.

My god is this actually happening or is it all one long dream...?

Now laying on the bed, he closed his eyes, resulting in the grey spectres swamping his vision. Counting became impossible. A fair estimation would be that he had at least two hundred before his dream began. The content of which was so enticing that it caused him to remain asleep.

Now stood inside a cave on the eastern side of the Isle, the rock formation, wind noise, even the overwhelming smell of damp, felt real.

Although I am dreaming, I may as well be awake, such is the similarity.

Footsteps echoing around the walls interrupted his thoughts.

He froze.

The sound of Bran's heartbeat dominated at the sight of William Cranson standing at the entrance. Alone, carrying a small leather bag and a pickaxe, he began to dig a hole. Once finished, he placed the bag inside, hammered the loosened grit back with a hand-sized boulder, then covered the dig with a stack of rocks. Satisfied, he then scaled a large rock and hid the pickaxe inside a crack on the cave wall. Without looking back, he left.

Bran's heart continued its high-octane rate.

Is it possible to interact within the dream?

As he nervously stepped forward, a dancing light cast eerie shadows about the walls. Anxiously glancing towards the entrance, two men, dressed in long black capes holding lanterns, entered the cave. As they began a search, Bran, feeling vulnerable, eased to the rear.

Seconds later, drawn to the pile of rocks, the taller of the two called out to his colleague. Bran's renowned sense of justice rose to the fore.

They have no right to disturb William's property.

Without logic, he stepped from the shadows. On sight of Bran, a sheer terror overwhelmed both men. Petrified, they crossed themselves, then bolted from the cave.

Shocked at how his intervention had affected the men, Bran walked towards the entrance. The men were nowhere to be seen.

Why did they react so fearfully?

As a strong wind swirled inside the cave, he shivered. Now turning to look at the stones, a sudden fatigue engulfed him. Instinct warned it was time to leave before an image of the barn at Cliff Cottage entered his mind. Bran somehow understood what it represented.

Thank you William.

Once awake, he shook uncontrollably. With his mind frantically questioning all that had happened, he pushed a few moments of deep breathing to ease himself back to normality.

His watch gave 6 p.m.. Forcing himself to relax, he attempted to rationalise the event.

Time passes so fast in the sub-conscious state... Why? Why were those men petrified? I have to speak with Arlo, before I lose the plot.

Outside, the weather had worsened. Ross, washing his hands in the kitchen, having seen him leave, opened the window. His sharp command prompted Bran's return.

I can't afford to appear anxious.

'Sorry dad, it'll keep till morning.'

Now back inside, the smell of cooking instigated a nausea, to which he ran back to the den and vomited as quietly as possible. On his return, as mothers do, Isla showed her concern over Bran's pale complexion.

'Not feeling well?' she asked.

'Just a little off today, no worries. I'll have a light supper, then slip off to bed if that's okay.'

Isla would serve him one of her *magic* broths with a little toast. One hour later, he retired. Once in his room, the sight of his bed provoked an extreme dread.

Too many questions beyond normal parameters. I've interacted with people inside a dream, taking this to another level. They appeared to be terrified. Almost as if...

Bran paused before speaking aloud.

'They had seen... A GHOST!'

Shocked, he continued to talk aloud. 'My god? Did they actually see me as a ghost?'

The thought made him shudder.

Have I interacted with the past? If so, this changes my entire perception... this is no longer a fairy tale – this is an unknown phenomenon, and I am the only human able to solve its mystery.

A surge of adrenalin rushed through his body.

Spectres... realistic dreams... Void... recall and now ghosts. Not forgetting the image inside the barn revealed to me during the recall... I am a living Paragon!

Bran eased onto his bed. A rapid heartbeat was certainly not conducive to sleep. Breathing slowly helped.

If I am to succeed, then I must learn to control my anxiety.

Thoughts of a smiling Christie helped as he forced his mind to wander into less stressful recollections. Sleep came. Remarkably, the spectres stayed away.

The questions would continue on his waking.

Eight

Cliff Cottage, 9 a.m. the following morning. Bran knocked on the door, then stepped inside, followed by Loki. His agitated demeanour caused Arlo concern.

'A development already?'

'You could say that.' Bran paused before scolding Loki, who had begun an exploratory sniff of the cottage.

'Sorry.'

'Don't worry, he's fine. Please take a seat.'

'Thank you,' said Bran, who, after a deep breath, explained his experience.

Severely agitated by the development, Arlo disguised his concern.

'The cave exists?'

'Yes, we have to travel there now?'

'Right, I'll get my coat.' Pausing, he looked at Bran. 'What's your instinct for why the men became scared?'

Bran rolled his shoulders. 'Simple... they believed I was a ghost. Do you understand the ramifications of what I am saying?'

Arlo failed to conceal his shock.

Our world is about to change. This is just the beginning.

'Let's find absolute proof William buried an object before speculation.'

Over rough terrain, the drive would take twenty-five minutes.

As they stood at the mouth of the cave, both held a slight hesitation to enter. Not so Loki, he had areas to mark.

Bran spoke. 'Theoretically I've travelled back in time?'

Arlo failing to reply, switched on his torch then stepped forward. The bright light, bouncing off the cave walls, made Bran shudder for a moment before the torch illuminated a simple depression surrounded by a cluster of hand-sized rocks. 'Is that the spot?' asked Arlo apprehensively.

With his stomach in turmoil, Bran nodded, then climbed onto the rock just below the crack in the cave wall. Moments later, he gingerly pulled out a rusted pickaxe head. The wooden handle had long since rotted.

'Are you certain I haven't passed back through time?'

Arlo looked astonished. 'Right now, not entirely. How were the men dressed?'

'Both wore black robes.'

'Did either wear a cross or necklace?'

Bran's memory was exact. 'One held a cross, the other... rosemary beads.'

Arlo's tone amplified his concern. 'Then the Vatican, have possession of William's book.'

'That's not good, is it?' questioned Bran.

'No, and this event explains how, after many searches, we could not locate it.'

'What now?'

Stepping outside, Arlo pulled out a sat phone from his coat pocket. The recipient answered promptly.

'We have a setback. I believe the Vatican has possession of *The Last Book*. You understand what you have to do.'

A momentary pause led to a firm reply. 'I'll begin preparations.'

'Be careful, my friend.'

Call ended; Arlo closed his eyes for a second before speaking.

'It would be negligent on my behalf not to assume they know I've made contact.'

Bran's brow furrowed. 'Their intentions should they discover I am a Paragon?'

Arlo's expression betrayed the reality of the situation.

Bran raised his arms into the air. 'The fun has just gone outta this.'

Taking hold of Bran by the shoulders, Arlo spoke reassuringly. 'Understand this, the ¥ is more powerful than you can imagine. We have contacts seated in many halls of power. Finance is unlimited and for centuries we have dedicated our lives to protect the Paragon.'

'Then you had better make sure I don't add to your fifteen percent...!'

'You have my word, but right now you must speak with your parents.'

Bran's reaction was sharp. 'NO! I will not involve them until we have answers, therefore tonight I will attempt another recall.'

Arlo, although surprised by Bran's quick temper, he remained calmed. 'For you to dictate a recall, well, that's impossible.'

'I will not trouble my parents – not until I have concrete answers. This is none-negotiable!'

Arlo paused just a moment. 'Very well. Then we must return home.'

As they left the cave, Bran had calmed and spoke in a whisper.

'If I appeared as a ghost in their vision, then the spirit world becomes reality?'

After pulling out a tablet, Arlo swallowed it whole as he tried to remain in control of his whirling thoughts.

'Time and your senses will produce the answers required for this conundrum.'

'You say this as though I have the means to do so.'

'Trust me, once you have sourced the void, the answers will come thick and fast.'

'You mean that place that might exist and may be accessible for an instantaneous moment...!'

Arlo tapped Bran's leg.

'You're thinking consciously – your abilities lie in the sub-conscious.'

Bran shrugged in frustration before an odd thought popped into his mind.

That last image presented during that recall, why did I not disclose it?

The drive home seemed to take forever.

Back inside Cliff Cottage, Arlo towelled off the rain.

Bran rolled his shoulders. 'Pointless me drying as I fancy a run back... I need the release.'

Arlo took a wistful breath. 'Oh, for the exuberance of youth... I was a runner in my time. Unfortunately, I developed an arrhythmia – irregular heartbeat, around eight years ago. Tablets and more tablets, alas, but enough of my ailments! Go for your jog.'

A meaning embrace ended, with Bran sprinting from the cottage. On reaching the den, he allowed himself a few moments to catch his breath, then sat down and closed his eyes.

I have to learn to stay calm...

Ross, seated in his land rover, always enjoyed the sight of a vessel approaching his jetty, even though the wooden structure had seen better days.

If these bookings continue, I'll soon be able to fix this.

After Jim McTay moored his boat, two men stepped onto the landing and unloaded several large rucksacks, both looked mid-thirties and in excellent shape. A sharp demeanour suggested a military background. Ross climbed out of his land rover. The shorter of the two men spoke.

'Mr Cranson, Mike Tate and Tom White, thank you for accepting our booking.'

Ross took the handshake. 'No Mike, thank you for the visit. Don't get many in March. Call me Ross.'

'We're working on a survival course for corporates and hoping the Isle is as harsh as advertised.'

'Harsh is one word – an absolute twat would be more apt.'

The men laughed their way over to Ross's land rover. Ross paid McTay, who beamed.

'Hope this little idea works out as if those lads bring the corporates over. I may get a new boat.'

'Down to our Bran building a website to cut out the middleman.'

'Yes, I heard. How is the young genius?'

'He needs to be seventeen for a while Jim, can't blame him, the attention he gets can be frustrating.'

'That's the truth Ross, tell you what next trip I'll stop over so we can pull a wee cork and have a crack.'

'Make a change from talking to your sister all day.'

'Can't argue that point.'

The men shook hands.

Tate and White, having stowed all but one of their rucksacks in the rear of the land rover, set to walk. Ross, noticing, felt no need to warn of the trek ahead.

'I've prepped the log burner, plenty of stacked wood and there's a basic food supply in the freezer – enjoy the breeze. Oh, the generator may need a kick now and again!'

'We'll manage. Cheers.'

Ross tooted the horn as he drove away.

Bloody hell, Scarth becoming busy – well, I never!

He could not possibly understand just how busy it would become.

Seventeen hundred miles away, in a small office within the Vatican, an elderly gentleman received a phone call.

'Two men have joined Professor Norton on the Isle. What actions should we take?'

The elderly male began tapping his fingers on the dark oak desktop. A sound that echoed against the matching panelled walls. After a few moments, the tapping ceased.

'Nothing, just observe. Let him determine if the boy is a Paragon. If so, we live in hope he is just another sleeper that dies. Meantime, plan meticulously for taking the family from the Isle if required.'

Nine

4 a.m..

After trying for over two hours, Bran had failed to break into recall.

It appears Arlo was correct; or is this inexperience on my part? The cave scenario, random no. I believe it had a purpose – a warning, maybe? If so, by who? William? Time travel? As we reminisce, we travel back in time. However, it's impossible for me to have a memory of that event. To say I'm confused would be acceptable.

On the sheet of A4 paper, alongside the word recall, he drew a short line then the word *Memories?* Determined, he set to sleep again. The grey spectres began their torment, but rather than concentrating on the images, he looked towards the area in which they appeared to dissipate. Instantly, a tiredness swept over him, but like an exhausted motorist, he forced his eyes to stir harder. The next few moments became a battle in which sleep took the victory.

Arlo closed his satellite call to Professor Watkins, the principle of Robert Gordon University. Unknown to the Cranson's, the sponsorship for Bran's admittance had come from a company owned by Arlo. Watkins, embedded into the ¥ through historical family ties, pondered over Arlo's *sensitive* but vital request.

I'll have to resolve this pressing issue rather tactfully.

Standing before the log fire at Cliff Cottage, Arlo breathed out a sigh.

I believe Bran will develop quicker than any other Paragon before him, and if so, will he perish earlier than the others?

Another satellite call lasted over an hour. The ¥ was now on full alert!

Bran woke in a confused state, having just experienced an African safari. On his arm, he had penned the words "wrote this b4 sleep" and so, for several minutes, he enjoyed the sheer realism of the safari experience. Without doubt, he preferred the purity of these dreams, as he suffered neither anxiety nor fear, just an unnerving sense of happiness.

Uncanny, it's as though I have actually travelled to Africa and experienced a safari. My understanding of why the Paragon sleeps excessively is expanding, as these dreams appear as reality and lodge into my mind as a genuine experience. This is mad!

A sudden vision of the grey spectres produced a numbing feeling in his stomach.

I fear the explanation regarding the spectres will not be so pleasant.

Mike Tate and Tom White, the Isle's guests, sat in front of their log burner. The walk had been worth it. Scarth most definitely suited their rouse of corporate instruction. Both men had served in the military and were experts in surviving the most inhospitable of landscapes.

The ¥ had planned well...

Arlo had invited the Cranson family over to Cliff Cottage – his turn to cook. They arrived promptly at 6 p.m.

Bran's thoughts appeared to be elsewhere. However, ignoring the current circumstances, he found the family to be genial company. He concluded that those who chose a simple existence appeared more contented. A small part of him held a slight envy, but no question, restricting his lifestyle to the basic simplicities of Scarth was impossible.

Irrelevant, for if Bran reaches his potential, then all our lives will change!

The night was a roaring success cut short when the generator revealed its temperamental side. An hour later, Bran would begin another assault on the grey spectres.

Ten

Seated on his bed, Bran counted to five, then gingerly eased back onto the pillow.

What exactly do I seek? The void, is it another world, an extra dimension? I have to accept that whatever happens will be extraordinary.

The routine of peering through closed eyes was becoming natural. Immediately he switched his attention away from the horror of the grey spectres, which were becoming less distinguishable such was their volume. After fighting like a man possessed, the inevitability of sleep came. Waking himself, a wild anger forged through his veins.

Why can't I control my entry into sleep? I see the spectres; I fall asleep. Perhaps my mind processes sleep to escape the horror? Therefore, I must shun their approach with a certain nonchalance? I can but try.

With eyes closed, they came. Effectively working *ad lib*, he cautiously eased his hand forward to wave the spectres away. Inexplicably, an intense surge of evil flowed through his body, forcing him to snatch his hand away. In shocked repulsion, he gritted down and tried again. Such was the sense of evil he processed a harrowing thought.

Is this to be my death?

With his heart rate now racing to over one hundred and eighty beats per minute, he opened his eyes as a paralysing fear enveloped his body. Now lying on the bed unable to move, thoughts turned to his past.

Moments preceding my first fist fight, I remember freezing before my father's words echoed through my mind. 'Son, when fear rears its ugly face, remember – losing is the worst option.'

The sentence bolstered his mind.

'This evil will not defeat me.'

Using every fibre of his willpower, he forced a modicum of control back into his paralysed body and slowly lowered his legs over the bedside. The moment his feet touched the wooden floor, a welcomed calmness enveloped him.

If I'm to become a Paragon, I must remain in command of my senses. I feared the grey spectres and the evil they exude – no more! Ignore them and look beyond for this so-called Void.

He closed his eyes.

I will not sleep.

The spectres came in an ever-increasing flow, determined to envelop Bran within a cocoon of evil. This time, he stood firm.

It's as if I'm facing a raging blizzard, but instead of snow, I sense evil.

As the seconds passed, he became overwhelmed, leading to another moment of panic, resulting in him being cast asleep. Waking, he began trembling, not from fear but anger.

I cannot keep repeating the same actions and expect the solution. I need another angle.

Now concentrating, his mind wandered to his conversations with Arlo.

You're processing with your conscious – try your sub-conscious.

Bran climbed out of bed and walked to the window on shaky legs. Now peering into the night sky, he spoke aloud.

'Just how do you activate the sub-conscious?'

The question produced a viable solution.

The human sub-conscious sits in the background, performing tasks without conscious actions. Can the Paragon activate the sub-conscious... consciously? Only one way to find out!

A deep breath led to closed eyes. As the spectres came, Bran faced the grey blizzard, looked forward and attempted to imagine the beyond... Nothing! The grey assault took effect, implementing one thought.

Take me beyond this moment.

The instantaneous change in surroundings to an inky blackness snatched away his breath. Not daring to move, his mind desperately fished for sensory activities such as sound, smell, or touch – nothing. Rather unnervingly, he now feared he was blind. Devoid of all sensory activity, he raised his hands to establish exactly where he was.

Nothing...

Such was his sensory breakdown, his mind questioned if he was alive. With a fear escalating in the pit of his stomach, he snatched open his eyes. The muted moonlight shimmering through the window, followed by the night's sounds and smells, brought a calming relief. Breathing hard, he switched on the bedside lamp, and for a few moments bathed in its comforting light.

That was absolute terror. I've never experienced such vulnerability. How is it possible to lose all sensory activity?

He reached for a glass of water and downed half before stopping.

The greys disappeared, and I did not fall into sleep.

A mixture of both anxiety and excitement flushed through his system. Slowly finishing the remaining water, he placed the glass down.

I was neither awake nor asleep, therefore I may have found the void, that neutral point between "on and off". No matter how intimidating, I have to keep going.

He grinned.

I just wish I could take a torch.

A stride to the mirror prompted him to nod to his own reflection.

Losing is the worst option.

Stepping to the bed, he then turned off the lamp. Settling, he took several deep breaths, then closed his eyes.

The greys came. However, before he could process a thought, the darkness enveloped him. As before, all sensory activity ended.

Losing is the worst option.

A feeling of complete helplessness passed over him and so he continued to repeat the words in a desperate effort to maintain his composure. Seconds ticked by, each one edging him to his breaking point. As he forced another sentence, his eyes detected a white mist forming in the distance. Immediately, the light produced a settling effect on his emotional state.

Weird, it's like the creeping sea mists that often invades our shores.

Transfixed, he stared open-mouthed as a shape began developing from the mist. Moments later, he gazed at what appeared to be a white tunnel, radiating a shimmering light from within. Rather peculiarly, although the light was exceptionally bright, it was not blinding. The *sea mist* continued rolling forward until it immersed Bran up to his waist. Cautiously moving his hands, the contact did not displace the bizarre mist, to which he found peculiar.

Although this appears to be a mist, most definitely it is not. However, it has opened my sense of sight to which is extremely comforting. Interesting. Apart from this approaching light, I am surrounded by an impenetrable darkness.

He drew a breath.

Am I actually in the void? Certainly I'm not in a dream, nor do I feel tired.

Thoughts returned to the light.

The object appears to be shifting but without diverting from its "tunnel" shape. I would estimate its circumference to be around the size of a London subway.

Bran shuddered.

If this is the void, then could the tunnel be an exit portal? If so, to where?

Tingling at the thought of an extra dimension, he then shivered in the realisation that the *sea-mist* had lured him closer to the mysterious passage, producing an overwhelming sense of vulnerability.

My instinct is telling me this is a danger. I must leave now, that's presuming I can!

After crossing his fingers, he opened his eyes. The sudden appearance of his bedroom caused an outpouring of emotion, triggering a nervous laughter. Sweat had soaked through his bed shirt. Outside, cloud cover had erased the moonlight and so with shaking hands, he grappled with the lamp switch, before gleaning a comfort from the light. Daring to recall his experience, he then gasped.

I beat the spectres, sleep and... I entered the void.

Bran looked at his alarm clock, then scratched his head. He had been *dormant* for over seven hours.

My god it feels, but just a few minutes.

An overwhelming sense of achievement consumed him before he passed into a sleep that would last for at least fourteen hours.

Eleven

At 2 p.m. the following day, Ross and Isla were beside themselves. After trying to wake Bran several times, both harboured thoughts of the family curse. Sensing his parents were in the room, Bran woke without fuss and began yawning, a challenge in its self, considering last night's experiences.

'Wow, that's a student's sleep. What are you two doing here?'

Isla's voice sounded strained. 'We couldn't wake you and...'

Bran yawned again, eased up, then stretched.

'Nothing to worry about, am guessing the Isle is de-stressing me.'

Ross's expression was one of relief. 'Are you sure everything is normal?'

'Absolutely.'

Bran seldom lied to his parents, but for now, he must.

Isla gave the bed a nudge. 'I talked to the new guests about a get together.'

'Great. I've some work to finish, then you have me, okay?'

As Bran dressed, a fearful thought enveloped him.

Am I pursuing my death? Well, tonight will no doubt provide that answer.

6 p.m..
A bold chicken curry was the serving. The new guests were polite, drank moderately and showed a strong interest in Scarth.

'The amount of woodland that's on the Isle pleasantly surprised me...' stated Mike Tate.

Ross answered with a hint of pride. 'We can toast my ancestor, James Cranston, for that. The bosk he planted as a windbreak for the house. Next, hundreds of beech, birch, alder, and elm across the middle of the Isle, before introducing rabbits as a food source. We have Red Kite, occasional visits from Osprey, a huge seal population on the east coast and several families of otters. Sheep and red deer graze over the west side and not forgetting my fine colony of honeybees. We are self-sufficient in veg, tomatoes, spuds, apples, and pears... Not bad for a once bleak Isle. It was our James that built this house.'

We also have a fourteen-point Stag, but I will not divulge his location.

'It's a millionaires paradise.' praised Tate.

Ross laughed. 'Aye, in the summer, but the winter kicks up a fierce deterrent.'

Tom White spoke up. 'Have you ever considered selling up?'

'Och no, where would we go? Nay, I'm to be buried alongside the rest of the Cranson's.'

'Well, never say never. We like this place. It's perfect for our project. Who knows what the future may bring?'

Ross turned a little serious. 'We don't provide sport hunting or trapping... over the centuries the Cranson's only kill to eat – don't have time for that sort!'

Tate nodded. 'Trophy hunting is not on our to do list!'

'Glad to hear that.'

Fearful that they would address the subject of William. Isla offered dessert. She need not have worried, as neither Mike nor Tom would broach the subject.

Meal finished, Ross, Mike, and Tom continued a discussion about the habitat. Arlo turned to Bran, who had remained pretty muted during the meal.

'Chess young Bran? I need to claw some credibility back?'

'Not tonight thanks, I've a headache from hell.'

'Probably saved another defeat.'

Something has happened, but I won't push for now. This has to be on his timeline, nothing else.

Isla, having enjoyed cooking for guests, was brimming with smiles, as just occasionally, she yearned to be amongst people.

Could we sell up and move? Nay, life's too fast on the mainland.

As the generator stayed loyal to its primary function, the evening eased nicely into its conclusion.

At 11.30 p.m., after scribbling a short sentence on his arm, Bran turned off his bedside lamp. Never in his entire life had he felt so anxious.

If I access this void again, at least I know I can exit at will...

Closing his eyes, all he could hear was his heartbeat.

The spectres came, but in that exact moment he was facing the *white tunnel.* A sudden thought prompted him to look down, confirming he was hanging in the mist, producing an emptiness in the pit of his stomach. A double take brought the realisation that his form had become translucent – a ghostly spectre.

I'm floating. Am I breathing? Hell, I don't know?

With panic rising, a horrifying thought jumped into his mind.

Am I dead?

Instantly snatching his eyes open, the sight of the bedroom prompted relief. Now gazing at his physical self, he ran a hand over his chest.

This is madness! How can I become a spirit? Did that actually happen? Calm down and work this out.

Hurriedly moving to the open window, he took several deep breaths, allowing the night air to boost his system.

I'm alive and my physical form is unharmed. Then I should try to embrace the experience, not fear it.

Back on the bed, he whispered the words, 'losing is the worst option.' Still nervous, he had to dare himself to close his eyes. Now facing the bright tunnel, a nervous glimpse confirmed his status as a spectre once again.

Just to be certain – test my ability to return to consciousness once more.

In that split second, he was sitting upright in bed with his heart beating almost through his ribcage. For the first time, a confidence purged through his system.

I can switch scenarios at will. This is definite progress. Keep level-headed and study.

After checking the time, he closed his eyes. Back inside the *void,* facing the bright tunnel, he settled to study his spirit.

My human form is now defined by an iridescent white border, enshrouding a body of glistening colour, all of which is transparent. This "spectre" is truly a wonder of creation which actually produces a warm serenity. Could this be my spirit or soul? There are definitely two separate entities. A body of shimmering colour, silhouetted by a white aura, defining my natural shape. I appear not to breathe, but within my physical form, I must be.

A deep breath produced a peculiar sensation, as no physical effort took place, yet it still activated a natural calming.

To use my physical senses in a spiritual form is fascinating and no doubt will be a comfort as I progress.

All thoughts shifted as the urge to move inside the mesmeric passage pulled to his very core.

To ensure maximum survival odds, I need time to plan.

Bran woke and looked at his alarm. He had been *asleep* for almost nine hours. In moments, the overwhelming tiredness that seemed to follow entry into the void lured him into a natural sleep. Yet again he would slumber through to the late afternoon.

Twelve

Arlo had connected to the internet via a satellite dish brought over by his men. One email raised his anxiety.

I expect entry into the lottery draw this week – fingers crossed.

The ¥ would begin infiltration of the Vatican. After shutting down the laptop, he drifted into thought.

Suspicions will become aroused if our attempts fail, but it is imperative to find the Last Book, as it may hold details to help extend his life. My atheist leaning prevents me from praying, but hell, we need a batch of luck just now.

Bran woke at 5p.m.. The set of words scribbled on his arm gave confirmation he was conscious. A dream of climbing to base camp three on Everest, once again, had appeared realistic. Even so, his mood was flat.

I dislike leaving the dream world. Arlo was correct. This is becoming an issue.

Setting aside his concerns, he understood both parents would not accept continued deflection over his sleeping patterns.

Get away for a few days!

On entering the lounge, he yawned, then spoke. 'Mum, I'm visiting some pals staying over in Wick – a break from study will do me good. Err, do you think Uncle Jim can make a trip over?'

'I'm sure he will.'

'Ta – has Arlo popped over?'

'Yes, he's helping your dad fix the seat on the JD, as he almost slipped out of the cab.'

Bran stifled a chuckle. 'Okay – please do contact Uncle Jim.'

Isla tutted, but as all mums do, she obliged.

Ross and Arlo stepped in.

'Afternoon all.'

'Afternoon. Arlo, would you look at a calculation I'm working on?'

'Delighted.'

Ross shrugged his shoulders. 'I'll settle for a brew.'

Isla popped the kettle on. 'Hurry you two.'

Inside the den, Bran immediately jumped to the point.

'Can you arrange a place for me to crash? I need to lock myself away so as not to cause problems with oversleeping.'

'Not a problem. I own a holiday cottage on the outskirts of Wick.'

Bran looked surprised. 'No stone unturned, I see.'

Arlo shrugged. 'Never. I'll make the call. Can you get a passage over today?'

'Already sorted.'

'Then I'll have you met on mainland and taken to the property. Inside there is an encrypted mobile phone programmed with a number. Whatever you require, use that, nothing else. Give the mobile number to your parents to avoid worry. I may add, the cottage will be under twenty-four-hour surveillance. Apologies for smothering you.'

'I'm a tad overawed, but I understand.'

Arlo smiled. Although he would not ask questions, every fibre in his body wanted to.

'It's my job, oh and there is ten thousand pounds cash in a safe housed in the main wardrobe floor, code is YX12Y#21. It's yours to use in times of emergency.'

'Ten thousand! What would I do with all that?'

Arlo shrugged. 'Hopefully, you'll never need it.'

Within three hours, Bran, seated in a luxurious cottage, stared at the mobile phone.

Arlo has planned meticulously around my life; it feels odd, but he is a much-needed consigliere.

After a tour of the property, he decided such opulence was not a necessity. A call to the family felt good. Isla seemed happier with him having friends. He would negotiate around her request to meet them. As he walked down the hallway leading to the bedroom, a wave of expectation swept over him.

I have a destiny to fulfil and as no one before me has succeeded, I'll not make rushed conclusions until I have approved the possibilities presented.

He exhaled.

Am I scared... Absolutely bricking it!

Thirteen

Lamberto Pugliesi had lived at the Vatican since the age of six. Now aged seventy-two, he had served the Catholic church his entire life. The funerals of his parents had been the only occasions he left the city. Although they abandoned him at five, he had wanted to pay his respects. After holding the title of *Cardinal in Pectore* (secret cardinal), for seventeen years, ill health had forced his retirement. Non the less his status within the hallowed city was legendary. Today he would meet with his sister, Madalena, who visited him once a month. Their meetings followed a simple routine that hadn't changed for many years. They would sit in the gardens to share a light meal and a glass of red wine. This would last around seventy minutes, after which they would move to take coffee inside his living quarters. The walk from the gardens took its toll on the ailing Pugliesi, as he doggedly refused to adjust to the restrictions his illness caused.

At the table, Madalena unpacked their picnic hamper. Today's meal would be home-made chicken soup, with bread and olives. She always felt proud of how many people paid tribute to her brother as they passed by. After a catch up on the past month's news, Madalena topped up her brother's glass.

'We have to ask you for a favour, Cardinal.'

Pugliesi understood. 'Then whisper closer to my ear, sister.'

Madalena clasped her brother's hand. It felt weak, weaker than last month.

'The Columnae may possess The *Last Book* and, as we have discovered an unblemished Paragon, confirmation of its existence is required.'

Pugliesi exuded a smile of unbridled relief. 'Then I shall make enquiries.'

Madalena held her brother's hand tighter. 'Please be careful. If it's a risk – do not take it.'

Pugliesi shook his head. 'Our parents gave me up in order that we had someone inside this corrupt establishment. It would please me to make their sacrifice worthwhile.' Pugliesi coughed before taking a sip of wine. 'This is precisely why I committed to a life inside these walls.' He coughed again.

Madalena frowned. 'Cardinal, your strength is my inspiration.'

'And yours mine, dear sister.' He paused. 'My word, an unblemished Paragon, you understand the consequences?'

'Let's trust it's for the good of humanity...'

Slowly standing, he gestured for a hug. Both shed a tear. They would not discuss the task again.

In 1776, five members of the Pugliesi family were burnt alive in their own home by disciples of the Columnae as punishment for the actions of their eldest child. The Paragon, Antonio Pugliesi, aged fourteen, had drawn pictures depicting another life outside normal belief. That he was blind terrified the locals, forcing the church to condemn him as a disciple of Satin. Despite their best efforts, the ¥ could only save their youngest child. The Pugliesi's hatred of the Catholic faith became all-consuming. Over the centuries, they infiltrated many official positions within the Church, plotting both political and mercenary attacks against the leaders. Just after the second world war Lamberto Pugliesi Snr inserted his first-born son into the belly of his sworn enemy. For Lamberto Pugliesi, finding the *Last Book* would become his zenith.

Brother and sister walked arm in arm back to Pugliesi's apartment. Madalena hoped this would not be their last time together... No one within the ¥ ever prayed!

Fourteen

After sitting on the sofa for an hour with an aching stomach, Bran regretted gorging on microwaved junk food. His watch gave 10 p.m.. Making his way to the bedroom, he fist pumped.

I am the only human capable of entering the void. Time to go...

After writing something on his arm he laid his head back down on the pillow. A shuffle into comfort led to closed eyes. Without a glitch, he was back in front of the gleaming passage, which now projected a vision of supreme precision, cutting deep into the surrounding blackness.

A glance at his spectre filled him with a glowing confidence.

Perhaps 'the void' is simply a hub, a place that gives access to other worlds or dimensions which may not fit the human understanding of space, time, and movement.

He paused.

Again, no sound, scent, warmth, or cold.

Suddenly, his mind presented a thought that shocked.

Is this the white passage witnessed in near-death experiences? My god – Williams "Mortis Lux..." Then entry becomes inevitable? But does this mean my death?

Immediately opening his eyes, Bran sat up and began nervously striding around the room and speaking aloud.

'What the hell should I do? If I enter this tunnel, I could die. Should I just walk away? Losing is the worst option, but in this case, losing is death! But then, if I am a Paragon, I have to trust my ability to negotiate the obstacles set.'

After five minutes of intense consideration, he huffed.

'Let's do this...!'

Determined, he strode to his bed, laid down and closed his eyes.

The sight of the sheer clarity of the bright tunnel prompted butterflies in his stomach, but as he looked down to his spectre, he actually smiled. Who else can become a spirit at will? I am a Paragon therefore I must progress.

After a moment of measured breathing, he turned towards the tunnel. The urge to move inside had now become insatiable. Moments later, without thought or calculation, carried on the mist, he eased inside the brightness. In the same instant, a huge torrent of grey spectres surged towards him. Shocked by the sheer intensity of the grey onslaught, he intuitively held up his hands as a shield before realising that the grey force was being extinguished at the entrance. Dumbstruck, Bran was now witnessing two unknown forces engaging in a brutal conflict. The event was breath-taking.

This is actually an extermination of the grey spectres. I cannot say I am saddened. Why?

With the battle at the entrance continuing, he turned inside towards the shimmering light. The experience was comparable to looking through a raging waterfall, only this was pure light.

The other side of this light-fall portal holds the key to many questions. None the less, the overwhelming lure to pass through is a torment I must ignore for now, for whatever lies beyond this light, not a single Paragon has survived the experience!

After a brief pause, he wondered.

Have I uncovered the mystery of the death sleep?

The hypnotic effect of the light-fall portal flooded his thoughts to a point where he was moments away from entry.

NO! I must return home.

Eyes opened; the time lapse back was infinitesimal. Sleep was immediate.

On his awakening, the unfamiliar surroundings of the cottage agitated him before an outburst of emotional uncertainty began. The written words on his forearm did nothing to ease the confusion, and so, for several minutes, his mind fought against the terrifying reality of the *Mortis Lux*. With a sudden urge to vomit, he rushed to the bathroom. Now shivering uncontrollably, he crawled to the corner and wrapped himself in a bath towel.

A second vomit strained his gut, yet still the nausea remained.

Mind must trump the physical.

As a steely determination descended, he compelled himself to recall images of play with Loki. Comforted, he cautiously made his way to the basin. The sound of running water helped as he washed his face and hands.

Menacingly, whatever lies beyond the light-fall portal has claimed the lives of many Paragons and possibly contains the answer to the finality of death. The return to consciousness was unpleasant, but to be expected, considering the discovery. My mind has to cope with the backlash resulting from the impossibility of my experiences. As a human, this may be impossible, but as a Paragon, I have a chance.

The thought brought on an intense irritation, and so he gazed at the normality of the room to regain composure. A glance at his watch showed 12 p.m., only one hour had passed.

Perhaps time lapse is normal inside the tunnel?

He shivered a little.

My every fibre became drawn towards that portal. However, my instinct warned that what lies beyond is a danger. Then why unbridled contentment...? I'm parched, I need to drink.

Three glasses of water later, he picked up the mobile. Oddly, the battery had drained. After a few minutes on the charger, he switched the device on. Twenty-two missed calls and various texts from his parents shocked him, but not nearly as much as the date. He had been asleep for five and a half days...

After reading the texts, the furore to follow would become problematic. Isla had informed the police, who, after failing to track his mobile, listed him as missing. As he pieced together a solution, the mobile rang. Arlo spoke in a reassuring tone.

'You've been on a bender with two pals named Len Harrows and John Barron. They're outside now and will knock just three times. Take the default chastise from the authorities, act shameful and move on.'

The call ended. Moments later, Bran answered the three knocks. Within ten minutes, the cottage looked like it had catered for a student's all-nighter. Harrows suggested Bran rang his parents.

Rather uneasily, he did so.

After their relief came the shouts. Ross's understandable anger hurt Bran.

'Dad, please, to be a daft teenager occasionally is acceptable. I'll pack my things and travel home now.' As he closed the call, the doorbell rang.

Police take exception of time wasted. Bran took the caution.

Now alone, he began recalling his experiences.

Until I am prepared both mentally and physically, I must put my next visit to the void on hold, as I believe no other Paragon has returned from that portal alive. Am I scared? Oddly, since I experienced my spectre, my nerves have settled during sleep. In fact, I'm more secure in that state rather than my physical self? Full control of my human emotions that are hard-wired to fear the unknown is imperative. If this means confiding in my parents, then it's time to face all consequences. Ultimately, I shall prepare like no Paragon before. If I fail... or die in my death sleep, it will not be from lack of preparation.

He sighed.

My god, with every passing second, my need to return to the void intensifies, as does the expectancy of discovery.

A car horn broke his thoughts.

Bran stepped outside and waved to Jim McTay, who shouted over.

'Welcome to the world of alcohol, young Bran. How's your head?'

Bran grinned.

Uncle Jim – you really don't wish to know...!

Fifteen

3 a.m. The Vatican.

Lamberto Pugliesi and the Pontiff often shared nightly conversations over religion, politics, personal and even the important matters of Italian football. Both had trusted the other implicitly, especially with their personal thoughts and problems.

Pugliesi drew a breath.

'Your holiness, we both know my time is near.' He paused. 'I've devoted my entire life to the Church, so before I pass, I have just one request?'

The Pontiff, stifling his sadness, replied affectionately. 'Lamberto, I doubt our Lord is ready for you just yet? But how can I help?'

Pugliesi straightened his posture. His solemn expression instigated a minor concern from the Pontiff.

'Lamberto – what is the problem?'

'Your holiness, I know we have *The Last Book* and so before I pass over I wish to study its pages.'

The Pontiff couldn't have foreseen the question. As a result, he failed to disguise the shock on his face. Several moments passed before he composed an answer.

Pugliesi's expression did not waver.

'Lamberto, I will not insult you by denying the existence of this book, but how do you know we hold it at the Vatican?'

'Whilst the Columnae keep our secrets from the outside world, within our walls is different. I also understand you refused to read the pages – that I admire.'

With having fabricated the entire sentence, Pugliesi had taken the gamble of his life.

The Pontiff's expression changed to one of dismay. 'Why would you wish to read the devil's work?'

Pugliesi had his answer. 'I wish to test my faith before I die.'

The Pontiff shook his head. 'But our Lord will accept you with open arms for your devotion.'

'When my family rejected me, the church took me to her bosom. And so, I repaid their kindness with my service and so the test they set for me was a simple one. But now I wish to examine my resolve.'

The Pontiff's brow creased. 'Lamberto, how does reading the devil's work cleanse your soul?'

Pugliesi's reply was a little terse. 'Before I die, I require that right to examine my faith.' A tear tracked its way down his cheek. 'This is all I ask.'

The Pontiff moved to a window; His mind did not wander to the view. The silence lasted almost a full minute.

'You understand, I have no control over the extraneous forces that govern the Catholic order. I promise to ask, but we must wait.'

'But time is something I lack; therefore, I must beg you to grant me a personal reading tonight.'

The Pontiff, looking distinctly ruffled, spoke tensely. 'Tonight! Lamberto, you ask too much of me.'

'Then I must leave the order to find other ways to fulfil my last days.'

The Pontiff looked to the heavens. 'You're serious, Lamberto?'

'I am but a dying man who needs answers.'

The Pontiff sighed. 'Very well. We'll take my buggy to the Mater Ecclesiae Monastery?'

Pugliesi allowed his relief to show. 'I cannot thank you enough, your holiness.'

'Our friendship is greater than the ripples that will follow my actions. But Lamberto, I warn you there will be consequences.'

'Consequences are ineffective, as I will be complete when I renounce the devil's work.'

Both men knelt to pray.

Within thirty minutes, Pugliesi was alone in a small reading room at a felt clothed table. The single door opened and two priests who he had never seen previously entered. Respectfully, they placed a glass case containing *The Last Book*, together with a hard-backed manuscript, in front of him.

One priest spoke.

'Cardinal, as the book is too fragile for reading, we use a copy. The content is exact. There are just twenty pages.'

Pugliesi stirred at the glass case containing a ragged binding of brown, time-aged papers.

There it sits, the most important book in the history of humankind and they deny the world its content.

Pugliesi turned to the priests. 'Have either of you read the pages?'

Both shook their heads. The taller priest spoke. 'No Cardinal, very few have... May I ask a question?'

'Of course.' nodded Pugliesi.

'Why do you choose to read the book?'

Pugliesi allowed his head to drop a little. 'I am but a man. All I have known is this city and my belief. I wish to read the details of which I've heard many whispers.'

The priest bowed his head. 'Then we will leave you in peace, Cardinal.'

Both backed out of the door and closed it quietly. Pugliesi shut his eyes and prayed. Then, with shaking hands, he began.

One hour later, he eased the book aside, then broke down and wept. It would be ten minutes before he regained his composure.

I now understand why religions have feared the Paragon. Could the world cope with the revelations written inside these pages? I have serious doubts, however people have a right to the knowledge. Several pages contain an unknown language. Instincts suggests a message; therefore, I must commit these to memory.

Searching through his pockets drew a blank locating his mobile phone. Cursing absentmindedness, his shoulders slumped. At least twice a week, they would return it to him, having left it elsewhere. He baulked at the time – 5 a.m..

Brother Michael will serve my breakfast at seven... and most likely return my mobile. I can wait.

Pugliesi addressed a priest as he exited the room.

'We chose the correct path – have no fear in meeting our maker.'

The priest bowed his head a little, masking his genuine reaction to Pugliesi's concocted statement. 'Thank you for that admission Cardinal, your words will stay with me forever.'

Pugliesi nodded before asking the priest to accompany him to his apartment.

Back in his living room, although fatigued, he moved to his worktable and began writing the strange characters from memory. Once finished, yet again, tears flowed.

I have serious concerns over the events that will follow an "Awakening" triggered by the Paragon. No question this will be "earth changing". That I will have passed before the consequences impact gives me relief.

A knock on the door broke his thoughts.

'One moment Michael.'

Pugliesi stood and moved to the wash basin, refreshed his face, then called for Michael to serve his breakfast tray. Camomile tea with a single poached egg on brown toast, no butter.

'Ah, Michael, have you seen my phone? Once again, I have mislaid it.'

Michael, looking apologetic, reacted. 'I'm sorry, not as yet, but I'm sure someone will find it soon.'

'Thank you, I'll need to nap, but please do wake me when you have it.'

'Of course. Do you require anything else?'

Pugliesi opened his arms. 'Perhaps my youth.'

With a warm smile, Michael left.

Pugliesi moved to his writing table. The top drawer contained a small wooden box shaped like a pirate's treasure chest. Inside lay a *baby* photograph of himself with his family, a ring, and two gold coins. Carefully, he tucked his written work underneath a layer of felt lining the bottom of the box. Contented, he lay on his bed, and once again recalled the pages of *The Last Book.* A single tear passed down his cheek before he sipped on his tea. Although he found it to be slightly unpalatable, he finished the brew. Pugliesi closed his eyes.

They would never open again.

Sixteen

The journey over the choppy North Sea back to Scarth felt like a lifetime. As they approached the landing jetty, Ross's land rover pulled to a halt. The main beam of the vehicle shining across the water caused a sudden flashback to Mortis Lux. Once again, the urge to return to sleep became overpowering. Boat secured, he stepped onto the rickety jetty, then approached his father, who thankfully did not appear angry. The warmth of their hug was heartfelt.

Jim shouted above the harsh gale.

'Ross, this trip is on me. Put it down to young Bran's enrolment to the hangover. Go easy on the lad – you were a lot worse!'

A grinning Ross waved a thumbs up. 'Cheers, I owe you one.' Turning to Bran, he exhaled deeply. 'Booze is something we all try lad and I have no craw with that. But putting your mother through worry, no, we can't have that – deal?'

'Of course, I'm sorry and if this is what a hangover is like, I may give the booze a miss – I need to crash.'

Ross couldn't help but smile. 'We all say that. Come on, let's get you home.'

Ten minutes later, Isla, as all mums do, forgo the shouts and smothered Bran with hugs. After a snack and warm drink, Bran retired. The prospect of confessing to his parents was daunting, and so he ignored the spectres and drifted into a welcomed natural sleep.

Seventeen

Michael rapped on the door of Lamberto Pugliesi for a third time. He had called to inform the Cardinal that his mobile was still missing. Concerned, he stepped inside. Now standing in the small entrance hall, he listened for sounds or movement... nothing, and so he began an agitated walk to the bedroom. Fears confirmed, he looked down on the body of his friend. Tears flowed for a few moments before he blessed the Cardinal then raised the alarm. The Vatican would, in most corners, begin its mourning.

Within hours, Madalena Pugliesi was standing over her brother's body in his bedroom. Guilt rushed through her as she understood her request had caused his death. Turning to the priest who had accompanied her, she politely asked him for a few minutes' privacy. As the door closed, Madalena moved quickly to her brothers' desk and located the small treasure chest. Carefully lifting the loose felt, she pulled out the note. Before reading, she swallowed hard.

I drank the tea knowingly, as my physical pain will cease. They keep the Last Book at the Mater Ecclesiae Monastery. My sister, ensure that brother Norton keeps an influence over this Paragon as I believe the initial consequences of his discoveries will trigger an "Awakening" of catastrophic events. I believe the unknown symbols used to write the last pages are a hidden message. Now, my sister, you must accept my death as natural without question. Show sorrow, not anger.

I love you deeply.

Lamberto

A gentle knock prompted Madalena to pocket the papers. After drinking water from a bedside glass, she answered the door.

As the Pontiff held his arms open, Madalena, weeping, fell into his embrace. Their moment of grief was genuine.

'I am so sorry, Madalena. Lamberto was a unique person and one of my closest confidants.'

Madalena stepped back and wiped her tears. 'Your companionship was something that comforted him through his illness and for that, I thank you.'

'There is no need to thank me. I received much from our friendship, more than I gave.' The Pontiff paused. 'Let us pray for your brother?'

Madalena smiled. 'Yes, I would like that, your holiness – thank you.'

After linking his arm to Magdalena's, the pontiff set to walk.. 'Allow me to escort you to the place your brother found the most soothing.'

As the two eased away at a pace suitable for the aging pontiff, Magdalena understood he would not be directly involved in her brother's murder; however, he would suspect his death may not have been by natural causes.

The Columnae, mindful that Madalena was her brother's only contact with the outside world, would keep a close eye. If evidence tied her into the ¥, tea would be the least of her worries.

Eighteen

9 a.m. the following morning.

As a deep sadness passed through him, Arlo closed a call.

You gave an entire lifetime to our cause, my dear friend. Your sacrifice will become legendary amongst our ranks.

A sharp knock on the door interrupted thoughts, followed by a hurried entrance by Bran. His agitated expression told him it had begun.

'I'll make you a drink.'

Minutes later, as Arlo placed a pot of tea on the table, Bran stared at the trail of steam for a few moments, then spoke.

'To quickly summarise. I have passed the spectres and entered the dimension of what I believe is the illusive void, the infinitesimal moment in between consciousness and sleep. Once inside, a bright translucent spectre replaced my physical form, to which I found extremely comforting! The void is a darkness that prohibits all sensory perception except sight. Within this "dark void" sits a bright tunnel, sealed at one end by a *lightfall* portal. After much consideration, I eased inside this tunnel only to witness the termination of the grey spectres as they attempted entry.' His eyes glazed over. 'This event brought on a satisfaction I did not expect.' Again, his expression changed to one of contentment. 'The lightfall portal is so captivating it took all my will to avoid being drawn in. Whatever is behind this portal has taken the lives of all Paragons who died during their *Death Sleep.* This is the Mortis Lux, my ancestor William, announced so dramatically.'

Almost unable to comprehend Bran's spoken words, Arlo stirred blankly, as his entire nervous system ignited, triggering an icy shiver.

The beginning of the truth. Is it possible that he can survive the death sleep?

'Words fail me – please, expand on the entire experience.'

Bran began. After an hour of a one-sided conversation, Arlo stood and bowed.

'I can only imagine the courage required to embark on such a journey. I'm astounded.'

Bran lowered his head. 'My whole being is pulling at me to return to this darkvoid to pass beyond the lightful portal. The lure is bordering on obsessive.'

Now standing with his hands clasped on the top of his head, Arlo spoke.

'Have you given thought to what the grey spectres actually are?'

'They represent evil. However, I will confirm nothing until I complete the final stage.' He grimaced. 'Of course, which may be my last.'

Arlo threw his hands upwards. 'That, my friend, is not in your remit.'

'Perhaps, but countless near-death experiences come very close to the description of the spectacle I witnessed, suggesting death waits behind the portal.' Arlo looked heavenward. Bran continued. 'What I find intriguing is that when I enter this *Darkvoid,* I am stronger mentally, causing resentment of the natural apprehension seated in my human mind.'

Arlo thought for a moment. 'Perhaps the clash is between your conscious and sub-conscious thought?'

'That is a strong possibility! It also appears that once I have experienced a stage, it then becomes natural.' He changed the subject. 'When I attempt the death sleep, I will require a setup similar to an intensive care unit, solely for the benefit of my parents.' He fell silent for a few moments. 'Ideally I would prefer to undertake this task alone, but I have to involve my family to say my goodbyes – you understand?'

Arlo frowned sympathetically. 'Yes, of course.'

'Then please begin your preparations, whilst I take time to confide in my parents.'

'Moral support?'

'Thank you, but no. I wish to speak to them alone and, of course, I'll explain your status and how you have helped my transition.'

Bran moved to hug Arlo, who gratefully excepted the show of emotion.

'I could not have progressed this far without your guidance,' said Bran sincerely.

'Thank you for your trust. As for the equipment, apologies... ninety percent is already on the Isle. I always expected a *medically assisted Sleep*, but perhaps not so staged.'

Bran grinned at the Professor's penchant for planning. 'Meet tomorrow – Oh and bring some Horlicks, I may need it.'

Both laughed, which felt good. After another firm hug, Bran prepared to jog home.

Ten minutes later, Arlo's sat phone rang.

My brother left a warning – you must maintain complete control of the Paragon, for his quest could trigger catastrophic events across the globe because of the Awakening. He also made a copy of the contents of the last pages written in ancient symbols to which he could not translate; I will send a scanned image of the wording. Please forward instructions on how you wish to proceed. Be warned, if he moves to the grey side, the world will suffer.

Message ended; Arlo took a deep breath.

Control the Paragon! That will depend on his metamorphosis, when or indeed if he returns from behind this portal. Regardless, there is much I cannot disclose, for he must discover his own true path.

Arlo breathed deeply, before assembling his satellite dish for an internet feed. One moment later, a notification pinged into his laptop. Arlo accessed the image. Moving hurriedly to his rucksack, he pulled out a large Tupperware box. Holding it closely for a few moments, he then removed the lid and carefully eased out an ancient leather-bound book.

No other living person understands the mystical language of the Paragon. Therefore, I am confident that the Vatican has not deciphered these characters.

Thirty minutes later, having decoded Lamberto's message, he felt a shock wave shiver its way through his body.

He spoke out loud. 'Brother Lamberto, I wish I could tell you how important your brave sacrifice has become. For what it revealed is possibly the saving of the Cranson Paragon.'

As another shiver passed through him, he paused for a few seconds, then continued.

But written in the last passage are devastating consequences far beyond anything man has experienced.

Arlo dialled a number and left a message.

'The book has revealed invaluable information; your brother's sacrifice has not been in vain. Destroy the note and all copies. Stay safe!'

Closing the call, his mind began.

His sensory advancements will evolve far and above any previous Paragons. I hope with all of my heart he remains of the white.

After pouring a large glass of wine, Professor Arlo Norton broke down in tears.

Ross watched Bran jog up to the back door. 'That lad, if he weren't so bright, I'd bet on him to make it as a sportsman.'

'What's the hurry?'

Bran stopped. 'Mortis Lux...!'

The words were enough for his father to call Isla from upstairs. Moments later, all three sat at the breakfast table in a calmed manner.

Isla broke the silence. 'This is about your dreams?'

'My apologies for concealing the truth,' said Bran quietly.

Ross took hold of both Isla's and Bran's hand. 'Let it all out, son.'

Over the next few hours, he spoke of the entire events, including Arlo and the ¥. His tone was one of command coupled with passion, but most of all, it portrayed an unwavering determination. The compelling presentation seemed to have a calming effect on both parents, who remained silent until Bran's last sentence.

Ross spoke first. 'Your mother and I have known this day would come.' Nodding to Isla, he moved to the oak cupboard, eased out a drawer, then thrust his arm into the back, pulling out an old parchment. Bran looked decidedly curious as Ross passed it over. 'From William's father, Gregor, its short and to the point.'

Bran closed his eyes for a moment before reading the words in silence.

Excus any mistaks in spellin I'm a crofter not a scoler.

Our William is differett to any child befor but not evil. And is cleverer than what we understand. He asleep most of the time and visits us when we asleep. When he dreams, he can hear and speak. We enjoy our sleep time better. He rites book after book all the same. I have red but no, this cannot be red by others, so I burn every copy. In his dreams he tells us that another boy is born to our line, a much cleverer boy than him and one who will change the world. He asks that this boy be protec at all costs until he finds the truth. I don't know what that truth is. I always thort somehow he got us this Isle. William passed during his sleep, but that night he came to us for a last time in our sleep. His words were exact "Wen the perfec child is born trust him for he wil be the one who understands."

One thing I no is that William does not talk of good and bad he talks of white and grey. Pass this down our family line and let no generation forget the sign speak.

Gregor Cranson 1712.

Bran blew out his cheeks. 'The spectres are certainly grey, and whilst in Darkvoid, my outline is white.'

Isla moved toward her son. 'You're not the devil, nor are you sick. You have a unique gift, and we stand by any decision you make.'

As one, they burst into a warming embrace before Ross spoke.

'Well son – as mum said, it's your choice to what happens from this point.'

Bran choked back. 'One thing is for sure, with my family behind me, I simply cannot fail. Oh, one thing... I didn't get drunk when I was at that cottage – apologies, I lied, but may I have a scotch now – I bloody need one!'

All burst into nervous laughter, which helped.

'My word, this explains why for generations our family has practised sign language. I did often wonder, as you never gave me a satisfying answer.'

Ross made a toast.

'To the most unique bloodline ever created – The Cranson's'.

'The Cranson's...'

After the first sip, a moody silence began.

At precisely 3.30 p.m. Jim McTay dropped off the latest guest to book a cottage on the Isle. Jim commented to Ross as he helped pack the five large suitcases into the rear of Ross's land Rover.

'Townies and baggage, what is it?' whispered Jim.

'They need shit loads of kit, as we are Neanderthals over here.'

Both men laughed as Ross slipped Jim his fare.

'Keep em coming Ross, keep em coming.'

The two men shook.

'Dr Massam, welcome. Arlo has prepared a bedroom for you at Cliff Cottage. I'll drop you there.'

Dr Massam smiled. Born in the UK, raised in Texas, he was a senior member of the ¥. His overall demeanour oozed a clean lifestyle.

'Mr Cranson, I'm privileged to help. Please, my name is Walter Massam, so plain ole Walt works for me.'

Both men smiled. The hand shake meant a lot to both.

Thirty minutes later, after settling into the cottage, Walt, holding a cup of coffee, listened intensely to a precise summary of all that had happened. For a few moments, he remained silent.

'Have you discussed the *Awakening* with the boy?'

Arlo shook his head.

'No – after much internal debate, I felt the information would induce negativity at this stage. Tell me if I'm mistaken.'

'I agree – absolutely. We must await his return from the sleep before considering this stage.'

'Thank you.'

Walt frowned. 'Is he the one?'

Arlo moved to gaze out of the window.

I must control my urge to reveal the closing chapters of the Last Book and allow the forces behind this journey to continue unfettered.

'I won't attempt to influence your mind on this. Once you have met him, you must make your own decision.'

'Fair enough. Oh, incidentally, Professor Watkins has been successful regarding the task you set.'

The news came as a welcome relief to Arlo.

'That, my friend, is a colossal headache avoided.'

For Bran to begin a sleep that no other had survived, that afternoon his bedroom would become an emergency crash theatre.

Nineteen

Hidden amongst the corridors at the Vatican, a small room, rarely used, housed three gentlemen, none of whom held a rank within the Catholic church. All were members of the Columnae, the eldest, and sitting chairman, Vincenzo Giordano, spoke in a tone that demanded attention.

'So – I'm informed that the wonder boy, Cranson, left university to be with his parents. Now Norton, Massam plus two other men, are living on the Isle. Coincidence? No! Are they awaiting his *Sleep*? If so, why have we not reacted? Tell me.'

The men looked nervous. The tallest spoke.

'He is too young to attempt the Sleep.'

Giordano slammed his fists onto the table. 'And you know this how?'

'All before him were well past their nineteenth birthday.'

'Correct – but they were all flawed. This boy has no defects. So that makes him different and with his IQ, he will be a threat. Trust me, Norton believes the Cranson birth line has spewed up another Paragon.'

'And if he makes the Sleep?'

'If he survives, remove him from the Isle and safeguard at our refuge. As for the parents, arrange the accidental sinking of their relative's boat when they make a crossing.'

The two men left. Within three hours, six men would make a covert insertion into Scarth.

Twenty

7 p.m. The Cranson household.

Bran had spent an hour with his parents before introducing Walt. With everybody inside the house, he addressed all.

'Mum, Dad, this has been our family's destiny for centuries. Let's take pride, not hesitancy in this final stage.'

Isla lovingly embraced her son. Loki, not to be outdone, badgered for his attention. One by one, he shook everyone's hand. Ross pulled him in for a final hug. At that moment, Bran wished his dad could be with him. To shake the feeling, Bran gave thumbs up to Walt, looked up the stairs towards the bedroom and smiled.

'Saddle me up!'

Twenty minutes later, they had connected Bran to the various equipment set in place. The bleeping pulse of the heart monitor gave the room a cold, clinical atmosphere. O negative being the blood group of two Paragons exhumed (as was Bran), was available from a cold store.

After adjusting for comfort, Bran laughed aloud. 'To infinity and beyond.'

Walt and Arlo politely left the bedroom to allow family privacy. Now alone with his parents, Bran ensured his tone exuded belief, but inwardly he was *paddling* like hell.

'I have no fear – none. Trust me, and on my return I want a full brekkie ready and waiting.'

Ross, holding Isla's hand firmly, understood she was close to a break down. As they hugged, Isla hoped it would not be their last.

A wait unlike any other would begin shortly.

Outside, two hundred yards away on a hillside, three men were observing the house through infrared binoculars. One picked up comms.

'Alpha One to Bravo team – sit rep.'

'Bravo reporting. All cottages are empty, assuming occupants at the Cranson house?'

'Received – Alpha Bravo teams, surround the house on all points. Advise when in position.'

'Rodger that – out.'

Twenty minutes later, Alpha One dialled his sat phone. 'All targets gathered inside the Cranson house, over.'

‘Monitor closely, the Sleep may have begun.’
‘Received – out.’
Alpha waited for Bravo team to confirm position before easing down towards the house. Threading his course upwind would help reduce scenting from the Cranson’s dog.

Bran drew comfort from the chilly breeze that crept in through the window left open by a reluctant mother. His emotions were on the brink.
Just now I’m a little petrified, but I understand this to be my human nature. Close my eyes and everything will be fine.
After writing *I’ll be back* on his forearm, it began!

Now in touching distance of the lightfall portal, Bran closed all thoughts of how he would return from the other side, before gazing at his spectre.
A perfect tranquillity, coupled with a lack of fear, is overwhelming. I have to move inside – now!
With a rapidly increasing pulse, he braced before moving into the lightfall. On entry, the sensation of being propelled forward was immediate. Barely a moment later, he burst from the light and plunged into a vibrant body of shimmering colour, stretching infinitely outwards. Now stationary, he calmed.
I’m surrounded by a visual sense of coloured movement, comparable to the Aurora Borealis (Northern Lights).
As his gaze swept all in front of him, sprinkled amongst the coloured phenomenon were thousands, perhaps millions, of star-like forms, materialising and disappearing almost in the same instant. As a purity of extreme contentment flooded into his mind, he opened his arms to embrace the experience. The physical action produced no resistance and yet he still felt cocooned within the vibrant colour. Ultimately, no scholar could summon the words to describe this phenomenon to its exactness.
My comparison to the Aurora Borealis is accurate, except this is infinitely more vibrant, portraying the sensation of, dare I say it, life. Curiously, the coloured splendour has a similar tinge to my inner spectre, but again, markedly more intense.
He smiled at a bizarre comparison.
This brings back recollections of the tranquillity radiated by the wax inside a lava lamp, buoyant in its prismatic prison.

Fixated on this mysterious dimension, he doubted if anything on planet earth could produce such contentment.

What have I done to deserve this experience...? Just watching the dynamic array of colour produces a stimulation impossible to describe.

The sense of supreme privilege ended abruptly as an overwhelming exhaustion, coupled with an urge to sleep, consumed him.

No! I am already asleep. Something is wrong... very wrong.

'I have to leave now!'

Opening his eyes had no effect. A glance around confirmed the white tunnel was no longer in view, whilst the lure of *sleep* was becoming irresistible. Now fighting to stay awake, a glaring realisation flushed through his mind.

This is not sleep... this is death calling!

Back inside the bedroom, Arlo, extremely agitated, spoke.

'Bran's brain activity is at its highest since he began. Whatever happens from this point, we cannot interfere?'

With eyes locked onto their son, neither Isla nor Ross replied as Bran unexpectedly stopped breathing. In seconds, the heart monitor registered a numbing, continuous tone. Bran had flatlined!

Isla rushed to her son's side.

Walt stepped forward; 'Please, you will endanger his life if you interfere.'

'But his heart has stopped!' she screamed.

Ross looked hard at Arlo. 'Tell me for certain our son won't die!'

Arlo replied with a genuine compassion. 'To say I'm certain would be a lie, but right now, he is fighting events beyond our understanding. Interference with his physical form will affect the outcome in only one way... his death!'

Ross bit down and tried his best to comfort his distraught wife as the monitor continued uttering its morbid tone.

'We must wait...'

Loki, unconcerned, set for sleep.

Outside the cottage, with the wind occasionally shifting the curtains, Alpha One, after scaling an outlying barn, had observed the emotional scenario with some relief. When easing back to cover, he made a call.

'Alpha One reporting. Boy must be in the Sleep; the bedroom looks like an operating theatre. The good news, he has just flatlined.'

'Excellent. Stay for confirmation, then make a clean extract?'

'One hour then I'll exfil.'

'Received – out.'

Bran, now seconds away from death, produced one final thought.

Take me beyond this moment.

In that instant, *death* vanished. Now back in Darkvoid, facing the bright tunnel, the urge to vomit consumed him. Until the nausea ended, he remained motionless. Minutes later, looking at his own form, he let out a nervous sigh.

I appear to be alive if only as a white spectre.

He grinned.

How bloody stupid does that sound? If I'm alive, then I should...

All thoughts paused as he focussed on a mist approaching his front on a continuous path.

This is the exact sequence of my initial experience with Mortis Lux. Therefore, I understand what I must do!

With the mist flowing ever closer, a second portal formed. Once level with Mortis Lux, Bran shook his head in astonishment.

Its composition is identical to the Aurora Abyss I experienced beyond the lightfall in Mortis Lux.

The temptation to enter became overwhelming and so, without hesitation or fear, Bran released into the depths of the portal. Once inside, he became surrounded by the coloured *Abyss,* with the star-like forms appearing, then disappearing in a display of light never seen. As the indescribable euphoria returned, he bathed in its unbridled elation, for some time.

Instinct tells me by using this second portal, I eradicate the burden of a premature death, a death that every Paragon suffered who reached this point. I am both saddened and elated, so I bow as a matter of respect for my ancestors.

Bran held his bow for some time before relaxing back into thought.

Inside this wonderment, although I'm "physically" asleep, I'm mentally awake. Is this heaven? If it is, where is everyone?

Although I have concern over my return to consciousness, I have attained a level of contentment never experienced.

He shivered as his mind drifted to the point of his near death.

But then I was so close to death, so close. Have I experienced how life ends? But now, in order to become the first Paragon to succeed, I have to return to my conscious form.

Opening his eyes – nothing...!

Back in his bedroom, an hour had passed with no response from Bran. With all monitors now switched off; the grieving had begun. Ross, having come to blows with Walt, had to be restrained by Tate and White, resulting in Isla hyperventilating. Walt, ignoring a rapidly closing eye, brought her back to normal. Both parents were now sat blankly staring at the lifeless body of their son.

Whilst observing the events inside the house, Alpha one had instigated the team's withdrawal after confirming that Bran had been unresponsive for over an hour. News of the death brought a smile from Giordano. Red wine to hand, he sat back in his chair to gloat.

'This Paragon must have ventured further than the others. Perhaps it's time to eradicate this bloodline. No need for complications, I'll allow the parents time to grieve, then we can arrange a sinking of that ferry boat.'

Seated on the porch with clenched hands, Arlo swallowed another anti-arrhythmic tablet. On every minute he had looked to his sat phone wishing it to ring. Thoughts snapped back to the present after a hysterical scream from Isla. Another glance at his phone with pleading eyes ended in frustration.

Minutes later, it rang.

Arlo twitched as a commanding voice spoke.

'Their team has extracted from the Isle.'

A rush of adrenaline flushed through his system.

'Confirm again.'

'I repeat – the six have made exfil.'

'Great work.'

Arlo, heaving an enormous sigh of relief, rushed into the bedroom, and asked Walt to switch the heart monitor on. Ross screamed.

'What the hell are you doing? My son has been dead for over an hour. Have you gone insane?'

Arlo looked awkwardly at Ross. 'Please, for now, just wait, watch, and hope.'

As all eyes fell on the monitor, Isla remained traumatised. For thirty minutes, they sat in silent trepidation before Ross stood up.

'This is madness! Switch it off – NOW!'

A single beep from the monitor pierced all ears like a gunshot, interrupting Ross's tirade. Shocked back to reality, Isla turned to Arlo.

'Is there hope?'

'As long as we keep getting a response from the machine, I believe Bran is still on track. However, I must warn you – we'll have a long wait.'

Ross spoke in anguish. 'Arlo, this is beyond cruel. If you had hope, why the hell did you allow us to suffer?'

Arlo dropped his head. 'I am truly sorry. Please allow me to explain.'

With a temper at breaking point, Ross sat down; Isla's gaze stayed locked on the monitor. Arlo began.

'The machines were Bran's idea to make you both feel a little safer.'

Ross, shaking his head, replied. 'That lad...'

Arlo sighed. 'That lad indeed, but to further explain. I received a message found in William's book.'

'William's book?' quizzed Ross.

'Yes, he wrote, a Paragon could remain in a "death state" for many days, even weeks.' He exhaled. 'Therefore, in the belief they had died, many suffered the fate of being buried alive.'

Ross looked horrified. 'Why did you not tell us?'

'As I explained, there are many dark forces at work. We had information that a covert team infiltrated the Isle tonight.' Both parents looked shocked as Arlo continued. 'I knew they would observe the situation before making their move. As a result, after watching the *death* of Bran play out, coupled with our reactions, they left the Isle in no doubt that Bran had died during his death sleep.'

Ross's brain ticked over. 'Our anguish had to be realistic?'

'Yes – and again I apologise for my misdirection.'

'You knew?' said Ross, looking directly at Walt.

'No. But it was the correct decision.'

Ross held his hand out to Arlo. 'That took a lot of courage and Walt – I'm so sorry about...'

Isla interrupted. 'Are you saying that because of Bran's *dream* you located William's book, which helped to save him?'

Arlo's expression exuded pride. 'That is exactly what happened.'

Another beep interrupted the sentence to the instant euphoria of the room. Arlo looked at his watch. 'Ninety-two minutes from the last beat.'

A sudden knock made everyone jump and set Loki to charge the door, barking frantically. The voice of Mike Tate calmed all, including Loki, who trotted back to his bed. Tate, Tom White, and another man stepped inside. Loki remained silent as Tate introduced the stranger.

'Dav Branson. He kept track of the men who came for us.'

Welcomes and handshakes followed before all turned to the monitor.

Ross looked to Arlo. 'Is there hope for our Bran?'

'Beyond any doubt. However, I cannot predict how long this period will last.'

Without taking her eyes from the monitor, Isla spoke out.

'He will be back!'

Ross cradled her. 'He wouldn't miss that brekkie.'

The wait began...

Twenty-one

Just moments had passed since Bran had opened his eyes and failed to return to a conscious state. Now staring into the matrix of flickering lights, his mind was in overdrive.

Failure will not intimidate, as I feel no threat to my life. However, I must remain calculated to find a way to my conscious state. Energy has a start and finish point. Lightening an example. My end target is my physical form! But there are billions of conscious states. Facts are facts. My sub-conscious has drawn me to every stage of this journey; therefore, I must allow it to seek a pathway back.

The thought resulted in a concern.

What timescale in the natural world will this sleep represent? Days? Weeks even? There is also a fear that the euphoria of my return would disrupt my family's composure, unsettling the process. So, if I hit a "home run," I must bounce back to this Abyss to ensure my stability.

His thoughts stalled as, once again, the enchantment of the coloured abyss consumed him. Sometime later, he snapped back.

The Abyss overrides all negativity and stimulates a tranquillity that is difficult to ignore, but I must, once again, seek my return...

Take me beyond this moment.

As Bran engaged his sub-conscious, an indescribable rush of colour enveloped him before he was back in the depths of Darkvoid. A fist pump suited his elation. Looking straight ahead, both portals shimmered ominously as they cut into the surrounding blackness with an unerring precision. The once eerie silence had become a comfort. The second portal matched the size and shape of Mortis Lux but with a "*Borealis*" *like* mass as its centre.

By defeating the onslaught of death, direct access to the Abyss is possible through this second portal, confirming that Darkvoid is a hub to other dimensions. My urge to discover is relentless, but right now, it is imperative that I revert to my conscious form.

Upon opening his eyes, the pulse of the heart monitor invaded his ears. After three beeps, he closed eyes and returned to Darkvoid.

Isla, Ross, Arlo, and the rest had gasped when Bran's life force returned. His body had shuddered aggressively as it registered three consecutive heartbeats before returning to its coma-like state. Shocked to her core, Isla stood quivering, whilst Arlo erupted with a triumphant shout of "Yes"!

With anticipation, Walt anxiously checked the data from various equipment and spoke excitedly.

'Bran's reconnected. He's found a way back. However, allowing time for him to adapt to the conscious world is vital. If he wakes, don't rush him. Let him dictate the protocol.' Shaking, Arlo popped a tablet into his mouth. 'Ross – Isla, your son is a miracle.'

Isla's shoulders shook as she tried to contain her sobs. The couple, in emotional unison, stared at the prone figure of their son.

Bran had held a death-like state for twelve days. During this period, his heart had beaten once every ninety-two minutes. Arlo's statement was correct; they were all witnessing a miracle.

Now gazing intensely at the two *portals,* Bran recalled the experience of his *deathly* journey through Mortis Lux, resulting in a deep remorse.

Passage through this dimension has taken all before me, therefore I must continue to reinforce my command of my ability to manoeuvre through both portals.

High on confidence, thoughts turned to home.

The Bosk became my sanctuary when I was a child. I called it Nemkis, a name suitable for this wonderful abyss. My entire being is willing me to embrace this feeling of euphoria, but my family is waiting. And so, one more flashed return, before I complete this enlightening journey.

The beat of the heart monitor began. After six, he returned to *Darkvoid* triumphantly and opened his arms in exultation.

The time I now take to switch is infinitesimal. Home is now, but a thought away.

Back in the bedroom, nine hours had passed since the last *return,* taking the parents to an extreme level of anxiety. With a brutal honesty, Arlo brought a sharp reality to the situation as he explained the full ramifications had the Columnae witnessed Bran's survival of the death sleep. After several worrying discussions, a cover story emerged, being a new identity and location. Both Ross and Isla, although in full agreement with the subterfuge, had found the reality difficult to process. However, after witnessing the apparent *reincarnation* of their son, his anonymity was paramount.

Now feeling ready to enter his physical form, Bran set himself. Closing his eyes, his return to conscious state was without a timescale. For a few seconds, he shuddered as his heart adjusted to normal sinus rhythm. After a sharp gasp of air, he eased himself upright, shivered a little, then blinked several times. Isla, shaking, held her hands to her mouth to stifle a vocal reaction.

With the euphoria of his return to a conscious state, combined with the knowledge gained, Bran broke down. Both parents, understanding their son's mind was in an emotional turmoil, felt helpless.

As Bran's human mind battled to cope with the verifiable facts of a mortal death, his sub-conscious eased him into a tranquil sleep to prevent lasting damage to his mind.

Walt looked at the monitor, which brought an almighty relief when the machine's consistent beep began.

Isla moved to feel her son's brow. 'Is he safe? Is he sleeping normally?'

Walt spoke up. 'He'll sleep for some time after such a complicated encounter.'

He was correct; it would be six days before Bran woke.

Twenty-two

3p.m.. Sixth day of the recovery sleep.

Bran woke. Seconds later, the enormity of his journey took a hold, creating an overwhelming relief. Understanding he was now in a conscious state, his mind, settled by the *after* sleep, began processing.

I'm alive! Back in the physical world. And I sense there is no longer confusion regarding my conscious or sub-conscious state – a welcome fact. Have I actually uncovered the truth behind death? Hell fire!

Of the medical equipment, only the heart monitor remained. In his current emotional state, a pulse rate of one hundred and thirty would not be a concern. Ross and Isla, seated at the end of the bed, remained motionless, unsure how to react. Upon looking at his parents, Bran began rubbing his eyes anxiously. After several deliberate blinks, he stared hard, as they appeared to be silhouetted by a bright *aura* that replicated the white perimeter of his spectre when in *Darkvoid.*

Is this a side effect?

His own features had also become shrouded by the mystical aura to a depth of three inches, with a *fuzzy* edge. Gentle rubbing made no effect. A swift scan around the room confirmed normal vision with inanimate objects.

What the hell has happened to my vision?

Confusion was such that it stalled the euphoria of his return to consciousness. With nerves on a knife edge, he snatched off the electro pads from his chest, eased off the bed, then moved tentatively towards Ross, whose concern at his son's bewildered expression was obvious.

'Son – your back with us... are you alright?'

Still rubbing his eyes, he stepped closer to his parents.

'My vision appears to have altered as I now see a glowing white aura around us all – can either of you see it?'

Confused and ignoring the sound of their racing heartbeats, Ross and Isla looked at each other questioningly before shaking their heads sideways in a silent no.

'Then please don't move. I have to see if I can touch it.'

Holding still in nervous apprehension, both nodded.

After a steadying breath, Bran touched Ross, then Isla. Half expecting a shock, relief flooded in as his hand passed through the aura with no effect. Satisfied they were in no immediate danger, his nerves eased.

'Well, it is not hazardous, so can I have a bloody hug?'

Happy to have their son back and safe, neither parent asked questions. The hug was pure emotion. A stampede on the staircase gave notice to Loki, making his bid for attention. As the dog bounded into the room, followed by Arlo and Walt, Bran's stomach churned over.

Arlo, Walt... even Loki radiates this bizarre aura.

Upon stroking Loki, as with his father and mother, the aura gave no effect on touch.

This is just a visual phenomenon.

A man hug with Arlo and Walt confirmed this thought. Bemused, his eye caught a sight through the window, forcing him to move to peer outside. Now staring out towards the bosk, he became mesmerised by a scene of pure enchantment. The white aura shrouded all living vegetation. Gazing skyward, he watched as several crows hounded a common buzzard in an air battle that was a delight to witness with the radiant aura enhancing their shapes.

Unbelievable! All life appears to emit the same aura. Is what I see the aura that encapsulates the spectre? Could the coloured internal mass be the soul? Where the hell is this going?

For a moment Bran stood transfixed as the birds continued their acrobatic display, the beauty of which disguised its violent intent. All in the room noticed his obvious detachment, prompting Walt to shake his head at the others to dismiss any interference.

With a bark hinting at a walk, Loki nudged Bran's hip, breaking his concentration. Smiling, he patted his dog's head before moving to the sink. Three glasses of water and a flapjack would ease hunger pangs for now. Understanding that everyone was on edge, he turned to speak.

'Don't concern, I'm fine – this peculiar change to my vision is both unexpected and a wonder. However, I need to run....' Turning to look outside, he spoke again. 'On my return, I'll attempt to explain.'

Bran's offer helped appease the tension, prompting Ross to speak, albeit with a tinge of anxiety.

'Son, it'll be pitch dark soon. Take a head torch.'

'I will and please, everyone, I'm okay!'

After rushing downstairs, Bran grabbed his running jacket and torch, then took off with Loki.

Back in the house, Isla had wept.

'Love, he's safe. That's all we need for now,' said Ross, easing her down on the sofa.

'I know – I just wish he were a normal young boy, and this was all a dream.'

Turning to Arlo, she wiped away her tears.

'He's survived the trauma we all dreaded, yet he only shows concern over this light *thing*. What is it?'

Arlo moved to sit on the chair opposite.

'I really don't know, but you're correct. This issue has dominated his thoughts, so we must assume it has an elevated level of importance. But for now, let's be joyous he beat the curse of the Paragon.'

Isla shivered. 'He has, hasn't he... beaten it... my god our son!'

Now motionless in the centre of the wooded bosk, Bran had become awestruck by the gentle sheen shrouding all life forms.

The light from this aura doesn't illuminate the immediate area like a normal light source. How peculiar!

A curious urge to gaze upon the herd of red deer triggered him to set off running. With every pace, the fascination of the aura intensified, building a euphoric emotion that increased his desire to see more. As the herd grazed on the low area of the Northside in winter, locating them would not be difficult. After twenty minutes, he stumbled headlong into the main herd, alerting the alpha stag, which turned to face him.

Bran froze.

I wouldn't have chosen The Major to greet me.

The stag, a prime male, whose fourteen-point antlers gave him the imperial title of *Monarch*, raised his head to take scent. A two-hundred-pound stag was impressive but viewed with a surrounding aura. The vision became amplified. With breath billowing from flared nostrils, the Major eased forward.

Grabbing Loki by the collar, who had set his stance, Bran took a breath.

Do not run or he will charge me down... do not run!

After a moment, without thought or calculation, he heard himself command Loki to stay. On shaking legs, he moved towards the stag. Loki growled, to which Bran gave another sharp command. The stag stopped, grunted twice towards his herd, before continuing forward.

Loki remained silent.

Time stood still as the distance narrowed. At five feet, the Major paused, stomped his hoof, and let out a low grunt. Bran now gazed, trance-like, at the spectacle of the Majors' surrounding aura. After a few seconds of an impassive stand-off, without fear, Bran moved to touch the stag. As he approached, the stag lifted his head in a passive action to reduce the threat from his antlers. The act was one of enormous trust, to which Bran's entire nervous system ignited. As his hand touched the cheek of the stag, it exhaled from his nostrils. The warmth of his breath relaxed Bran further. Slowly he brought his left hand up to the other cheek, creating a tender moment lasting a few seconds before the stag billowed, then backed away to return to his herd. Bran dwelled on the moment he would never forget. An impatient bark broke his concentration. A shrill whistle from Bran resulted in Loki displaying the exuberance all dogs do when their master had shunned them for a moment. Seconds later, the two leapt about, exuding frantic excitement, each for a different reason.

I connected with the most powerful animal on the Isle. Two different species, one special moment.

The jog for home began.

Thirty minutes later, as he passed through the bosk, a rotting oak lying against the backdrop of the shimmering aura of the surrounding trees caught his attention.

The fallen tree emits no "light," so I must conclude that an aura signifies life itself. This being true, trees and vegetation must also have a link to the Nemkis? How is this possible without conscious thought? I am drawn to follow an instinct; this is my way of learning.

A young oak glowing with the aura became his task. Setting his balance, he then placed his palms onto the tree before relaxing into a state of absolute calm.

I feel a connection but it's sporadic, almost as though the link has a loose wire!

Upon closing his eyes, the serenity of the Nemkis engulfed him. Although the transition had been instant, Bran understood he had travelled via Darkvoid through the *coloured* portal.

Once again, my connection becomes natural. In recalling The Major, my emotions appear to intensify within the Nemkis. For the stag not to show aggression is... remarkable. Does he see me as a Paragon?

Bran eased into a state of harmony. After some time, he returned to consciousness to become enthralled at how the dark of night enhanced the aura of the trees and vegetation, producing a dramatic display.

This is beyond all imagination – a light source that provides zero illumination beyond itself...?

After switching on the head torch, the beam revealed a sight that disturbed him. The young oak tree had withered and died. Something had processed a fast forward of its life cycle.

Loki began wagging his tail, instigating Bran to move the beam toward footsteps, causing Ross, Arlo, and Walt to shield their eyes. Bran lowered the beam.

'Over here.'

As Ross approached, the gnarled oak tree drew his gaze.

'What happened to that oak?'

Bran, looking distraught, spoke.

'I've experienced many things – but this?'

Both Arlo's and Walt's expressions questioned the discussion as Ross crouched down for a closer inspection.

'This was a young oak until I touched it moments ago?' said Bran.

Ross ran his hand over the withered bark.

'You've been outside for over six hours. Son, I'm at a loss how or why this has happened.'

Becoming used to shocks regarding timescale, Bran ignored any concerns.

'I do not know. Let's get back.'

As he stepped forward, his legs gave way. Moving quickly, Ross braced his fall, then eased him to the ground. Walt rushed to examine him.

'Don't concern, he's just fallen asleep.'

All flushed with relief as they set to carry him back.

Bran would sleep for some time.

Twenty-three

The following afternoon.

Bran woke, dressed, and sat for a moment.

I feel... different, in a way I believe is positive, but I can't put my finger on why.

Confused, he moved downstairs to be met by everyone standing in passive apprehension.

The white aura is still in my vision.

'Did you carry me back from the bosk?'

'Yes,' said Ross.

'Ah, my apologies. Well, I best explain my experiences, otherwise my mind won't clear.'

Isla moved to the gas hob. 'You look drained. I've grilled some bacon?' Cooking was her way of staying calm.

'Thanks mum, I'll grab a drink as well.'

At the sink, he allowed himself a quick glance outside to confirm his previous vision. The aura once again dominated, but his thoughts lay elsewhere.

The oak tree perished. Why? There will be a reason, one of enormous significance, so for now I must keep my explanations simple whilst my understanding is limited.

Bran moved to the kitchen table and devoured a bacon sandwich before asking for a second. Once finished, he invited all to be seated, being he could almost taste their anticipation.

'I will be brief, as I have yet to absorb the experience.' Concerned at the nervous expressions portrayed by his parents, Bran shuffled to get comfortable.

They're scared! Keep it simple.

He began.

'Entry into a dimension between our conscious and unconscious mind is possible. I now call this *Darkvoid.* From here, a bright passage leads the way to an *abyss* of sheer wonderment I have named Nemkis. The only other phenomenon that comes close to its visual splendour is the aurora borealis.' Bran rested his hands on the table. 'This journey is not without danger.' Another pause. 'The onslaught of death begins when leaving this bright passage via a portal that is best described as a "waterfall" of light. I believe this is the stage that claimed all previous Paragons who attempted the journey. As I tried to return to a conscious state, death was but moments away. Thankfully, in the last second, my sub-conscious thwarted death's clutches by transferring me back into Darkvoid.' Bran shuddered as his mind recalled his emotional state. 'During my near death, I felt no pain. The expression I would choose to describe the event is a sense of *dispersal.*' With a drying mouth, Bran asked for a drink of water. Isla obliged. The break helped, as all had held a muted silence as their minds built a picture of Bran's preternatural discoveries.

After coughing several times, Bran wiped his mouth, then continued. 'Upon re-entering Darkvoid, a second portal manifested alongside the white passage. The size was the same, yet its appearance was reminiscent of the colours of the Nemkis. This, as I discovered, is an entrance to the Nemkis without the risk of death. Entry is instantaneous. I cannot put into words the sense of contentment this dimension provides; its purity enriches your mind. Joy is a thousand times more intense and does not diminish. It is an everlasting utopia!' His expression lingered for a moment.

It is hard to encapsulate the true magnitude of the Nemkis. Proceed before this engulfs me.

'Mixed amongst this wonderment is a matrix of star-like objects appearing then vanishing in a unique display, which for now remains unexplained.' As he looked at each person, a deep sigh preceded his next statement. 'I cannot confirm that travelling through the white passage explains death, as my experience was one of a living Paragon, but it is a distinct possibility.'

Walt spoke out.

'I think I speak for all. Is the white passage many claim to see during near death situations?'

'Again, I cannot confirm this as fact, however if I allow my instincts to answer – I would say yes, and perhaps the Mortis Lux, William foretold!'

The words hit hard and so all remained in a brooding silence as minds dared to imagine the actual route from their own life. Understanding that nerves had become fraught, Bran changed the subject.

'Since my return, I appear to have gained a sense that views the world *differently*. Upon entry into Darkvoid, I become a translucent spectre.' He paused. 'Imagine the same coloured mass that forms the Nemkis, surrounded by an aura of white light, defining my natural shape, and you have my spectre.'

Each now drew upon their own assessment of Bran's description, producing expressions of wonder. Bran, closing his eyes, exhaled. 'Now things become a little more complicated, as in my vision, all life now radiates this *white aura,* silhouetting the entire form.'

Arlo, clearly excited, spoke out.

'Even plant life?'

'Yes, every living organism appears to exude this aura. As a result, I met and stroked the Major!'

'What.. *our* Major? Are you telling me you approached the stag?' said Ross, slightly sceptic.

'With an overwhelming desire to see the herd's aura, I ran to the lower north side, pitched over scraghill headlong onto the herd. Dad, I crapped myself as the Major scented us. But amazingly, he just plain walked over to greet me!'

Ross shook his head in disbelief. 'Are you certain you were not dreaming?'

'No, since my return, I can decipher my exact state of consciousness. I tell you as a fact. The Major strode close enough for me to feel his breath. He grunted, eased his head back to reduce the threat of his antlers, and allowed me to touch his cheeks. Can you imagine how I felt? Contact lasted but a few moments before he turned and led the herd away.'

'That is absolute madness,' said Ross, throwing his arms up in amazement.

Bran grinned at the irony of his father's statement, with him having just listened to his explanation of Death, Nemkis and the Mortis Lux.

Expressing the same level of enthusiasm, Arlo pitched in.

'If this outline, the *aura,* is visible to you, can you also see the coloured mass?'

'No, but I am presuming it is within us all.'

Isla, rather white faced, spoke timidly.

'Could the aura be the soul?'

Her question maxed everyone's anxiety.

Aware that this answer would unlock issues deep in their psyche, Bran deliberated momentarily.

This is an enormous step for the human mind.

'Mother, forgive me. I can only answer this question when I understand the truth. Assessments at this stage would be non-productive.'

Isla pushed. 'But again, what is your instinct?'

That his mother's question was more of a plea, Bran sighed.

'My instinct could be incorrect, but yes, I would say the coloured form contained within the surrounding aura may be what we understand as the soul. Therefore, I intend to prove this as fact.'

All as one looked directly at their own body.

Walt spoke in a tone that was a little rushed.

'We're all bloody shaken by this, but I agree we must not dwell on the assumption.'

Isla spoke again.

'What you have achieved is a miracle. You're bound to solve the questions we all have. My fear is that in finding the truth about death.' she baulked. 'Will knowledge of death affect how we live? Will this become an albatross around our necks?'

With his mother's obvious distress, Bran became caught in his own human reaction to her question. After concealing his concerns, he moved to hug his mother.

'Until we know the verifiable facts, it's impossible to make that judgement.'

Arlo spoke out.

'A burden of centuries released, and for that, I thank you. And you're correct, time is required to decipher the facts. However, with control of entry into Darkvoid, I am certain that whatever answers you seek will appear naturally in a sequential timeline. As well, dreams and recall experiences will come at you thick and fast. Therefore, I would advise to hold the soul as your primary task. Anything else is secondary, to be expanded on at a later stage.'

'Wise words to which I agree, for the soul is truly the holy grail of human curiosity, so yes, given the chance, this will be the direction I take.'

Arlo, aware nerves were becoming fraught, cleared his throat, then switched the topic back to the *normal* world.

'It is also important that we address the present and explain the developments that occurred during your sleep.'

Bran listened in silence. Once Arlo had finished, the realisation of the trauma he had caused his parents resulted in another emotional surge, albeit without shedding tears.

Mothers' hugs helped and for five minutes he became her little boy once more.

Ross spoke out.

'Son, you have negotiated a journey that took all before you – but now I must ask you one question.' Pausing, she clasped his hand. 'Do you wish to continue? Our preference is against, but please, mother and I will support you either way.'

Bran grimaced.

'My human side is fighting the verifiable facts of death; however, the Paragon resents this and continues to urge me back to the Nemkis. I must find a balance in this struggle to establish my advancement. Am I scared? Again, perhaps in my human mindset – but!' Not wishing to be swayed by the concern his parents would show at his next statement, Bran moved to the window to gain comfort from the wonderment of the aura. 'All my life I have searched for fresh knowledge. My mind demands information. It's always been that way. In front of me is the ultimate discovery and as a Paragon, I crave to explore; deep inside there is no fear, just an overwhelming urge to continue.' Bran turned to face his parents. 'I apologise, but I have to forge on.'

Isla spoke out, her voice now sounding resolute.

'Now that we understand your need to continue, we remain behind you.'

Ross felt Isla's grip tighten on his own, understanding that her speech was for Bran's state of mind, not theirs. Both wished it would all go away.

'We're with you every step of the way.'

My parents are suffering, and yet they still show support. Family is my indispensable foundation.

'In that case, can I eat again?' Bran laughed, hoping to put the dialogue on pause.

Isla closed her eyes briefly, then ventured to her domain. Arlo peered into Bran's eyes, indicating they required a clandestine discussion. Walt set to explain the cover story for Bran's demise. Once finished, Bran stayed in reflective silence for a few minutes before speaking.

'No corpse avoids complications, so as the current takes everything out to sea, my thoughts favour a *probable* cliff accident on the northern side.'

Arlo nodded. 'I agree, saves a challenging post-mortem. Isla... Ross, can you cope with this?'

'If it keeps our son safe, we'll be fine,' Isla responded.

Ross nodded positively. 'The accident will set off a frantic exploration of the Isle and its adjacent ocean, lasting for three to four days before they conclude it. The wait will then begin for the body to be washed ashore, which, of course, it won't. Sea life *feeding* would be a plausible explanation. I'm happy we take this line.'

Pleased, Bran stood. 'I'll lay a scent to the cliff point and throw some random clothing over the edge, then I'll slip off the Isle with Mike and Tom. Arlo, can you offer a place to stay?'

'Already in hand, a property just next to Loch More.'

'Fine, but once the furore settles, I'll return to Scarth, and that is non-negotiable!'

Arlo wanted to argue, but let it drop for now. Ross and Isla just smiled.

'Then no time like the present.' As he moved to embrace Arlo, a flood of visions ripped through his mind. Although shocked, he called for Loki, said his goodbyes, then set off for the cliff.

I connected with personal memories deep within the psyche of Arlo. How is for another time, as what I saw was devastating... but why has Arlo concealed this? No – this revelation cannot unsettle plans for my disappearance. My god, when will this chaos cease?

Bran's absence spawned a profound silence that lasted nearly five minutes as the gathering struggled to accept the gravity of his statement.

Isla broke the ice. 'He will uncover everything man has feared.'

Ross drew a breath. 'Does this worry you?'

Isla cast her gaze to the ceiling before speaking. 'My concern is how will we react to understanding death...'

Arlo sat down. 'Aye, even for me, the concept of understanding our end is more pressing than the thrill of its discovery.'

Walt pitched in. 'I'm also finding this extremely difficult. I mean, we have actual answers regarding the mysteries of our existence. Christ, it's so bloody surreal!'

A new hush descended before Arlo shifted direction. 'Ross Isla, amongst all this turmoil, your suffering over the last few days has been relentless. Are you both coping?'

Isla shrugged. 'After believing your son has died, then getting him back is the absolute range of our emotional tolerance, so anything else we'll manage.'

'The family connection is the mainstay Bran requires. May I suggest that Walter and I return to Cliff Cottage to give us all some time to ponder on what has happened?'

'Yes, we would all benefit from a little space. Thank you,' acknowledged Ross.

Minutes later, as Arlo started the JD, Walt raised a question, which both had been considering.

'Dare we reveal the devastating senses he may inherit?'

'As much as I crave to interfere, we have to let nature dictate his development. It is a blessing that his aggression in the past has been to protect others.'

'Do you wonder if that fact is pre-ordained?'

'I hope so, or the shit storm of all shit storms will be upon us.'

Walt made no reply, as both men drifted into personal thoughts about their own mortality.

Back at the house, Isla voiced her concern that if this knowledge were to be made public, he would be subject to persecution.

Ross grimaced. 'Or worshipped. I'm not sure which is the lesser evil!' He paused before continuing. 'I'll admit to finding the thought of understanding my demise fulfilling.'

Isla's grip tightened.

'Well... I'm not in that camp, but at least we can give him different perspectives.'

'Haven't we always...'

Both smiled.

Within three hours, Bran was on a boat heading for Tod's Goat, a small coastal inlet south of Wick. As agreed, the authorities were called by distraught parents at 7 p.m.. Mountain rescue, along with a dog team, assembled on the Isle within two hours. Later into the night, the team confirmed a suspected cliff fall. A full search of the Isle's coastline in daylight would confirm their suspicions.

Seated alone in the small bedroom at the rear of the cottage, Bran had shown little interest in the building, nor had he chatted with Mike and Tom. His mind had become overloaded. To determine where to begin was proving difficult as his emotional state continued to flux between his human and Paragon mindsets.

I have to stay within the mindset of the Paragon to suppress my natural concerns. That being, at least I have some insight into how the human mind will cope. Sadly, I have grave doubts the knowledge will suit the masses. This aside, linking to Arlo's memory, has alarmed me. So, given all these facts, I have one conclusion. All contact with the ¥ must end until I have a valid explanation.

Bran nodded to himself.

My parents will know where I'll take refuge.

Before retiring, he insisted that Mike and Tom should not enter his room unless called. Mike rang Arlo to confirm, who, after a little thought, instructed them to check occasionally.

Thirty minutes passed before he penned a note explaining he needed time alone and slipped out of the window. A mountain bike stored in the lock up caused a smile – wheels!

The next day, the news of Bran's probable demise reverberated through the academic institution and intellectual community. The identification of his hat, ensnared on boulders at the Northern coast, had magnified this probability.

Jim McTay had remained with the family to support them. Isla vomited the moment he left. However, after witnessing the miracle of their son's return, both parents understood the need for Bran becoming anonymous.

Earlier Bran had emailed Christie to ask her to ignore the subterfuge, but to tell no one. Christie, having read the email, had one thought.

Life or death, whichever is to be my fate, always trust my word forever.

His disappearance came as a complete shock to his family. Arlo had left the Isle immediately to organise search efforts. Now alone, Ross and Isla embraced. Isla spoke softly.

'Why would he forgo the ¥ and the protection it offers?'

Ross shrugged. 'Bran does not act on a whim; he has motives. I've an idea where he will be?'

Isla thought for a moment. 'Our Jim's bothy?'

'Without a doubt. Love, it's our task to maintain the cover of this accident and keep his location safe – that's how we can help for now.'

'I know you're right... but I'm at a loss to what Bran is experiencing.'

'The main thing for now is he won't die prematurely, and that's our starting point.'

Both looked towards the drinks cabinet...

In an apartment within the Vatican, Vincenzo Giordano, chairman of the Columnae, closed a call, then smiled.

Impressive move by the ¥! A cliff accident! Saves any hiccups in the coverup. I can wait a month or so before ending the Cranson blood line.

Twenty-four

Jim McTay's two-room abode, set approximately five miles away from Lybster, Scotland, was spartan. The spare key was in its usual place behind the woodshed. First task – a warm fire, followed by a brew and a beef ravioli.

An hour later, Bran moved closer to the fire, looking puzzled.

I must accept who or what I am and follow the unrelenting urge to return to Nemkis – nothing else matters. Selfish perhaps, but this is now my utopia. For every moment spent in the physical world promotes negative thoughts regarding my discoveries.

After piling a heap of logs onto the fire, he moved to the bedroom and clambered into the single bunk bed. The bedding felt damp. No problem. Within a moment, Bran was staring at the wonderment of Nemkis. For some time, he enjoyed the emotional surge that generated a sense of unbridled euphoria.

The blended movement of colour, being the living pulse of Nemkis, synchronises with my own "soul". I am it – it is me, creating a sense of unbridled fulfilment without engaging in anything. This consuming emotion is constant, adding to its irresistible lure. If this is the "afterlife," could I remain in this state forever? Absolutely, but that answer isn't important yet. No, I must turn my studies back to my near-death experience to understand the process. For that, I need to return to Mortis Lux.

By a virtually incalculable time span, Bran returned to Darkvoid. Mortis Lux hovered menacingly, enticing his entry, forcing Bran to concentrate hard on his task.

Before I understood the portal's purpose, its presence held a certain enchantment. Now the fear of death raises a nausea in the pit of my stomach. Although the sensory value of scent is zero in Darkvoid, I attach a stench to the experience. It is time to comprehend the process of death in its entirety.

As soon as Bran entered, the grey spectres disintegrated as they encountered Mortis Lux.

Ying and Yang, the white and the grey are opposites? Good and evil...? Yet another question – move on.

Although he felt a slight uneasiness in the presence of the light-fall portal, his need for knowledge prompted him to move forward.

If I die, all my efforts will come to naught. Therefore, I must forge a confidence in my capability to survive the onslaught of death once again.

As expected, the glare of the Nemkis' coloured display overwhelmed him, as countless millions of the star-like forms appeared and dissipated in moments.

Perhaps the star-like flickers are the "Mortis Lux" for other life forms?

The ghastly thought caused another bout of nausea before the inertia of death began its call. Immediately, his focus became attracted to the white border of his spectre, dissipating like the fuse cord of an explosive device. The ever-expanding gap allowed his inner colour to merge with Nemkis.

As I am dispersing, my imminent death brings no pain. Nevertheless, the will to survive is quickly weakening... I must end this before I am fatally consumed!

Bran's sub-conscious took over and transported him to Darkvoid, rendering the death call inoperative. Now stationary, the experience evoked a distinct melancholy. To neutralise his dour mood, he returned via the Nemkis' portal. In that moment, all negative emotions ceased, allowing a recall of the event without the negativity of anxiety.

Death was a unification, like a single raindrop entering an immense ocean. The droplet integrates with the larger body. Once more, my intuition tells me that this is the spirit reverting to its roots. Do we secure a memory of life in this "repatriated" state? Or is this unification a journey in its own right? Time and persistence will unearth the answer. Without doubt, I must stop risking my mortality to gain evidence of its final state.

With pushing thoughts of his near death aside, Bran settled to study, fishing for answers, building conclusions.

Can I confirm that the "inner form" of my spectre is a soul? I concur with Arlo's counsel, and it shall become my primary focus. Our existence comprises two parts. The physical body and the celestial soul. Certainly, for now, I will refer to this energy as the soul unless I prove otherwise.

Could we perceive Nemkis as a Heaven? It definitely provides a spiritual experience, perhaps even divine. A deity? Again, time will tell.

He paused for just a moment.

Those who have lived through a near death experience reported the same thing – a white tunnel! After passing through something similar, I am convinced that they were accurate in their assessment, and I will stand by this as fact.

Bran's visions flashed back to Mortis Lux as it decimated the grey spectres.

Opposites... Ying and Yang, white and grey, good and evil. Is there a hell for evil? No, from evidence witnessed, just absolute extinction! Then I must conclude, only a pure existence will return the soul to its beginnings. However, as the soul returns to Nemkis during the process of death, I cannot confirm if it keeps a memory or blueprint of its life. Perhaps only in death will I understand. So many possibilities. A complicated conundrum, for sure.

With a mind on overload, his sub-conscious drew him back into a much-needed sleep.

With no further news of Bran's location, Arlo's concern had become heightened.

I must return to his parents and disclose my darkest secret.

Mobile to hand, he dialled.

Ross answered and applied his most distressed tone for effect. 'Have you found him?'

'Not yet.'

'What about your place in Wick?'

'The cash is still in place. Would he trust anyone else?'

'Only our Jim's family, but he wouldn't risk the contact.'

'Understood – I'm leaving for Scarth now as I have to speak to you!'

The anxiety in Arlo's tone caused Ross to snap his reply.

'Can we not speak over the phone?'

Arlo paused for a second. 'What I have to disclose – it's difficult. I'll be there as soon as I can.'

Ross looked at Isla.

'Arlo's coming over. Something doesn't sit right.'

'In what way?'

'I don't know – guess we'll have to wait and see.'

After three hours of restful dreaming, Bran yawned and stretched before being overcome by a wave of apprehension, causing his body to twitch involuntarily.

I am in utter shock that I have stumbled across the ultimate voyage that leads to the end of life. The thought is extremely intimidating. I need to calm.

In order to release his nervous tension, he peered outside to view the aura surrounding all living forms. After a few moments, he could feel his self-control regaining the status quo.

The aura reveals itself, whilst the soul remains hidden. Perhaps the aura is a protective force, only releasing the soul on its return to Nemkis? All to be proven.

His mind suddenly gave birth to yet another shocking breakthrough.

Given that the soul returns to Nemkis after death, it is reasonable to assume it originated there. This means that a soul that has been reborn could be the root of a new life. Does this signify reincarnation? Perhaps. However, the probability of regressing back to a human form when having access to the multiplicity of life forms would be exceptionally low. This verifies the lack of true reincarnation stories.

Bran felt a shiver wash over him; such was the effect of his discovery.

The existence of reincarnation. My mother is correct in her assessment. What would be the psychological response? How can I verify this to be factual? No question if I published my experience's, I would become either heralded or damned!

After a few moments, he stood up.

I have failed to ask one of the most obvious questions during my search for answers – where are Nemkis and Darkvoid? Can I only experience these dimensions through the subconscious? Perhaps they are just varying interpretations of the universe? I'm left with so many questions. Will I ever find the answers?

I need to calm – I need my utopia.

He moved to lie down on his bed and closed his eyes...

Twenty-five

As the helicopter touched down only a few yards away from the bosk, Isla couldn't help but stare with a feeling of dread at the pending conversation. Ross, having ventured out to greet Arlo, stood several metres away from the rapidly spinning blades. As soon as he entered the room, Arlo immediately began a conversation with Isla, who had made herself comfortable on the sofa beside a blazing log fire.

'My apologies for not being more explicit when we spoke on the phone. I have many things that I need to admit.'

Isla shifted her attention in Ross's direction. 'I suggest you go grab a bottle of red – having a drink can help us all relax.'

Arlo nodded in agreement. 'May I sit down?'

'Yes, of course,' said Isla.

After Ross poured, everyone took a mouthful. Isla's wistful look gave Arlo the motivation to take a deep breath and begin.

'I have a sole mission in life. To ensure the ¥, keep looking for and observing any Paragon born. Why? You will comprehend my explanation better than most people, because two Paragons have been born from our family line.' Ross and Isla, shocked, took another sip of wine. Arlo continued. 'When my only son was born. I knew he followed the line. I also understood he was a malevolent child.' Arlo's turn to take a sip. Isla and Ross remained silent. 'His educational opportunities, as you would expect, were exemplary, however in every stage of his life he fought against society and its compliant ways. From the age of six, he exhibited a brutality that raised its head in many guises. As with Bran, he had no physical deformities and intelligence that gave him an edge. During his development, he became a concern. Why? You may well ask.' Arlo took another sip. 'There are two separate paths the Paragon can follow. White or grey. I knew he would take the grey, presenting a danger to all.' He paused for yet another sip. 'As you already understand, Paragons have command of various new senses. However, as no one has completed their long sleep, we cannot calculate their full potential. My son, at the time of his demise, was the most advanced.'

'I'm so sorry Arlo...'

Arlo's expression became dour. 'I pitched his ashes to sea forty-six years ago, having died in a car accident of which I instigated.'

Enraged at Arlo's confession, Ross jumped up. 'You murdered your own son?'

'I arranged his death and carry no guilt or burden in doing so. He was a monster. But I still hurt from the very depths of my heart – he was my son!'

'Your wife?' said Isla.

'Our son set fire to our house aged thirteen. She perished alongside our maid. Never proven, but I knew.'

A few moments of stunned silence passed before Ross said something.

'It is inconceivable that something like this could happen, but yet you still took the life of your own son... your own flesh and blood!'

'I'd make the same decision if time allowed. In layman's terms, Ross, Isla – the Paragon, evolves into a super being with remarkable powers. My son's inclination towards sadism would have caused him to go down a destructive path, and that was something I could not allow.'

'And if Bran takes the grey line?'

'Then you must not hesitate to stop him. I ask you this. Would Hitler's parents have taken the same measures had they of known...? I would think so!'

Ross looked towards Isla, opened a cupboard, and produced a shotgun. Without emotion, he shoved the barrel firmly against Arlo's forehead, who froze.

'You say you knew your son to be evil?' Ross nudged the shotgun again to prompt an answer. Arlo winced, but answered without fear.

'Yes, with no doubt.'

'Understand this, with no doubt there is no evil abnormality in our son – ZERO! If you even think to harm him, I will kill you stone dead.' Ross prodded again. 'Clear?'

Arlo's reply carried a certain dismay. 'Yes, I understand. He is your son.'

Isla spoke in a stern tone. 'If my husband is unsuccessful in accomplishing the task, I will finish it.'

Arlo showed his disapproval with a frown. 'Please, you must understand – be he white or grey, people cannot comprehend their abilities and will fear the Paragon. Without guidance, Bran could become a danger to himself and this world.'

Ross looked directly into the eyes of Arlo and pulled the trigger. The dry click echoed menacingly around the room. Arlo twitched before letting out a relieved breath, triggering Ross to lower the barrel.

'They will cease to search for his body tomorrow. We'll then travel to the mainland and join in with the people of Wick as they offer their prayers. Then, we will make a solitary journey to our son to tell him of your family's death and its implications. It is up to Bran to decide the path he will take. If you give any instruction to tail or trace us, we will make sure Bran never returns to the ¥. Is that clear?'

Arlo silently acknowledged by nodding his head. 'Without a doubt, but he will already be familiar with my history.'

Isla wondered, 'How?'

'Bran is the only one who can answer that question, but if I had to guess? His leaving was based on a lack of trust in my integrity. I give you my word, I will respect his judgement.'

Arlo rose to his feet and offered his hand. Ross disregarded the shake.

'When he is safe – not before!'

'I respect your wishes and will bid you both a goodnight. Oh, may I stay over at Cliff Cottage?'

'Of course.'

'Thank you.'

Ross's forehead creased as a sad expression crossed his face. 'My deepest condolences for all that you have lost. Nobody should have to endure such suffering.'

Arlo's manner showed his appreciation. ''I talk to my wife every single day without fail. The sorrow of her absence still resonates within me. I'm so grateful to both of you and I wish you a pleasant night.'

A deep feeling of sadness swept over the couple as the door closed.

'My god, that man lives in torment,' said Isla.

Ross lowered his head. 'Yet he is the only one who can help Bran!'

Outside, Arlo eased into the JD before collecting his thoughts.

I must refrain from introducing the full truth about my son, as well as any information about the "Initiates" and the

Awakening. Without question, I must only act if the conditions are impossible to disregard.

Bran had remained transfixed by the enchantment for the longest period since he had discovered its existence.

With each passing instant in Nemkis, my Paragon character is growing increasingly powerful. No hunger, no thirst, just an enrichment of my mind. But what of my physical form which rests in a deep sleep? How do I survive for what may be weeks? Why is sleep forced upon me after leaving Nemkis? During this sleep, my dreams are so vivid, in contrast to a typical dream which is irregular, unreal and virtually incomprehensible? Sleep is a requirement for both the Paragon and the regular person. Despite this, it takes significantly longer for the Paragon to recover. Is it a consequence of the realism? Does the restful mind of both Paragon and the human link to Nemkis to rejuvenate their energy? Arlo suggested I find the answers we seek if I allow them to manifest naturally – let us see if this is true!

He returned to his physical body to drift into a dream. Now, watching the start of a Formula 1 race at Silverstone, a wish of his since he was a boy, he became mesmerised by the sound and velocity.

Bran shook his head.

Don't get too wrapped up in this dream – find the connection.

As he envisioned Nemkis, his dream became fragmented as racing cars turned into shopping trollies. Concentrating, he gasped as the racecourse shifted into a grocery store with Arlo standing at the entrance handing out posters of missing persons.

My god?

As he approached, Arlo drifted further away, causing annoyance.

Forget the dream – take me beyond.

Darkvoid appeared as expected. The Mortis Lux and Nemkis portals shimmered ominously. His intuition told him to wait.

Time ticked before a sea mist on the horizon revealed a third portal. Immediately, memories of his previous experiences brought calm.

I have no fear. This "creation" will have a purpose.

The central composition of the new portal was identical to Darkvoid, yet surrounded by the coloured splendour of Nemkis. Bran's anticipation was at an all-time high as it locked into position. When he reached the count of three, he opened his mind and allowed his sub-conscious to take over. At that same moment, he passed through the portal, then found himself within.

For a few moments, the multi-hued exterior held his attention before a small, white globe caught his eye as it streaked across the internal darkness and *adhered* to the surrounding Nemkis. Then a second and a third, followed by hundreds, thousands, and onward to an innumerable amount. Concentrating hard, he focused on a specific area to assess the peculiarity.

The rapid formation and disappearance of these spheres make their evaluation difficult. They stay singular, but attach themselves to the surrounding Nemkis like limpets to a rock, drawing up nourishment.

Bran reorganised his thoughts.

My aim was to uncover a relationship between Nemkis and the sleeping unconscious. Then is this the dimension of dreamworld? If so, then the spheres must be the sleeping minds of the human, and confirms my belief that we draw energy from Nemkis during sleep.

For the next few minutes, the intensity of the mysterious spheres became frenetic.

I am witnessing sleep replenish both mental and physical energy levels by drawing directly from Nemkis.

Bran laughed.

Like driving up to the fuel pump, I guess.

His observations formed conclusions.

The spheres materialise and dissolve in an instant, far beyond the human brain's ability to process. Undoubtedly, this explains why humans cannot recognise the shift from consciousness to sleep. It is now imperative that I confirm the "spheres" are actually slumbering minds, but how?

A moment's reflection yielded the answer.

Could I, as did the Paragon dream walkers, enter another's dream?

Bran worked through the process.

Is my access to these "sleeping minds" a matter of chance, or can I choose which one I would like to enter? The most basic method of deciding would be to select something at random. Follow my usual pattern. Use the subconscious.

Now gazing across the Dreamworld, Bran allowed his thoughts to drift amongst the billions of spheres. In a flash, the situation changed into a primary school football match. Bran did a double take when he saw the grass on the pitch towering to two feet high, creating a ridiculous playing environment. The groundsman dashed on, summoned a suspension of play, before endeavouring to shear the grass. Bran roared with laughter as the man's scythe seemed to be made of rubber, exasperating him to the brink of tears. Unexpectedly, the children morphed into hungry rabbits, devouring the succulent blades at a startling rate. The exasperated groundsman shook the scythe at the rapidly increasing multitude of munching bunnies.

The epitome of madness!

With a cheerful face, Bran withdrew. Still chuckling at the ridiculousness of the subject's dream, he focussed once more. On this occasion, the narrative was female-driven, as the main character was in Harrods of London, endeavouring to purchase a Louis Vuitton handbag. Bran roared with laughter as each time the female attempted to lift the bag, the handle extended like a bungee cord, making the purchase impossible.

Now confident, he tried a third scenario, only this time, the participants were naked!

'Oops, no need to see this one.' Slightly blushing, he laughed heartily before recalling the previous encounters.

As expected, human dreams make no sense, but why? Why is the subject so abstract?

Bran pondered for a moment.

The human mind cannot possibly function normally in this dream dimension, causing the disjointed nature of dreams.

As his mind flashed over conclusions, he glowed with excitement.

'Have I explained the sheer insanity of the dream?' *Absolutely! The Paragon has a heightened sense of awareness that allows them to remain in control of their mental faculties in any dimension, something the human is incapable of.*

Now charged, he continued on this thread of thought.

Therefore, the scattered information from their dreams makes it difficult for humans to recall them accurately. Bugger me, this makes perfect sense!

Bran reassessed his interpretations once more and concluded that he had solved some of the mystery behind sleep and dream.

In conclusion, the mind replenishes its energy reserves by linking to Nemkis through a subconscious process we know as "sleep". With lacking the required senses, the event becomes distorted and jumbled, resulting in the bizarre dreams we experience.

After reflecting on his theory, he found it to be without fault. Satisfied, his mind swerved to another tangent.

Am I now able to locate my slumbering parents? If asleep, they are somewhere in this dimension inside a dream-sphere?

Focusing solely on his mother, he suddenly appeared inside a scenario seated opposite Isla in their garden, which, for some bizarre reason, had an abundance of tropical fauna. The speed of their connection caught him off guard. Frantically suppressing his rising excitement, he took control.

'Mum – it's me, Bran! We're both asleep, but with me being a smart arse... I've joined your dream.'

Isla, looking confused, squinted as she stared quizzingly at Bran. 'Is that you? I couldn't sketch you as you're a lot taller.'

Her abstract words produced a smile. 'Mum, tis aye, please don't fear, I'm safe and at Uncle Jim's bothy chilling, but I would be ever grateful if you could bring me some fruit?'

'Are you floating or swimming?' said Isla, quizzingly.

Not wishing to place any further anxiety on his mother's sleeping mind, he withdrew after one last message.

'I have to leave you now, say hello to dad and don't forget the fruit – love you.'

Isla woke bolt upright, then shoved Ross, who cussed and turned over.

'Wake up. You won't believe what's happened.'

Still half asleep, Ross sat up and yawned. 'What?'

'Bran has been in my bloody dream! I saw him – well, kinda... I think it was him. It's difficult to remember.'

The sentence shocked Ross into words. 'You sure this isn't the wine playing tricks?'

Isla's expression confirmed her claim.

'It was Bran in my dream... but he was different, if that makes any sense?'

'Go on then. What did he say?'

'Err – I can't recall all of it but... I think he said bring fruit?'

'Bring fruit? What the hell!'

'Well, true or not, I'm taking some and then we shall see. Anyway, William was able, so why not our Bran?'

Ross shrugged. 'Point taken.'

For the next few moments, both lay in silence as their minds attempted to process Bran's visit. Dumbfounded, they got up to make a brew. Anything to help remain calm.

Back inside the sleep dimension, visiting his mother's dream had boosted morale.

Confirmation of my interaction will be if mum actually brings fruit. I would have tried Dad also, but I've absolutely no doubt mum's awake now and putting him through the mill. Hell fire, I've actually entered my mother's sleep, set in a dimension which supports the human dream. Mind blowing.

After a moment of self-congratulations, he replayed the events before deciding to wake and make another attempt to get into the dream dimension. Jolting awake, he banged his head on the bunk. As he rubbed, he felt the knock was more painful than it should have been.

Peculiar. The impact was minimal but the pain severe. Water required.

Three glasses later, a tin of peaches also took the hit. A decent belch worked, but the thumping headache begged for paracetamol. From the medical tin, he swallowed two tablets before stopping in his tracks.

I'm not tired! Yet I've been active? Does this mean I forgo the "replenishing sleep" by connecting to the dream dimension?

His return to the dimension was immediate.

As before, once I have experienced a dimension, entry becomes instant. To be a Paragon is breath-taking.

Bran woke, then waited thirty minutes for his mind to grasp at sleep, only it didn't.

Then, travelling through this "dream dimension" negates the necessity for restorative sleep – a major development! Am I now able to interchange between all dimensions at will?

After looking at his watch, he closed his eyes.

For a fleeting moment, he visited Darkvoid, Mortis Lux, Nemkis, and finally, the Dreamworld. Travel time to each dimension had become infinitesimal. On waking, normal time had logged forty minutes. His yearn for sleep had vanished.

One last test.

Bran entered Nemkis, stayed for some time, then exited via dreamworld to Darkvoid. Now looking at the three portals, he observed they had formed a triangular formation with the Mortis Lux at its peak, whilst the Nemkis and Dreamworld portals lay bottom left and right.

Their symmetry is exact, it is a wonder of natural engineering. I am questioning if there is intelligence behind this phenomenon?

Upon waking, yet again, his desire to sleep was zero. The time scale was three hours.

There's no doubt that entering this Dreamworld prevents restorative sleep.

The thought produced a surge of emotion.

My entire perception of death, the soul, sleep, ghosts, reincarnation, and dreams is being challenged. Yet I crave for more. I am now curious to discover how and when a soul enters a new life. Would this be at conception or birth? Before I can study this, I must first confirm the existence of the soul. Arlo's assertion was correct. A chronological order of discoveries will continue to unveil new insights. The possible aftermath of revealing the truth concerns me. And so I must be vigilant and oppose the malevolent forces that will obstruct my progress. I sense that this "battle" will be a crucial moment in my progress, temporarily outweighing the importance of gaining further knowledge.

A visit to Nemkis would settle emotions before his return to Scarth.

Twenty-six

The parents' guilt was magnified by the significant presence of Wick's citizens and the intolerable media coverage. Immediately after the service, they slipped away quietly in Jim's Land Rover.

Thirty minutes later, fruit in hand, Isla knocked on the bothy door. With no immediate answer, her stomach churned over. Ross ran back to the Landrover. The ignition key was one of five, the fourth opened the front door. Rather gingerly, both moved inside to find Bran fast asleep. Relieved, Ross locked the door, whilst Isla set about to make a brew. Two hours passed before Bran stirred. On sight of his parents, he jumped up and, yet again, banged his head. As before, the pain seemed exaggerated. Rubbing his scalp, he eased from the bunk rather shakily. As his eyes cast upon his parents, the sight of their surrounding aura gave them a distinctly saintly presence.

'It's a treat to see you both.'

After a hug-filled reunion, Isla timidly displayed the bag.

'You asked for fruit?'

Bran felt a sense of satisfaction overwhelm him.

'I hope I didn't scare you?'

'No love, but it was weird! How on earth?'

With a satisfied grin on his face, Bran chomped away on the apple. 'Wow...! I entered your dream... bloody hell, I'm a dream walker! It's been an eventful journey to get to this point. The discoveries I have made are absolutely mind-blowing.'

He paused.

Ross frowned. 'Why do I feel there's a *but* coming?'

Bran's face marked a look of awkwardness.

Until I have a greater knowledge of the circle of life, I will not engage in any discussion about it. Although dreams can be unnerving, they are a less disruptive topic to discuss.

'It may take some time to understand this.'

Both parents, albeit apprehensively, settled to listen. One hour later, questions began. Ross first.

'You're saying that when I fall asleep I pass through this *Darkvoid* – but cannot see it?'

'Correct! Darkvoid is the moment in which you switch from conscious to sleep, and since it occurs so quickly, your brain cannot process it. Think about it. Can you ever recall falling asleep?'

Ross held the thought for a second.

'True. One minute I'm awake, the next asleep... weird. So, when I fall asleep, I go...'

Bran interrupted.

'Think of it in terms of sight. You can focus on one object before switching to another without moving. The sub-conscious merely switches dimensions, not images.'

Bran's simple interpretation helped the parents.

'Where are these places?' Isla wondered inquisitively.

'Wish I knew, let's just say... somewhere!'

Creases formed on Ross' forehead, as his mind became awash with thoughts. 'And we sleep to recharge our soul?'

'Well, yes, be it the soul or physical energy.'

How is it that our dreams are so peculiar? And how did you find the way to enter our dreams?

'In the dream realms, your mind cannot function normally, causing the experience to be distorted beyond recognition. As for becoming a dream walker. Well, from Darkvoid, I pass into a dimension I've named the dreamworld. Once inside, my sub-conscious targeted two random dreams. Both were absolute nonsense, but amusing. With my subconscious aiding me, I was able to connect with mum and have a brief conversation with little trouble.' He shrugged. 'It seems nonsense, but as you brought the fruit...!'

Gathering herself, Isla made a statement.

'Mortis Lux, a mysterious tunnel associated with death, Nemkis, a spiritual realm, and now a Dreamworld.' Pausing, she lifted her shoulders before opening her palms. 'There's a pillar missing?'

Bran looked quizzical. 'A pillar?'

You have identified the three dimensions which are integral to the structure, but in order to make it complete, a fourth is required. So I ask, is the fourth pillar the creation of life?

Ross, impressed by Isla's assumption, waited for Bran's answer. Equally surprised by his mother's assessment, Bran took a moment before answering.

Four pillars... My mother's assertion is correct, I am lacking a fourth portal.

'Mum, I agree. However, let's not dwell on the uncertainty of guess work, we'll leave it open.'

The parents gave the same answer in unison. 'Okay.'

Isla continued to talk. 'How do you cope?'

Bran spread his arms and smiled widely. 'I descend from remarkable Cranson ancestry. We are masters at coping!'

A sharp knock at the door ended the smiles.

'Jim? Is that you?'

Ross gestured for Bran to sneak into the bedroom, then hastened to answer. Isla kept herself occupied.

When the door opened, a small but burly man, garbed suited to a Highlands farmer, stood in search of answers. Ross offered his introductions.

'No, it's Ross Cranson, Jim's my wife's brother. We're staying over for a night, and you are?'

The farmer's attitude eased down a notch. 'Oh – err right, I see, yes I'm Rob Tate from over the Glen there. Apologies Mr Cranson, with the Rover being parked I thought...'

'Of course, thank you for your concern.'

'No problem and I'm so sorry about your son...'

'Thank you. We really needed a break from the press.'

'And here's me chuntering on. I'll be away then.'

Five minutes later Tate met with a news reporter whose complexion hinted at an alcohol problem.

'Are they in there?'

'Aye.'

'How long are they staying?'

'Day or so I reckon.'

Handing Tate one hundred pounds, the corners of his eyes creased.

'Cheers pal, they won't give interviews, but I'll try my luck when they set to leave.'

Tate snatched the cash. 'Well wrap up mate, there's a storm on its way.'

'Bollocks. I'll stay put in the car on the road out. That way, they'll have to pass me.'

Tate shrugged and left feeling a little guilty, but in the winter months, one hundred pounds would come in very handy.

Bran stepped from the bedroom as he heard Ross enter the main room.

'Let's go home. Hiding in plain sight is the better solution. Fact is, no one actually turns up on Scarth, do they?'

Ross gave a shrug of his shoulders. 'I guess that makes sense. Let's sleep over and return tomorrow, Mum?'

'Alright, but what about Bran's return? Our Jim's no longer an option.'

Bran moved to the window. 'And I have a problem with Arlo.'

Isla peered at Ross, her expression giving the thumbs up to open dialogue.

'Arlo called to the Isle yesterday and spoke at length about his life and its appalling tragedies.'

'Did he mention his son?' said Bran, sounding perplexed.

Ross raised his eyebrow a touch. 'He suggested you may already be aware. Hear his story out, then we can discuss?'

'I'm all ears,' said Bran.

Isla rustled up a cuppa and a snack. With his headache worsening, Bran took two more paracetamol. Ross began. Bran had conflicting emotions after the explanation.

'I somehow sensed that his son was a Paragon, but I did not see his genuine pain. I feel much sorrow for Arlo, but also a wonderment on how I interacted with his past. The *greys*, as he mentioned, represent evil, and thanks to my parents' evil is not my trait, his concerns are unnecessary. I'll visit him in sleep and smooth this over.' Bran stopped talking and began laughing. 'Did I actually just say that?'

All three burst into laughter at the sheer lunacy of the statement.

Ross folded his arms. 'Perhaps you should ask him to collect you from Tods Goat at 8 p.m.? If they show up tomorrow, you're definitely a dream walker!'

Bran gave his stomach a light tap with his fingers. 'Challenge accepted, I'm hungry.'

Isla huffed with a smile. 'My son, be patient. There are much better ways to cook than using a wood-burning stove. Ross, best you rustle up a night's worth of logs.'

Nodding, Ross set to the task. Bran moved to a cupboard; inside he found a bottle of Scotch and a pack of cards.

Family time...

Some four hours later, Bran lay awake on his bed.

Drifting back into normality has been uplifting. Now then, Professor Arlo Norton, let's see if you're asleep.

Upon entering Dreamworld, a sense of pride surged through him, followed by a wide smile. Thoughts of the Professor entered his mind, resulting in an instant connection. Now watching Arlo, walking on the grounds of Cambridge University, he took a breath.

Connection is natural. I have become a dream walker!

'Professor, can I have a minute?'

On hearing Bran's voice, Arlo turned to look; his confusion was obvious.

'Bran, is that you? I can't make out your features?'

'Yes, it's me. We're dreaming. I'm sorry to hear about your family's tragic history, but please have no concerns about my allegiance. It will always be of the *Whites*. I'm with mum and dad now but I need a pickup... 8 p.m. tomorrow at Tods Goat. I repeat, 8 p.m. at Tods Goat.'

Bran faded from the dream which led to Arlo waking in a sweat.

'Impossible, a dream walker! How can he have achieved this so early in his development?'

Struggling to recall the dream, Arlo strained at his memory. One set of words remained in his mind: Eight goats?

Meet me with eight goats? *What does this mean?*

Arlo pondered for several minutes before his mind worked out a possibility.

Perhaps Tods Goat? Yes, has to be and so, Tods Goat at 8pm. Fascinating, truly fascinating.

After making his calls, he reached for a tablet.

Whilst I'm thrilled, I cannot help but wish my son had taken this destiny. But that is in the past! I'll do my utmost to make sure this boy fulfils his fate and becomes a Paragon.

Parked a mile down the track leading to Jim's bothy, the reporter woke from a snatched sleep as the storm began its delivery of high winds and torrential rain.

Bollocks! To make my story worth this discomfort, I need to link this death to the last time a young boy died on Scarth. Will need to add a little bullshit, as folk do love a cursed tale.

Twenty-seven

The following morning passed quickly. At 1p.m., from behind a curtained window, Bran watched his parents drive away. He would leave for Tod's Goat around 6 p.m. As the vehicle slipped from view, one sentence sprang to mind.

Consciously controlling my subconscious has become second nature.

With his mind feeling positive, he gazed at the scenery through the window.

Understanding all life emits the same aura, affects the mindset. I love the animal world, but I eat meat, or used to. But life must kill life to survive. Will I ever solve this conundrum?

Ross honked his horn to alert the BMW that was blocking his way down the narrow lane. The reporter smiled and waited. Had he known of Ross's temper, he would have taken another angle. Ross stormed out.

Isla called from the side window. 'Do not make a scene!'

The reporter stepped from his vehicle and held out his hand. 'Mr Cranson, Mike Cookson from the Herald.' Ross, remaining silent, ignored the shake. Cookson pushed.

'Without appearing to be discourteous, I would like to talk to you about the tragic events concerning your son's recent *disappearance.*'

Cookson's tone in presenting the word *disappearance* was a distinct hint of foul play.

'The Herald.' said Ross through gritted teeth.

'Yes, the Isle would appear to be a curse to your family, given its history of mysterious deaths.'

Cookson never saw the blow which knocked him stone cold.

'Bastard!' screamed Ross, standing over Cookson's unconscious frame.

Isla, rushing from the vehicle, took hold of his arm. 'For god's sake, check he's okay.'

Ross turned coldly. 'Go back to the car – he'll be fine.'

Isla gave an indifferent shrug. Arguing with Ross in temper mode was a pointless action. After giving him *that look,* she moved back to the passenger's seat. Ross angrily dragged the unconscious Cookson back into the rear of the BMW. A groan gave notice he would be okay. Slightly calming, Ross gave a nonchalant shrug before driving the car off the path and into a field.

As he re-entered the Land Rover, Isla gently patted his leg. 'As long as he's not injured, I'm glad you punched that snide.'

'He'll be fine, but his jaw might need a wire.'

'You'll need one if you're arrested. That's a promise.'

Within two hours, they had boarded Jim's boat. Three hours later, Jim returned to the Isle accompanied by two police officers who promptly arrested Ross. The online edition of the Daily Herald posted the following headline.

"Ross Cranson assaults Herald reporter Mike Cookson after being questioned regarding the mysterious disappearance of his gifted son."

The article also included information on the history of Scarth and the shocking details regarding Devil Will.

Arlo's barrister took the case. His initial background study revealed the reporter to be obnoxious with a penchant to "create" news rather than report it. His quote of *fear not – I will crush the bug,* helped. As suggested, Ross took a plea of not guilty, claiming self-defence as the reporter threatened both for declining to speak with him. With his bail approved, Ross stayed the night at Jim's and would make the trip back to Scarth the following day.

At 8.01 p.m. Bran eased aboard the boat moored at Tod's Goat, pulling a smug grin, with confirming his abilities as a dream walker.

Tate passed him a flask of soup.

'Cheers Mike, hungry is me...'

Mike gave a thumbs up before bringing Bran up to speed.

Bran tutted. 'The Cranson's temper at work again.'

'Most dads would have reacted the same way, the reporter's trash. Social media has already attacked the paper for its lack of empathy and demanded a written apology.'

Tate's words were a comfort, for Bran required peace to fall on the Isle, not a barrage of reporters. Now, more than ever, he needed the comfort of Nemkis.

As each moment passes, I crave the dimensions. This is escalating into a disturbing issue!

The hug from Isla felt good.

In order to avoid arousing suspicion from Vincenzo Giordano and his organisation, Tate and White decided it was best they left the Isle. The ¥ would covertly insert two new operatives the following afternoon. Arlo would also have to be seen *elsewhere* until the dust settled.

'Dad can be a dick,' grinned Bran.

'Truth... I'd have struck the man if your father hadn't.'

'The fighting Cranson's – go easy on him.'

'Not a chance. He'll be expecting a volley from me and will bloody get one. Enough of your daft father. What did Arlo say about you appearing in his dream?'

'I haven't talked to him about it yet. But within the dream, he looked as bewildered as you.'

Isla flicked a tea towel at Bran. 'Cheeky – it's difficult having a magician as a son.'

Both laughed, which felt good.

'I'm knackered. Would you mind if I had an early night?' said Bran wearily.

Isla, looking anxious, whispered.

'Will you be going *there* tonight?'

Bran could not lie. 'Yes, but I've discovered a way to prevent those dreadful recovery sleeps, so don't worry.'

Isla glowed inside. 'You'll solve this mystery, won't you?'

'Mum, I believe the answers will come quicker than we ever expected.'

'Then isn't that a good thing?'

'Perhaps, but I fear the world may never be ready to accept the truth.'

Isla hugged her son. 'Until you've answered all the questions, there are zero positives to considering the future.'

'Aye, that's a fact.'

Hug completed; Bran would address Nemkis. Isla would address a large glass of red.

Vincenzo Giordano clicked on a link to the Daily Herald article. His grin became sardonic.

'My term is now secured, as I doubt I will see another Paragon in my lifetime. The article provides enough speculation to make people believe in the double suicide of the parents. Is it a gamble? Hell no, the timing is perfect.'

He dialled. 'Put our best men on devising a suicide for the Cranson's with immediate effect. Zero mistakes. This has to be clean. Any cock ups, heads will roll. Do I make myself clear?'

'Sir.'

Contented, he closed the call.

That's one less bloodline to worry about...

Twenty-eight

With Bran knowing his father would have zero concerns about being charged, he was certain he would be fast asleep. After initiating a mind search, he grinned at his father's dream scenario, situated inside a *saloon* in a town called El Dorado. Ross's predilection of the actor John Wayne often led to him experiencing vivid dreams involving the wild west. He couldn't help but smile as his father's holsters appeared to support two cans of WD 40.

'Pa it's me.'

Ross squinted as he struggled to form a clear image.

'Our Bran...?'

'Reckon so dude. I'm back at home. Mum's fine, but you can expect a rollicking. Oh, and no more temper fits. We can't afford the publicity.'

'Son, I can't make you out. Can you hear me?'

'Aye, can't stay. Catch you tomorrow.'

As Bran fizzled out, Ross sprang upright on his bed and questioned the experience.

'What the hell, that is so God damned spooky? Well, I never, my son... a dream walker.'

On attempting to look through closed eyes, Ross scolded himself for being stupid.

I'll leave that stuff to our Bran...

Every moment spent in Nemkis increased Bran's desire to learn. From nowhere, a memory bludgeoned its way back into his mind. Waking, he sat upright and for the first time since day one, an unnerving fear overcame him.

With experiencing the process of death but not death itself, I cannot complete the true circle of life, but when death arrives, will I be aware of the transition?

A gentle knock on the door broke all thoughts.

'Son, are you asleep?'

The gentleness of his mother's voice soothed. With trembling hands, he took a breath, counted to ten, then answered. 'No mum – fancy a brew? Sleep is proving to be a tad difficult.'

Both moved downstairs. Loki, by default, followed.

Whilst making the tea, Isla turned to Bran, who expected a grilling.

'This is the first time your father, and I have slept apart since we married?'

Not having considered his mother's feelings, Bran felt a wave of guilt wash over him.

'Gosh, I'm sorry, I'm so wrapped up in myself...'

Isla wagged her index finger. 'You have enough to worry about, besides your dads in the doghouse.'

'I spoke to him earlier...'

Isla's expression quizzed.

Bran chuckled. 'In his dream.'

Isla shook her head. 'Of course you did – silly me.'

Both laughed at the sheer ludicrousness of the statement relaxing Bran considerably.

Don't dwell on death. There is too much to learn. Time will dictate the answers to Mortis Lux. As Arlo wisely suggested, I must make it my mission to gain a greater understanding of the soul. Besides, the fourth pillar will eventually reveal itself.

After tea, a conversation about his time at university brought back fond memories. Isla asked a question that had been hanging in her thoughts.

'Is it that amazing – Nemkis, I mean?'

Bran leaned back in his chair. 'Visually, it's exhilarating, but it's the level of contentment that overwhelms. It's unlike anything I've ever experienced. It's a marvel!'

'Better than life itself?'

'That question opens a can of worms.'

'And one you must seriously consider, if Nemkis is the heaven you say...'

Bran prompted. 'We would rush to be there.'

'Exactly.'

A few moments of silence passed before Bran spoke again.

'At this moment, I've no proof we keep conscious thought after death. If we don't, then perhaps the experience differs from the one I faced.'

Isla sighed. 'How will you find this answer?'

Bran fought to remain passive in his expression.

I do not have the heart to tell my mum that the only way to find the answer may be upon my passing away.

'Step at a time mum, I've only scratched the surface, but to answer your question... if I'm destined to understand, then I will.'

Isla looked into his eyes as she held hands. 'Be careful with all this knowledge.'

'Of course.' Pausing for a moment, he then continued. 'Are you afraid?'

Isla folded her arms. 'Your father and I promised honesty when you asked a question, enabling you to gauge *human reaction.* So, my answer. Yes, I'm scared, as *knowing* changes my mindset about our *physical* existence. Your father is the opposite. The prospect of understanding excites him.'

'The understanding that just the pure will make their way to Nemkis may help in your reasoning.'

Bran's words struck a chord with Isla. 'That would certainly impact on how people lived their lives.'

'It's a fact to ponder over for sure. Shall we sleep on that thought?'

Isla, brushing a little dirt from Bran's sleeve, smiled. 'You know, you will always be my little boy.'

'Wouldn't have it any other way.'

Both hugged, then retired to bed, where each pondered the conversation. Isla gave thought to the possibility of her own immortality but decided unless her family was at her side, it could not offer her ultimate satisfaction. A peep through closed eyes proved futile.

At 9 A.M., Ross returned home to find both Bran and Isla still asleep. Not wishing to disturb either, he took Loki for a brisk walk around the bosk and to tend his bees. After speaking with Arlo via the sat phone, he was to expect two replacement guards to insert onto the Isle by 2 p.m. An email with details of their names and identity arrived. As requested, Jim had stopped all ferry movement to the Isle. The search and rescue team had stood down; it would be a week before the community would hold a *burial* service at Wick.

An hour later, Ross returned with the smell of baking drifting teasingly around the kitchen.

'Miss me?' asked Ross, smiling passively.

Isla turned, then spoke her mind before allowing a loving cuddle. Ross took the verbal torrent, then gave a look of hunger.

'Mrs Cranson, baking a cake?'

'For Bran – you're not off the naughty step. What have you done with Loki?'

'Just having his brekkie in the kennel, I'll let him...'

Loki's aggressive bark interrupted, causing Isla to look out the window at two men leaving the bosk. 'Ross, there are men walking this way?'

'Arlo's sending two new lads to keep tabs on us. He emailed their details – would be polite to know their names.'

Wiping her hands, Isla moved to the laptop. 'One mo.'

Ross opened the door.

'Morning. A little early, but do come in.'

The larger framed man looked quizzingly at his colleague, shrugged, then stepped inside. That neither returned pleasantries, annoyed Ross.

After checking the images, Isla became concerned. 'I'm guessing these men are reporters, as they don't match the photos.'

Ross stiffened. 'Just who the hell are you?'

The larger man coldly drew a handgun from his jacket.

Ross stepped purposely in front of Isla. 'What the hell?'

The man spoke in a tone that offered no empathy.

'Both of you, sit at the table, shut up and listen.'

Nodding to Isla to be compliant, Ross regretted not loading the shotgun after scaring Arlo. A concealed pocketknife was his only comfort.

Now seated, he spoke. 'So?'

'You don't ask the questions!' snapped the tall man.

Ross bit down and tightened his hold on Isla's hand. The taller man peered through the kitchen window.

'Who were you expecting and why?'

Ross, for a fraction, debated on making an attack but feared Isla being caught up in any gunfire.

'Funeral directors to discuss our son's memorial service.'

'Not much to bury I guess,' replied the tall man, grinning.

The cruel jibe, rather than hurt the parents, forged a calmed steeliness inside both. The taller man turned to his partner.

'Check the rest of the house.'

'No one else here,' said Ross calmly.

The tall man barked his reply. 'Shut the fuck up! One more word and I'll put a bullet through your wife's knee.'

Bran stepped into the room, causing Ross and Isla's heart rate to skyrocket.

Both men, speechless, stared in utter disbelief when recognising Bran.

'You're supposed to be fucking dead?' questioned the second man.

Bran stared at the men without replying.

A murky, grey shroud of energy envelops both these men. Could evil inflict damage on the soul, causing it to lose its purity?

With his firearm pointed at Isla, the tall man spoke. 'Kid, sit with your parents and keep it shut.'

Without showing fear, Bran slid next to his father. Ross tapped his leg to give reassurance.

Tall man spoke out. 'This is a bonus. We came here to build a suicide for grieving parents... then we get the mother load.'

As the realism of their predicament struck hard, both parents felt numbed.

Ross, through gritted teeth, spoke out. 'You're to end our bloodline!'

Tall man pulled out his sat phone. 'Nothing personal.'

Giordano answered. Tall man spoke.

'The boy's alive. Have all captives in hand – advise.'

With zero empathy, Giordano reacted. 'Throw the couple off the cliff and confirm their death. As for the boy, as he is supposed dead – make him so! Bury him offline... never to be found.'

With a wry grin tall man replied coldly. 'Message understood.' Call closed, he looked directly at the parents.

'We can make this messy ` or...'

Ross stood up aggressively, forcing tall man to take aim at Bran's head.

'Chill dad! Messy is not good. Now listen. You will both walk off that cliff. Do that and my friend won't cut the boy up, bit by bit, until he dies an excruciating death.'

Seemingly oblivious to the situation, Bran continued to gaze at the two men. Isla, yearning to hold her son, began fighting a mother's urge to attack. Ross bit his own tongue in frustration, causing blood to seep from his mouth. The second man brandishing a knife, placed it against Bran's throat, yet Bran still showed no fear.

'I'll start with the smaller muscle groups, then I'll cut him down to the bone.'

With a drying mouth, Ross spoke.

'My choice – I'll go down fighting. Guess it will piss off your boss, not producing the perfect suicide.'

'And I'll not be jumping off any cliff – fact, you bastards,' said Isla stubbornly.

Tall man laughed as he jabbed his firearm hard into Isla's temple, causing her to squeal.

In that same moment the Cranson's way of life would change forever as Bran's eyes widened momentarily before he blinked.

Unexpectantly, both the men's arms dropped to their sides in unison. The sound of metal on stone filled the room as their weapons clattered to the floor. Ross's gaze drifted to Bran, who silently urged his parents to remain still. The two men, now dribbling saliva from open mouths, slumped backwards into the corner. With eyes devoid of life, both stirred blankly at nothing.

Ross, although shocked, moved to grab both the gun and knife. Understanding the event to be completely abnormal, he turned to Bran.

'Son... what the hells happened?'

Bran's reply was completely void of any emotion or care.

'My sub-conscious intervened. They are now an empty shell. No memory, no experience. They exist as babes fresh from the womb.'

Ignoring Bran's macabre explanation, an unbridled relief flooded into Isla, causing her mind to dismiss the absurdity of what had happened.

'I don't care; we're safe.'

Concealing his rising confusion, Ross, directing the firearm towards the men, moved to check them. After examining both closely, Bran's explanation appeared to make sense. Although they were breathing, they appeared to be in a deep coma.

'I'll tie them all the same,' he said, shaking his head.

After a few minutes, with both men restrained, Ross reached for the bottle of scotch. After filling two tumblers, he handed one to Isla. Both downed in one. The scotch had an immediate calming effect. 'I'd best call the professor.'

'No need. We're safe, and I'm hungry,' snapped Bran.

Outside, Loki's barking made all but Bran jump. Ross gripped the firearm. Bran moved to the bread bin.

'Both of you stay inside,' whispered Ross.

'Be careful,' said Isla, as her hands turned into fists.

With a determined expression on his face, Ross quietly exited the side door, eased around the corner, then brought the gun up.

'Don't you move one fucking inch!'

Neither man flinched as both recognised the safety was on.

'Mr Cranson – please, check your emails.'

Isla burst out of the front door, causing all three to twitch just a little. 'Ross, it's okay, they're Arlo's people!'

'Names boys,' questioned Ross.

'Andy Sutton and Pete Tate.' answered Sutton.

Isla, visibly relieved, nodded confirmation.

With care, Ross lowered the firearm. 'I need to speak to Arlo now!'

Sutton's voice was oddly deep for a slightly built man. Certainly, it was more suited to Tate, who stood six inches taller.

'Mr Cranson, I'll call, but I have to reach inside my coat, okay?'

'Fine.'

Sutton dialled. 'Sir, I have Mr Cranson on the phone. You're on loudspeaker.'

Nervously, Ross explained the event.

Sickened to the core, Arlo took a breath.

If I was a praying man...

'Ross, do exactly as I say!'

'Go on...'

'It is of utmost importance that Bran sleeps immediately. If he refuses, force him. Clear?'

'What?' questioned Ross.

'Take Isla with you and ensure Bran goes to sleep. I'll be with you as soon as I can.'

The call ended. Ross, turning to Isla, gave her a slight shrug, then walked inside. Ross and Sutton moved quickly to confront the two trussed men, who, although alive, now resembled ghoulish corpses.

Fuck! Said both in tandem.

In a hushed voice, Isla spoke to Ross. 'What the hell do we do?'

Ross, shaking his head, looked at Bran, who was buttering toast.

'Son, I've just got off the phone with Arlo. He suggested you need to sleep?'

'It's okay, no need.'

Ross's expression asked for backup. Isla responded by moving towards Bran.

'Arlo says it would be good for you.'

Without warning, Bran became hostile in his demeanour.

'What the fuck would he know? I'm the Paragon...'

Neither Ross nor Isla had ever heard Bran use such aggressive language, let alone aimed at them. As Isla moved closer to her son, Ross eased alongside.

Bran, I'm begging you to please consider your father's words and...

With a swift turn, Bran shoved Isla. 'Fuck off from my space!'

Reacting sharply, Ross caught Bran square on the jaw with a right hook, knocking him out cold. Time stood still for both parents.

Sutton's shout brought them back. 'Get some rope. We must restrain him to the bed before he wakes up.'

Ross quickly obliged. Minutes later, Sutton secured the last knot, then called Arlo, who began an explanation.

'In connecting to those grey souls, evil has tainted his mind. He must fall into a nightmare, then leave by his own free will. I must warn, the distorted horror we humans endure is profoundly more terrifying for a Paragon. In our case, as the *mare* hits its peak, the mind wakes us. The Paragon, however, has to fight their own exit, otherwise he aligns to the grey.'

Deeply upset, Isla spoke.

'Our son will never become evil. Whatever is put before him, he will overcome.'

'I too believe in his capabilities. But what of those assassins?' said Ross.

Sutton spoke. 'Boss, the men have zero output. They're fucked! I've seen nothing like this, ever!'

'Keep tabs on them till I arrive.' The call closed.

Ross turned to Tate. 'Chaps downstairs for a moment?' The men looked quizzingly but duly obliged.

Downstairs, Ross drew the firearm.

'Those two bastards would have thrown my wife off a cliff and cut up my son. Fucked, they may be, but I'd feel a lot more relaxed by making sure they don't function again.'

Sutton replied. 'Understood, but not your call.'

'Do you have a family?' Snapped Ross.

'Not the point, trust me, keep your soul free of the burden and wait for Arlo!'

'Andy's talking sense Ross, these shits are not worth it,' said Tate compassionately.

Ross, staring hard at the vacant men, exhaled, then laid the firearm on the table.

'I'm down. Thanks, lads.'

Vincenzo Giordano, having not heard from his team, concluded the mission was a failure.

If it's a botched operation, I'll cope with the fall out. But my instinct tells me something unearthly has occurred. God help us!

Irritated, he dialled the leader of the insertion team that watched over *the sleep*.

'How close did you get to confirm his death?'

'Twenty yards from the window – he was dead, no question, and backed up by the parents' grief.'

'Was he cold?'

No answer.

'I'll ask you again, was he cold?'

'Truth – I don't know.'

Giordano closed the call. 'Mistakes? Why always mistakes? If this Paragon has released from the Sleep, then my God, you will need *our* help.'

Twenty-nine

Bran was running hard. Deep in his psyche he had always feared the grey spectres, and now a hoard was chasing him through the marshes of Rannoch Moor, Scotland. The sound of dozens of feet driving through the marshland ripped through his soul, galvanising his efforts to keep moving. After five more gruelling minutes, his legs ground to a crawl whilst the demonic screams from the chasing hoard grew ever closer. Without warning, the marshland swallowed him knee deep, causing his body and face to smash forward into the cold mud, where his immediate concern became suffocation.

Move slowly. If I keep struggling, I will sink.

Bran did so and eased himself up right only to see the hideous creatures frantically wading towards him. With every aching muscle, he strained to pull himself forward, but found movement caused him to sink deeper into the mire. Waist high in mud, he gave up all movement. The pack of grey-faced ghouls was close enough for him to see their expressions, screaming a determination to kill. Now chest deep, Bran thrashed around, hoping to slip under the mud before the pack devoured him. Choking as the sludge invaded his mouth, he felt a hand grip at his hair, then another around his neck. The first bite ripped flesh from his forehead, causing his system to command a scream, but the cold sticky mud had clogged his airways. A second and third bite took his consciousness. Now, moments from death, memories of his life flooded in, his childhood, the Isle, his parents. As the mists of thought dissolved, Mortis Lux formed and drew his soul inside. Now in front of the lightfall portal, one final thought entered his mind.

I am a White Paragon. Evil will never taint my soul.

The exact moment the singular thought formed, he returned to Darkvoid, then Nemkis, replacing the horrific nightmare with its serene wonderment. All fear and torment ended.

Bran calmed.

The event of releasing from that nightmare has shaped my Paragon status to the true white line. Somehow, I now control an arsenal of senses of frightening potency that leaves me feeling fearful. What transpired earlier with the two men is only a mere snippet of the absolute devastation I can now affect to protect myself and loved ones. Such power is a deep concern.

Bran woke.

Ignoring the numbness and severe chaffing caused by the binding, he called out.

'Mum – Dad, your son's back, any chance of a hand?'

Bran had been asleep for twelve hours, during which his screams and violent struggles had sickened his parents. Arlo, having arrived with Walt and four men, all armed, moved to the bottom of the stairs. 'Bran, what line have you taken?'

Bran closed his eyes.

In becoming a White Paragon, all ties with normality are severed, as I am no longer shackled by human emotions unless I choose to do so. My future is now forged.

Bran straightened his back as he spoke. 'Don't stress, I'm still the perfect kid.'

Isla shoved past Arlo and dashed upstairs; Ross followed. Nervously placing his hands on his head, Arlo breathed hard.

I hope for all our sakes he's speaking the truth.

As the parents burst into the room, Bran spoke softly.

'I'm sorry to put you both through so much continued stress.'

'We're all safe, and that's what counts,' said Ross as he set about untying the rope. With Bran's struggles causing the knots to tighten, Ross cut the bindings then looked at his son's face.

'How's your chin?'

Bran shrugged.

'Had to be done. Can't thank you for my stonker of a headache, though!'

Isla's expression became sullen. 'Bran, are you aware of what happened?'

'Yes – everything. It's complicated. Let's move downstairs.'

Now in the kitchen, Arlo and the rest remained silent, allowing the family to dictate the events.

With all seated, Bran began.

'Where are those men?'

Sutton answered. 'Locked in the kennel. We intend to take them ashore and leave them on a bench somewhere.'

Walt spoke up. 'They won't be responding for some time, if ever.'

Bran gave an indifferent shrug before moving on.

'I have become a White Paragon. Evil can no longer distort my mind.' He shifted. 'I am now more Paragon than human in both my mental and emotional state, which will help considerably.' Another pause. 'The manipulation of those men instigated my change. I have no remorse.'

Isla broke down.

'I weep over the fact that you are the first to experience this gift and survive. God damn, I'm so proud.'

Bran did not hide his relief.

'Well son, that's you told. Now, what the hell happened?'

Bran closed his eyes before making an extraordinary statement.

'During this latest experience, I have made several sensory advancements, one being the ability to manipulate other people's thoughts and actions. I can now implant a memory to explain all I have experienced. The input will feel natural, but should anyone not wish this intrusion, speak now.'

Each looked around. Ross spoke first.

'Do it son.'

As all nodded reluctant permission, Bran blinked once.

In that instant, every person had an exact memory of Bran's discoveries. Moments passed as they digested the details. Ross was the first to speak.

'My god, this is staggering. It's as though I've actually experienced everything?'

Arlo shook his head. 'Even if it is a touch unnerving, this is truly remarkable.'

Bran could hardly contain his exhilaration at this captivating phenomenon.

'Could Nemkis be heaven?' Asked Walt.

Bran rested his hands on the table. 'In death, all religions promote a utopia and promise hope of immortality. Obviously, I was alive during my experience of Mortis Lux, so it may be different.' He sighed. 'But it is becoming increasingly possible that the soul exists and returns to a state of harmony to a place we could call heaven. But I impress not in the way we perceive.'

Ross shared his thoughts. 'Then death – holds no fear?'

'Physically? Yes, of course. We fear the pain of passing and losing the physical world we exist in. But as the soul appears to be absorbed back into Nemkis, we may, in fact, become immortal. However, with having no experience of death, I cannot confirm the exact meaning of *immortality*. To reiterate this point. Our understanding of immortality is likely to be flawed and may not match the reality of it.'

Bran looked at Arlo, who had remained silent.

'Questions?'

Arlo stood and looked at Walt, who nodded approval. With a deep breath and a wry smile, he began.

'Before we continue, I must, once again, come clean.'

Bran's expression remained passive. The rest – not so. Isla placed her hand on Ross's arm to hold him back.

'I withheld the genuine tragedy of my family, as I did with some of the information regarding the development of the Paragon. Why? You rightly ask, and so I shall explain.'

All became silent as Arlo began.

'To become a true Paragon, you embark on a journey inside a dimension the normal human cannot access. There is no clear or singular route to this dimension. Each Paragon discovers the various mysteries in a sequence unique to them. My son experienced images of death, and so his sub-conscious revealed the sense he coveted most – manipulation of life, a similar sense of the one you exacted today. He revelled in the power this gave him. One particular night I will never erase from my mind.'

Arlo's expression became deeply harrowing...

On September 25th, 2001, Arlo received an excitable phone call from his son demanding he returned home. Concerned, he made his excuses and drove back to be confronted at the front door by his son.

'Dad, I've accessed my first sense. The power it has released is awesome. Come and see.'

With a pain in the pit of his stomach, Arlo followed his son to the garden to be confronted by his wife and housekeeper in tears, cradling the family dog, who was clearly dead.

'I killed her with my thoughts. Dad, I can kill anything I choose! Hell, how awesome is that? It is now my time to sleep and on my return, I will dominate this world.'

Arlo's expression told of his anger at his son.

'Father, are you not happy for me?'

'Happy! You've lost your mind? Why would you choose to kill anything, let alone our Sheba?'

Arlo froze as he saw a raging disappointment flood through his son, who stepped back a few paces.

'Just once, could you stand by me? No, you're jealous because I have the power.'

Arlo's wife spoke up. 'You're mistaken! Father has always attempted to help you fight your evil nature, but what you have done is heinous, truly heinous. I never wish to see you again.'

As Arlo moved to comfort his wife, his son began laughing.

'When I look at the two of you, I am astonished at your feebleness and unimportance. You make me want to vomit.'

Arlo took a deep breath. 'Leave our home now. I cannot stomach you anymore. Go, take the sleep and I hope with all of my heart it consumes you.'

'Yes, that would suit, wouldn't it? And mother, you pathetic bitch, you say you never wish to set eyes on me again...'

The son's haunting laughter prompted Arlo to stand.

'No, I forbid you!'

'You forbid me... Fuck off!'

The son ceased his laughter and shut his eyes. In that moment, Arlo could not move or react as he witnessed his wife and housekeeper succumb to death. Devastated, Arlo slumped to the ground, and held the body of his wife, the finality of her death weighing heavily on him.

Overwhelmed by his own power, the boy sank to his knees and raised his arms skyward.

'This is incredible! Father, this power will change the world, but first I will sleep. When I wake, you can join me or die...'

As Arlo eased out of his emotional recall, tears flowed. Isla moved to comfort him.

Mortified, Bran lowered his head. 'Arlo...'

Acknowledging Bran's sympathy, he spoke. 'Please allow me to continue – it would help!'

Ross slipped him a neat scotch, which was consumed in one. Another breath and he began.

'I both rejoiced and wept when he failed to return from his encounter with the death sleep. The ¥ help concoct all their deaths as a tragic road accident to keep our secret safe. Time has not helped my wife's passing.' Turning to Bran, he smiled. 'Your journey had to be of your own making, not staged managed. You experienced the grey spectres; nine others began with the same. The tenth was my son. An instinct we all have, natural survival, awakened a sense that lay dormant inside you. Saving your family was not an act of evil. However, the grey aura that passed through your mind infected your personality. Had you succumbed, you would have entered the grey side. I care not to imagine the consequences.' Arlo rolled his shoulders, then huffed. 'I find myself again, apologising for my deception, and so I promise never to lie nor deceive this family knowingly. Bran Cranson, I bow to your achievements.'

Arlo then poured a hefty measure of scotch, downed it in one, before sitting down with his head held low.

With a sorrow that was so profound it was almost palpable, Bran spoke.

'The sadness you have endured is beyond words. That everything has been for my benefit, you don't need to apologise. Please – your honesty or loyalty is not in doubt.'

Ross stepped forward and gave a man hug.

'Please forgive my past actions; I am deeply ashamed. I can only thank you for helping my son achieve so much.'

Bran's level-headed approach helped to return the group to a level of equilibrium amid their highly charged emotions.

'Those killers informed someone I was alive, meaning my concocted death is now worthless. To remain deceased will add to my difficulties, so I suggest *marijuana*!'

Confusion and bewilderment adhered to the expressions on the faces gathered.

Bran laughed aloud. 'I got *stoned* for a week in Amsterdam. Kinda, the next step up from my drunken spree. I'll take the flak, not a problem.'

Walt shrugged. 'Not watertight, but uncomplicated and acceptable. I'll have a mobile ring on Ross's sat phone from Amsterdam in five. We can helicopter Bran over there, a few press interviews, the ferry back – job done.'

Isla spoke up. 'They will try again?'

Arlo could not lie. 'Yes, they will, but also the ripple effects of this information reaching the major forces of the world will undoubtedly bring about the inevitable consequences. If any government attempts to capitalise on Bran, it will completely overshadow all issues related to the church. Therefore, after we have successfully completed Bran's return, to prevent any further kidnap attempts, we must conceal you at a safe house.'

The statement hit hard; Isla shook her head. 'They will come, be it to destroy or manipulate.'

Bran stood.

‘Please, let’s not get consumed with what could happen. For now, let’s settle on what we have uncovered to date.’ Without warning, a severe migraine instigated a sickening nausea. ‘Mum, have we any paracetamol? I’ve another headache from hell?’

With a sense of unease, Isla walked to the kitchen. Bran turned to Arlo.

‘We have much to discuss, but for now I ask you a simple question and I require an honest answer with no stalling and not one question in return?’

Arlo looked a little surprised, but agreed.

‘Vincenzo Giordano, is the man who pulls the dark strings for the Columnae?’

Arlo’s expression gave away his shock at Bran’s knowledge.

‘How did you know he was the elected chairman?’

‘I just do.’

Standing, Bran called Loki and left for a walk, leaving Arlo decidedly edgy.

Has he begun the path to which Brother Pugliesi warned? Then I must keep him safe from all influence but my own.

Sutton and Tate moved to the kennel...

Thirty

Two days later, with the euphoria of Bran's miraculous return from Amsterdam becoming old news, Arlo arranged for Ross and Isla to join a Caribbean cruise under false identities. Saying goodbye to Bran had turned both into emotional wrecks, but as he had insisted, they complied. Both were finding it difficult to cope with the knowledge, causing long bouts of silent thought each day.

After having worked on a diary of events, Bran and Arlo set to chat.

'Questions?' Asked Bran with anticipation.

Arlo released a deep sigh. 'Too many.'

Bran's jaw tightened. 'Then I suggest we discuss how, not why.'

'But that was my first question. Will we ever understand why?'

Bran made a gesture of denial with his head. 'Tell me how you would explain the workings of the combustion engine to a worm?' Arlo's expression queried his statement. Bran continued. 'Point being – are we that worm? My conclusion is simple, our intelligence may fall short of answering why?' Arlo nodded but remained silent, allowing Bran to continue.

'Humans understand the physical world around them based on the senses they can access. While extraordinary senses exist across many species on our planet, humans are lacking in comparison, especially in terms of sound and smell. No, the power of humanity lies in its intelligence. Ironically, this intelligence has enabled the human to endanger the co-existence of all life on this planet. The Paragon is not the epitome of intelligence, but their superior sensory enhancements raise them above the regular. But again, I revert to the worm. Within the micro-world, we see life in its most basic form. Life with low intelligence. As a rule of thumb, size plays its part, being – smaller equals less intelligence. We are colossus compared to the spiders and insects that lurk in the dark corners. But if we reflect on our comparative size within the universe, that comparison is pointless. Intelligence is often based on a level. For instance, does the mole think the grub to be stupid when it drops into its burrowed tunnel to be consumed? Therefore, I say again, is the level of human intelligence sufficient to understand the bigger picture?'

Arlo gave a half smile. 'You are in a unique position to argue that point.'

'My experiences so far have been introductory. Nemkis pulls at my soul, prompting me to wonder if it is intelligence. What if Nemkis is God? We covert the human form, when in fact all forms on the planet contain the soul. So, my intention is to maximise my potential, then answer questions based on experience, not opinion.'

'Do you believe this Nemkis to be a living form?'

'It provides celestial energy, which suggests a structure. But again, I am only making this assumption based on my current perception.'

'And death?' pushed Arlo.

'The only genuine answer will come from death itself. Yet another quandary,' sighed Bran.

'And to change the subject, your survival is a major concern; I need to move you to a...'

Bran interrupted sharply. His tone was one of no compromise.

'I understand a fight is coming, but nothing must prevent me from expanding the knowledge I am predestined to learn.' He paused as a thought jolted his mind. 'Nemkis... it ends the grey souls like a germ.'

His concentrated expression disturbed Arlo.

'Bran?'

Bran was on a high. 'Of course! The Mortis Lux are the Sentinels of Nemkis, tasked with stopping the grey spectres from entering.'

Arlo gasped. 'But that most definitely implies intelligence?'

'Exactly. During the onslaught of death, as a natural occurrence, white and grey souls return to Darkvoid. *The Sentinel* provides a pathway for the white soul to enter Nemkis. The grey, however, cannot. And, as I have witnessed, they face total annihilation. The conundrum I now pose is... Is it the result of evolution, instinct, or necessity that has brought the Sentinels into existence?'

'Back to the worm effect,' mused Arlo.

'Sadly, yes.'

Both slipped into deep contemplation for a few minutes before Bran finally spoke up.

‘Evil is incapable of entering Nemkis... Therefore, it only exists in the physical world.’

The statement moved Arlo. ‘A heart-warming possibility which opens up yet another thread of questions.’

Bran gave a nod of agreement. ‘When considering Sentinels, death, and the soul, a multitude of questions come to mind that need to be answered. Ghosts, for instance? How was it possible for me to see William bury his book? What caused the oak tree to wither and die? Is there a celestial God? And of course, where exactly is Nemkis? My list of queries has grown significantly since I achieved Paragon status.’

‘Nevertheless, your ultimate quest remains the soul and its mystery,’ suggested Arlo.

Bran placed his hands on his head and exhaled. ‘No pressure then...’

Arlo smiled as he gently patted Bran's shoulder.

‘This is what you were born for.’

‘Exactly, and that's why I need to disappear.’

Arlo looked puzzled as he asked, "Disappear?"

‘To remain in Nemkis for extended periods, my system can enter a state of hibernation by reducing its metabolic rate by a factor of thirty. To safeguard everyone, it's best if my location remains unknown.’

‘I will abide by your wishes, but should the dynamics change, so must your security.’

Bran locked eyes with Arlo. ‘The depth of my potential to guard myself and my family is beyond your understanding, and it is something I will not waver on. Don't be concerned.’

Arlo's insides curdled, causing him to pop a pill. As he swallowed, the sound of a helicopter intruded into their conversation. Bran directed his gaze towards the sky and smiled.

‘Both pilot and co-pilot emit the white.’

‘Some radar you’ve got there,’ said Arlo.

‘A wonder and a curse.’

‘I don’t understand?’

Both looked back towards the helicopter as it touched down. For a few moments, Bran pondered in uneasy thought.

‘Had they been of the grey and become aggressive?’

Arlo raised a brow. ‘That would become a dilemma for you?’

Bran’s tone offered zero empathy. ‘No dilemma.’

Arlo's skin tone whitened as a chill passed over him.

He understands!

Bran noticed the flinch in Arlo's expression.

'You're aware of the full extent of my sensory capabilities?'

'Brother Pugliesi warned me that the consequences of your discoveries could be catastrophic, and that I must keep full influence over your actions. I recognised what carnage my son would have reaped, so when he entered his last sleep I had armed men on twenty-four-hour watch, with orders to shoot him dead the moment he woke.'

Bran's expression did not falter. 'Your son's obliteration by the *Sentinels* was always to be his outcome. I apologise for the harshness of my statement.'

Arlo accepted Bran's show of empathy with a nod. Now staring at each other, both held a slight reluctance to speak. Steeling his nerve, Arlo broke the stand-off.

'I ask you this question... is the white Paragon to become an avenging angel?'

Bran grimaced a little. 'Men of the grey dispatched operatives with the sole task of forcing my parents to jump from a cliff face to their deaths on the rocks below. When my sub-conscious dismantled their minds, I felt no empathy. After my release from the nightmare, I became aware of defensive senses that are truly apocalyptic. Is it my divine task to eliminate all evil? Am I capable?' Bran drew a breath. 'Yes... but not by choice. Only the actions of others can awake my sensory retaliation.'

'First blood...!' said Arlo.

'Precisely.... If I'm threatened, my sub-conscious activates these defensive actions. It's a ticking time bomb; one I will try my hardest to defuse.'

Arlo, fighting to stay calmed, replied. 'But where does this take us?'

Bran frowned. 'Time will answer that question, but I see in your eyes you have doubt?'

'As a human, I too experience a certain amount of tension, even being the head of the ¥.'

Bran nodded his understanding. 'Of course, but please never attempt to harm myself or my parents even if you feel you must, for it will be your demise. The speed and time scale of this defence reaction is beyond all human comprehension. It has no boundaries, no conscience. I have no choice. For example, the men ordered to shoot your son. They would have died the instant their minds programmed an attack had this been my sleep. Can the Paragon see the future? No. However, the sheer speed of reaction would give this assumption.'

Arlo now understood why Lamberto Pugliesi feared the Paragon. That the white Paragon could only eliminate evil was the redeeming factor.

'Your wrath is upon the grey and I have no issue with that, but can you align the world without a genocide?'

Bran expelled a deep breath. 'When they send men to end my life, I hope the abnormality of my retaliation dampens their resolve. But I have concerns, in that... where is the line drawn that separates grey from white? Is a young child that stamps on a beetle evil? Is a lion evil for killing prey to feed its cubs? Also, the possibility that Nemkis has created the Paragon as its terminator on planet earth is another suggestion of intelligence. These are the questions that raise my anxiety.'

'I understand, but does not mankind have an entitlement to the truth behind their existence?'

'Yes, of course, but if mankind cannot accept this truth?'

Arlo's expression saddened. 'I have to believe we will find a solution.'

'And we will.' He paused. 'But one event must not manifest. They must never proclaim me a deity!'

'It's natural for people to follow,' Arlo said with a shrug.

Bran replied with a tone and expression that left no doubt over that topic.

'I will never allow it to happen.'

Arlo smiled. 'Thankfully, that issue is far from becoming reality.'

Bran puffed out his cheeks, then calmed.

'Thank you for your council. I need these conversations and opinions to maintain a clarity of thought. I'm certain that it will be possible to draw you into my dream, so during the next few weeks we will converse during slumber.'

An expression of dread passed over Arlo.

'Really?'

'You will be fine, but you MUST follow my instructions to the letter when I try. Heed my words, or you will lose your mind, then the will to live.'

Arlo took a deep breath. 'I feel both excitement and trepidation.'

'Then welcome to the club.'

With a firm handshake, Arlo made his way to the flight. As the helicopter began its ascent, he gazed down on Bran.

I've waited so long for the truth... But now I wonder, is it too high a cost for humankind?

Bran watched the flight until its disappearance from sight.

Whatever lies ahead, nothing must prevent me from gaining the knowledge I seek? Evil men will come at me, but as their attacks escalate, they will experience annihilation in a form they cannot comprehend. Can I prevent this? History suggests not!

Once back in the house, Bran gorged on food and water. After ablutions, he collected a sleeping bag, water bottles, rucksack, and various tools. Satisfied, he set off for Cliff Cottage.

If my dream about William's book is accurate, I will solve an issue that's been playing on my mind.

The stone outhouse next to Cliff Cottage was in excellent repair. Used as a wood store, its history would provide an interesting tale. Moving inside, he placed his sleeping bag and rucksack on a stack of logs, then swept the dusty floor in the far northern corner. Once finished, he began a fingertip search within the stonework of the wall. Two minutes later, he tapped at a hollow spot with his hammer. In moments, a rush of relief passed through him as the plaster fell away to reveal a small brass lever. Moving to his rucksack for a tin of WD40 and a stiff wire brush, he then cleaned away the debris. After a burst of spray, followed by a patient wait, he cautiously pulled the lever forward, resulting in a firm click. The sound of a set of brass cogs whirling into action made Bran smile contentedly as a small section of the stone floor receded.

Straight out of Raiders of the Lost Ark – magic!

In a few seconds, a trap door measuring around three feet square had opened. A torchlight search revealed a basement measuring eight feet long, six feet wide, with a head height of five feet. There was nothing in the room except for a bed with delicate carvings on its wooden frame.

Finally, I get to see Williams hide. Not even my parents knew of its existence.... does this confirm that deceased Paragons maintain the ability to communicate?

Bran lowered his head further into the room to become entranced by the abundance of tiny, shining auras.

The souls of insects are as mine. A sheer wonder. Now settle and concentrate.

The hide held a musty odour but was at least dry. Several chains dangling down the wall appeared to be part of the mechanism for the floor hatch. As his torch exposed a single air vent, a slight draft came as a relief.

Climbing back up, he looked for the air outlet both inside and outside to ensure it was clear. Thirty minutes later, the vent still evaded his search. Glancing around, he stepped to the wood burner before pulling it free of the stone chimney to reveal the elusive vent. Satisfied it was free from any blockage, he pushed the log burner back into place, then climbed down inside the hide with his rucksack..

Bran felt sickened.

William's hideaway. The Paragon. Unjustified beliefs held by the church led to torment, death, and extreme prejudice against those who were different.

After spraying the chains in WD40, he tested their reliability by opening and closing the hatch several times. Satisfied, he rolled out his sleeping bag on top of the wooden bed.

Comfort is not a necessity; however, my personal safety is.

After gulping down a bottle of water, he pulled out a dust mask, earplugs, and goggles.

This should keep out any inquisitive insects during my time on the Nemkis.

He shivered slightly.

Am I closing my tomb?

A final click led to silence.

Humour of the situation caused a chuckle.

It's not the Crown Plaza.

Now shuffling into his sleeping bag, he pulled on the mask and goggles before inserting his ear plugs. Settling, he shone his torch around for a last check before switching it off.

'Now that's dark.'

Closing his eyes, he peered...

Thirty-one

The following day, the Daily Herald continued in its attempt to raise the profile of the Isle, but the might of the ¥'s social media attacks effectively forced a climb down.

Ross and Isla were aboard the cruise liner 'Allure of the Seas' sailing the Mediterranean under false identities, along with three close protection operatives from the ¥. Both detested the fact they had left Bran but understood the necessity. Jim agreed to look after Loki and keep one eye on the properties whilst the family *moved away* to allow the dust to settle. Arlo had returned to his home at Lake Lincoln, Nebraska, USA. Known as "Fort Norton", the land spread over five thousand acres and had the infrastructure to repel a full assault to the main house, such was the security. Without question, all were suffering mentally from the disclosures regarding Nemkis. Everyone encountered difficulty in understanding and accepting one point... That the mysteries of life were unravelling! Yet all continued their attempts to peer through closed eyes at sleep.

Vincenzo Giordano had returned to his home in Sicily. That a Paragon was now active, tormented his mind. After the failure of the attack on the parents, he was certain that Bran would have been taken to the Professor's estate. No question he had to attempt an assassination. With a whirling mind, he retired to bed. It would take him an hour to fall asleep...

In the middle of a vast ocean, stood on a jagged rock measuring six feet square, Giordano stared in stunned silence. Deep within his diaphragm, a scream built.

When aged nine, Giordano became lost at sea for several days in a rubber dingy after the tragic sinking of his cousin's yacht, a hundred miles off the southern coast of Sicily. As the only survivor, he failed to recover from his guilt and had since suffered a debilitating phobia about the ocean. So intense was his fear he refused to lay eyes on any large body of water.

Now staring blankly, he became traumatised to the effect that he was incapable of speaking. With a mind unable to process how he had arrived in the middle of an ocean, his legs buckled, causing him to slip. As the rock's jagged edges bit deep into both knees, he winced. Unable to stand, he sobbed, when from nowhere he caught sight of the dorsal fin of a great white shark. In seconds, others appeared and, as a collective group, they circled. The realisation they had scented his blood caused him to vomit, after which his terror exploded into a blood-curdling scream. At that moment, Giordano stirred in absolute horror as, inch by inch, the sea reclaimed the jagged rock base.

No – No, this is impossible; how can this be?

The sharks, sensing a kill, thrashed their tail fins on the surface, stimulating bursts of random aggression from the larger males. Bordering on hysterical, Giordano screamed upwards to the heavens for help. With only a few feet of rock remaining above the water, one shark made an exploratory lunge. Giordano's instinct was to jump backwards, and so he plunged into the water. As he tried in desperation to scramble onto the rock, the first bite took his right leg clean from the mid-calf. The heavy blood release ignited a violent feeding frenzy, during which shock ended his pain. With life fading, his concluding thoughts were of how this had happened?

'Vincenzo – Vincenzo – wake up, whatever is the matter?'

Giordano sat bolt upright in his bed and screamed in unbridled terror, resulting in his wife stepping back in shock. Then, after gathering her nerve, she slapped his face. The tactic worked. Giordano shook his head, then gazed frantically around the room.

'It was real – I'm telling you now, I died in the ocean – eaten by sharks!'

His wife's voice offered calm. 'No Vincenzo! You're at home in your bedroom.'

Giordano rubbed his eyes to dismiss the gory experience lodged in his mind.

'I'm telling you that was real, it – it was not a dream – it was real.'

Now holding him, his wife whispered. 'You've had a terrible nightmare, nothing more. You're safe now, relax.'

Such was his anxiety, Giordano wept for a moment, before requesting a stiff drink. Ten minutes later, he had calmed and moved to the balcony to admire the surrounding mountains and take a few deep breaths. Down below, his wife's cat caught his eye as it set off for a night of hunting. With a severe dislike of all domestic animals, he hoped it would become the hunted before his mind snapped back to being the prey.

I can remember every horrific detail. That was real, my god, I never want to suffer that again.

Giordano called out to his wife. 'I'll take a couple of your sleeping pills?'

'You sure?'

'I'll never get back to sleep if I don't, and I've an early meeting tomorrow.'

As his head touched the pillow, his mind grasped at the memory of the dreadful nightmare he had experienced.

No dream can be so horrifying.

Thoughts broke as his wife passed him a pill and a glass of water.

'Sorry for disturbing you, my love.'

'Sleep soundly. It was all a dream.'

Giordano swallowed the tablet. Slumber came fairly quickly, as did the nightmare, as once again, the agony of his flesh being torn returned with a vengeance. Such was his terror his wife resorted to pouring a jug of water over him. Waking with a jolt caused him to strike his head on the wooden headboard. In his unconscious state, the rock base returned. Minutes later, his wife's frantic efforts pulled him from the dream. Thrashing his arms as he woke, Vincenzo knocked her to the floor. Then, in a fit of insanity, he charged to the balcony and flung himself to the ground below. His wife, now in a state of hysteria, rushed to the edge of the patio, only to witness Giordano's last movements as he lay motionless on the stone surface with a broken neck. The cat strolled onto his torso, scented, then returned to the foliage – critters to hunt.

Vincenzo Giordano's death hit the media within the hour. Reports of a tragic accident at the family home gathered pace. At 5.30 A.M., Arlo received a call.

I understand why, but how?

Two hours later, an extraordinary meeting was called at the Vatican. *The Columnae,* seated at a table chaired by Giordano's only son, Stefano, began discussions.

'To clarify. My father threw himself from his bedroom window after suffering a sequence of horrific nightmares.'

A shocked murmur spread around the room. Stefano held his hand up.

'Mother has confirmed that prior to his death, he maintained that his dreams had become reality. In which case I fear the Paragon has acted his revenge. Gentlemen, this is a warning!' Pausing, he sipped at a tumbler of brandy. 'Now, before the death of my father, he had proposed a covert infiltration to the home of Norton. The Paragon must die!'

The bold statement triggered a heated argument within the room. Stefano shouted for calm above the verbal commotion before asking the judgement of the eldest member of the board – Marco Russo.

Aged seventy-three and riddled with chronic arthritis, Russo remained seated as he held his arm aloft.

'Brothers, this is a time for calm minds, please, no more shouting. It's a strain on my old ears.' Russo paused as the room eased into silent compliance. 'History dictates that violence solves most situations, but now we face a unique adversary.' A slight cough made him pause for a sip of water. 'This Paragon, apparently, can unbalance the mind of his enemy, which is extremely disturbing! However, one factor gives hope. He has chosen not to attack our entire structure, to which I believe equates to negotiation. That being true, our best option is to open discussions with the ¥.'

Immediately, several men voiced their disapproval.

Russo continued. 'Who amongst us has read the Last Book?'

Not one person raised their arms.

Russo's expression changed to a grimace. 'I will send for it now, so we can all read the words of the Cranson Paragon. Once digested, we then vote on violence or dialogue.'

Some three hours later, the room was of mixed emotion. Some openly wept, others remained silent. Russo began.

'First we eat, contemplate, then I'll ask for a final vote.'

Supper was served. Vincenzo's eldest cousin, Custanti Giordano, a member of the committee, had not spoken a word during the entire meeting. Custanti's individual perspective on religion clashed with the church, yet his effectiveness in resolving conflicts for the Columnae had opened the door for him to join the board. His primary interest was financial gain, which prompted the idea that many governments would offer a significant reward to gain further insight into the mind of the Cranson boy.

I might as well turn this into a financial gain. The ¥ believe they are invincible. However, my family has long prepared for such a time...

A knock with a spoon on the table by Russo broke his thoughts.

'Brothers, the Last Book is a frightening read. I fear the future, especially regarding the *Initiates* and the *Awakening*. So please, can we vote for those who prefer dialogue?'

One by one, they raised hands. At the count of five, Custanti Giordano raised his arm to make the vote in favour. The rest followed, not wishing to be isolated.

Custanti smiled inwardly.

Excellent, this allows time to explore my options.

Russo eased himself to standing before he spoke. 'The vote for discussion was unanimous. I'll leave you now to pray to our lord in order that we are successful in our battle against the devil's spawn.'

Thirty-two

7.30 A.M.

After a lengthy two-hour Skype call, Arlo and Walt closed discussions. The question, "Is a young child that stamps on a beetle evil?" stirred up serious concern in Arlo.

There must be a dividing line.

His mobile vibrated. Gerry Dee was the head of his security.

'Get this... the Columnae have requested a meeting.'

Such was the shock at Dee's statement. Arlo took a moment.

'They're running scared...?'

'The bottom line is they have to shut down the Paragon. You understand that much?'

'Of course, and most likely myself. Still, can we set this up? I'm intrigued.'

'I'm one hundred percent against a meeting in the flesh boss, I'll confirm a conference call.'

Of all of his employees in the USA, Dee was his most trusted. Over the course of the last twenty years, he had thwarted several attempts on Arlo's life. As a result, he never ignored his advice.

'You're in charge. Do we need to increase our levels of security?'

'Already set in motion, I'll confirm your decision to the Columnae.'

'Excellent.'

Arlo sat back in thought.

The death of Giordano has unsettled nerve ends. Dee is correct... they have to eliminate Bran. Stalling is their play.

Dee called back.

'They pushed for the face to face – I slammed the call. However, as we figured, they're running scared, and agreed to a video conference in thirty minutes.'

'Keep this to yourself.'

Dee's historical timeline would reveal the brutal murder of three of his ancestors. Without doubt, he would relish seeing the Columnae on the back foot.

Bran had been deliberating about the details of his attack. The death of Giordano had left no mental scars or regret. Thoughts changed.

Since the discovery of Dreamworld and its purpose, my sub-conscious has continued to expand my sensory capabilities. The way it manipulated Giordano's dream is frightening. Now I find I can maintain a 24/7 link with any person of my choice. Meaning, if an aggressor processes a destructive thought relating to my parents, my sub-conscious will react. How is this possible...? One obvious explanation – we are all the same soul! That the possibility of Nemkis being an intelligence is menacing. However, when I'm within its calmness, all issues become less of a concern.

I have to accept that whatever I experience is fact and I have no choice in the sequential timeline of my discoveries. But yet I still feel I must concentrate on the soul. The search for the fourth pillar, the "birth of life", can wait.

1.55 p.m.. USA time.

Dee had all systems set for the conference call in the main working office on the grounds. The moment the meeting began; Arlo turned to address Russo, ignoring the natural successor.

'Signor Russo, I will forgo pleasantries and ask why the Columnae wish to open communications?'

Before speaking, Russo glanced at Stefano in order to stem his temper at the obvious insult.

'I see you offer no condolences to the Giordano family and by that, I assume you are aware of the true cause of his demise?'

'Had the murder of the Cranson family been successful? Would he have shown sympathy? Signor Russo, if it is sympathy you seek, then I will bid you good day.'

Arlo held for Russo's reply. Russo counted to five in his mind before speaking.

'Your Paragon is now pure. Therefore, we have concerns, concerns that go beyond our own interests. We require reassurance over his intentions and, of course, the facts surrounding the Awakening. In return, we will proclaim a *ceasefire* for the good of mankind.'

Inwardly, Arlo smiled.

'The Paragon is not under my control. Since your aggressive actions, he has disappeared off the radar. If your attempt on his family turns him to the grey side, then we will all suffer.'

Russo thought for a moment.

Norton, you play the game well; the Paragon is white, no question, and I would bet my life he has full contact.

'And if he is of the white? What then? Where does revenge stop? What are his intentions regarding the Awakening?'

'Signor Russo, you ask me questions I cannot answer... But I have some advice.'

Stefano broke his silence, much to the disdain of Russo.

'And that is?'

Arlo looked at Dee, who nodded.

'Prepare for the truth, a truth that you and your kind have suppressed since your very existence. All religions promote their gods' divine ways, yet they manipulate with fear, dishonesty, and damnation. This merciless deceit will be your downfall. Hear this... God fearing, will become obsolete.'

Stefano took the bait.

'One Paragon cannot affect our faith that has dominated for centuries. The devil's spawn will not intimidate god's will. So, hear my words men of the ¥. We will send this offspring to hell as was your son's fate and from this day forward we will end all blood lines of the Paragon. As my father lies in rest, this is my promise.'

The reference to his son produced a zero reaction from Arlo. A broad grin then formed on his face as he observed Russo deal with Stefano's outburst.

'You have broken the will of the Columnae... unforgivable!'

Turning his gaze around the table, his tone dropped.

'Does anyone else disagree?'

Regardless of their opinions, none of the remaining men would back Stefano's act against a carried vote. Russo nodded at the men's acceptance before turning back to Stefano, who remained silent.

'Leave the room and await our decision.'

Stefano looked at the others, who ignored his stare.

'You can all suckle on the devil's teat; my family will stand alone.'

Stefano's first cousin, Custanti, stood.

'Stefano, you're my blood, but I will not turn against the will of the Columnae. I beg you to ask for forgiveness.'

After staring in shock at his cousin, Stefano spat and left the room. A bated silence lasted for a few moments. Custanti concealed his satisfaction.

I now have the trust required and nullified the stupidity of my cousin.

Russo turned to the screen, hiding his own temper – just.

'Professor, please forgive that distasteful outburst. The decision by the Columnae does not echo the thoughts of a grieving son. Fact being – we wish to negotiate with, not against, the Paragon.'

Arlo held his reply for a few moments.

'Then I say again... accept the truth and prepare for change.'

He ended the connection, then closed his eyes for a few moments.

'To educate mankind, I fear will require an epidemic of death. One thing is certain, the religious structures will have to change.'

Dee spoke out. 'For centuries, our families have waited for the chance to repay the pain of suffering. This event is not on our conscience. We can both take solace from that. I'll have security placed on full alert.'

Letting out a sigh, Arlo acknowledged they were just waiting for the unavoidable to happen.

After the shutdown, Russo listened on as the fallout from the meeting erupted into heated debate. He allowed all to let off steam before banging his spoon on the table.

Russo spoke in a reassuring manner. 'Brothers, I hear your words and agree we need to become pro-active. However, I will not endorse a full-scale attack at the home of Norton. There is another solution. Twenty years ago, I inserted a sleeper into the ¥. The moment he discovers the Paragon, he will end *its* life.'

Russo looked at Custanti. 'Stefano was correct, but his open threats will have prompted defensive actions, making our task extremely difficult. However, I propose Stefano to be recalled after submitting his apology and resignation as acting chairman.' The room acknowledged agreement. Russo turned to Custanti. 'This position now falls on your lap.'

Yet again, Custanti concealed his delight.

'But, Signor, I am not worthy of such a hallowed position. I must decline.'

Russo bowed his head. 'Your family has served the Columnae for centuries. Custanti, I trust your judgment and the experience you can draw from.'

Custanti *reluctantly* nodded. Russo called the vote.

'All in favour, raise your right hand.'

The vote carried. Russo thanked each man, then spoke.

'It is done... congratulations Signor Custanti, you now chair the Columnae.'

Depicting a fake humility, Custanti bowed in meek acceptance.

'Brothers, I am humbled by your confidence, please I will devote my time to the Columnae and attempt to steer us through this challenging time. Of course, my first decision is simple. Who is in favour of placing our faith in Signor Russo and his covert operative?'

Eight hands carried the vote.

'Signor Russo, we await your progress.... Failure, then we will have no alternative other than a direct assault.'

Russo nodded his thanks. Custanti walked to the *chair.*

'Brothers, I conclude this meeting with one final thought. We have fought against this curse for centuries. I, for one, shall pray to God for his divine intervention. Let no man lose faith in what we stand for. God bless you all.'

The room applauded, leaving Custanti feeling ecstatic.

Unexpected, but I'll take this as a bonus. Time is short. I have to contact willing ears, then placate that short-tempered cousin of mine.

Four hours later, Stefano and Custanti, seated in the sparse living quarters of the deceased Vincenzo at the Vatican, held a glass of red wine in hand. Stefano's mood had not improved.

'You turned your back on me and then climbed into the chair. My father will turn in his grave at your treachery to this family.'

Custanti, remaining calm, sipped, then spoke in a tone depicting a sympathetic firmness.

'My cousin, we are away from attentive ears. Our family is about power and finance, religion is but our tool.' He accepted a nodded approval from Stefano. 'As we enter this unprecedented period, our followers will question their faith. I fear the Paragon will make his mark and begin a new era.

Therefore, it is necessary to transform the Paragon to nothing more than a scientific study.'

Stefano's mood shifted.

'Explain?'

As Custanti lifted a briefcase onto his lap, then tapped it once. 'Inside is a copy of The Last Book. My role as president has yielded its first assist.'

'And?'

'A senator from the U.S., blessed with an open mind, has shown interest. The book will help bring him on board.'

Stefano threw his arms up. 'What the hell are you thinking? The U.S. will bury us once they have the Paragon.'

'I have my back covered, trust me on that, but would one billion sterling tempt you onside?'

'One billion?'

'I've asked for five! Rather, a bargain for an assassin who can kill by using a dream?'

Stefano shook his head. 'Impossible to pull off.'

'Your father was aware of the operative implanted into the ¥. And as I cloned his laptop, then intercepted coded messages... I have a couple of key snippets that will do for now.'

'That being?'

'I've located the parents on a cruise liner and have intelligence that the Paragon may still be on the Isle.'

Stefano grinned. 'You always were a devious child.'

'Not devious cousin, just single-minded. So, can you cope with an injection of one billion?'

Stefano poured a top up. 'Absolutely – Signor!'

'Excellent, once the USA is on board, I'll present the parents as a persuasive negotiation. This lever on the Paragon is paramount...'

Both chinked glasses. Custanti smiled.

'Now to appease the Columnae! Can you please lay your apology on the table alongside your official resignation? We need to keep them in line, as I need time before they grind into action.'

'For one billion, why hell, I'd blow them all off.'

Both grinned.

Stefano's smile was false.

If that bastard is on Scarth, I will avenge my father.

Thirty-three

With having slipped into recall, Bran was now standing inside a bedroom in Cliff Cottage, albeit several centuries ago. Confident that the reason for this event would reveal itself, he settled into a corner. Not long after, Gregor, the father of William, made his way into the room. At the sight of his elderly ancestor, Bran's face lit up with joy and was in awe of the beauty of the moment.

I am no longer intimidated by the random circumstances that evolve. However, meeting Gregor is pretty awesome.

Without rationalising the sheer complexity of the event, Bran watched on as an exhausted Gregor climbed into bed, then closed his eyes for a much-needed slumber.

Will his sleep pattern fit into the modern theory of the "four stages", not five, as once believed?

Time ticked on and with stage one and two completed, Gregor entered stage three.

This is when the brain moves into a deeper, more restorative stage of sleep, allowing the body to repair itself. In the young, this stage stimulates growth and development, but for adults, it recharges physical energy.

Ninety minutes later, stage four – REM sleep (rapid eye movement).

As brain activity is at its peak, this is the most interesting stage, especially as dreams are more likely to occur during this period.

At that precise moment, Bran's subconscious drew him into Gregor's dream.

Cursing, Gregor had become agitated whilst attempting to plough a field using an irate rooster. After an angry tirade, the rebellious bird paused in its tracks and pecked fiercely at its leather bindings. As the harness snapped, the pecking bird gave a mighty crow before fleeing the field at speed, with Gregor in hot pursuit. Bran could not help but grin at the sheer lunacy of the dream. As the scene faded away, he became drawn into Dreamworld, where a *dream-sphere* manifested itself to his right side. Set against the dark, its perfect symmetry seemed to emphasise its significance. With the dream-sphere remaining singular, a curiosity washed over him.

To focus on a sphere at close proximity is astounding and something I could never do previously. Is this the slumbering mind of Gregor? What has become of the other spheres?

Concentrating, he became dumbstruck when realising that its internal structure was identical to Nemkis. Scarcely believing his eyes, he watched the internal mass of the dream-sphere become absorbed into Nemkis. Transfer completed; the sphere disengaged, flashed across the darkness, then disappeared from view. Suddenly, an intense wave of nausea left him feeling helpless and overwhelmed.

That's impossible! The mind does not transmit energy, but extracts it. Yet... I have seen it with my own eyes, and it is true. Hell, this changes everything we understand.

Before shock took hold, he was back inside Gregor's bedroom, who woke, broke wind, walked to the door, then looked at Bran.

'Another wee ghostie come to see our William! I have ne seen ye before. I hope ye find yer answers.'

The door closed.

Bran wanted to scream. Concerned that he may suffer a breakdown, he returned to Nemkis.

Medical science explains that we replace physically during the third stage of our sleeping sequence, with the fourth period replacing mental energy. I now discover that Nemkis actually "extracts" mental energy from the sleeping mind. Given this, becoming mentally tired must result from over production of energy and not, as we believed, diminishing levels.

Bran's sub-conscious brought up an image of the deceased oak tree on the evening of his return from the death sleep.

By keying into the oak, I likely created an abundance of energy that caused its ultimate destruction. Therefore, the compulsion to sleep starts when energy levels increase beyond the sustainable point. Getting rid of the "overload" leaves you with a "revitalised" mind once awake!

He paused in shocked thought.

Then all living organisms produce celestial energy for Nemkis?

Now questioning his own decision, he searched for facts to confirm his hypothesis.

Insomniacs! How can they sleep if they lack the extra mental energy that is necessary to fall asleep? Therefore, not sleeping leads to the severe physical exhaustion they experience.

Such was the tension he was feeling. Bran clenched his fists.

This parallels flawlessly! The question I now ask is extremely disturbing, for if Nemkis draws celestial energy from a physical life, did it, in fact, create life for that purpose? This being true, then Nemkis may be the divine creator the entire human race coverts.

His next thought made him tingle.

Is this the reason for our existence? Are we born to process celestial energy that we understand as the soul? But what of the grey? The Nemkis would not harvest corrupted energy.

An explanation formed quickly.

As we produce the resource daily, Nemkis would harvest before corruption takes place.

After ten minutes of contemplation, he delivered his summary.

The physical is disposable, but the soul... immortal? I wondered if Nemkis held intelligence. My answer now is absolutely, but on a scale far and above human comprehension; no question, as I once said to Arlo, "we are that worm". My next question has to be... how would a human mind react to this knowledge? I must subject my human side to test the water...

Bran opened his eyes.

The black of the basement was reminiscent of Darkvoid, creating a state of confusion which caused him to shake uncontrollably. Not since he had first entered Mortis Lux had Bran felt so alone and vulnerable. His 'human' mind, fearful of the reality of his experiences, fought against accepting his conclusions and so he quickly changed back to the Paragon state. As he switched on his torch, the effect of light induced a slight calm, not so for the creatures that lived in the dark hide. As his sleeping bag had become layered in spiders' webbing, rather than brushing it off, he eased slowly upright to allow the insects to take a safe passage from the moving giant. The shine of their aura pleased him. His watch gave 10 A.M.. The date told him that sleep had lasted for eleven days.

I need to talk with my parents, breathe fresh air, and sit with my dog.

After pulling on the chain to release the trap door, climbing out felt uncomfortable, as his renewed blood flow exacted pins and needles around his body. Now standing upright, he stretched, then froze as he noticed the barn door was ajar.

Without a doubt, I closed that door.

On tingling legs, he walked outside. All seemed quiet. Taking a deep breath of fresh air, his need for food and water struck him. Another recce followed before he moved to the cottage. The front lock had signs of damage. After a slight pause, he moved inside, ran the cold-water tap, then drained three full glasses. A tin of luncheon meat, followed by canned peaches, eased his hunger. Now feeling the cold, he set about rustling up a fire on the lounge wood burner. Ten minutes later, the warmth of the spitting logs settled him into thought.

Gregor's dream and its momentous implications have impacted on my mind to where I must recall the entire event... Rather like the hair of the dog.

Moving to the sofa, Bran laid down, but then eased back up as his stiffened body rejected the sleeping position.

I suppose eleven days of complete motionless have an effect.

Settling upright in a chair, he closed his eyes, and began a full recall of the disturbing revelations.

Around half a mile away, one man, from a team of four, caught sight of the smoke trail bellowing from Cliff cottage. Grinning, he called to the others.

'Has to be the Paragon?'

All three gave a thumbs up.

'Split and surround, I'll take the front with Cami. On comms at my command, we hit front and rear... kill shots gentlemen – lots of them... we don't want this kid starting any weird shit!'

All gave a confident nod, primed their weapons, then moved in tandem towards the cottage. Five minutes later, the first man settled at eighty yards from the front door and waited for confirmation of the rear assault team. It came.

'Target asleep upright on a sofa in the lounge.'

First man moved to his left.

'I have clean sight on target. On my first shot, go in hard and empty your magazines.'

'Be our pleasure.' came the reply.

After checking his weapon, the first man whispered into his comms. 'On three... two...' Before finishing the count, a vision caught his eye, prompting him to empty his magazine into the sky. Cami, leaping from the crouch position, also fired at the heavens. Seconds later, with expressions depicting absolute fear, both men continued to "dry click" their rifles into the air. Fear turned to insanity as the men began running towards the cliff edge. Cami, without changing stride, launched himself over with an unnerving silence, followed by the first man. Over one hundred feet below, the jagged rocks ended their lives, alongside the broken bodies of their two comrades, who had already made the *silent* jump. Successive swells of the North Sea rinsed away blood, bone, and sinew before fully claiming the contorted figures, much to the annoyance of the rock crabs.

Bran opened his eyes, walked to the lounge window, and peered outside; The scene felt calmed as he gazed over the cliffs. Moving back into the kitchen, he poured a small scotch.

I lit the fire, knowing it would draw anyone on the Isle to the cottage and end with their brutal demise. The sea and its inhabitants will conceal the event. This confirms I do not need to lie in a dark hole, as the grey cannot harm me. I will return home to face the facts of our existence.

At the precise moment the team had taken aim to process the kill, Stefano Giordano was talking to his cousin Custanti via Skype. Present in the room was his personal assistant, positioned behind his PC screen, teasing Stefano by revealing her stockinged clad legs. Stefano's voyeuristic leer changed to one of absolute terror as a vision appeared in front of him. The intensity of the shock caused him to fall off the chair and utter the same words repeatedly.

'You cannot be alive...! You cannot be alive...!'

He calmed, stood, then threw himself out of the office window. Twenty-seven floors passed before the pavement ended his silent descent. The female, now staring at the open window, remained motionless in complete shock before breaking into absolute hysteria.

Custanti flinched as the scream of the female burst into his earphone. Blinking hard, he shouted at the microphone.

'Has he fucking jumped?'

As the manic screaming escalated, other employees entered the office and attempted to pacify the distraught female. One employee looked down at the pavement before turning to the front of the PC screen. Recognising Custanti, he spoke.

'Signor – Stefano has leapt from the window. I don't know what to say...'

Custanti, suppressing a rising fear, spoke. 'Please calm down. What is your name?'

The man took a breath. 'Galrani Fanello, Signor...'

'Well Galrani, can you find me the best in IT we have in my cousin's office?'

Galrani nodded. 'You're looking at him, Sir.'

'Excellent. Send me any footage and tell no one the clip exists. I do not wish this to become a paparazzi feeding frenzy Are we clear, Galrani?'

Galrani stuttered his answer.

'Of – of course, Signor, I understand.'

'After you have sent a copy, erase everything.' Custanti paused for effect. 'Galrani.'

'Yes, Signor?'

'You understand my family does not like mistakes...?'

Galrani gulped hard. 'Signor, I won't let you down.'

Custanti ended the connection. Within twenty minutes, he had viewed the stream several times. Downing a brandy, then drawing on a cigarette, he accepted the reality.

Stefano's expression tells me his mind was elsewhere – this is the work of the Paragon.

His mobile rang, causing him to flinch. A brief conversation led to information regarding a hit team placed on Scarth by Stefano. All had failed to return comms. Custanti closed the call, took another brandy, then slumped into thought.

My uncle, the assassins, all dead. It would appear that the same fate has befell my cousin. Rosso was mistaken! The Paragon did not hold back for the sake of negotiation; he only eliminates threats on himself.

Custanti made two consecutive phone calls before calling Russo.

'Signor Russo time is crucial – I witnessed Stefano jump from his office window to his death whilst on a Skype call. My belief is that the Paragon took possession of his mind because Stefano dispatched four of our elite to the Isle of Scarth. Short story – the team has vanished.'

Russo looked shocked. 'The devil is now unshackled; our God must stand up to this evil. Custanti, what power can make a sane man leap to his death?'

Custanti cursed under his breath.

'We are dealing with the unnatural Signor, please capture his parents as soon as.'

'Pray to our God for his help against this evil.'

'For now, I'll pray that you capture his parents. Contact me when you have news.'

Call closed, both men sat in feared silence for several minutes. After which Russo gave the green light to pick up the parents.

Custanti dialled the number of his contact in the United States.

'I'm sending you a file of the latest kill by the Paragon. Have it examined, but trust me, it's not faked. Work quickly. This is beyond anything we've ever experienced.'

Galrani Fanello had viewed the suicide tape several times and was utterly shocked. He concluded the authorities had to be informed, regardless of what the repercussions were. Moving quickly to the staff room, he felt relieved that security had calmed the hysterical female.

Close to her side, he whispered. 'I've watched the security tape; we have to show the police how this happened.' The P.A. stared vacantly at Fanello, who whispered again. 'Please, I believe his death to be abnormal.'

With a sobbing grimace, she drew a stuttering breath, then mouthed an okay. Within ten minutes, both were on their way to the police station, having agreed the situation was well beyond scare tactics. Five minutes into their journey, an articulated truck wrecked Fanello's vehicle. The P.A. died instantly. Fanello, although trapped and bleeding, attempted to send the file to his family's *Whats App* group. Death prevented his bravado as fire engulfed the overturned vehicle.

News of the mysterious demise of Stefano Giordano caused pandemonium amongst the various media outlets. Conspiracy theories surfaced, linking his death to his fathers. As a deflection, Custanti contacted the authorities to log his *concern* over the relationship between Stefano and the female. To why Stefano jumped from the building baffled the police, as did the accident of Stefano's P.A. and senior IT consultant.

Custanti relaxed, as without doubt the chance of a detective uncovering the truth was zero.

Thirty-four

9 A.M. the following day.

Ross and Isla, aboard the cruise liner *Allure of the Seas*, were laying on their bed talking. Neither had ventured onto the decks as the Nemkis and its secrets had become all-consuming. Two of their three-man protection unit waited in the adjoining cabin. All were over six feet and could pass as brothers, although *Bilks*, the team leader, having ginger hair, threw a spanner into the works.

Stood on the forward deck, Bilks had latched on to a heated discussion between an engineer and a young HLO (Helicopter Landing Officer) below on the Helideck. Turning seaward, Bilks noticed a helicopter approaching from the starboard side, causing him to feel uneasy. Identifying the aircraft as a military Agusta Westland, flying Italian colours, he called Kyle.

'What the hell is a Westland doing scouting our ship some thirty clicks from Barcelona?'

'Can't see it from our cabin, but I don't like the sound of it.'

'Nor me. I reckon their HLO is going by the book as the D-circle of the Agusta may exceed the helideck.'

Bilks immediately decided.

'Have Jock prep to turn off all internal CCTV. Once down, extract the parents to a random cabin asap; I'll see what I can recce on the chopper crew.'

'Rodger that.'

The pilot eased the aircraft down to the relief of the *HLO*. Four men stepped from the chopper, all looked in shape. The appearance of the captain added to Bilks concerns, and so he dialled Arlo on his sat phone. After listening, Arlo replied.

'We've received intel that Stefano sent operatives to Scarth. All believed to be dead but not confirmed.'

Bilks spoke up. 'The Paragon must be on the Isle?'

'It's a possibility.'

'Shall we get a team out to him?'

'No need. He's quite capable of looking after his corner. Our problem is on board your vessel. Location?'

'I'd say we're thirty clicks from docking at Barcelona.'

'Well, whatever story they've concocted it will lead to extraction by Heli or turnover in port. Keep the parents secure till you dock. I'll arrange back up.'

'Boss.'

Bilks had kept half an eye on the helideck. As one man had passed the captain several documents, he surmised they were serving arrest warrants on the parents. The captain, happy with the men's credentials, escorted them back to the bridge.

He will provide passenger lists. Next question... How did these guys get their intel?

The captain of the vessel, following normal protocol, had contacted the shipping company. That they had produced undeniable proof that *Mr and Mrs Holding* were, in fact, Ross and Isla Cranson, sealed the deal, along with anti-terrorist identification papers produced by the men. Russo had played his cards well. Two men set off for cabin number 14568.

Bilks made comms.

'Kyle, we're compromised. Have you re-homed the package yet?'

'Going dark now.'

Ross and Isla, remaining as calm as possible, held hands as Kyle closed the call. Jock moved to hold the lift. After giving the go-ahead. Kyle set.

'We'll have around two minutes before they override the glitch – we go in five seconds.'

Side arm checked; he took a breath. 'Okay, turn right, grab the lift, we drop to deck ten, then turn right on exit – stay tight, okay?'

Still holding Isla's hand, Ross nodded their readiness. After checking the corridor, Kyle called to go.

All three rushed to the lift and stepped inside. Another couple, smiling, called for them to hold the doors. Not a chance. Kyle hit the button. Seconds later, a pleasant electronic voice called *Deck Ten.* As the doors slid open, four people were waiting. Expressing no pleasantries, they turned right. As Kyle knocked on a cabin door, Jock rushed to rendezvous with Bilks. The cabin opened, revealing a well-presented elderly lady.

'We haven't called for room service?'

With zero time to go soft, Kyle pushed his firearm at the lady's forehead.

'Sorry sweetheart, back you go.'

The lady warned her husband before being muffled by the firm hand of Kyle. As he pushed inside, the Cranson's' followed. The husband, seated in a wheelchair, was a single amputee. Showing no fear, he spoke in a controlled manner.

'That's a Glock, but your safety's on, so I imagine you're going to scare us a little. That's achieved, so I'd appreciate you eased the weapon away from my wife's head. Major John Kline, ex-navy seal... We all good here?'

Kyle, nodding his respect, holstered his firearm, then checked his watch.

Just about beat the reboot, I reckon.

Turning to the major, he smiled. 'My apologies, major – then I'm guessing you heard the chopper land?'

The major looked out of the porthole towards the ocean. 'Aye, what's the Itia's doing strong-arming near Barcelona?'

'Always switched on, you boys. Okay, I'll level with you, – we're tasked to escort these witnesses to Barcelona. Some bad, bad people have other ideas. Can't say much more...'

The major frowned, then turned to his wife, who had settled down after her initial shock.

'My sweet, best break out the red wine. Looks like we have company till we throw down anchor. Mr and Mrs, please take a seat.'

The Majors calm manner, relaxed everyone at least two notches. Ross and Isla both felt the need to apologise to the elderly couple. A glass of red helped. Kyle, placing his ear to the door, looked at his watch. The time matched the last breakfast sitting. Footsteps, non-rushed, pleased him. Bilks and Jock, unaware of their location, would remain so until he made comms. The major pointed to Kyle's ankle.

'If they are really *bad* and try to enter, I'll take your boot-arm if you don't mind. It's a Glock 26?'

Kyle grinned. 'I'll think about it.' He said before pointing at the major's leg. 'Serving?'

'Fell off my Harley ten years ago, wife warned me when I passed sixty to give it up.'

A knock on the door halted discussions.

'Room service.'

The wife's reply gave no concern. 'Fine today, thank you.'

'Okay, Mrs Kline.'

Kyle, grateful to hear the maid knock at the next cabin, sighed.

'Any chance of a coffee, Mrs Kline...?'

Bilks met with Jock, who had hacked into the CCTV to search the decks for the intruders. Five minutes later, he located all four of them back on the helipad in discussion, which ended in the pilot extracting alone.

Bilks frowned. 'This will go to the wire when we reach dockside. Keep tabs on that lot.'

The sat phone rang out. Arlo spoke immediately.

'We've *unofficial* help from the Spanish police.'

'Well boss, it's definitely a shore snatch as the chopper took flight, leaving the four x-rays aboard. Bottom line – they need the parents in good health.'

Call closed; Bilks waited until he had a close visual on the coastline, then rang Kyle.

'Spanish feds are onside, but we'll have to tread carefully till we get the parents ashore. I'll call nearer docking.'

'Received, out.'

Isla felt relieved that Arlo had commandeered the Spanish police. Ross, not so.

'Those men have to try – fact.'

The Major spoke. 'Tugs have us. Be stationary in about thirty minutes. My advice, join one of the shopping parties to disembark. You're welcome to take my wheelchair and borrow our duds.'

Kyle nodded; he liked the idea.

Now on top deck, Bilks watched on as the four men moved towards gangway two. He was in no doubt they would have onshore operatives on standby. Twenty minutes later, he called Kyle, who fed him the plan.

'Ross in a wheelchair, Isla pushin. Both dressed as biddies, will join up with a party hitting the markets. The old boy's idea, ex seal. We'll need the Spanish on the ship side of the security checks.'

Bilks ran the situation through his mind. No question it had merit.

'Okay, take the play.'

Kyle closed the call and turned to the major. 'One day, the beers will be on me.'

'I hope so son – just don't fuck up my wheelchair.'

Both laughed, then shook hands.

Five minutes later Isla's heart rate maxed out as she pushed Ross towards the group gathering in the middle bar. After a head count, they moved on, with Kyle in close attendance. As Isla reached the outer deck, she stopped pushing.

'Ross, I could not live with myself if one of these people gets hurt. I won't do this.'

Ross sighed. 'Your right love, but what's our options?'

'We walk right off this bloody ship. Stand up, you look like a twat.'

Ross chuckled, having never, in his entire life, heard Isla cuss.

Moments later, as the party began to disembark. Kyle approached the two and spoke under his breath.

'Get back in the chair.'

Ross spun around in anger. 'Back off! Nobody will get hurt because of us.'

Kyle, fuming, had no choice and shrugged as Bilks glanced at him quizzingly. Now aware of the developments, the kidnap team's leader made comms, prompting rushed movement on the docking bay in the area behind the ship's exit gate.

The sudden movement caught Bilks' eye.'

And no sign of the Spanish Feds!

In a typical British manner, the shopping group filtered casually through security. As Ross and Isla nervously stepped onto the gangway, Bilks and Kyle followed. Spread amongst the other passengers, the attackers calmly followed on. As Ross reached the exit gate, he raised his arm to alert the four policemen who had just arrived. With the domino effect of reaction now set, Bilks braced for the first push. Just twenty feet from Isla, the leading enemy, gripped a female passenger and slammed his firearm against her temple. In tandem, his operatives on shore drew down on the policemen who had failed to react. Bilks, Mike, and Kyle drew against the men on the ship. A tense standoff was now in place.

Above the screams of the nearby passengers, the assailant called aggressively to Bilks.

'Send the parents to my men so we can all stand down.'

Aiming at the kidnapper's head, Bilks spoke. 'Not going to happen.'

To the shock of all, Isla turned and ran towards the assailant, who grinned. Ross, missing in his attempt to grab her arm, followed.

The assailant called out.

'Get your ass over here.'

Narrowing the distance and displaying no fear, Isla yelled. 'Put your gun down!'

As Ross drew near, his aggressive manner forced the assailant's mind to process the action to pistol whip Isla.

In that instant, his expression turned to one of absolute terror. Dropping his firearm, he patted frantically at his clothing, which, in his mind, appeared to be burning. Now screaming and thrashing at the *flames*, he ran and launched himself off the port side. For those watching, time stood still as his men, including those ashore, also began beating at their *blazing* clothing. One by one, they plunged into the dock, desperate to quell the pain. The flames, however, continued their torment and so in moments, with no attempts to swim, the sea devoured all.

As mass panic erupted around them, Ross reacted by shoving a shocked Isla towards the exit. Bilks, recovering from his own disbelief, rushed alongside them, weapon still drawn. Shouting to his men, they sprinted past the policemen, three of whom were still trying to process what had happened. The fourth, a sub-inspector, motioned for Bilks to follow. One minute later, they piled into a police vehicle bound for Barcelona-El Prat Airport to board a private flight. All sat in stunned silence before Bilks dialled Arlo. The short de-brief prompted Arlo to swallow one of his tablets.

This event changes the field of play – for all.

Isla asked for the sat phone to be placed on loudspeaker. Bilks, albeit gingerly, obliged.

Her tone was non-compromising. 'Get us home. No arguments.'

Just now Arlo could not dispute the safest place for the Cranson family was the Isle.

'Isla, it is inevitable the conflict will continue to escalate!'

Ross butted in sharply. 'We don't want to listen. Get us home!'

'My apologies, yes, of course.'

Isla snuggled wearily into Ross' shoulder as Arlo began discussions for their return to Scarth. The Cranson's raised a contented smile, then closed their eyes.

Call ended; Arlo looked to the heavens.

Mankind has always feared what they don't understand. Today, that fear has become warranted.

Thirty-five

The remaining senior members of the Columnae had assembled inside a board room at the Vatican. Custanti opened discussions.

'Stefano's P.A. has become the prime suspect over my cousin's death. We have attributed the suicides of our operatives in Barcelona to the drug Pervitin X. A similar strain to the one the Japanese used in World War Two. Considering the extreme circumstances – it's the best we could do.'

Concerned voices raised the volume in the room. Custanti held his hand up.

'In all missions, the Paragon has manipulated our operatives to the point of death. Ominously, the incident at the dock proves he can protect those close to him. This, of course, may include members of the ¥.'

Russo raised his hand.

'Gentlemen, we are without doubt,' he paused, then began brushing his hands against the table as though he was shooing something away, producing a blank silence from all. He then spoke with a sense of agitation and a tinge of panic in his voice.

'How did these bees get in? You know I'm allergic to stings... get them away from me! Get them away from me – NOW!'

Custanti, understanding the Paragon was at work, snapped a command.

'Signor is in a trance. Wake him now!'

Two men rushed towards Russo as he began swatting at the air manically. Inside his mind, a swarm of African bees had engulfed him. With each sting registering as reality, swellings on his hands and arms appeared. In moments, the angry bees were crawling over his face. A scream invited entry. Now manically chewing the invading bees, he shuddered violently. With the two men attempting to calm him, Russo arched his back, took one huge gasp for air, and was gone.

Custanti had already called for a medical team, who arrived promptly and set up the defibrillator.

Ten minutes later, the lead medic shook his head, then spoke.

'I am so sorry the Signor has passed.'

That a post-mortem would confirm a heart attack was the only positive. After thirty minutes of thought and several large brandies, Custanti had one conclusion.

'If we are to protect the future of our organisation, we must recognise the work of the Paragon as a genuine threat. As of now, we must stay in a passive state and refrain from any plans of aggression. Senior Russo has now gone to a better place. First, we must make sure that his family receives our support and then dedicate some time to review our circumstances. In light of this, I am concluding the meeting so that we can reconvene tomorrow.'

The room emptied quickly, leaving Custanti alone.

Money is of little use if I perish.

Now dialling his contact in the U.S., he chose his words carefully.

'I strongly advise that any contact with the Paragon is peaceful and there is no intention of violence, considering he has just murdered Signor Russo by controlling his mind.'

Custanti closed the call and then destroyed his sim card. Senator Finney tried a redial to no avail – the hum of a *closed* line made him smile.

These religious types are always a touch overzealous in their belief of their almighty. If this Paragon can do as claimed, it's worth a punt.

Finney dialled. 'Insert an eight-man team covertly into Wick Airport, Scotland, immediately. Once in situ, I'll update intel on the target.'

Finney sat back in his chair.

Let's see how this so-called wizard deals with our "all mightiest".

Thirty-six

After a restful night's sleep, Bran awoke and stretched to his full length before heading to the kitchen to indulge in an enormous feast.

Each time an incident occurs, I appear to grow closer to Nemkis. Although I feel no empathy, how many more deaths will they suffer before realising the futility? The greed of evil men throughout time has been prohibitive to common sense.

The distant sound of a helicopter abruptly interrupted his thoughts. Five minutes later, the family was rejoicing in a tearful reunion. Ross made a phone call to Jim, asking him to bring Loki over the following day. Bran beamed, then spoke serenely.

'Without sounding belligerent, we are now protected by a sense that is beyond normal comprehension. I have no conscious connection to the event it all happens within my sub-conscious mind.' Looking at his parents' concerned expressions, he raised a smile. 'Although it may seem like your son is a crazed killer, he is really just a guardian protecting us from the malevolent.' He took a breath. 'I am truly sorry for all the added stress that I have brought into our family. It was never my intention.'

Isla poked Bran on the shoulder rather firmly. 'They didn't think twice about attempting to kidnap or murder us, so apologies are not required.'

Ross shrugged. 'Your mother has been on one for a few days.'

Isla let out a chuckle and poured two enormous glasses of red wine and one of scotch for Bran before she spoke her mind.

'What really happened?'

'The quick version. My sub-conscious can create a *dream like state* whilst the recipient is awake. Of course, the illusion appears as reality, resulting in death if that is the scenario presented.'

Both parents took a large mouthful. Isla, placing her glass down, looked at Bran.

'I sensed they would die. How?'

'Possibly because we are family, therefore connected.'

Ross frowned. 'Son, you seem depressed, which is natural given the circumstances?'

Bran forced a smile.

I dare not confess the true devastation the sub-conscious can unleash.

'Another absolute stinking headache. Guess the knowledge weighs heavily on my mind. Family time is my need for tonight – tomorrow we can discuss my experiences.'

Isla downed the remaining wine. 'Then we shall. Do you fancy another nip?'

Bran grinned. 'I'm only seventeen and already forming a liking for scotch.'

'Hardly surprising,' shrugged Ross.

With drinks to hand, Bran spoke solemnly.

'There will be more deaths.'

Isla looked into her glass. 'Providing it's not ours. We'll cope.'

'I can guarantee absolutely no harm will befall this family, but once we are at peace, the actual battle begins.'

'Battle?' asked Ross nervously.

'Conveying the truth to the world.'

Isla looked concerned. 'And if they refuse it?'

'Let's not dwell on that!'

As though he was in pain, Ross placed his hands on his head.

'Will the good suffer?'

'No, father. If I may quote... *the meek*,' he paused, 'no, *the good* shall inherit the earth.'

'Then all will be fine, now enough. You need to relax – Cluedo?' challenged Ross.

'Scrabble board?' Countered Bran, smiling.

'Bugger off! You whacked us at that when you were just three.'

Isla chirped in. 'Cluedo – that's a two-to-one vote.'

Bran scratched his head. 'I best have another wee dram.'

A few hours of joy and normality were just the remedy Bran needed. Now staring at his bedroom ceiling, he felt relieved that his parents had coped with the horror. Turning his thoughts to Loki triggered an idea.

Dogs dream! My god could I connect to Loki? I dare not try yet, as I would never forgive myself if I unbalanced his mind. That's for another time. Looking at his watch, he calculated Arlo would be asleep. Well then, I will pay him a visit.

Bran closed his eyes and peered. In moments, he had invaded Arlo's dream, set on a rubber dingy floating in a large steel tank filled with sand. Bran dismissing the ludicrous scenario spoke.

'Arlo, please listen.'

Extremely confused, Arlo continued his attempt to paddle.

Bran began.

'I am to bring you into my dream. Once inside, you will believe you're awake.'

Struggling to focus, as his oar had turned into a brush, Arlo half nodded, then set to sweep.

Moments later, with both seated in Cliff Cottage, he stared in nervous disbelief at his surroundings.

'Are you telling me I'm dreaming?'

'Look at your left little finger. It's missing.'

Arlo quickly shut both eyes before nervously opening just one.

'What the hell? How did that happen?' he asked, perplexed.

'This dream will log into your memory bank as reality. Once awake, it will trigger severe mental conflict as you fight to understand how you transferred from the cottage. The missing finger will separate the dream from reality.'

Arlo, breathing hard, held out his *mutilated* hand. 'I understand the reasoning behind the illusion, but... it is bloody awful!'

Bran's tone became serious. 'When you awake, look at your finger before you recall the memory. Now say to me a dozen times. *Look for my finger.*'

Although feeling awkward, Arlo did so, then took a breath.

'Is this really how you dream?'

'It has its advantages. Now I'm going to release you back to consciousness. When I do, you will instantly panic. Do not let anxiety override your composure.'

Arlo spoke up. 'And look for my finger.'

'Perfect... are you ready?'

Arlo stood and opened the back door.

I feel the cold and smell the fresh air – my god.

'Are you absolutely positive this is a dream?'

Bran smiled. 'When awake, look for your finger...!'

Now sitting upright in his bed, Arlo froze as a raw anxiety gripped his nervous system.

'What the hell! Bran... where are you? What...? I was just inside Cliff Cottage...!'

Standing, he questioned his sanity. 'Have I gone mad? I was definitely just talking to Bran on Scarth, but now I'm in my bedroom.' Rushing to his window, he raised the blinds. 'This is my home, yet moments ago, I was opening the rear door at Cliff Cottage?'

As his mind struggled to knit the two memories together, shaking, he collapsed forward onto his hands and knees. A sharp pain in his left wrist led to him rubbing the strain. Now staring at his hand, Bran's voice appeared in his mind.

Look at your finger.

As his memory replayed the dream scenario at the cottage, Arlo wept unashamedly.

That was truly frightening. For a moment, I thought I'd lost it. That entire episode at the cottage was a dream, yet it wasn't. How on earth does Bran keep his sanity? What next? Hell, back into the frying pan, I suppose.

With his mind in overdrive, Arlo took an age to fall asleep.

Cliff Cottage returned.

Rather gingerly, he moved to the back door, breathed the air, then faced Bran.

'I am glad I've no left little finger.'

Bran laughed. 'Are you stable?'

'It was touch and go, but yes, I'm fine. Hell – how do you cope?'

'I'm a Paragon.'

'Daft question if ever there was!'

Bran set to the point. 'I have so much to explain. Please take notes and later transfer to our language. Remember, this will become a powerful memory, therefore you will recall all the material you require. I warn you now, nothing is as we expected. When we are done here, leave for Scarth at once and fear nothing as my sub-conscious protects the ¥, except one who is of the grey.'

Arlo's expression depicted his hatred for the traitor. 'We had our concerns about how they found your parents. May I have a name?'

Bran's reply was extremely cold. 'No need.'

Arlo would not press the issue. Bran continued.

'The next few weeks will be extraordinary. Now, are you ready for my experiences?'

Arlo nodded. It took many hours of discussion to finish the notes. On the final full stop, Bran, without warning, closed the dream.

Arlo woke. His first reaction was to hear the dawn chorus before a twinge of panic surfaced. Now breathing rapidly, he looked at his hands.

'Ten digits – I'm awake.' Trembling, he grabbed his phone and called Dee.

'I need to be in Scarth ASAP. Make this happen and wake Walt.'

'Boss.'

Arlo closed the call and placed his head in his hands.

Nemkis farm's our excess energy...! Is this really why we exist?

As his mind went back to the conversation, one particular memory caused him to shake his head in surprise.

We have always assumed that life requires a form. We even see aliens as mis-shaped humanoids. Nemkis has intelligence far beyond our own, and yet it has no physical shape? As Bran once surmised – are we that worm? These chapters will become the most important novel the world has ever seen, but proving their authenticity will become mission impossible. I have to stay the scholar and record everything I've learned. However, at this present moment, I cannot decide if the knowledge is beneficial to our existence. But first I have to put in writing the Awakening before detailing Bran's findings.

Arlo moved to a wall safe and removed an enormous leather-bound book, secured by a brass clasp. After a brief pause, he began and would continue to work until he stepped onto the soil at Scarth. During writing, his mind would continue to struggle to process the enormity of the discoveries.

The calm and peaceful atmosphere of Nemkis allowed Bran to clear his mind and think with clarity.

The dreamworld, although complicated, is clear in my mind, but I believe there are more answers yet to release from this dimension. Grandpa Gregor appeared to be used to such ghostly sightings; who were they? Certainly he was a wise man, for keeping this knowledge within the family circle was paramount. Again, I wonder who the other ghosts were? Yet another thought to dwell on. Unavoidably, death will play a part in the rebirth of mankind. I wish there were another way, but until I force the power men into submission, I cannot concentrate on discovery.

Thirty-seven

Sat at the breakfast table the following morning, the family heard a sound that caused Bran to dash towards the back door. Loki's bark was unmistakable. Jim had let him off the leash upon landing at the jetty. The direct route taken by the Schnauzer at full pace easily beat the cycling efforts of a rotund boat captain. The reunion made Isla smile. Loki was a headstrong dog to which she found difficult to manage, but his relationship with Bran was truly uncanny. Ten minutes later, Jim appeared on his mountain bike blowing like a Scottish piper.

Ross snickered. 'Bloody hell, what's this about?'

Jim's expression needed no explanation. Isla, grinning, waited for the tale.

'Wife's idea, says I'm overweight and need to get in shape.'

'So, you won't need the full cooked our Bran declined?' Teased Ross.

With the poise of a walrus, Jim dismounted. 'Let's not be too hasty. I'll take a plate.'

Isla winked at Ross. 'Not likely. If Mary wants you slim, then it's porridge for you, James McTay.'

Ross batted back Jim's pleading expression.

'Sorry Jim, is that with milk or water?'

Laughter ensued. Bran grabbed his coat. 'Out with Loki for a while.'

Isla almost said, *be careful* but settled for, *enjoy the walk love.*

Extruding obvious pangs of hunger, Jim sat at the table.

'Anyway, what's with this helicopter flight? You trying to bankrupt me?'

Ross thought on the hoof. 'It's that Professor... thinks we may sell up?'

Jim's reply stalled as Isla placed his meal on the table. Immediately chomping on the first of four sausages, his face became a picture of contentment.

'Buy the Isle for what?'

'Survival school.'

'Oh Jesus – what next?'

No need for Jim to ask about their intentions. Besides, he had breakfast to devour.

Bran had walked due south to sit at a small loch in which, as a young boy, he learnt to fish. Seated at the water's edge on a boulder, he became enthralled at the constant flicker of fish just under the surface.

I cannot face meat when I see the aura emitting from all life.

Loki barked, as was his nature to remind Bran he required sticks to be thrown into the water. Bran laughed.

'Hell Loki, it's bloody freezing?' Loki boomed another bark; Bran collected, then threw a stick and watched on as Loki plunged and made like a paddle steamer, causing the illuminated fish to dive for the depths. As he laughed aloud, for a while the teenager returned. Around thirty minutes later, the chilly wind dictated a return to home. Smartly dodging the expert shaking from the wettest dog on the Isle, Bran stood.

'Come on boy, let's jog back.'

A barked agreement ensued, and so the two set off. Twenty paces into their run, Bran stopped dead in his tracks...

Two hours earlier.

An EC225 Super Puma helicopter landed at the north corner of Wick's Airport. The eight men aboard, dressed in full combat rigging, began checking their equipment.

Captain Rick Davis, a rugged, bull shaped man, dialled the sat phone. Senator Finney answered.

'All present and correct, captain?'

'Yes sir, awaiting orders.'

'Excellent, now inside your brief case is the coordinates of a private Isle named Scarth, two miles off the east coast. Your primary target is a youth named Bran Cranson. His parents, Ross, and Isla are secondary. We have intelligence that a relative named Jim McTay is currently paying a visit and believe his return to the mainland is imminent. Another flight is due to land on the Isle in six hours, this we wish to avoid. Wait for one hour only for the relative to leave. Should his capture be unavoidable, drop him out to sea. It has been determined that this boy is the one responsible for several recent fatalities, including the Barcelona dock mystery, so it is of paramount importance that we apprehend him with due consideration and respect, and that we keep him alive at all costs. Do I make this absolutely clear?'

'Yes sir – are they armed?'

'Possibly a shotgun or two and a male Giant Schnauzer, the boy's threat, or so I'm told, is via his mind.'

Davis remained silent for a moment.

'Sir, repeat that threat?'

'His mind, captain! Our sources inform us he is some kind of fucking mutant.' Finney laughed. 'But as yet, he aint met men who can shoot straight. The code for the case is C3471. Read the intel thoroughly. But seriously, captain, dart him on sight just to be sure and keep him under till we have him below base.'

'The secondary targets – are they also live capture?'

'Yes, need them as working bait.'

'Understood, we await the go.'

Call closed; Davis studied the full operational details. Closing the brief case his mind ticked over.

I've never felt as uncomfortable over an op – how fucking odd.

Intelligence digested. He looked towards his men.

'Straight forward lift, body bags not required! Primary is a seventeen-year-old kid, a mental job our employers wish to examine. I want six on darts, the rest standard kit. His parents are on the Isle. We'll pick them up cleanly for the leverage. Anyone with eyes on their Giant Schnauzer, top it!' The team nodded their acceptance. 'We're to be dropped on the east coast, leaving a tab of seven clicks over rough terrain. Check your laces boys. Questions?'

'Eight specials for a seventeen-year-old staying with his parents? Just how mental is this twat?'

Davis sighed. 'Intel states he is some kind of mutant, not my words.'

'Fuck off Boss. They're having us off here?'

Davis looked at his men. 'That weird shit in Barcelona where those agents offed themselves. This is the bastard they suspect.'

'They blamed a strain of Pervitin, the shit they gave to Kamikaze pilots in World War Two.'

'Well, apparently, that's bollocks, so we dart him on sight, absolutely he remains alive at all costs – do I make myself clear?'

'Ok to spank him though?'

The team laughed collectively. Davis didn't.

'Check your gear. We fly within the hour...'

When Davis left the flight to urinate, his action produced concerned looks from his men, who would have expected him to pee in a bottle. Now behind the plane, he dialled his wife.

'Hey Joan, I'll be back sooner than I thought. I'll make our anniversary for once.'

Joan screamed her delight. After a pleasant exchange, he closed the call, then looked at the sky. 'Not this time, big man, eh?'

Forty minutes passed before his sat phone rang.

'McTay is returning to the mainland. I repeat. Do not harm the primary.'

'Roger – out.'

Fifteen minutes later, the team had deployed on the east coast. The tab was as expected. Upon reaching the outskirts of the bosk, they split to surround the Cranson house. A close recce showed the parents to be at home with no sign of their primary target. Davis set the command.

'Darts, one front, one rear, three with me. Lead... one with me. The rest stay in the trees. Do not put any holes in the primary!'

All nodded confirmation.

As the *external* team made position, the rush to the house was rapid.

Isla yelped as she glimpsed the men approaching fast. Before Ross reacted, both front and rear doors were burst open.

Davis spoke in a calmed manner.

'Ross, Isla please relax, it is not our intentions to harm.'

The parents, showing zero panic, moved to sit on the sofa, surprising Davis somewhat.

'Where's Bran?'

Ross, looking directly at Davis, swallowed before speaking.

'My advice is this. Call your contact and tell them the boy is not on the Isle.'

Davis ground his teeth. 'Ross, I'll ask you just once again!'

Comms came alive. 'Boy and dog jogging in, half a click away – orders?'

'Let him pass.'

'Rodger that.'

Davis turned to his men. 'Take out the dog, leave the boy. He won't gamble with his parents in play.'

Isla stood, then looked at Davis. 'Sir, please, for the safety of your men, do nothing but speak. I beg you.'

With a tinge of adrenaline forging through his veins, he replied sternly. 'You have my attention. Let's see how this pans out. Tie and gag the parents... dart the boy and top the dog on entry.'

Isla and Ross remained compliant as the men taped their mouths and slipped plastic ties on their wrists, perhaps too tightly. The external team came on comms.

'Primary approaching the rear.'

Moments later, the sound of pounding paws raised the hairs on the back of Ross's neck. Bran called out.

'Parents – I'm home.'

Ross and Isla, recognising the unnatural tone in their son's voice, tensed.

As Bran stepped into the kitchen, his expression was best described as vacant. Loki, glued to his side, did neither bark nor growl. From the kneeling position, the shooters mentally processed their shots...

The unexplained creates a turmoil that even the combat worn soldier cannot suppress. Both men dropped their weapons, curled up on the floor, and began vomiting. In reaction, Davis drew his sidearm and aimed it at Isla.

Ross attempted to stand, resulting in the soldier behind him driving his rifle butt hard into his back. Falling to his knees, Ross's muffled groan echoed around Bran's mind. His voice changed to one of calmed menace.

'I tried to minimise the effects of this attack, but enough. It has become essential that you people understand!'

After blinking, Bran shuddered. And then it happened...

All the soldiers, excluding Davis, disappeared completely, leaving no evidence of their existence. The atmosphere in the room filled with a peculiar type of nothingness – no sound, no visuals, just an eery emptiness that made little sense.

Ross and Isla gaped in astonishment. Davis, traumatised, dropped to his knees as his mind failed to process the moment.

'What the fuck just happened...?'

With a muted demeanour, Bran moved to his parents and released their bindings. Isla, close to tears, began shaking uncontrollably, whilst Ross stirred blankly at the space once filled by soldiers.

Fighting to stay in reality, Davis looked at Bran.

'Just what the hell are you?'

Ignoring Davis, Bran spoke softly to his parents to bring them back to normal thought.

'These men have left our world forever. I hope this example will curtail any future acts of aggression.'

Ross, now visibly shaking, moved to Isla and held her lovingly. Neither spoke. Davis, even with a grounded ability to control emotions, was teetering on the edge of his logic. Standing, he peered outside – no one was in sight.

'Where are my men?'

Exhibiting zero remorse, Bran replied. 'They are now all extinct.'

Davis's brow furrowed. 'Extinct! What the hell do you mean?'

'My explanation is time-consuming, so I offer you the certainty that they are all dead.'

'Give me one reason I should not put a bullet in your head.'

Loki growled. Bran stroked his ear, pacifying him immediately. 'Because I need you alive!'

Understanding he had to stay passive if he were to survive, Davis spoke in a measured tone.

'Alive – why?'

'To prevent more death.'

'You're the one doing the fucking killing!'

'Retaliation, captain, nothing more. I only end those who display the grey aura and show intentions to harm.'

Davis's puzzled expression prompted Bran to continue.

'All humans begin their lives' emitting a ring of white aura, or as you may understand, their soul. Sadly, those that choose an evil path corrode this purity.'

'You've lost me, my friend. Don't forget I'm from earth!' said Davis.

Ignoring the comment, Bran spoke firmly. 'Remove any weapons, place them on the table, and sit down on that chair. My father will bind you. Trust me, this is for your safety, not ours.'

Davis paused, contemplated all actions, before petulantly tossing his side arm onto the table.

'And the knife tucked behind your back?'

'Whatever...'

Ross walked to the scotch bottle, took a large slug, then moved to a drawer to collect a length of nylon cordage.

His knots would hold.

Turning to Bran, he asked a question that was on all their lips.

'Son, what the hell just happened?'

His words caused Isla and Davis to stir blankly at Bran in expectation of an explanation.

With understanding the trauma behind their expressions, Bran spoke subtly.

'The mind feeds Nemkis' celestial energy, my sub-conscious can reverse this process. When it detects a threat, it delivers an extreme overload of energy directly into the soul of the aggressor.' He paused. 'We cannot comprehend how fast this happens. In layman's terms, the timescale is beyond infinitesimal. This results in the body, and anything attached becoming vaporised... no extinguished.'

All remained silent as Bran's words rattled around their minds. Davis responded first.

'I've not a clue what you're on about, but if you're saying, you have the ultimate defence system. Hell fire, you're going to be in high demand.'

Isla moved to Bran and held him close.

'Just the evil son?'

'Thankfully yes.'

'Then I'd call that a gift.'

Davis laughed. Ross spoke out.

'Do you have the choice to use this?'

'No, my sub-conscious controls the reaction, but I have zero remorse, none!'

The room fell back into silent thought. With another headache developing, Bran moved to take both paracetamol and ibuprofen tablets.

This ache is unnaturally intense. Is it a product of my defensive actions? I need fresh air.

'Have to walk.'

Loki followed...

Thirty-eight

As expected, Isla, Ross, and Davis had all gone into a state of deep thought. The trauma of the event had left them with an awkward alliance. Three people, incapable of processing the impossible. A bottle of scotch placed dead centre of the kitchen table was now three-quarters empty. Ross held a glass up to Davis's mouth, who gulped down yet another sip, then nodded his appreciation. The lapse into alcohol mode helped ease the mental trauma for all three. Davis spoke.

'This makes little sense. You're just a normal family?' Ross fidgeted in his chair, then took another sip. 'Please understand, however peculiar this appears there is good reason.'

Davis snapped back. 'Good reason? I doubt if you've ever lost comrades to weird shit like this?'

Isla cut in. 'My son is a unique human being, so even in your grief, try to remain open-minded.'

After shuffling to ease his bindings, Davis spoke. 'You're either nut jobs or aliens! This cannot be happening...'

As the sound of a helicopter reverberated around the structure, Isla prevented Ross from having another refill.

Davis became irate. 'Don't let him kill again!'

'Captain, the chopper is ours,' said Ross.

Davis relaxed before mentally chastising himself for his weakness.

Outside, after ordering Loki to stay, Bran walked to the chopper and climbed aboard. Arlo's anxious demeanour did nothing to improve Bran's mood.

'Is your family safe?' shouted Arlo above the engine noise.

Bran closed his eyes for a moment before answering.

'Thank you and yes, they are fine, but the situation has escalated.' A deep sigh punctuated his sentence. 'Eight U.S. soldiers attempted to take us – only one remains.'

Arlo shivered. 'How?'

'My sub-conscious can obliterate in micro-seconds.'

'Obliterate?' Arlo uttered in shock.

'Absolute! There is no trace left of their existence, no sound, no visual, just... gone! In a nutshell, my subconscious can overload the soul with a colossus burst of raw energy direct from Nemkis. No matter how many people it impacts, the result stays the same.'

Now struggling to remain calculated, Arlo forced himself to deliberate over the consequences, not the cause.

'As the facts stand, you have eliminated seven U.S. soldiers, which will trigger a backlash and will escalate both violently and politically. I can handle the ¥, but the might of the U.S....!' Arlo paused. 'If we approach the UK, we'll have to disclose the U.S. entered the country to kidnap or kill UK citizens... politics and publicity we don't need! Do we know who dispatched this team?'

'A senator Finney.'

Arlo swallowed a tablet without water. 'Powerful but a vile man, his interests are invariably financial. Odds-on Custanti Giordano will have instigated a deal. It's his nature. Positive side, we can beat them to the punch and take this to the top.'

'The negative?'

'Once the top brass has knowledge of your abilities, the consequences will be both complex and problematic. At that level, nothing but their objectives count. In effect, you will become a commodity - unique, but none the less a commodity. Our success balances on a disclosure, whilst sidestepping the controlling influences of the power men.'

Bran shrugged. 'If they send an entire Marine Corps battalion, jets, and all, they will perish! So, make this meeting!'

The sound of Isla's agitated screams interrupted the conversation. Without a moment's hesitation, Bran leapt from the chopper and saw his mother running towards him in a state of intense agitation.

'The house... it's come alive!' she shouted hysterically.

Bran's expression hardened. 'Alive? What do you mean?'

Isla winced. 'I can't explain, but Dad's inside untying the captain. Loki is acting like a banshee!'

As Bran rushed to the house, Ross and Davis dived out of the door seconds before it slammed closed.

'What's happened?' said Bran, confused.

'The kitchen... it's bloody moving, Loki's still inside!'

Arlo moved to just steps away from the window when a wine bottle suddenly came crashing out, barely missing him. Guardedly, he gazed inside to see something so disturbing it felt like it had come straight from a horror movie. Ornaments, plates, cups, and glasses were careering around the room. As a carving knife plunged menacingly into the window frame, he dropped back sharply. Now traumatised, he stuttered his words.

'My God – that's demonic lunacy.'

With a disposition suggesting his sub-conscious was now in control, Bran replied in a tone, confirming the fact.

'All move away from the building... now!'

Isla and Ross both stood firm. Bran's eyes narrowed.

'Please...'

Arlo pushed at both Ross and Isla to coerce them into moving.

Davis stepped forward. 'I've got your back.'

Bran did not turn to face him as he spoke.

'This is not your world. Stay outside!'

The ominous wording prompted Davis to pace backwards.

As Bran stepped inside, a multitude of grey spectres were agitating around the room, each screaming silently at their apparent entrapment within the kitchen walls. Loki, with hackles raised, rushed to his side, and continued barking in a tone that was purely feral.

Hell – Loki can see the spectres – how?

Bran observed that any movable object that came into contact with the spectres was randomly flung aside. Rather curiously, he noticed they appeared to avoid contact with himself. With eyes fixed on the spectres, he picked up a fallen stool, placed it in the corner, and sat in order to process the event. Loki moved between his knees and ceased barking, prompting Bran to rest his hand on his back, comforting both.

The grey souls of the fallen soldiers. But how have they become trapped?

Bran watched on for several minutes before he arrived at his conclusion.

The speed of their annihilation was faster than the process that returns their Aura to Nemkis via the Sentinels. Trapped on the earthly side, these spectres now suffer the agony of "perdition." Even the grey does not deserve such damnation.

Closing his eyes, his sub-conscious instigated the demise of the *lost spectres* by drawing them towards a Sentinel. After each had disintegrated, he reflected on the experience.

Both menacing and bewitching, one of the unknown mysteries, the Poltergeist... solved.

Upon opening his eyes, Loki began panting, whilst his Aura had dimmed. After a hug and a gentle stroke, his tail and shining aura gave notice that all was well. The action provided a warming moment between the two. Bran turned to look around at the devastation, then raised a wry grin.

'Gifted, na – if I were Harry Potter, I'd clear this mess up in a jiffy!'

A slight chuckle at his sentence brought back a little normality. Stepping outside, he held his hand up.

'Normal service is now resumed.'

Keep this simple.

'Static electricity, a reaction to the event.'

'More fucking Disney tales,' snapped Davis, shaking his head in disbelief.

Bran sighed. 'Thank you for your offer of back up.'

'I would have taken the first chance to top you!'

'An hour ago, you would have tried. But now, perhaps not.'

Bran moved back into the building, leaving Davis agitated. Arlo, Ross, and Isla followed rather cautiously.

Astounded at the bedlam, Ross gaped at Bran.

'Son – the truth please, as this had nothing to do with static.'

Arlo's expression depicted *spit it out.*

Bran looked at the heavens. 'Oh, just a batch of Poltergeists that's all!'

Ross frowned. 'Explain.'

'In simple terms, the dissipation of the men was quicker than their soul attempting a return to Nemkis, resulting in them becoming trapped on *our side*. It was the grey spectres blundering around the kitchen that caused everything to be thrown about. My sub-conscious ended the turmoil by drawing the souls to a Sentinel to put an end to their suffering.'

Davis, standing in the doorway, felt a fresh swell of rage rise in his body.

'Those are my men you're spouting shit about.'

'My apologies, captain. Trust me when I say this, your men would thank me. I speak the truth.'

'Truth – bollocks! You're a bunch of fucking aliens, that's what I think!'

Bran frowned. 'Captain, it would be much easier to explain if we were.'

Davis picked up a chair. 'I'm going to sit outside, so tie me back up and hit me with another scotch.'

Ross duly obliged.

Now calmed, Bran had an overwhelming urge for solitude!

'Mum, Dad, I need to chill if that's okay.' Both nodded permission. Ross rubbed his forehead.

Our boy eliminated seven soldiers and dispatched their ghosts to hell, yet he still asked for permission to go out! My word, we will always be his mum and dad.

Upon reaching the bosk, Bran noticed many freshly snapped branches and uprooted plants.

Caused by the spectres of the exterior soldiers? I wonder to what extent their entrapment on the outside would have been. More questions!

With his mood diminishing, he moved to sit against a tree, whilst Loki began a sniffing recce of the nearby area.

I've seen that look of horror on spectres many times, yet having seen their human form before death, underlines they are physically, mentally, and spiritually erased. The finality of the grey death is truly a "Hell". Despite that, the event hasn't affected my emotions. Seven men gone, in the most dramatic and perhaps awe-inspiring way – yet nothing...

Bran flipped his thoughts.

Another deep-rooted question answered. Poltergeists are a reality! But in confirming their existence and why, I must then ask who created previous poltergeists? Has to be a Paragon, but who?

The thought dropped his mood down even further.

Loki, having *covered* all scents, charged over. With his black coat surrounded by a white aura, Bran opened his arms to prime a cuddle. Loki snuggled close, causing Bran to double take as their aura combined, forming a single sheen. Immediately, the joy of their *hug* soothed away his cloud of sorrow. In effect, their connection had cheered him up. A sudden surge of excitement flushed around his body.

This moment proves we are all connected... a stunning revelation. The blending of the soul triggers emotion between two life forms. This opens up a whole new world of how we interact with our loved ones. The sheer joy of Loki eased my own dour mood, presenting a new understanding of a "comforting cuddle". Of course, the "ying and yang effect" dictates that a grey aura will also be able to effect a negative mood change.

Loki flopped his considerable paw onto Bran's leg, who snatched at a thought.

If dogs can see a poltergeist, they must see an aura, explaining how they can understand our moods. This would also explain why they bark at random people... they see the grey! Do all animals naturally have this sense? If so, why not the human?

A thought crashed into his mind.

While humans require sleep, it is widely known that dogs, cats, and the majority of other animals sleep for longer periods. Are they able to access Nemkis during this time period? Might this explain why they sleep so excessively? The significance of this will exceed my current understanding. This is escalating at an incredible speed and exceeding all my expectations.

His next thought hit hard.

When, like souls connect, does this create the feeling of love? Yes, I believe this to be true... It would certainly explain the pain we suffer when losing a loved one.

My god!

Standing, he set for the house.

Arlo, seated next to the captain, held a concerned expression as Bran approached.

'The captain's sat phone has rung twice. Guessing our *friend* is getting anxious. Thinking logically, he's the one guy who could get a bigger fish to the table.'

'Well, no time like the present.' Bran moved to Davis. 'Seeing you have drank most of our scotch, I don't suppose you would mind calling Senator Finney?'

Surprised that Bran had knowledge of the Senator, Davis attempted a one finger.

'Fuck right off.'

'Finney has intelligence regarding my status. After today, I need to dissuade him from escalating his current line of thought.'

'Of course this will escalate. You've just executed seven U.S. soldiers!' screamed Davis.

'Captain, if he sends men, they will die. Do you want that on your conscience?'

Wishing his men would just pop-up from wherever Davis gazed blankly.

Isla stepped outside and knelt in front of the captain.

'Please make the call. Aren't seven deaths enough?'

Davis snarled, then paused before replying. 'After another scotch.'

'Make the call.' snapped Isla.

Davis relented, then nodded his head, causing Arlo to snatch the sat phone and dial the last call on speaker mode.

The senator answered. 'Captain we good?'

Davis's reply had the slur of half a bottle of scotch. 'They're gone! Every man, vanished right in front of my eyes. So, fuck *need to know;* this shit should not be possible!'

The senator felt a shiver pass over him.

'All dead?'

'In the words of the *mutant*, extinct!'

'Where is he now?'

'Stood next to me. They want a word!'

Arlo interrupted the conversation.

'Senator, Professor Arlo Norton, we once met at a senate function. I require for you to meet with the young man whom you have just tried to kidnap.'

Finney attempted to appear unnerved. 'Nothing can connect to me, professor. You, of all people, will understand that. So, mission failed – we move on.'

Hardly able to contain his anger and agitation, Arlo fumed. 'Did you pay attention to what the captain was telling you? He used only his mind to obliterate your men, and he will do the same to any other group you send. A word of warning to you - all those tied to the attacks on the boy have since died.'

Davis asked to talk to the Senator. Arlo gave a nod of approval.

'What he did to my men was inhuman. My advice: meet him and sort this shit out.' Davis pulled away from the phone and beckoned for the scotch bottle.

Arlo spoke again. 'I need the Chief of Staff to accompany you. And I warn you, any escalation of violence will react in a hostile defence.'

'Threatening the U.S. is not the way forward, I assure you, Professor?'

'Do not underestimate the capabilities of this boy, Senator. I expect a reply within the hour.'

Finney was aloof in his reply. 'I can't make any promises...'

His manner resulted in Bran entering the fray. The unnatural tone had returned.

'Senator, no need to speak, just listen. Men have died because of your greed. But others' suffering has never bothered your kind, so allow me to bring you into my world for a moment.'

Dropping the phone onto the ground, Finney began scraping his head as an apparition appeared in the blackness of his mind. Senator Finney now endured a sense of impending death as he stood at the entrance to a Sentinel, his soul drawn by an invisible force. The sound of Bran's voice lingered above his screams.

'Senator, if you value your life, then you must comply with what I am asking of you - this will be the only request I make. Following all of Professor Norton's guidelines is of utmost importance to you. Failure to do so will trigger a torment you will not survive, and cease to exist in this world and the next.'

Bran kept Finney at the point of death for over a minute before pulling him back to consciousness. On his release, fighting for his breath, Finney collapsed to the floor. After struggling to grasp reality for a few minutes, in absolute desperation, he clutched at his phone.

'Please, I beg you, do not send me back to that place. The meeting will happen.'

'One chance Senator – one chance!'

Bran closed the call, then turned to the captain.

'I believe it's your anniversary in three days – I'll try my utmost to have you home.'

Davis, shocked Bran had that information, spoke passively. 'This shit is well beyond my pay check, if you get my drift?'

'That's the world you live in, and I intend to change it!' Bran suddenly flinched, then grasped at his head as he asked for another paracetamol.

Isla questioned.

'These headaches are becoming far too frequent; you need to rest?'

'In time mum – in time...'

Under normal circumstances, Senator Finney would have covered his tracks, but knowing this scenario was incomparable, paranoia was taking hold!

That experience was ungodly; once I have arranged this meeting, I want no part in it. First problem, how do I convince the Chief of Staff to accept my words are true? I'll call an old colleague for the solution.

Thirty-nine

Finney received a green light for his meeting with Tom Rialto, the Chief of Staff. Ten minutes into their conversation, Rialto suggested he check into rehab. A long sigh preceded Finney's reply.

'This shit goes back a long way. Check the document 1049-1B linked to the Vatican files. Granted a little tongue in cheek, but none the less its listed. I also recommend you speak to Captain Davis, the only survivor of the mission – Tom, do this for me and I will clear all debts.'

Rialto's brow furrowed as he turned to his aides. 'Gentleman please, allow us a moment.'

Two men left without question. Rialto stared at Finney.

'All debts?'

'You have my word. Shake my hand, and I'll make the call!'

Rialto tilted his head. 'Your actually serious about this shit?'

'Never more so...'

Known as the persuader, because of his uncanny ability to trouble shoot, Rialto had been fast tracked to the top. However, a murky secret hungover his political career, therefore a welcomed relief flooded through him.

'Deal! However, if he has murdered seven of our boys, there will be consequences.'

'That's your shout Tom, but trust me, you don't want to underestimate this situation – not one inch.'

Finney made a call. 'That data on our mutual friend – it's called in. Destroy all copies and I mean all, or...!'

'You sure?' came a quizzical reply.

'Absolutely, and send me your invoice.'

'That'll do it,' laughed the respondent.

Finney closed the call and looked firmly at Rialto. 'Tom, one word of advice, this *boy* – zero aggression, promise me that much.'

The tone and expression of Finney caused Rialto to feel a touch uneasy. 'You seem scared?'

'Tom, I'm absolutely petrified... we all should be!'

'Well, we shall see, won't we?..'

Finney left, leaving Rialto extremely pleased.

With my past now brushed neatly away, finally I can set my eyes on the main title... Just to be cautious, I'd best have someone close to me peruse over this document 1049-1B.

One hour later, Davis's sat phone rang. Arlo answered. Bran was out with Loki.

'Tom Rialto, Chief of Staff, I need to speak with Captain Davis.'

Arlo stiffened a little before walking outside and switching to the loudspeaker. 'Go ahead.'

'Tom Rialto. Captain, please explain the mission in full.'

The rank of the caller surprised Davis. Ten minutes thereafter, he finished his explanation.

'Captain, your assessment of the threat level to this country?'

Davis considered for a few moments. 'None if you do not agitate.' He paused as a memory of the event appeared in his mind. 'Otherwise, a shit storm of the worst kind.'

The line held for a moment.

'Put them on.'

Arlo took a breath.

Something will backfire... always does.

'Professor Arlo Norton speaking.'

'Tom Rialto. We have a situation in progress, one I am keen to navigate without further incident. I grant you immunity to enter our country without prejudice to establish the verifiable facts.'

As his expression of relief was clear to see, Arlo was thankful he was on a call.

'In order to do so, the attendance of Senator Finney and the remaining committee of the Columnae, a covert society attached to the Vatican, is required. I'm sure you'll have them on file. I recommend the CIA step on their toes as some will take flight at the mere hint of this meeting.'

'In some areas, securing Italian citizens could be interpreted as an act of aggression.'

'Sir, forgive me for being direct, but our meeting is not too smooth over the attack. No, it is to prevent an apocalyptic event... I offer this advice. Forget offending anyone and pull all these people together by tomorrow and finally... at no stage, become hostile towards the boy!'

For effect, Arlo closed the call. Moving inside, he grabbed the scotch, then returned to sit on the floor next to Davis. A slugged shot straight from the bottle did the trick.

With having stirred at the phone for several moments, Tom Rialto allowed his anger to subside.

If this boy is all he is cracked up to be, having him as a tool is an opening for me to exploit. For now, I must keep this from Potus, as he will act on this by the book.

He grinned.

I certainly won't!

Bran, tailed by Loki, returned to the house.

'Any news?'

'I've just verbally threatened their chief of staff, then cut him off.'

Bran shrugged. 'That's your green card in jeopardy, well I suppose we just wait.'

Arlo took another swig.

Davis remained silent as he stared vacantly at the scotch bottle. His adrenaline had long faded, and losing his men was hurting. Bran noticed, grabbed a chair, and sat next to him. Davis, looking disgruntled, disregarded his presence.

'Captain, I understand your grief and whilst I cannot expect your forgiveness, I wish to help you understand.'

After a silent pause, the captain replied.

'No thanks, just get me home; I'm done with this shit, as they say – I'm out.'

Bran's expression acknowledged his reply.

'What will you do?'

Davis reflected for a moment. 'Guess I'll spend time with the family, dads at stage seven of Alzheimers.'

'I'm sorry to hear that...'

Without replying, Davis drifted back into thought.

The sat phone rang. Arlo looked at Bran, who shrugged. 'Go on then, sort the world out...'

The voice made no introduction. 'Plan to fly to Langley Airport. Once you have an arrival time, call us back.'

The line closed.

'Touché! Well, we have their attention... Langley, my word, they will take us underground, my young friend.'

Bran smiled. 'Lead covered walls and gamma rays at the ready, I would think.'

Arlo blew out his cheeks. 'We're in with the big league now, that's for sure.' His face turned bland. 'Guarantee me one thing?'

'Being?' quizzed Bran.

'For now, stay in the physical, as we cannot determine what other sensory escalations you will expose.'

The lines on Bran's forehead deepened. 'An experience with Loki has opened up another facet to the soul.'

Arlo's eyes glinted. 'Do tell.'

After listening intensely to Bran's explanation, he closed his eyes.

'When understanding we all have the same soul, one cannot but help to wonder why nature evolved so cruel a system.' He frowned. 'So many organisms feeding on each other just to survive.'

Both held that thought for a moment before Arlo spoke again.

'Another question to ponder over, but back to what's at hand. Success will depend on the U.S. reaction.'

Bran cast a wry smile. 'Our fate rests in the hands of humans, not exactly a perfect scenario.'

Sighing deeply, Arlo lowered his head. 'I'll arrange the flight.'

Loki rushed to Bran, who immediately spotted that the dog's aura had dulled a little.

He knows I'm going away!

Patting Loki, he walked inside the house and threw his hands in the air.

'Looks like I'm away to the land of the free!'

His parents smiled, but as with Loki, their aura dimmed.

I'm uncertain this sense is a blessing, as I feel like I'm infringing on my parents' personal feelings.

Isla moved closer. 'Do you really have to travel?'

'Nothing would please me more than to stay on this Isle and continue my journey of discovery. But I must prevent this escalation of aggression; you have seen what can happen!'

'The planet is better off without those types.'

'I can't disagree.'

With his mother's words echoing around his mind, Bran once more wandered outside.

Nemkis farm's pure celestial energy, the soul. The grey spectre, tainted by evil, is a waste product of no value, eradicated in both celestial and physical forms. Am I to become the avenging angel, as the professor once questioned? Liberating the planet from evil would be a blessing, but I question again – just where exactly is the line drawn?

A wet-nosed nudge from Loki broke his thoughts. Bran sighed. 'I promise, after this trip, we'll never be apart again. Come on, let's get your *dinner* sorted.'

The two left for Loki's kennel.

Arlo ended his phone call, then faced the parents with an expression that depicted fatigue.

'On the flight over I compiled the sequential timeline and as a scholar I am truly marvelled.'

Ross interrupted. 'But?'

Arlo looked at the sky. 'I have worries about the repercussions of the truth.'

His answer shocked both Ross and Isla, Isla especially.

'You have concerns about the repercussions of the truth... but humanity has forever suffered the repercussions of lies.'

Isla's sentence hit Arlo like a bolt to the head.

The systematic annihilation of the evil is just reward for all the suffering they have caused.

He bowed.

'Isla, thank you for your wisdom. I deserved that kick up the backside.'

As the three burst into laughter, Bran stepped inside.

'Laughter is good. Arlo, expect zero conversation on this flight. I need sleep to shift this damn headache!'

'Son, just bloody dream. No more upsets!' sighed Ross.

'Don't worry, I promise, besides I have a speech to prep.'

Thirty minutes later, with goodbyes said at least three times, the helicopter pulled away into the distance. Ross and Isla returned to the house, where finally a nervous exhaustion took its toll on both. After five minutes of weeping, Isla spoke.

'How much more can we take?'

Ross threaded a hand through his hair. 'I know. But our boy has the world on his shoulders, and we are all he has.'

Isla cast a morose eye about the walls and shivered.

'I can't stay here tonight.'

'Agreed. There's definitely a strange feeling about the place. Hardly surprising though. Fancy the cottage for a few days?'

'Would you mind?' asked Isla, hopefully.

Ross cast a glance at the bottle on the table.
'I'll grab the scotch.'
'I suppose it will take the edge off this mess.'
The two hugged, grabbed their coats, the scotch, and collected Loki, who showed little enthusiasm for moving.
Later, they would not chink their glasses, but stare into them.

Forty

After consuming two tumblers of brandy, Custanti Giordano poured a third.

'I thank all for joining me at such short notice, I will get to the point. We have little choice but to meet the Paragon as requested.'

All nodded in disgruntled agreement except one man, Antonio Beneventi, a wealthy wine merchant with a strong connection to the Sicilian mafia.

'There is always a choice, Signor.'

All looked towards Giordano for a reaction, who paused long enough to maintain control.

'I advise caution in your suggestions, Antonio.'

'Thank you for your concern. That said, my understanding is that only a direct threat activates his defensive strategy.'

'Meaning?'

'I assume he can die of natural causes, accidental death, or illness?'

'Of course, but nothing you mention is likely to befall him in the immediate future, so what is your point?'

'If intent triggers this supernatural defence, would he be able to detect a person who *unwittingly* transferred a fatal disease or virus?'

Giordano rolled his eyes. 'He detected those who ordered the attacks, or have you forgotten the revenge exacted on my family?'

'Forgive me Signor.' He paused for effect. 'But revenge on the instigator would appear to be after the event. Therefore, if the carrier succeeds, then revenge becomes impossible.'

Giordano thought for a moment before speaking.

'The theory allows hope. Are you prepared to take the risk?'

Beneventi shrugged. 'High risks deserve high rewards – so I ask, what is my incentive for such a perilous task?'

Giordano smiled. 'Write your own cheque?'

Beneventi raised an eyebrow. 'There is insufficient ink in your pen to write the true cost of defeating the threat.' He paused. 'Should I undertake such a task, I require three hundred million on success and one hundred million for my family if I fail. This is my last offer. Reject it and I will retire to my vineyards and let the world deal with it.'

Giordano stood. 'No one in this room can agree on this course of action for the safety of their souls... however, I believe it cannot harm us for allowing hope into our minds.' Pausing, he took a breath. 'With hope in our minds, we wish you success.'

Beneventi nodded. 'That aside, perhaps the Awakening is our best chance?'

Giordano made the sign of the cross.

'That event does not evolve until the Paragon releases his world upon ours.'

With a nonchalant shrug of his shoulders, Beneventi showed his indifference. 'Yet he may not survive the onset.'

Giordano poured another brandy. 'A risk too far, I feel.'

'Then we take this opportunity to meet the Paragon to assist my research,' said Beneventi.

After swallowing the brandy, Giordano sat down to address the room.

'Again, I suggest we make this trip, not that I fear the wrath of the CIA, but as brother Beneventi stated, it may well be to our advantage to toe the line and meet this Paragon.'

One hour later, on a private flight to Langley, Giordano rejected all thoughts regarding Antonio Beneventi.

Forty-one

The bespoke Gulfstream G650 aircraft, belonging to a company owned by Arlo, had been in flight for about seven hours. Bran had drifted into natural slumber in a private compartment the moment they had boarded.

Untethered, Davis listened in fascination as Arlo explained the Paragon and wanted to deride the information, but an open mind was the sensible decision.

Arlo looked at Davis, who appeared troubled.

'Are you a religious man, Captain?'

Davis didn't answer. Undeterred, Arlo waited. One minute later, Davis began.

'A soldier either carries a cross or not. In my eyes, if a god exists, then soldiers should not be required.'

Nodding, Arlo replied. 'Then we understand religion is a wistful attempt to explain life, and a discipline to keep the masses in check.'

'It also gives hope and there is nothing wrong with that. Of course, the radical element spoils the ride, always have.'

Arlo raised an eyebrow. 'You have listened to me for over four hours, yet I see neither denial nor acceptance?'

Davis looked hard at Arlo. 'I saw a ghost when I was a kid. Funny thing, every single person I told either laughed, called me a liar, or put forward an explanation for what it could have been. Point being – my men vanished in front of my eyes and yet I still don't believe it happened. In a nutshell, convincing Tom Rialto and his people... well, good luck with that!'

Arlo frowned. 'If you could eradicate evil – would you kill...?'

Davis couldn't help but chuckle. 'Hell. I've killed a parcel of people and it aint fixed nuthin! Ultimately, without psychopaths, the world ceases to function. I mean, who else is going to hold it together? You're fucked without a blanket deterrent to maintain order in any society. Violence in its raw form runs this planet, be it to feed or control. Hell, those nuns dished it out – right? What you need to end is violence for individual gain, being monetary, power, or pleasure.'

Arlo shuffled a little. 'The Paragon could exterminate all evil in a fraction of a second. Think about that!'

Davis moved closer to whisper in Arlo's ear. 'I have – ever since he killed my men, but I'm guessing, those deaths will be a drop in the ocean for what's coming. Fact is, I have feared no man as I have the measures to kill. This boy... I can't, and that scares me. Now, forgive me, my mind's popped and needs sleep.'

'Agreed, a nap will do us both the world of good. Nothing stupid Captain... please, for your sake.'

Davis shrugged. 'Live to fight another day has always been my motto!'

Deep in a dream state, Bran watched on as Ellenweorc Mendenhall's husband fought to save their Paragon child. Even when a lance was driven through his shoulder, he hacked down the priest holding their daughter. The melee resulted in several deaths on both sides before the surviving family members made good their escape. The disturbing vision changed to a young male burning at the stake in front of a baying crowd. Bran baulked as the smell of burning flesh and screams invaded his mind. Over the next hour, at least a dozen visions of torment and murder emerged, shocking Bran to the core. On waking, although traumatised by the horrific murders, he understood this to be a reminder of the suffering endured by the Paragon.

No question, the flashbacks were to steel my resolve. Yet who creates these visions?

The pilot's voice bellowed out via the speaker system.

'Professor Norton, we land at Langley in a few minutes. Please fasten your safety belts, thank you.'

Arlo's expression showed concern as he called out to Bran, who stepped out of the sleeping cabin.

Yawning, he spoke. 'That sleep has focused my mind somewhat.'

'Wheels down, hold tight,' boomed the pilot.

Bran strapped into a seat and mused over the horrific visions he had suffered.

I will not waste the sacrifice of brave people. Nothing will prevent me from finding the truth.

The Chief of Staff, Tom Rialto, even after viewing the clips of Stefano Giordano and the operatives at Barcelona, held a little scepticism.

'Madness, sheer madness?'

A female aide spoke out. 'Sir, just to summarise once again. Senator Finney attempted to pull the boy in for *assessment.* However, the operation resulted in the death of seven special force soldiers in the most unusual of circumstances. The boy wishes to prevent further threats from the U.S., the Vatican and any others who may jump into the frame.'

'The Vatican?'

'To rephrase their *trouble shooters,* a clandestine organisation named the Columnae.'

Rialto shook his head. 'That prick Finney, his capacity to piss me off, is legendary.'

Kurt Zachary, the secretary of defence, spoke up. 'Finney had a point. If this tale is fact, we have some fascinating research ahead... he would make one hell of an asset.'

Rialto frowned. 'Christ, why are we having this conversation? The U.S. cannot bow down just because he is some kind of freak. Show him common curtesy until we establish the facts, then take him down without causing a fuss. Have we leverage over him?'

Zachary listed the details. 'His parents are on the Isle. The only other people to connect to the boy are Jim McTay, the mother's brother, and a college *girlfriend* named Christie McCall. We have assets close to all. Professor Arlo Norton, head honcho of the ¥ organisation, apart from losing his family to an R.T.A., runs a standard ship.'

'Okay, I want them all in scope and double our security.'

'Darts or lead sir,' asked Zachary.

'Lead, if he turns out to be superman, we can't make mistakes!'

His personal aide interrupted. 'Sir, having spoken to Senator Finney, the boy petrified him. Therefore, I recommend minimum security.'

'Are you serious?' barked Zachary.

'Senator Finney is a thick-skinned rat who would sell the soul of his mother, but after his incident, he's a few notches from being sectioned.'

Rialto looked at the ceiling. 'Jesus, this is lunacy. Get Captain Davis on the phone now!'

Several minutes later, Rialto was speaking to Arlo, who was now sat with Bran in the rear of a black Ford Cruiser, the fourth in a line of a six-car motorcade.

'Mr Norton, time is of the essence, so I will forgo the pleasantries. I require another discussion with Captain Davis before we meet.'

Arlo looked at Bran. 'And we're off.'

Rialto asked one question.

'Captain, confirm the explanation over the deaths of your team is as you explained is fact.'

'Sir, by my family's lives.'

The line fell silent, then died.

Bran shrugged as he looked at Arlo. 'It wasn't ever going to be pumpkin pie and butter milk.'

Even after the oath of the Captain, Rialto still held his doubts, such was the difficulty in believing the facts.

'I don't care if he's Merlin himself. If this kid has murdered our boys, I want him in our cells after this meeting. And if he steps out of line, save us the expense of a court case!'

'Roger that!' snapped Zachary.

The aide asked a question. 'Is the president aware?'

Rialto's look made her cringe. 'Not yet. If this ends up as a damn pantomime, it's getting rubbed out, end of.'

The aide's reply to the answer was a wry smile.

I fear this is going to end in tears.

Rialto left the room, deep in thought.

Linked to this development, document 1049-1B, is an eye opener. Fact being, if I can gain control over this freak, then the top job is mine... and much, much more!

Forty-two

As the convoy entered Langley, the sight of several attack dogs with their handlers provoked a comforting image of Loki for Bran.

After this is done, I'll never leave our Isle again.

Ten minutes later, they entered an area five floors beneath ground level. The room had concrete walls, a low ceiling, a large window with tinted glass, and a single steel door. Captain Davis had been spirited away for a debrief.

Both Bran and Arlo ignored the armed guards positioned behind straight-backed chairs placed around a long wooden table curiously set for dining. Twin chain guns mounted on the walls did little for the room's ambience. An LED light on a metal box positioned over the weapon suggested control from elsewhere.

As Custanti Giordano, Senator Finney, plus nine of the Columnae, entered the room, neither Arlo nor Bran uttered a word. Only Beneventi had the nerve to stare.

Minutes later, Tom Rialto, Kurt Zachary, the aide, accompanied by her secretary and two CIA operatives, took their positions.

The female aide and her secretary were the only two of the white aura. Although what fascinated Bran most was the range of tone in the grey.

Light grey to dark, does this depict a level of evil? With Beneventi radiating the darkest tone, this makes sense.

Rialto, seated, felt for the firearm mounted underneath the table. With it pointed directly at Bran, he began the discussion.

'Given the rationale of your alleged actions, the president will not be involved until we are clear of the circumstances and your motives.'

Arlo, remaining calmed, replied.

'Mr Cranson is here for discussion and presents no danger unless threatened.'

Rialto's reply was sharp. 'You do not dictate! Mr Cranson murdered seven U.S. troops on UK soil in bizarre circumstances, so please, your explanation.'

Bran sighed. 'Then I shall.' Pointing firmly at Finney, he began. 'You attempted to kidnap me. Explain why.'

Everyone gasped as Finney, after a tirade of apologies, crawled under the table.

Bran now turned to Rialto.

'The Columnae attempted to murder or kidnap my family, as did your senator. Subsequently, this resulted in an act of self-preservation, in which I terminated all assassins, including the senators' team. Perhaps a demonstration is in order.'

In recognising Bran's sub-conscious had become active, Arlo stood up, resulting in several guards drawing their firearms. Now becoming hysterical, Senator Finney screamed, *"let me out,"* then clambered from under the table to grab at a guard's weapon. The guard, blocking the attempt, forced an armbar on Finney, only to find he was now grasping at thin air. Horrified, he fell to his knees and froze in nervous disbelief. A stunned silence hit as each person took a double take. Arlo slumped back into his seat and felt for his tablets. The aide screamed, triggering four of the guards to take direct aim at Bran.

The chain guns twitched.

Bran remained silent. Tension was now on a knife edge.

After swallowing a tablet, Arlo spoke as calmly as his nerves allowed to placate the confused looks around the table.

'Do not react with further aggression. I beg you all to calm down, relax and take stock, or what just happened to Senator Finney will befall anyone who processes thoughts of retaliation.'

Rialto, trembling, peered under the table, hoping Finney had attempted a simple rouse. After a few awkward seconds, he took a deep breath, moved back to his seat, then addressed Bran.

'We control the chain guns from another room; you cannot stop the operator should you activate another...' Rialto paused as his mind looked for a word. '*Disappearance*. In addition, we have people close to those you care for.'

A nod gave approval for an operative to place his sidearm against Arlo's temple.

'Mr Cranson, now that I have your attention, please look at the monitor on the wall.'

The screen flickered, then revealed a close-up of Christie McCall's shocked expression as a male operative held a gun to her head in the rear of a vehicle.

Arlo closed his eyes. Some of the Columnae gasped. Antonio Beneventi concentrated on every micro twitch Bran made, probing for a way to complete his task without implementing his own death.

Bran's demeanour remained the same as he spoke.

'Mr Rialto, you have my undivided attention, please may I have your permission to speak with Christie for a moment to settle our nerves.'

Confident he had retaken control, Rialto relaxed, then spoke with authority. 'After the call, on the floor, hands behind back.'

'That's seems fair,' replied Bran in a submissive tone, settling the entire room.

Kurt Zachary instigated a video call. The driver complied.

As the call connected, Bran beamed his finest smile.

'Wonderful to see you, Christie. Apologies for this shameful incident, *life, or death, whichever is to be my fate. Always trust my word forever.*' Aware she had recognised his words, he continued to speak. 'Close your eyes tightly, count to twenty and all will be fine, my promise!'

Zachary nervously called to his men. 'Keep her tight!' As his sentence finished, Christie, with tears flowing down her face, closed her eyes and began a silent count.

The men were gone. Neither of the chain guns twitched. The agent holding the firearm to Arlo began trembling.

Christie grabbed the fallen mobile. 'What happened?'

Bran's tone became cheerful. 'They've just buggered off, so take their vehicle, drive home, but say nothing and I'll call back as soon as I can... Christie, please do this for me.'

'Tell me you're safe?'

'All is fine... for both of us.'

Christie nodded nervously before closing the call.

Whilst Rialto attempted to contact his men on another line, everyone, apart from two agents, had backed against the walls, arms aloft. One agent, sweating noticeably, aimed dead centre at Bran. Rialto made a hand gesture towards the tinted window. All jumped when metal shutters clattered down, covering the door and window. As the silence returned, one of the CIA operatives called out.

'Take the shot.'

The agent and two guards disappeared.

Screams of absolute despair now flooded the room. Three of the Columnae dropped to their knees and began praying.

Rialto pulled the trigger only to have a misfire. Now with nerves in tatters, he wrenched his hand away from the weapon. In a separate room, a man shivered uncontrollably. Seconds earlier, his colleague, whilst attempting to fire the chain gun, had disappeared. As the shaking ceased, his expression glazed over as he moved to take control of the chain guns. His aim was now directed at Rialto, who grimaced nervously.

Amongst the bedlam back in the room, another guard screamed *"Fuck you"* as he processed a thought to draw his weapon... gone! As unhinged disbelief erupted, one man passed out, three began rocking in silent trauma, the rest kneeled and joined those men now chanting the Lord's Prayer.

Arlo fell back into his seat and placed his hands on top of his head. Rialto, staring at the chain guns, had one thought.

Thank fuck I didn't try a second shot... Fate or luck?

As Bran stood, his expression revealed his sub-conscious was still in control.

'This demonstration is not complete.'

The haunting words caused a whimper from the aide's secretary as she prayed. Bran, looking at her aura, which had dimmed considerably, whispered. 'Madam, no harm will come to you. That is my word. Please sit next to me.'

The secretary, trembling like a leaf, eased up timidly, but then stopped as fear gripped her nervous system. With a smile, Bran moved and placed his arm gently around her shoulders. 'Please, you are under no threat. Let's walk together.'

After easing her into a chair, he looked ominously around the room.

'I'm sure everyone is aware of the Poltergeist. Therefore, we sit and wait. I suggest you gather up any cutlery or glass close to hand.'

No one dared to move.

After a moment of silence, Bran spoke again. 'I implore you, once more, to pick up any loose cutlery and lay on the floor. Trust me on this!'

Almost immediately, the turmoil began.

Cutlery, now spinning wildly, impaled several still standing, adding to the hysteria that had erupted. With laboured breathing, Beneventi gazed at Giordano Custanti, who was lying face down with a steak knife driven deep into the side of his neck. He would not look at Bran again.

The chaos lasted for around thirty seconds before Bran dispatched the poltergeists.

All noise ceased as he made his way to Beneventi, leaving a blanket of silence in his wake. At that moment, Giordano's physical form disappeared from sight. Beneventi could not bear to lift his eyes from the floor, his face remaining in an expressionless gaze. Notions of revenge ceased.

Bran addressed Rialto, who had fallen into a state of shock.

'Request a medical team and refreshments. Remove all footage from this event. Providing no more acts of aggression occur, death will cease.'

Within the brief time span of ten minutes, medical personnel rapidly dressed wounds and handed out sedatives like candy.

'Settled?' whispered Arlo.

Bran frowned. 'Discussions took a path I never wanted; I just hope they are now pacified sufficiently.'

Rialto's mobile rang.

After a moment's discussion, he spoke. 'After watching the footage, Potus, despite advice from the secret services, will meet you alone, allowing everyone else to leave unharmed.'

Bran's expression was one of agitation. 'I requested all the footage to be destroyed. Is this the case?'

Rialto stuttered his reply. 'Please, we had to show Potus, but yes, we then deleted the footage.'

Bran pondered.

Protocol would have declined the Potus meeting alone. However, the human mind can become susceptible when faced with the unexplained.

'His word?'

'Given the circumstances... yes.'

'In addition, facilitate a protocol to keep everyone who has witnessed the events under strict lockdown with no external communication until we conclude.'

'Of course, this would be normal in such extreme circumstances.'

As the chain guns lowered their aim to the floor. Rialto's body language depicted enormous relief.

One hour later, Bran was sitting alone, opposite the president. Closing his eyes, he allowed a utopian moment to rush around his system. The president was of the white aura.

'Mr President, offering these terms after witnessing the events took a great deal of courage.'

The president replied in a somewhat nervous tone.

'Do you intend to... kill me?'

Bran looked appalled. 'No, Mr President, that is not, nor will it ever be, my intention.'

Failing to conceal his relief, the president spoke with a little more confidence.

'The death toll is now sixteen. What do you expect will happen?'

'Sir, I had hoped that discussion would be without violence or threat. This was not of my making. Look, you're likely bewildered, scared, and probably in shock. May I suggest we move to more comfortable surroundings, to be joined by Rialto's aide, her secretary, and my associate? Once settled, I'll explain everything. After which your emotions will allow the considered decisions, this situation requires. You have my absolute word, providing all violence ceases, nothing abnormal will occur, and I will remain under your direction.'

The president could hardly believe Bran had submitted to him.

I appreciate your thoughtfulness. 'May I ask why the aide?'

'Rialto is a dishonest man; I know you have questioned this many times?' The president's expression revealed to Bran all he needed to know. 'His advisor has been a source of direction and has the same shining white aura as you. She will be an invaluable source of support and comfort during our discussions.'

The president considered his response. 'Her name is Tess Mason, and she is indeed trustworthy, yet... What is the meaning of a white aura?'

'A pure soul, Mr President, something to be admired, and it is this which gives me hope. The grey soul is the opposite and symbolises evil. I must warn you that the discussions will be complicated, lengthy, and may resemble something out of a novel. This process will tax on your mental state as the mind struggles to cope with a deluge of inconceivable data.'

The president frowned. 'The footage I witnessed was neither fantasy nor fiction, so you take as much time as we damn well need!'

'Thank you, just one more requirement. No CCTV during discussions. I understand the secret service will resist, but please, my words are for your ears only.'

'I had to stand firm to arrange this meeting, as I'm pushing water uphill. However, I will try.'

'Understandable in the current circumstances!'

Immediately, the president made the call. One hour later, unarmed guards moved them both to a lodge set in ornate gardens one mile from the major complex. The guards confirmed Arlo's suggestion that they were private quarters reserved for visiting VIP guests. Bran noticed a raw anguish on every member of staff he encountered and had hoped with all his heart that his sub-conscious remained dormant.

Standing in a plush lounge, he played down the extravagance by picturing Loki lazing on the brown leather suite chomping on a bone. The unarmed guards remained and would stay until the president re-joined them *shortly*.

When Arlo looked at him with a puzzled expression, Bran responded with a comforting smile, then whispered words of assurance.

Forty-three

Two hours later, the president, Tess and her secretary, Shelly Lorenzo, arrived at the lodge. At how their auras had reduced in sheen, Bran had one thought: *fear!* In trying to relax them, he suggested they opened the bar. Arlo, smiling, seconded the notion. The president nodded approvingly.

'Under normal circumstances, I would decline, but right now, I feel we deserve a shot. Shelly, you know what I take, please gentlemen, speak your tipple.'

Bran made a joke after requesting a small scotch.

'You are aware you're serving a minor?'

Arlo laughed, sensing Bran's intentions. I'll have yours then.

With everyone's aura brightening, the simple rouse worked.

I continue to learn, fascinating!

Sipping eagerly, they moved to leather seats ergonomically placed for discussion. Bran set his drink down, then began.

'May I enquire the situation regarding Captain Davis?'

That Bran had shown concern towards a man dispatched to kidnap him threw the president a little.

'After his debrief, he remains in custody pending the outcome.'

'Yet he wishes to resign from active service?'

'Yes, I believe he has requested the process.'

'Process?'

'Black ops assets can find civilian life a little traumatic. Given his latest operation...'

'Ah, I see. Please, I do not wish any *harm* to befall him.'

'I assure you we are not barbarians.'

Bran frowned. 'Then forgive me for appearing mercenary, but may I suggest we discuss the deaths of Captain Davis's men after our explanation? After which, should you still wish to incarcerate me, so be it?'

The president, heartened at Bran's compliance, nodded in agreement. As a result, Bran clapped, causing everyone to flinch, to which he instantly regretted.

'Apologies for that. Presently, Arlo is better placed to explain the historical timeline of events, after which I'll take it from my perspective. Please, no matter how bizarre our narrative appears, every word we speak is the absolute truth. One thing – may I call my parents and Christie whilst Arlo narrates?'

The president's facial expression depicted amazement at the innocence of Bran's request.

'Regrettably, I'm clinging on by a thread, pushing my current line of action. Therefore, the *crisis committee* will monitor your calls.'

Bran shrugged. 'Expected, not a problem. We find ourselves in a situation that is unparalleled. Fear will take its toll on all decision making. Let's hope that these discussions appease everyone.'

Bran's passive mood gave all a lift.

'Arlo, over to you...'

After taking a small sip of scotch, Arlo initiated the conversation.

Bran switched on his mobile phone, then proceeded to an adjacent room and dialled. Ross answered. The sound of his parents' voices comforted. After a touching discussion, his explanation of the trip became heavily edited to the point he felt guilty. When speaking to Christie, he requested that she not share the specifics of her abduction. She chose not to engage in any type of speculation or conjecture. No, she would await his explanation in time. On closing the call, Bran found his feelings for her had become more intense.

Oh hell, is this the thing they call love?

After a final thought about Christie, he moved into the main room. Arlo had finished his summary of the historical timeline of the Paragon, therefore confusion had become the default expression. All looked at Bran.

He shrugged. 'That's us in a nutshell! However, your understanding regarding our existence is about to be shattered. Therefore, I suggest you top up your glasses?'

Sometime later, as Bran concluded, a confused silence descended on the room as they attempted to rationalise his claims. Questions began, to which Bran answered as simply as possible. Expressions were becoming exasperated.

The human mind seeks physical proof and so I must take a risk. In doing so, I can answer a question of my own.

'Sir, on entry into Langley, I noticed you employ handlers with attack dogs. Can I meet an overzealous pair?'

The president, looking quizzically at the bizarre request, replied firmly.

'Not if your intentions are to harm!'

Bran wrinkled his brow at the suggestion. I'm an extremely devoted dog lover, and I guarantee they'll be in safe hands.

Also curious about the request, Arlo wanted to know more.

A grinning Bran raised his hand. 'Everyone please... trust me. All will be fine, my promise!'

Well, at least I hope it will, Loki, if your kind are not all the same – I'm done for!

It would take around thirty minutes to bring in a handler, during which snacks were served. The mood had built, and so Bran expanded regarding the aura.

'As explained, the soul links all life. To observe this is a blessing. Recently, I discovered aura aligns with emotion, providing information about mood or state of mind. For example, when we first met, you all displayed a dimmed aura, and now? Well, they're a little closer to normal.' He grinned. 'Alcohol will have helped, but the upbeat mood is visible. Astonishingly, I believe dogs can also see the aura. Other life forms I've yet to confirm.'

A call to the president interrupted.

'Yes, but keep it leashed. Who are the pair?' The president grimaced. 'Josh and Duke – I see...' Looking concerned, he closed the call, then turned to Bran. 'You requested overzealous, in Sergeant Josh Moore and Duke, we have that in bucket loads. The pair always patrol my quarters when I am in residence on site. I ask once again, are you quite certain about this, Mr Cranson?'

'Yes, Sir and please – Bran.'

The president nodded acceptance. 'Well, Bran... over to you.'

Arlo, looking concerned, spoke in Latin.

'If the handler is grey?'

Before Bran acknowledged the question, Lorenzo replied... in Latin.

'Please speak in English.'

Bran smiled. 'Our concern is the handler may carry a firearm.'

The president replied – in Latin.

'Rest assured, he will not.'

All the people in the room burst into laughter.

A call to the president halted the conversation.

'Mr President, Sergeant Moore, I'm outside the door.'

'One moment, sergeant.' Placing his mobile on loudspeaker, he turned to Bran.

'It's your show.'

'Thankyou. Welcome Sergeant, first, may I ask – would your dog take direct command from a total stranger?'

Outside, Sergeant Moore frowned at the question. 'Absolutely not! He is impervious to command or affection shown by anyone bar me.'

Bran continued. 'And would you say on your command he would react with hostility towards me or even attack to harm?'

'Without question,' said Moore.

'Thank you, on my word, please enter the lounge after which, as I join you, set him against me whilst maintaining him on the leash.'

'No Sir – with respect, I do not wish to see my dog harmed.'

'Sergeant Moore, you have my word no harm will befall Duke, even if he attempts to gnaw my arm off.'

Taking a moment to clear his head, Moore inhaled deeply. 'Very well.'

With a commanding height of six feet three inches, Sergeant Josh Moore entered the room with the expected physical command. No one would have believed he was flapping internally. Duke, a prime male Belgian Malinois positioned exactly at his left side, sniffed the air. Josh, after saluting the president, who reciprocated, waited.

Bran called from another room.

'Sergeant, as soon as I open the door, please set him against me on a leash.'

Josh looked edgily at the president, who then nodded an uncertain *okay*.

Permission granted, Moore felt his adrenaline kick in.

'We're ready!'

As Bran opened the door, he gazed at the white aura surrounding both man and dog.

Is this fated...?

'Make the command sergeant.'

Upon the call of "WATCH", Duke, to the utter amazement of the Sergeant, acted like an eager puppy and pulled at the lead, expressing his delight. With a tone of annoyance in his voice, Moore pulled back on the leash and yelled, 'DUKE - WATCH!'

Ignoring the command, Duke relaxed into the "down" position, accompanied by a soft whimper of sadness that it could not greet Bran. Bran, having seen a dimming of Josh's aura, squatted down in response.

'Let him loose...'

Sergeant Moore, feeling annoyed, looked at the president, who shrugged permission.

'You sure?' gritted Moore, eager to let the dog free to attack.

'Of course.'

With a yell of "TAKE!" Moore released the leash.

The unthinkable occurred. Bran and Duke tussled around on the ground like reunited buddies. The level of joy that existed between the two was extraordinary.

Moore scratched the back of his head.

'God damn – Sir in all my life, I've seen nothing like that. Whatever you are – my dog loves the bones of you.'

Bran, smiling as he tickled Duke's chin, spoke up.

'Please call him back to leash and set him against Arlo, would you?'

Clearly not overly enthusiastic, Arlo gave a look of disbelief but stood as requested, albeit nervously.

Eager to regain respect, Moore called Duke back to heel. With Duke refusing to budge, Bran stopped tickling and pointed to Moore.

'Go see your dad.'

To Moore's absolute annoyance, Duke, showing textbook recall, ran to the right side of Moore, passed behind him, and sat on his left. Moore, albeit rather petulantly, patted his return, then snapped the leash back on before turning to face Arlo.

'WATCH.'

Instantaneously, Duke became a devil hound. Terrified, Arlo leapt behind his seat, along with the president, Tess and Lorenzo. Moore called "LEAVE" to which Duke eased down, before wagging his tail at Bran, who clapped enthusiastically.

'Thank you Sergeant, that's all I require and well-done Duke.'

Moore replied through gritted teeth.

'That Sir, is something I'll never forget.'

After saluting the president, he moved to leave, before Bran spoke out.

'Dogs are far more advanced spiritually than you can imagine. What happened is not detrimental to your ability. Trust me, when he leaves my presence, he will return to being Duke.'

Stepping out of the room, Moore nodded his appreciation. Once outside, he closed his eyes and exhaled.

'Jesus...!'

Bran's mind whirled over.

Proof that the soul interacts between species is enlightening and another breakthrough to ponder. I have so much to learn!

Turning to everyone, he exuded relief.

'I will confess to ab-libbing that.' He sighed. 'Duke evaluated me using his ability to see my aura, and being a pure white Paragon, no words of command would ever influence him to attack me. I recall a quote by the singer Lauren Jauregui...

"If only our eyes saw our souls instead of bodies, how different our ideas of beauty would be."

Since my return from the sleep, I see every living organism cocooned by this wonderment. We are all of the same spirit, bar none!'

Striding up to Bran, the president gently grasped his shoulders.

'This day has been unlike anything else. I'm scared, anxious, and yet strangely drawn to this, but accepting it as true is extremely difficult. I cannot deny that I'm deeply grieved by the deaths of our people. This is an obstacle that needs to be overcome. It might be beneficial to take a break. However, if I may ask you one question before we adjourn?'

'Of course.'

The president drained the last drop from his glass. 'What exactly do you require from us?'

Bran showed some relief at the question. 'An ally Sir, an ally that will allow myself and my family to complete this crazy jigsaw in undisturbed safety. Once achieved, I will need a strategy to expose the truth behind our very existence...' he smiled. 'Simple really!'

Unconsciously, the president made a sucking sound with his teeth. 'And if I refuse?'

'Sir you won't,' said Bran arrogantly.

Bemused, the president replied.

'How do you know that?'

'Because just now, your aura has become a shining beacon.'

The president replied with a gleam in his eyes. 'I wouldn't want to play Texas holdem with you.'

A serious look came over Bran's face.

'I'm guessing your emergency committee has raised Defcon Levels?'

The president cast a quick glance at Tess before speaking.

'Currently we sit at three. To say the military's twitching is an understatement.'

'Then your task is to prevent further escalation. Troop numbers, missile or air strikes make no difference. I do not wish to be tested by *gung-ho* military types, sacrificing young men.'

The president sat back down.

'Is this all real?'

'Absolutely! And as a mark of trust, I must advise you of another concerning fact.'

The president wished he had a drink to hand.

'Do tell.'

'Should you both take my side, you will, by default, become under my protection. Consequently, my sub-conscious would neutralise any intent or act of aggression in a manner suitable. Therefore, when appointing your advisory team, I would need to see every individual tasked. Please do not divulge this to anyone else – ever! Not even family.'

There was a pause in the conversation as the president remained silent for a few moments. 'How is this happening? I mean, this isn't reality, is it?'

'It is, Sir, that's a fact. Was it not once stated "*One small step for man, one giant leap for mankind*"!'

'Strong words indeed...' he sighed. 'You have our promise not to discuss the details of this meeting.'

Bran held his hand aloft. 'Oh, one other point of contention – the men known as *The Columnae*. My advice... keep them captive, but speak to the Vatican.'

'You mean placate them?'

'Yes. When we have an agreement, I'll speak to them.'

'The Columnae are utterly terrified... except one, Antonio Beneventi.'

'To be expected. Beneventi contemplated my downfall, but now understands this to be a pointless exercise. It will be this man whom I address... the others will follow.'

'Very well, I'll ensure they remain in comfortable lockdown for now.'

'Thank you and sleep well.'

The president pulled a wry smile.

'If I sleep tonight, it will be a miracle! As for you both, this facility is self-contained and well stocked. Please indulge. If you need anything, just use the phone. Unarmed personnel guard the outside area, keeping you completely secure.'

'Expected, and thank you for listening. But please, I must reiterate once more, convince your people that violence is not the way forward. If you fail, others will die...!'

The president, Tess and Lorenzo left the quarters with Bran's words etched into their thoughts.

Forty-four

Ten minutes later, as they neared the operations room, the president spoke in a whisper.

'My god, he's just a teen. How can this be possible?'

Lorenzo appeared to be lost to thought, Tess replied. 'Mr President, I've pinched myself many times and begged to wake, but here we are. Something is very extraordinary about that boy. To illustrate, if you analyse today's events without bias, at no stage did he take the offensive. And despite all hell descending, he is still in control of his faculties whilst showing zero signs of being psychotic. I did witness a mood change and wonder if he is schizophrenic, but I somehow doubt that.'

Turning to both Tess and Lorenzo, the president looked markedly dour.

'Today we've been told that upon death we enter an unseen dimension via a white passage, witnessed colleagues disappear into thin air and the damnation of the Poltergeist. But has it sunk in? No, I still hold doubts as I keep thinking this could be part of an elaborate scam, or maybe, as you say, I'll wake up. Of course, one fact remains, imagine the absolute chaos should this become public?'

Lorenzo spoke with an edge to her tone. 'Sir, that's for the future. The people behind that door require answers and a breakdown of the meeting... right now!!'

Shuffling a little, the president replied. 'We cannot discuss this, as we need his trust. And dare we risk the consequences should we break our word?'

'Ultimately, wild horses couldn't drag the information from me,' shuddered Lorenzo.

Each stood in silent thought as they faced the solid steel double door. After adjusting their clothing, Tess swiped clearance, then stepped inside the M.O.R. (Major Operations Room). The president and Lorenzo followed.

Tom Rialto, feeling war torn, nodded for everyone to stand. Representatives of the military, and the CIA, remained silent as the president took his seat and began to speak.

'We have all seen and felt the terror of the incidents that happened here today. Without a doubt, the losses we have experienced have caused us extreme sorrow. However, the deaths have to be set aside as the bigger picture is overwhelming.'

Raised voices cited objections.

The president slammed his fist down hard onto the table.

'Enough!' His enraged tone silenced the room. 'Our understanding of life shifts today. Forget your self-importance, forget politics, and dismiss any thoughts of reprisals. I cannot... no dare not, expand on the details of the meeting as yet.' Another chorus of dissent erupted. Understanding a need for answers, the president waited for calm before continuing. 'All I can confirm is that Bran Cranson is a *unique* human, exceptionally intelligent, cordial, and willing to work with us, providing all violent provocation ceases. We have scheduled a second meeting at 9 A.M. tomorrow to discuss our terms to move forward.'

Rialto thrust his hand up.

The president gave a silent sign of approval with a tilt of his head.

'Sir, you stated *our* terms. Are we back in control?'

'Provided we end all provocation to the family.' He stalled to look at Tess, who mouthed the word *careful.* After a confirming smile, he continued. 'And that I listen to the full explanation of his background and formidable *abilities.*'

A landline close to Rialto flashed a call. After a one-sided conversation, his expression was one of doom.

'Mr President, Michael Fanello, has requested an immediate update.'

As Fanello was one of the major financial supporters of the government and controlled one of the world's leading financial institutes, everyone was looking at the president, who seemed to be livid.

'Locate the mole asap. If this reaches the media, trust me, we will face a backlash of catastrophic proportions. Mobilise assets to Fanello's property immediately, then call him back.'

Shocked, Rialto made two internal calls, then dialled Fanello. With a submissive tone, he said, 'Sir, I have the president for you.' He smiled inwardly.

My take on the matter would undoubtedly be favoured by Fanello right now.

The president spoke in a harsh tone.

'You have breached a military lock down. I demand you reveal your source, and do not disclose any further information.'

Everyone could hear the verbal onslaught that followed. The president, remaining calm, waited for the tirade to dry up, then replied.

'Michael... Right now, you are insignificant, and your financial power holds no value, and trust me when I say this... I do not give one fuck if you pull support. Hold one moment!'

Shocked, all remained in glazed silence as the president addressed the head of the cyber team. 'Ensure nothing leaks from our bubble. Fail... trust me, you do not wish to piss this boy off.'

The president turned back to the call. 'Michael, do not leave your current position. Should you choose to do so, expect the severest of consequences.'

After closing the call abruptly, he took another deep breath.

'Now... is there anyone in this room who cannot grasp how fucking highly I rate the mystery of Bran Cranson?'

Above the shocked silence, General Ballinger spoke!

'With respect, Mr President, withholding information that affects our country's security is irregular.'

The president frowned, then stared hard at Ballinger.

'NO GENERAL! Irregular is the ability to terminate using just the mind! Now as your president I require – no demand – trust! You will step into line. Make no mistake, we are entering a point in our history never to be forgotten.'

Ballinger nodded passively.

Although relieved, the president understood he was skating on thin ice.

'Every person privy to the events earlier I want listed, checked, and grounded. I require this entire sector on full lockdown; I don't care about external issues – NO ONE LEAVES! And nothing, I repeat, nothing goes out, not even to family. If needed, we can start rumours of Cyber infiltration or similar, but I hope we won't require this deceit. So, I repeat, forget politics, finance and all the rest of the issues we manipulate. This agenda now takes full precedence!'

Nodding for Tess and Lorenzo to follow, he left the room.

As the door closed on a shocked silence, Rialto spoke up.

'My god... what on earth is that kid...?'

General Ballinger stood. 'Tom, the president is risking all sticking to this line. Suppose the kid has a hold on him and is working towards a greater atrocity? No, we must eliminate him! Call the vice, if we need to raise Section 4 of the 25th Amendment to the Constitution, I want to be prepared. And for those wondering why. The amendment states. If, for whatever reason, the vice president and a majority of sitting cabinet secretaries decide the president is unable to discharge the powers and duties of office, they can put that down in writing and send it to two people. The speaker of the House and the Senate's president pro tempore. Once the vice becomes *acting* president, we can ensure the safety of this government and its people. Those against, speak out.'

After heated debate, much against the *wishes* of Tom Rialto, the motion carried. Pleased, the General spoke again.

'I require a meeting with the Columnae to understand my enemy...!'

The general grabbed his papers, then left the room. Whilst he looked commanding; he was as terrified as everyone – bravado was his way of coping.

After a short walk, Tess spoke.

'Sir, that speech was right on the nail.'

The president frowned.

'Our people are reacting to fear, fear of the unknown. I just hope we can placate them until we have come to an agreement.'

Lorenzo gave a dismissive wave of her hand.

'Men will always use violence to solve their problems. History backs my statement.'

Each continued the walk to their accommodation in silent thought. None would sleep a wink.

Arlo placed the glass stopper back into the *Thistle Gold* square carafe by Saint-Louis. With having the same set in his Mayfair property, he smiled.

'This carafe costs two and a half grand. There are ten different whiskies on this bar top. That's twenty-five K for just this service alone.'

Bran enjoyed the sheer randomness of the sentence.

'We may get a bill in the morning.'

Both laughed heartily, which helped to dissipate their pent-up energy.

'You good?' asked Bran.

Arlo closed his eyes for a second. 'Truth... now that I have actually witnessed your defensive actions, my mind is failing to accept the reality. It's the *nothingness* Bran, it...' Arlo took the top off the carafe, poured another large scotch, then drained half a glass. 'It turns your mind *fuzzy*. For instance, say they had burst into flames, the mind could evaluate and file. Ultimately, it's the nothingness that is so terrifying, so "*what the fuck*"– I believe the brain attempts to erase the experience to stifle confusion.'

Bran placed the stopper back onto the carafe, adjusting its position to suit his eye.

'Even if slowed a trillion times, the brain would still not process the event. The speed is beyond man's comprehension.'

'That just adds to the terror.'

Bran gave a shrug.

'Struggling to come to terms with the impossibility of something has been a constant for mankind.' He paused briefly. 'Tomorrow, I will recreate the journey through the Sentinel for them via a dream.'

'Oh really! Then let's hope you don't scramble the mind of the forty-sixth serving president.'

A laugh escaped Bran. 'Well, we're already up to our knees, so why not?'

'Point taken. My goodness... *that journey,* I'm aboard for that!'

Bran frowned just a little. 'This will be no pleasure trip. Are you certain you wish to subject your heart to more stress?'

Arlo finished his scotch. 'I've waited too long to take a back seat, don't concern.'

His anxious demeanour worried Bran.

'Go on, spit it out.'

'In the eventuality of my heart failing...'

Bran reeled. 'Do we have to discuss this?'

'Wait, just listen... If I – no, when I die, can you track my soul, as you tracked the greys?'

Bran, having never considered this action, felt a little shocked he hadn't. A morose silence cast over both.

'I honestly don't know.'

'Then promise to track my soul and confirm it dissipates into the Nemkis, to make my passing worthwhile.' He said with a touch of desperation.

'I will try, dear friend, but later rather than sooner, eh!'

Arlo's relief was transparent.

Not wishing to dwell on death, Bran changed the subject.

'So many mysteries to solve concerning the soul and the way it interacts. That dogs see an aura is staggering. I have also witnessed the stag reacting to my aura. Why is this not gifted to mankind? And how many other species have this sense? Could it be something as simple as sensory communication? Since animals can't communicate as we do, it is possible that they use the aura to gain the knowledge they need to socialise and interact.'

Arlo thought for a moment. 'That's a valid point. In fact, it makes absolute sense.' He paused. 'To a dog or animal, it would be a prerequisite for survival, given their lower intelligence! Certainly, it explains their uncanny knack of assessing people. Huh, we consider ourselves the elite of the planet, but this suggests we are deficient in the sensory world. Bugger me. What else will the soul reveal...?'

'To find that answer, I need Nemkis and soon!'

'Then let's get some sleep, finish our work, and get you home!'

'Sleep!' Bran frowned. 'To drift into that realm and leave the physical... life would be simpler.'

Arlo bowed his head a little. 'I've never mentioned this but... Insomnia has blighted my life for many years now, but since I tried to look through closed eyes.' He paused. 'As I stir into the depths of darkness, I find myself drifting into the tranquil beginnings of sleep. Then, at some stage, my thoughts begin to distort and so I pass into full sleep. However, when insomnia strikes and I peer, my eyes ache as chaos seems to reign in the darkness. At this point, I struggle to fall into slumber. Yet, over time, by continuing to stir into the blackness, I have occasionally beat the chaos and drifted into peaceful sleep. What I'm saying is looking through closed eyes is gradually helping me to heal my insomnia.'

Bran appeared intrigued. 'You may have found a way to drift off to sleep when necessary - how incredible. I'm interested in finding out if sleep is attainable without having an abundance of energy to return to Nemkis. We can examine this in further detail when we get back home.'

'That would help, thank you,' said Arlo, pleased he wasn't imagining the process.

Both shook hands before retiring for the night. With thoughts swirling around in his mind regarding his own mortality, and alcohol working its magic, Arlo would not need to look through closed eyes to test his theory this night.

Forty-five

5 A.M. the following morning.

Ross had been up for hours, trying to make sense of the events. Upon Isla's awakening, she realised he was feeling down.

'Penny for your thoughts?'

After kissing her forehead, he spoke.

'I just wish we could do more to help Bran. Christ, the lads alone, with the burden of the entire world on his shoulders. How the hell will he become *our Bran* again? Once this hits the mainstream, some will worship, others... petrified! The extremists will denounce him as the anti-Christ or an infidel depending on which God they covert. Add to that, governments will claw after his mind. My god Isla... is this to be his life?'

Isla closed her eyes for a second before replying.

'Of the trillions that have walked this planet, Bran is the first true white Paragon. Think about that!'

'Kinda frightening and amazing, in the same thought.'

'That's a fact, but changing the subject, have you tried to look through closed eyes before sleep?'

'Yes, many tines – but nothing happens, of course.'

'I keep trying. It's so bloody frustrating.'

'Maybe, but to our son it's normal...'

'Normal is not a word you can attach to the Cranson's...'

'Isn't that the truth?'

While Bran was in a peaceful slumber, the Nemkis eased his mind to absolute stillness, allowing his thoughts to become clear and concise.

As I explored Dreamworld, I had a powerful feeling that I was being directed. I am confident that something has been controlling my journey to this point and providing answers when needed. By what or whom is another question? As to the fourth pillar, circumstances will dictate its presentation! Amongst the many questions, I continue to dwell on one. Upon death, will the soul keep its conscious state? This is the ultimate question for everyone, and so I will continue to make the soul my primary focus, since it has not yet revealed its true worth.

His gaze travelled across the infinite expanse of Nemkis, which caused him to ponder the mysterious whereabouts of this dimension.

7.30 a.m.
Alcohol had contributed to a decent night of slumber for Arlo, although just now his head would not agree. After rummaging through the bathroom cupboards, he stumbled upon a bottle of paracetamol.

My god I can't remember the last time I felt so rough. I suppose, like everyone, I desire an afterlife that gives hope. With only the slightest understanding, I feel optimistic that after death; the soul keeps a blueprint of life. That I may see my darling wife is something to cling to. Bran will complete his journey, of that I am certain, and so I must eventually expose the complications of the Awakening.

A knock at the adjoining door led to Bran entering with a broad smile.

'My word, Arlo, you look like shit!'

'After yesterday, you can't knock a man for having a blowout.'

'Perhaps a shower and a bite to eat would seem a logical move.'

'Shower yes. As for food...'

Both heard the phone ring. Arlo's headache, amplifying the ring tone, prompted him to answer. A full two minutes of conversation took place before he closed the call.

'They ask if we could move the meeting to 11p.m. as the president has some *internal* issues to deal with.'

Bran thought for a moment.

'Issues... there is only one issue on their table and that is one of violent action...' he paused again. 'Request that Sergeant Moore and his dog call to the lodge asap.'

Arlo, looking quizzical, relayed the request. The voice asked to hold. Confirmation came a few minutes later.

'Why the handler?' asked Arlo, closing the call.

'If successful, the president will require a confident, therefore the sergeant must undergo the same experience.'

Arlo frowned. '*If successful* sounds a little ominous.'

'Hell, I'm going to pull four people into my dream! A historical first and a gamble. That being, I ask you again – are you one hundred percent certain you wish to be included?'

Arlo wagged his finger. 'Risk frying my brain and becoming a vegetable, oh I can't wait. But seriously, don't concern, I've enough tablets to see me through.'

Both fist bumped.

Twenty minutes later, Sergeant Moore knocked at the door. On entry, Duke strained at the leash to greet Bran, frustrating Moore as he struggled to hold him.

'Let him go, Sergeant,' said Bran.

Apprehensively, Moore unclipped Duke. Now free, the dog ran to Bran to become embroiled in an exuberant greeting. After previously experiencing the dog's aggression, Arlo stood with one foot in his own room, just in case.

Bran's smile lit up his face. 'Sergeant, please confirm to my friend that Duke does not pose any threat.'

Moore, rigidly at attention, answered uneasily.

'Unless I give the word, not a chance, sir.'

Pointing to the sofa opposite, Bran sat. 'Josh, please relax. I just wish to ask you a few questions. Please speak your mind upon answering.'

'Yes, of course.'

'Thank you,' Bran said whilst whispering into Duke's ear, resulting in the dog bounding onto the sofa next to Josh.

'Josh, can you name the most important things in your life?'

Surprised at the question, Josh answered in a crisp, military-like tone.

'My family, which includes the Corps, the president, and dog, Sir.'

'Are you an honest man, Josh?'

Again, Josh looked a little awkward. 'Yes Sir, I try.'

'Then answer honestly, what is your opinion of me?'

Josh took a breath. 'You've killed my countrymen in a most ghastly, unnatural way, so how would you expect me to answer that?'

'Fair enough. Then, if men attempted to kidnap or kill your family, would you defend them in any way possible?'

Josh stood up. 'I ask you not to harm my family, sir. Take me instead.'

That Josh's aura had dimmed, resulted in a sadness flushing over Bran. As he stood, Duke wagged his tail – Josh stiffened.

'Josh, I apologise for instigating that thought. I have no intentions of causing your family or yourself any harm. You have my word.'

Now visibly relaxed, Josh sat down. 'Please forgive me, I was told to expect the worst...'

'By the president?'

'No, Top brass.'

'And yet you still came.'

'I'm a Marine. It is my duty when asked.'

'Indeed... However, my question was hypothetical. They have continually attacked my family without provocation and yesterday, my life and that of a close friend came under threat. Retaliation became unavoidable. I will be blunt. If you processed an attempt on my life, my sub-conscious would end yours. That said, I need you.'

Josh tried his best to dismiss the plausibility of the threat. 'Need?'

'Your passion for the president and country is commendable, and I believe, one hundred percent, that you would give your life for them as Duke would for you – correct?'

'Sir.'

'Then will you accompany the president and myself on a unique journey?'

'Not possible. You cannot leave this sector.'

Bran smiled before proceeding to explain the events of the Paragon. Sometime later, Josh held his dog closely as his mind attempted to process the bizarre information. While rubbing his head, he spoke.

'No bullshit. Is this for real?'

Bran closed his eyes and affected Josh's mind to recall an old memory. Now back in his childhood home, aged seven, he waited at the front door in total excitement as his first puppy bounded into the house. After dropping to his knees in delight, he opened his arms to allow the puppy to launch itself into his chest.

Bran closed the memory.

Josh, now back in the real world, was down on his knees with his arms open wide, awaiting the catch. When the puppy disappeared, he froze. Confusion stoked a panic. Duke, sensing his master's distress, nuzzled into his chest.

Bran spoke soothingly.

'Relax Josh, I influenced your mind to create the memory of the initial meeting with Ernie... your first dog. You experienced a dream, that's all.'

Convinced the puppy was real, Josh began looking around the back of the sofa, with Duke following in close concern. After a minute's frantic search of the room, he looked at Bran.

'A moment ago, I was a kid again – greeting a puppy and nothing will convince me otherwise. Tell me I'm not going mad.'

'Because of the clarity of detail within the dream, the brain treats it as reality and retains the memory, but none the less they are dreams.'

Josh shook his head. 'That's deep shit – deep, deep shit. I'll be honest... I feel quite sick.'

Arlo spoke up. 'Now do you believe?'

Josh didn't look up. 'Do I have to? That was unearthly.'

Pleased that Josh had quickly regained his composure, Bran moved to his side.

'If I bring you into a dream, you will have a vision of all that I described. Nonetheless, the process of withdrawing from this event will be highly traumatic and may affect your mental wellbeing. This has to be your choice.'

'And you say you're putting the president through this?'

'It is a requirement, and he will need a dependable ally.'

'In other words... me?' replied Josh, shaking his head.

Bran acknowledged with a nod. 'I warn that should you accept; your life will cease to be normal.'

After a moment of contemplation, Josh replied. 'I'll follow the president if he takes the plunge.'

The phone rang, causing Josh to twitch, then laugh. 'Apologies. To say I'm wired is an understatement.'

Arlo picked up the phone and responded to the call. The president's plans would be subject to further delay.

As he stood up sharply, Bran felt dizzy, then cursed as the headache from hell returned.

Concerned, Arlo spoke up. 'That's stress for you. I'll get the paracetamol.'

Clasping his head, Bran asked for ibuprofen. Arlo returned with both.

'Perhaps a doctor's opinion would be a help?'

Bran's expression gave his answer...

Forty-six

Some hours earlier.

The president, Tess and Lorenzo stepped into the operations room. A lack of food did not cause the immediate pang in their stomachs. With Michael Torrez, the Vice, and two congressmen present, the president instantly recognised the predicament he was facing.

Tess had just one thought.

Men of power have always endangered others to attain their goals. I can only hope the next hour will be a turning point.

The president spoke sharply, dismissing any formal introductions.

'Get on with it.'

Tom Rialto stood. 'Sir, as your chief of staff, I wish it to be known that I am wholly against the actions endorsed by the majority in this room. As a result, I will not make further comment, unless commanded by my president.' Nodding sharply, he sat down.

That Rialto had not sided with the mass boosted the president. However, his reasons for loyalty were purely selfish.

'Thank you Tom. Your allegiance is commendable.'

One congressman stood.

'Mr President, we have decided...'

Interrupting bluntly, the president spoke above the congressman with a calmed fury.

'You wish to implement Section 4 of the 25th – I get that, but before we begin the charade, I require a common courtesy in the way of my Vice answering a few questions!'

Clearly unsettled by the president's perception, the Vice frowned, then spoke.

'Very well.'

The president wasted no time. 'Confirm that lockdown is a success, and we have tethered Fanello along with the mole?'

Rialto spoke up. 'Sir, I can confirm that staff outside the loop are no longer on site. We are now in effect isolated. Fanello and the mole included.'

With a nod of relief, the president then turned his gaze steadily towards the Vice.

'And finally, what are your immediate intentions with the boy – I require complete honesty, not subterfuge?'

The Vice nodded at General Ballinger, who stood displaying his customary arrogance.

'Mr President, having spoken to the Columnae, we cannot allow this to escalate. Historically, they have eradicated the Paragon for the good of mankind. And whilst they have convinced me to his threat level, suggestions of how to end the boy have merit.'

The president shook his head in disbelief.

'The Columnae are the traditional adversaries of the Paragon, General. It is in their best interest for him to die. The boy has heightened senses, not a mutation, which has caused me to question logic and how we view the world. It's been a challenge, trust me. But a common thread runs through all discussions...' Pausing, his eyes met the generals. 'Did the Columnae advise against the boy being attacked? I ask for a truthful answer.'

The room waited silently for the General to reply, who coughed before speaking.

'Yes Sir, unequivocally they advised a passive approach, but if I may add to this statement?'

'Please do so General.'

'Are you aware that Professor Norton's son was a Paragon, and that the son killed his mother and housemaid?'

'I am General.' The president looked around the room. 'I asked for trust, and this is your response.' Not one person returned his glance, cementing a growing confidence. 'I put this down to fear. Fear of what we do not understand. Bran Cranson is.' After finding the correct words, he continued. 'Bran Cranson results from natural evolution in the human sensory progression. He is not a monster! Of course, this appears absurd, and yes, I also struggle to comprehend the facts. This being true, I need another twenty-four hours of discussions before I make any further decisions. During which I expect my government to stand behind me. If you cannot... leave now!'

After the Presidents assured delivery, the Vice spoke.

'Mr President, has the boy mentioned the consequences of the Awakening?'

The president, showing no signs that he hadn't, closed the question.

'Full disclosure will be after this next meeting. Are we all on board?'

The Vice looked for any unrest; a sullen nod from the General gave notice of compliance.

'Providing we get an hourly bulletin,' said the Vice demandingly.

The president snapped abruptly in a ploy to hammer down his growing authority.

'No! I require to be undisturbed, that is my terms!'

Now with the tension palpable, a deathly silence held before the Vice spoke.

'Very well, Mr President, you have twenty-four hours. I trust the faith we apply in your judgement becomes warranted.'

After glancing over at Tess, the president gave her a warm smile before responding.

'Not one person in this room can equate to the consequences of my failure, therefore I am committed to my decisions. Twenty-four hours gentlemen...!'

Forty-seven

The journey back to the lodge was in complete silence as the president, Tess, and Lorenzo recalled personal thoughts of the events. As the vehicle pulled up, Tess spoke in a whisper.

'Don't be too harsh on the rebellion Sir, the truth is... we're all bloody terrified!'

'There will be changes in personnel... fact.'

'And Tom?'

'I'm shocked, but proud.'

'He's changed, but I cannot put my finger on how?'

The president made no reply. Instead, he took a sharp breath as the door opened.

'Welcome,' said a smiling Arlo.

Stepping inside, they both drew comfort to see Josh and his canine. After polite exchanges and a welcomed coffee, the president took the lead.

'We have twenty-four hours before our emergency committee executes a decision I cannot prevent.'

The frank admission forged Bran's purpose.

'Then it becomes imperative I present my explanations within a dream of my creation.' Ignoring the shocked expressions, he continued. 'The experience is not without danger, as upon waking, your mind will undergo extreme chaos. Henceforth, if you survive, the knowledge will change your life forever. Subsequently, this is not for the faint hearted!'

The president replied first. 'For certain, you have just scared the crap out of everybody.'

As a group, they each expelled muted laughter, which helped. The president looked firmly at Bran.

'The Columnae mentioned an Awakening?'

Bran looked at Arlo, who replied nervously.

'The Awakening they refer to is the release of the Paragon.' With a churning stomach, he hoped Bran would accept his brief explanation.

Bran chose not to expand. 'This has no consequence just now – please continue with your questions.'

Arlo did well to hide his relief as Tess spoke up.

'Do we fall asleep first?'

'No, extracting you from a *normal human dream* would confuse. One moment you'll be awake, the next in a dream, experiencing the journey through a Sentinel, then the wonder of Nemkis.'

Arlo made himself heard.

'Will we encounter the journey leading to death?'

Bran's brow furrowed. 'Yes, but hopefully not the concluding act.'

'Hopefully?' Mused Josh.

A brief silence followed before Bran stood up.

'Anyone wanting to drop out? Please say now.'

'Will you find your answers if given time to do so?' prompted Josh.

'Absolutely, and what this group of people decides will affect our world dramatically.'

The president shrugged. 'Then how can we refuse...?'

Lorenzo, looking uneasy, spoke. 'Sir, forgive me! Since the onset of these meetings, I have become extremely uncomfortable. My religion plays a huge part in my life. For me, the belief I have lived with from childhood remains my priority... Respectfully, I wish to withdraw from further involvement.'

All looked nervously towards Bran, who simply bowed his respect.

'Shelly, I thank you for your honesty and respect the commitment to your belief.' Turning to the president, he smiled. 'I have no problem; this judgment is in your hands.'

The president decided.

'Shelly, I also thank you for your honest opinion and accept your wishes. Of course, you must remain within the lockdown until we reach a conclusion.'

'Sir, my commitment to your service will remain the same.'

A phone call led to Lorenzo's courteous dismissal to lockdown.

Belief is such a powerful emotion. This highlights the difficulties ahead, thought Bran, before speaking.

'Are we in favour?'

'Please continue, before I lose my nerve,' voiced the president, drawing a deep breath.

'Very well. Have we assurance that they will not disturb us until the final second?'

'Yes, but try to make their deadline!'

'I'll try.'

Moments later, with all doors locked, mobiles shut down, and the internal phone unplugged, Bran began.

'Listen carefully. When in dream, Duke will not be present, nor will anyone have a left little finger.'

Shocked expressions became default. Arlo laughed heartily.

'Trust me, it's a necessity to maintain your sanity within a dream.'

Bran continued. 'Apart from Duke missing and no left pinkie, everything will appear as normal! I'll assist in your initial confusion. On extraction, your fight to recover your mental state will be individual. Thus, enabling me to concentrate on each transition.'

All nodded, albeit half-heartedly.

'If it's possible, I'll lie on my bed; these old bones won't thank me for sleeping in a chair,' said Arlo.

'Of course,' responded Bran. 'But leave the door ajar. Anyone else care for luxury?'

Not wishing to lose the comfort of the group, the others abstained.

After shaking everyone's hand, Arlo hugged Bran, then walked to his room. Moving for his tablets, he stepped into the bathroom, tipped the contents down the loo, and flushed.

Could my death reunite me with my wife? Life has been too hard without her.

Next, he combed his hair, straightened his clothing, then placed a sealed letter on top of his leather-bound book, which lay on the bedside table.

'Good to go!' he called confidently.

'Okay everyone, please concentrate.'

Now standing in an identical room. Everyone looked at Bran.

Josh spoke first.

'Duke? Where's Duke?'

Bran's breathing quickened.

My god it worked; I've total control of the entire scenario. That knowledge appears when required appears to be true. But now – time is of the essence.

'You are inside my dream with your left finger missing. Once you can accept this, we can move on. Concentrate and pick up our last conversation. It's there, in your memory.'

As moments passed, one by one, each succumbed to the reality of their missing digit. As Tess dared to look at her finger, she let out a slight scream. Anxiously holding up her hand, she spoke. 'My god, apart from this, everything appears no different from moments ago. Now I understand why you left Duke behind, and my finger – hell, this is bonkers.'

The president moved to Bran and touched him.

'Your warm! Is this real?'

Tess pointed to his left hand.

'Sir, it's a miracle.'

Josh, also staring at his finger, shook his head in disbelief. 'So, what now?'

Bran called to Arlo. 'You with us?'

Holding his left hand up, Arlo shouted back. 'Been there, got the tee shirt! Take us to Darkvoid.'

With each having control of their emotions, Bran relaxed.

Stage one – acted out to perfection.

'Arlo, you sure?'

'One hundred percent.'

A thumbs up from Bran settled all.

To re-enact my entry into a Sentinel is a risk, but warranted. I hope they have the tenacity to cope.

'I am to create a dream inside a dream, a second layer in which you will experience the journey of your soul towards death before entering the wonder of the Nemkis. When I close the dream, once conscious, insanity looms as you fall from one reality to another. Look for Duke, seek him, for when he is in your vision, you are back to full consciousness. Check your hand. It will be as normal. I'll be there prompting your mind towards logic thinking. Again, look for Duke – check your hand.'

Before anyone replied, he pushed on.

As each strained to search the blackness, confusion reigned, prompting apprehension from Bran.

The Sentinel is a veritable nightmare, but the shift to Nemkis should soothe their minds with no lasting damage... hopefully!

Now speaking above the deafening silence, he began.

'You are in Darkvoid, a hub leading to many sub-conscious dimensions. Your form is now in a spectral state; a state we all assume when leaving the physical world. Next you will see a tunnel of light – a Sentinel. From this point, I need you to face the experience to its exactness. I wish you safe passage, for the next time we meet will be in the lounge with Duke.'

As each stared in nervous disbelief at their individual spectres, Bran let them free. Instantly, the greys came in droves. The first *silent* scream came from the president, surprising Bran considerably. The second from Tess. Josh and Arlo simply gazed in anxious wonderment. After a few moments, their Sentinels formed. Understanding exactly how each would feel, Bran grimaced.

Without pause, Arlo moved directly inside, followed by Josh, Tess and finally the president. The terror of the grey spectres colliding with the Sentinels caused everyone to exhibit fear except Josh, who braced for the fight. Now staring at the vicious struggle between the two forces, the grey's demise brought comfort to all. As their light-fall portals formed, looks of bewilderment became default as each approached the shimmering light. After allowing time to experience the spectacle, Bran moved each through their portals. Within moments, the stage of dissipation into the body of the Nemkis began. The president's expression now portrayed horror as he watched his soul ebb deeper into the Nemkis. Josh, however, began fighting to halt his demise, determined to go out like a marine. Tess's resistance broke almost immediately, and so she shifted into the pitiful turmoil of the unrelenting lure of death. Arlo, exhibiting the least resistance, displayed zero fear, slightly concerning Bran.

At the peak of their trauma, albeit without sound, screams became default actions, except for Josh, whose defiance continued. With all almost absorbed into the Nemkis, Bran switched the scenario. Now gazing at the wonderment, both Tess and Josh held their arms wide open to embrace the ultimate tranquillity, as had Bran. The president reacted by clapping, although no sound came from his actions. Arlo wept openly. That the sight of Nemkis had immediately erased the trauma of the Sentinel did not surprise Bran.

Even in an artificial state, the Nemkis presents a tranquillity we cannot replicate in the physical world.

Suddenly, Arlo's head slumped to his chest, suggesting a lost connection. Concerned, Bran immediately withdrew him from the dream. The lounge returned.

Bran rushed to the bedroom to find Arlo wheezing deeply. Hurriedly searching for his tablets, he found the empty bottle. Deeply alarmed, he rushed back to the bedside, holding the bottle.

'Why...?'

In between rasping gasps, Arlo smiled. 'It's time I saw my darling wife again.'

Bran grasped hold of Arlo's hand.

'What have you done...?'

His face twisted into a smile as he spoke.

'Make certain to research insomnia for me and I'm sure you will be a hero in solving it!' Arlo took another laboured breath before calming down.

'With this understanding, death holds no fear. This has to be a major concern. I implore you to be absolutely certain that mankind will benefit from the knowledge.' Another vicious gasp led to him clasping at his chest. 'Now follow me, you promised.'

In a fight to remain calm, Bran nodded. 'I will try. I just wish...'

As Arlo experienced the trauma of a cardiac arrest, his back curved. Moments later, his eyes rolled closed.

Regrettably, Bran closed his own.

Now inside a Sentinel, Bran watched on as the greys swamped the entrance, only to disintegrate as expected. Moments later, he shivered as a white spectre entered the passage at speed before slowing to a crawl as it passed him on its approach to the light-fall portal.

Arlo?

When Bran saw how young the features appeared, he did a double take.

I'm having a difficult time comprehending this! He has the look of a young adult in his early twenties. Does the soul transcend time when it matures? Could this be why the elderly exclaim, "I still feel young on the inside?" My goodness, he appears to be in a state of utter serenity and calmness.

In that instant, Arlo's soul became completely absorbed into the body of Nemkis. Shocked over the realisation of what he had witnessed, Bran fell motionless. With seconds from his own demise, his sub-conscious returned him back to consciousness. Now awake, he struggled to remain calm. With having clenched his fists tightly, a bout of pins and needles developed and for a few moments, an insecurity washed over him.

It was an incredible experience to be the first human to observe a death occurring in the present moment. We are no longer steered by suppositions or beliefs... This is a proven reality!

Now shaking uncontrollably, his mind fought for control.

I cannot allow my human nature to dictate my emotions – I require the mentality of the Paragon to eradicate this weakness.

As his sub-conscious *switched* to Paragon, his emotional equilibrium rebooted.

Turning to look at the body of Arlo, he sighed as the vision confirmed his aura was no more.

My dear friend. I will miss your earthly form and wisdom. However, the knowledge you returned to our spiritual dimension is a comfort, therefore I will not grieve. Confirmation that the soul returns to Nemkis is now complete. Even as a Paragon, I find it surreal that clarification of our ultimate demise now exists.

Bran took a moment to allow his mind to settle over the magnitude of his discovery.

My entry into a Sentinel was as a living being, subsequently fear became the overriding emotion. Arlo, however, entered as a dying being, but he expressed elation. Therefore, I can assume the soul has a conscious understanding of its return, producing the pure exhilaration I observed.

Bran's mind recalled an image of the exact moment Arlo passed over.

I would compare it to a single snowflake melting on the surface of a giant ocean. In one moment, the silhouette of pure creation was there, and in the next, it disappeared, becoming one with the greater body.

With his mind picturing Arlo's serenity in passing, an emotional warmth flushed over him.

Thank you my friend for this knowledge. I hope we retain conscious thought, but more so, that we connect with our lost loved ones. I now smile at the possibility you are with your beloved wife in total harmony.

Following a moment of holding the bow, Arlo's leather-bound book and the letter caught his eye. Understanding that Arlo had planned for his own passing, Bran released a deep, sorrowful sigh. Saddened, he reluctantly opened the letter.

Bran Cranson – my friend. If you are reading this, my heart ceased to beat. Please do not feel anger or sorrow, for I have longed for this day ever since he took my wife from me. It has been an honour to be your friend and confident, and hope you learn the truth about our last journey by following my soul. Just remember when you crack the code, I'll be waiting. One final warning, the knowledge I gained about the Nemkis, eased my fear of death. This may well be the case with the others after their experience. Bran, without the fear of death, life cannot survive! Please say goodbye to your parents and marry that girl, as fate dictates. Within the last pages of my writing, there are several chapters. Read only when required. You will know when!

Goodbye my friend... for now!

For a few moments, Bran allowed his emotions to release in the guise of a shiver, but stopped short of tears. Bracing himself, he carefully placed the letter inside the heavy book, bowed again, then moved to the lounge. Now seated, his mind returned to the dream. In real time, many hours would have elapsed. Within the dream, perhaps a few seconds. With the president, Tess, and Josh still under the enchantment, Bran stifled his trauma and turned his attentions to their return. Quickly settling, he set Duke in the sit position.

Moments later, the dream ended for Tess, who then woke with a vicious jolt, resulting in a gasp for air before absolute confusion. Now motionless, she mouthed what seemed like silent gibberish.

Her aura is as low as I have witnessed in a white soul.

Tess's gaze fell on Duke, which prompted her to mouth his name, although nothing audible sounded. Duke gave a nonchalant wag of his tail but remained stationary, as prompted by Bran. Turning her gaze to the floor, she then began squeezing the sides of her head in a bizarre attempt to correct her confusion. Now moving towards Bran, she continued to utter inaudible words.

Bran held firm.

With no response, Tess screamed like a banshee, causing Duke to set and bark, but a reassuring pat from Bran calmed him. Now transfixed with Duke, she called his name, in which, after three attempts, her first legible sentence echoed around the room.

'Duke, is that you?'

Now wide-eyed, Tess looked at her hands. As the connection to reality flooded her mind, Bran engaged.

'Yes, you're awake, and back into the physical world, hopefully undeterred.'

Tess, overwhelmed, slowly lowered herself onto her knees. 'My god, I remember everything, the darkness, the Sentinel, and that heaven. It's truly wonderful.'

With that, she broke down into tears of pure relief. Bran watched on as her aura returned to the white sheen normally displayed, producing his own period of elation.

'Please sit down. I have to bring the others back. We must let each find their own way unless I say so. Understood?'

Tess nodded; but her thoughts had transferred to recall her journey.

Moments later, the president jolted from the dream, walked to a wall, where he began to scream manically. The chilling shrill caused Tess to snatch open her eyes. Immediately, Bran signalled for her to stay still as the mournful screams continued. With one hand holding Duke, he watched on.

His aura has depleted dramatically.

The screaming ended as the president uttered a similar gibberish, whilst rotating unsteadily on the spot. Moments later, he slapped his own face several times, which, because of the fierceness of the blows, Bran commanded Duke to bark. After several sharp yaps, the president ceased slapping. A second command to Duke led to a shrill howl, prompting the president to look at his hands.

'Am – am I awake?'

'Yes, Mr President, you are... well done!'

Tess's emotions broke as she rushed to his side, resulting in an embrace of pure emotion. Once again, Bran's delight flushed through him as the bright sheen of the president's aura blended with Tess's.

Brimming with relief, the president looked at Bran.

'Arlo and Josh?'

After choking back his emotions, Bran woke Josh, who jumped straight out of his chair and stood defensively as he searched his mind for answers. Duke, recognising his master was stressed, rushed to his side. In the exact moment of connection, Bran watched open-mouthed as Duke's shining aura blended into the dull of Josh's, returning him back to reality without a blemish. Josh fell to his knees and hugged his dog with an intensity that brought tears.

'Duke – I'm back!'

Bran closed his eyes.

The soul is within all life. I experienced it with Loki and have now witnessed the same with Josh and Duke. That we are a separate species matters not – we are as one!

Seconds later, whilst looking at his hand, Josh spoke.

'Am I really awake?'

Euphoric, Bran replied. 'Yes. As are Tess and the president.'

A group hug provided comfort and instigated a cacophony of light to shimmer around their forms. The event elevated Bran's emotions.

Without them being aware, their aura merges, providing comfort. Ignoring sexual context, hugging a friend, a lover or family stimulates an unbridled joy, providing reassurance and protection in times of need. Our belief that a physical connection stimulates this sensation is incorrect. It is the merging of souls that creates the emotion. The quote "I can feel your pain" now makes absolute sense. But can only "like souls" form this bond? Certainly, it would explain why we can admire one person yet dislike another. I once discussed, animals must have this sense as they also greet or growl comparably. Yet I feel something else is staring me in the face. Time and patience will present this answer.

A few moments later, after composing himself, the president smiled, then looked at Bran.

'You are a miracle. I don't know if we entered heaven, but damn, I've never experienced such tranquillity in all my life. I could have stayed forever.'

Bran nodded passively.

Next, Josh moved to shake Bran's hand. 'Thank you for that experience. I don't quite understand the how's and why's, but right now – well, I'm buzzing.'

Tess's first words hit Bran like a locomotive.

'Death now holds no fear – how can it?'

Arlo was correct. The human must keep a fear of death or life will cease. This is a problem I never envisaged. I need to bring a reality back to death. Arlo's passing will jolt them out of their current mind set.

In a deeply morose tone, he set to disclose the sad news.

'Please, can we sit?'

Josh responded. 'What about Arlo?'

Bran took a deep breath.

'Sadly, Arlo has paid the ultimate price... his heart gave way during the dream; I am truly devastated.'

Bran's words, as he expected, rebooted normality.

With her hands holding her face, Tess spoke first. 'Are you saying – Arlo has died?'

Bran glanced towards the bedroom.

'His physical demise instigated a disconnection from the dream to reality, where he suffered a fatal heart attack.'

Josh moved quickly to the bedroom and peered inside. Bowing his head respectfully, he closed the door before nodding confirmation to the president. All sat down. The president spoke.

'My word... that's knocked the legs from under me. Although I have experienced this wonderment, death is still death. Its finality has recalled the horrors I suffered when inside a Sentinel.'

Both Tess and Josh nodded a silent agreement. Bran's thoughts kicked into overdrive.

Arlo's warning rings true. Without fear of death, life cannot hold the same value. For now, the truth behind our passing must stay within our circle.

After glancing at his watch, Bran spoke.

'Nineteen hours and thirty-five minutes have passed.'

Gobsmacked, all three checked the time. Bran continued.

'This event is now stored in your memory bank. Questioning thoughts will require answers, but first, may we respect my dear friends' passing? Mr President, if you can call in the medics to affect his death as a heart attack...' He took a deep breath. 'And can we agree not to divulge the circumstances that prevailed?'

Lost in thoughts of his own mortality, moments passed before the president spoke.

'The events of the past hours have taken a toll on us, and though I'm having trouble accepting the truth of what happened, I firmly believe in you.'

Bran allowed his expression to show relief. Tess, with tears rolling down her cheeks, spoke.

'This day has been like no other. The fact you keep a dignity and steadiness is remarkable. I now find myself in a state of pride, knowing I could be part of the process forward.'

Without embarrassment, Duke broke wind, jumped up, turned twice before rushing to the exit door.

A tactful smile from all became default.

'Well, that's brought us back to reality. My lad needs to poop,' laughed Josh.

Everyone stood, which ended in a group embrace. As they disconnected, Bran's thoughts turned back to Arlo.

Wherever you are, my dear friend, I'll find you, no matter what.

The president spoke in a tone of condolence.

'I will ensure we process this sad passing with the normality Arlo deserves. Let's call time for now to affect a respectful protocol. Our meeting will continue at your discretion, and as before, I will not expand on any details until our conclusion. Would you prefer time alone?'

Bran nodded. 'That would be helpful. Please, for now, do not inform my parents.' The president, although a little confused by his request, nodded his acceptance. Bran continued to speak. 'I advise you to contact a Dr Walter Massam who is as close to family as Arlo had. The number will be in his mobile.'

'Thank you and is he fully conversed in all matters?'

'His knowledge of the Paragon is on a par with Arlo's.'

'Then I'll call the doctor myself.'

After another group hug, they left.

Now seated next to the bed, Bran clasped his head as a headache with a severity he had never encountered took hold. Rushing to the bathroom, he vomited several times before passing out onto the floor. The trauma lasted for three minutes before he woke gasping for air. Struggling to regain his awareness, minutes passed before his system rebooted.

I don't know what happened or how I'm on the floor. That I have vomited is a deep concern.

Oddly, apart from the headache from hell, standing up felt normal, but his understanding was clear… the event was not natural.

Minutes later, a medical team removed Arlo's body. The moment they left, the reality of his death flooded back, resulting in Bran passing out for eight minutes. Once awake, he moved to Arlo's room.

Fingers crossed this problem is a simple blip linked to stress.

After placing the leather-bound book into his suitcase, sleep beckoned; he would not deny himself the Nemkis.

If ever I need my sanctuary, it's now.

Bran closed his eyes.

The president and Tess had become fixated over the lure of the *heavenly* Nemkis during their brief journey to the operations room.

'What if the events were purely his imagination?'

Tess paused for a few moments. 'Truth sir. Remove the mystery of Bran Cranson and you have one of the most gifted intellects on the planet. Fiction does not fit into his mindset; his reasoning will always be black or white.'

The president sighed heavily, his shoulders slumping in defeat. 'Am I not searching for ways to disprove his assertions?'

'That would be the straightforward solution.'

'Are you convinced?'

'The female is more often naturally aligned to a pure existence, so yes.'

Grasping at his phone, he dialled Josh.

'Sir.'

'Josh, I know you will answer honestly, therefore I ask one question.'

'Of course.'

'Do you believe in the boy?'

The line fell silent, long enough for the president to ask again.

'Apologies Sir, I was in thought. My answer has to be yes, I believe in him... one hundred percent.'

'May I ask why?'

'The boy has a natural honesty. When I wrongly believed he was going to harm my family, I saw a genuine sorrow in his expression. At that moment, I understood he was not a natural born killer. Sir, the boy cares. His blessing is not a random act. No, I believe this to be a divine choice. By whom? Perhaps the boy will find the answer.'

'Thank you. Are you coping?'

'Just – but I'm whirling in a cloud of confusion!'

'That I understand.'

'Sir. If I may speak?'

'Of course.'

'Whilst the boy is a wonder, he absolutely needs your help, protection, and guidance, for the world will grow to fear him and that fear will turn to hate. Sir, you cannot allow that, as this world needs peace, and I believe the boy is the answer.'

'Josh I thank you for your wise words.'

'Sir.'

After closing the call, he smiled.

'He chose my confidants well.'

After consecutive calls, the president turned his mind to setting a working protocol for Bran Cranson.

Forty-eight

Inside the ops room, the president stood confidently against a backdrop of silence. He took a breath, then began.

'Today, Professor Arlo Norton's life ended. Death's timing will never show empathy. The autopsy will confirm a natural heart attack. As a result, our meeting ended. However, I can confirm the following. Bran Cranson acted in self-defence against unlawful attempts to kidnap or kill himself and his family. There is no case to answer. I can also conclude that he is no longer a threat either to myself or this country.'

The furore began.

Above the noise, the president made a call and within seconds, ten secret service burst into the room. The internal guards, after listening to their ear comms, moved aside the president. Once again, a muted silence held.

'I will only say this once. Those who formally attempted to enforce Section 4 of the 25th I require to be detained for threatening the safety of this administration and their fellow countrymen until we have correlated the facts.'

General Ballinger stood to vent his anger. However, before he could speak, two agents handcuffed him at gunpoint. The president, unfazed, continued.

'Tom, those that stood against my government arrange their detention inside the Langley bubble. Those with us keep on standby.'

The two men nodded an acknowledgement.

'Consider this done,' said Rialto, concealing his delight in his play to remain loyal to the president.

The president left, followed by four servicemen and Tess. Outside, she held her hands up.

'Fucking hell Sir...!'

Having never once heard her swear, the president stopped in his tracks!

'My word that's some assessment – you approve?'

Being her response was out of character. She blushed, then whispered.

'It was exactly what was required, but the ripple effect, especially from the military, will no doubt cause severe issues.'

'The ripples from the Cranson boy would become more severe if that lot ran the show.'

Sergeant Moore's call interrupted.

'Duke is showing towards the lodge. Is there an issue?'

'Not to my knowledge, make your way over asap and report.'

'Sir.'

Call closed; the president shouted to the servicemen.

'Get us over to the lodge!'

Duke had forced a fast pace, pushing Josh hard, but as the lodge came into view, relief passed over him as nothing seemed untoward. At the front entrance, the external guards, looking puzzled at the urgency of Josh's approach, called out.

'Problem, sergeant?'

Just yards away, Duke began barking and pawing furiously at the front entrance.

'Has anyone else entered?' asked Josh.

'Negative.'

Josh opened the door, released Duke off leash and followed him to the lounge where they found Bran slumped on the floor lying in his own vomit. The guard immediately rang for a med team whilst Josh checked Bran's vital signs, which were nil. Instantly he began CPR.

As the president and Tess arrived just moments later, Bran was still showing zero sinus rhythm.

'Sir, it's been almost four minutes, and I am uncertain to when he stopped breathing.'

The med team entered the room and began prepping for emergency resuscitation. In that instant, Duke turned viciously on the men, driving them backwards before standing over the prone form of Bran. Josh, caught cold by Duke's action, screamed his command.

'LEAVE!'

Duke remained.

Josh called his command a second time, which was met by a low growl.

The med team leader, clearly concerned, screamed at his partner.

'Get your weapon from the vehicle.'

The soldier grimaced, then dashed outside.

As Duke settled over Bran, he whimpered softly, causing Josh to look at the president with a stony expression.

'Sir, my gut feeling is that Duke is protecting the boy. Why is beyond my reasoning?'

As the soldier rushed back into the room, the med leader gave the order.

'Take the shot!'

Josh immediately placed himself in front of Duke.

'You'll have to shoot me first.'

The soldier, confused, turned to the president.

Tess spoke out. 'Sir, look at Duke. He's appearing to be pleading.'

The med officer spoke coldly. 'Sir, you will lose this patient if we don't begin!'

Now looking hard at Josh, the president decided.

'Stand down, officer, wait in your vehicle. This matter is not to be discussed. Are we clear?'

'Sir, if you are certain?'

'I am.'

Bewildered, the med team packed away the defibrillator and left the room.

Duke stood, then moved back to Josh's side.

'What is it, boy? What the hell is it?'

Tess and the president held motionless as Josh tried to find a pulse before shaking his head frantically.

'Nothing! My god – the boy's dead...! I don't understand.'

The president slumped into a lounge chair.

'Not you're doing Sergeant, for whatever reason, your dog did not want the med team to interact – but why?'

Tess moved to Bran and located his mobile.

'Something doesn't add up... we should call his parents?'

The president agreed. After scrolling down the call list, he pressed *Dad.* Two rings later, Ross answered.

'How are you son?'

The president closed his eyes before speaking.

'Mr Cranson, my apologies. This is the president of the United States. Please sit down?'

A brief pause followed before Ross replied. 'Sir, you're on loudspeaker and my wife is present. Speak honestly.'

After listening to the explanation, Isla spoke up.

'Sir, I do not know what information you currently have on my son, but I can assure you he is not dead. Call it mother's intuition or whatever, but please trust me. If you attach a heart monitor and wait for a single beat, it will then happen every ninety minutes. Once you have confirmed this, call us back. And may I ask why Professor Norton has not informed you of this pattern?'

The president shifted awkwardly. 'Mrs Cranson, approximately one hour before Bran became unwell, Professor Norton suffered a fatal heart attack.'

Ross and Isla both suffered a wave of disbelief, then sorrow, before Ross snapped.

'Is this true or a cover up?'

'Trust me on this, Mr Cranson. Your son is a remarkable blessing, and I fully support the knowledge he has conveyed to us. As a result, I will adhere to your instruction without question. Again, I offer my condolences to you both.'

Both parents flushed with the sincerity of the president's words. 'Thank you,' replied Ross. 'May I ask if Arlo's colleagues are aware?'

'Not yet. Bran had suggested we contact a *Dr Massam*?'

'Then please allow us to break the news to him. However, I suggest you bring the doctor to Bran's side. His knowledge is as vast as was the professors.'

'Then we shall be in touch, thank you, and again, I am sorry to burden you with this sad news.'

As the conversation ended, Isla was too overwhelmed to keep her feelings contained, and broke down in tears. Ross, holding her tightly, gently kissed her forehead.

Loki wandered over and nudged Isla's side with his muzzle. She frowned. 'You would tell us if our son had died, wouldn't you boy?'

Ross nodded. 'That's for sure. Truth is, I also feel he's alive.'

Isla sighed deeply. 'But what the hell is happening?'

'Perhaps Arlo's death has induced a long sleep?'

'I hope it's that simple... my god, Arlo. I can't believe this has happened.'

Ross tightened his embrace. 'His heart was always on the edge. Hell, nature's timing can be ruthless.'

'We had best contact Walt.'

The president, over a call, began his demands.

'Do we have an at the base hospital?'

'Yes, Sir...?'

'Then clear that area from personnel apart from the senior consultant. What is their name?'

'Dr Alison Morley, Mr President.'

'Thank you. From this point we boost her security level, and I require that she make no contact nor speak to anyone regarding the patient, Mr X.'

'Sir.'

After forty minutes inside the scanner Bran's lifeless body registered a single heartbeat, leaving everyone shocked.

Stunned, Dr Morley tentatively asked a question.

'Sir, forgive me, but... this boy was *dead on arrival*. How is this possible?'

The president, lost for words, remained calmed. 'Please complete the scan and we shall see.'

Forty minutes later, Dr Morley stood in absolute confusion over the images produced.

'My initial response when told of his condition would have been a rare benign tumour. A hemangioblastomas, to be exact. However, that is not the case!'

Exhaling, the president sat in a chair. All waited.

'Mr X's pineal gland has expanded abnormally to the point it is affecting the surrounding area of his brain. Sir, I can confirm that there is no medical history of a pineal gland becoming so enlarged.'

'Dr, our knowledge of tumours is far greater than that of the pineal gland. Therefore, is it a serious concern? Is immediate surgery required?'

Dr Morley, looking extremely ruffled, replied.

'Without a case history, we are working on a new template. And as the patient is clearly *unique*; uncertainty has to be factored in. Being we cannot afford for him to move during any procedure we decide on, our key problem is how do we anesthetise Mr X?'

The president raised his hand. 'One moment I need to make a call to his parents.'

Isla answered. 'Has his heart sounded?'

'Thankfully yes, we now wait for the *ninety-minute repeat*.' The president allowed relief to flush through the parents before speaking again. 'However, a scan has revealed an abnormal enlargement of his pineal gland. At this stage, because of his... *difference*, normal medical treatment may not be suitable, so we need guidance on this matter. And for security, his identity is Mr X, with you both assuming Mr A and Mrs B.'

Isla and Ross, shocked to the core, stood in muted silence before Ross gathered himself.

'Sir, Mr X has entered... well, what you may perceive as *hibernation.* All systems are functioning, but at a significantly slower pace. This shutdown state enables him to sleep for extended periods without needing food.'

Dr Morley interrupted. 'Sir, may I?'

The president nodded. 'Our Dr Morley will speak.'

'Mr A... When your son's heart rate slows down to one beat every ninety minutes, does he ever move?'

'No, never. There are no signs of life when he enters this state of hibernation. May I suggest you ring Dr Massam? His knowledge may be of help. For your information, he is now aware of Arlo's passing.'

Ten minutes later, Walt spoke through a conference call after being informed of the details.

'We have always questioned if the pineal gland was, in fact, the mystery behind the Paragon. This confirms our theory. As for an operation, this is my best guess... Mr X's sub-conscious shut down his system in a defensive action against the abnormal swelling. However, my instinct is to believe that the growth matches his sensory advancement. Therefore, if you operate, he may lose all that makes him a Paragon.'

Isla spoke out sharply. 'But we lose our son if they do not perform the operation.'

Ross, holding Isla's hand, spoke.

'Walt, will there be a *reaction* if they attempt to cut him?'

With understanding the double-edged question, Walt paused for a moment. 'With zero intent, all will be fine. Dr Morley, is there an alternative to surgery?'

The Dr moved to the images and spent several minutes in thought.

'Calcification linked to the aging process is the common problem with the gland. This issue is distinctly an abnormality in size. However, the scan has revealed an excessive amount of fluid surrounding the gland. Draining this would certainly relieve some pressure.'

'And the prognosis?' asked Walt.

'I cannot forecast its success, nor how quickly the fluids will re-establish. Of course, we also have to factor in that the gland may continue to expand.'

Ross looked at Isla. 'Love, it is not our decision to make. Only Bran can make this choice.'

Isla spoke firmly. 'Then our answer has to be the drain. Temporary, this may be, but it will offer Bran his own choice. Mr President, please look after our son.'

'Mrs B, I assure you, he is in safe hands; shall we plan for your travel?'

'No Sir, you just get him back to us as soon as possible.'

'You have my word.'

Call closed; the president had a random thought about Duke.

How the hell did he know something was wrong?

After a shake of his head, he addressed Dr Morley. 'You have my direct command to put together a medical team immediately.'

'Sir, our best hope is the Johns Hopkins Hospital over at Baltimore, being one of our finest for neurosurgery of this type.'

'Then make immediate arrangements for the transfer.'

Thirty minutes later, seated in a room with just Tess and Rialto, the president spoke.

'Tom, we've had our moments over the years, but I am heartened by your loyalty, as I need all the help I can get. In short, we must *erase* the last few days completely. It's a blessing that the boy has appeared to *die, which* effectively ends this mess. It's my belief that if we closed investigations, they would become suspicious, so we will sweep all advanced studies into a specialist team to evaluate and determine the possibility of other Paragons officially. Meanwhile, underneath this *official* project, I want a small team assembled to support Bran, pending the success of his operation. Yes, I understand we are running close to the wind, but for now, it's the best route forward. As a top priority, can you make it work?'

'Yes Sir, I will make this happen.'

The president bowed his head.

'I promise you; your loyalty will be the best decision you've ever made.'

Turning to leave, Rialto's expression portrayed a certain smugness..

'Every cloud...'

The clock was ticking.

Forty-nine

10 p.m.

The president confirmed to the parents regarding the ninety-minute beat pattern and the procedures to follow. Now faced with the realisation that their son was about to undergo brain surgery, Ross and Isla were at breaking point. Agreeing they would feel better back in their home, they set off walking from Cliff Cottage. Neither would take a drink this night.

Walt had boarded a private flight to Langley. With being the named executor, he began the preparations for Arlo's legal requirements. Twelve billion fell to the ¥ trust, with properties and varying amounts to be split amongst his trusted staff. The Cranson family would inherit five hundred million! Knowing them, he understood they would give every penny away in a swap for Bran's health. He allowed a smile as, finally, they could buy new generators!

Both the president and Tess held their breath as Dr Morley and her team began the operation. With Bran remaining dormant, they exhaled. After leaving the theatre, a power nap was a top priority.

The drain lasted over two hours and with the postoperative scan completed, the entire medical team assembled to meet with the president.

'I'm sure you have concerns regarding Mr X.'

The staff's obvious confusion prompted the president to pause. Tess, who had also noticed the team's odd reaction, set to speak before a call from Tom Rialto rang out. Both feared the worse!

'Tom...?'

Rialto took a moment to compose himself.

'Sir, may I speak, or do you have company?'

'One moment.'

Turning to the medical team, who had remained unsettled, he dismissed them to an adjoining room.

'Go ahead Tom, you're on speaker.'

'Thank you. I don't know what to say. It's madness... We had nine senior ranked people held in isolation...'

Tess, looking mortified, spoke out. 'Do not tell us they have *disappeared*?'

The moment that passed before Rialto replied felt like an eternity.

'No, they are fine. Except not one has a memory of the past few days.'

'My god – really? Is this true?'

'Yes, absolutely. In fact, I'm recommending that we release everyone.'

Tess looked intrigued. 'Does this include the Vice and General?'

'It's as though it never happened.'

The president hurried to the next room to ask the medical team one question.

'Who is Mr X?'

Completely flummoxed, the anaesthetist replied nervously.

'None of us received a briefing over... Mr X?'

The penny dropped for the president.

'Sorry, yes, we had an issue which for now has passed, so please accept my apologies for wasting your time. You may return to normal duties.'

The team left with no questions sited.

In the holding room, the president, totally flummoxed, addressed Rialto.

'Again, anyone who met Bran over the past few days has no recollection?'

'Yes, apart from the Columnae.' said Rialto enthusiastically.

Tess spoke out. 'Lorenzo?'

'Zero recall.'

'If that's the case, then Bran must be up and running again, my goodness! Tom, I have to make a trip to see the boy. I'm entrusting you to make the right decision to close this.'

'Sir, it will be done.'

As will my collusion with Fanello.

An hour on, the president and Tess positioned themselves close to Bran, connected to a variety of medical appliances. Some five hours had passed since the operation. Tess spoke under her breath.

'He still looks... quite dead.'

Both jumped as Bran eased aside his respiratory mask, touched his head bandages, then spoke, albeit jadedly.

'But I'm not.'

Speechless, both watched in disbelief as the colour seeped back into his body. Bran's movement attracted his recovery nurse.

'Mr Boyle, nice to see your back with us. Do stay still whilst we make some adjustments.'

Bran addressed the nurse. 'Guessing my headaches resulted from a tumour?'

Dr Morley stepped into the room; her expression portrayed slight trepidation.

The president suggested he leave. However, Bran asked him to stay before addressing the doctor.

'How much of my tumour did you steal?'

'No tumour, Mr Boyle. However, your pineal gland is approximately ten times larger than normal, which is a medical first.'

This confirms the gland is the key to the Paragon. For now, I'll shrug this off.

'Really? The prognosis?'

'Your parents decided not to remove the gland in order that we first performed a drain to relieve the pressure. Temporarily, this appears to be a success. If you continue to show no effects, I expect at least three to five months before a further fluid imbalance causes issues. Of course, should the gland continue to expand, then we have to explore removal.'

Bran took a sip of water before speaking.

'I see. Well, for now I'm alive, and that's a bonus – thank you.' Sighing deeply, Bran's voice tailed off as he passed into slumber.

Dr Morley moved to his side to adjust his pillows. 'Sleep, that's fine. The next time he wakes, he will be stronger.'

'How long will that be, doctor?' asked the president.

'There is no definitive answer – my best guess, possibly a maximum of forty-eight hours. After this, he will require around eight weeks of rest to fully recover. Of course, this is providing the gland does not continue to grow, or produce another build-up of fluid.'

'Thank you doctor, please. I wish to be informed the moment he becomes coherent.'

'Of course. I'll leave you for now, as I wish to discuss all possibilities with the most prominent people we have in this field. Sir, we will cover every angle.'

'Excellent, and thank you for your work.'

After the door closed, Tess whispered.

'Why is nature taking the boy back after giving him these gifts? This is sheer madness.'

The president's eyebrows wrinkled as he stared quizzingly at Bran. Moments later, he spoke solemnly.

'I'm both shocked and scared, Tess. If we lose him, where does that leave us?'

Tess shook her head. 'In a deep, deep void!'

Dr Morley was some way out in her assessment, as on a Tuesday morning, seven days after the operation, the president's phone rang – Tess.

'Sir, Bran has finally woken. A full scan shows no further swelling, and that his physical condition is excellent?'

'Great news. We leave in thirty.'

'Sir.'

Closing his eyes after the call, he whispered under his breath.

'Here we go again.'

Fifty

Bran, having bathed, eaten a full meal, and spoken briefly to his loved ones, asked if he could exercise by walking along the corridors. Permission granted, but, as a caution, he was to be chaperoned by Kate Novak, his recovery nurse. The news that Arlo's funeral had passed was the only negative. He would find the time to pay his respects at his resting place, alongside his beloved wife.

As they walked, Novak tentatively asked how he had recovered so efficiently.

Bran's reply oozed *matter of fact.*

'My family are excellent healers... and lots of sleep.' Wanting to change the subject, he gazed into a rest room and caught sight of a family huddled together. Disturbed that their aura had formed a dour sheen around them, he turned to Novak and spoke in a whisper.

'Have they lost a loved one?'

Novak cautiously glanced up and down the corridor before replying.

'They're waiting for results for the removal of a malignant tumour from one of their twin daughters... who's just fourteen!'

As she finished her sentence, the family's consultant walked into the corridor. By the brightness of his aura, Bran understood he was about to present good news!

Moving closer to the window, he watched on as the consultant stepped inside and announced that the operation was a complete success. Now shedding tears of joy, the patient's twin rushed to the consultant and embraced him tightly. Such was the intensity of their aura as it combined. Bran gasped. The entire family now rushed to form a group hug, resulting in a spectacular glow silhouetting the family as the unbridled exhilaration bled into all.

To witness the connection of the white soul is a wonder and an honour. I observed a professional man deliver good news with an unbridled passion to a family in deep sorrow. He visibly transferred his joy to all. Even though I am outside, I experienced their warmth and intimacy. Whilst he used physical mannerisms linked to verbal exchange to communicate the news, it was their connection that enhanced the mood. Having the ability to decipher this communication by sight is awe-inspiring. With all souls being connected, the "spiritual pain" of losing a loved will always remain, unlike the physical memory, which, given time, fades, enabling us to continue on our own life journey.

Pausing, his mind shifted to another angle.

That the Sentinels exterminate souls tainted by evil, I conclude that, during its existence within the physical dimension, the soul must preserve absolute purity for its return after its physical death.

A rush of adrenaline flowed through his system as he realised the consequences.

The fear of absolute termination would intensify our desire to live a pure existence. For only the truly deranged would risk the extinction of their soul preventing immortality within the afterlife. That may include the act of suicide. Undeniably, this effectively ensures the human will seek a pure existence to achieve the holy grail – immortality!

His concluding thought sent a shudder around his body.

Novak did not speak, as her own understanding of the situation was that Bran's recovery had finally hit home.

No question. It had certainly contributed to the emotional cocktail that had fermented inside him for some time. Stepping back from the window to compose himself, he breathed slowly.

Turning to Novak, he smiled. 'I'm okay.'

Novak nodded. 'Life is the greatest gift ever given.'

Bran beamed over her statement.

The consultant, after hugs in abundance, turned to leave, then stepped into the corridor. Bran held out his hand.

'Sir, I have just witnessed something so special. I congratulate you.'

'Why thank you, Mr Boyle. May I say how intrigued I've become by your return to complete fitness?'

Not surprised by the Dr's knowledge of his medical condition, he smiled. 'Thank you. I am just feeling extremely grateful and humbled by the work you all do.'

The consultant gave a slight nod of his head in appreciation. 'Whilst our work is not always pleasant, days like today help us focus.'

Perhaps one day I will share a coffee with you and explain how you opened my thoughts with the purity of your soul.

An array of dark-suited men interrupted the mood as they entered the corridor, followed by a smiling president and Tess. The consultant shook his head in disbelief.

'My word, Mr Boyle... is that our president?'

Bran grinned. 'Yes – I believe it is.'

As they approached, he beamed.

'Mr President, may I introduce the consultant who has just gifted the life of a daughter back to her loving family?'

The Dr flushed as the president offered his hand, thanked him whole-heartedly, then walked into the room to speak with the family. Now watching their joy as the president sat down for an unscheduled chat, Bran became enriched. Once again, a bright aura became entwined within the group.

The president is not perpetrating a PR stunt – he is acting as a caring human being; this man will become my backbone.

With everyone returning to his room, and refreshments at hand, Bran spoke up.

'Please, before we effect a de-brief, thank you for everything you have done for me.'

The president sighed. 'Thank your parents and Dr Massam. Their information was invaluable.'

Bran smiled as an image of his parents swept into his mind. 'I understand the complications. Has Dr Morley a long-term strategy?'

The president bowed his head a little. 'A specialist team is currently working on various treatments, excluding removal, should the swelling continue or, of course, a fluid build-up.'

'I see, then should removal become a necessity, it now becomes my choice.'

'That was everyone's wish.'

Bran smiled. 'Possibly not mums. She would have had the sucker whipped out.'

'Correct!'

'That aside, for now, my life expectancy is the least of our concerns.'

A sharp knock on the door led to Rialto stepping inside. Bran, staring ominously, stepped towards him. Concerned, the president spoke out.

'Bran, please... Tom is now fully behind our work.'

Ignoring the president, Bran continued to stir intensely, causing everyone to hold in fearful apprehension. A few awkward moments passed before he broke the tension.

'Mr Rialto, I'm fascinated. Your aura has reverted to its white beginnings. What's changed your nature?'

Rialto's colour had drained from his face. His reply disguised a cautious relief.

'Aura? I'm sorry I don't understand, but as to your question regarding my nature.' Now breathing rapidly, he continued. 'I became extremely traumatised, as all did, by the... *events* that happened during that horrific meeting. Of course, I understand why Senator Finney acted to enhance his power and finance. Sadly, I too became blinkered with how we could utilise your... shall we say, *talents?*' Pausing again for a few seconds' composure, he continued. 'And then I watched our president volunteer to face you alone to secure the release of his staff, even though he feared for his own life. That single act portrayed a depth of character so strong and true; I became ashamed to the point, my values changed.'

Bran's features remained quizzical.

'Have you ever killed?'

The direct nature of the question made everyone uncomfortable. Rialto grimaced and looked to the president for help.

'Truth Tom.'

'Sir,' he replied bowing his head.

'I was a Marine for ten years before entering politics, so as a soldier, I served my duty. Nine months after leaving the service, my wife was at home... alone.' He swallowed before continuing. 'Three men who broke into the house raped and murdered her.' Again, he steadied himself. 'She was seven months pregnant.' Bran replied, but Rialto held his hand up to continue. 'Those men no longer breathe.' He looked directly at Bran. 'I would do it again!'

Bran moved closer to Rialto, who remained motionless as a fear swept through him. In a tone that oozed compassion, Bran spoke.

'Relax Tom, as you have witnessed, I acted in the same manner when my family became threatened. So please, I am truly sorry for your loss.'

The relief in Rialto's expression was clear to see. Bran, however, continued to gaze at his aura as it glowed ever brighter, matching the relief shown on Tom's features.

His aura was light grey. I questioned if there was a definitive line.

Now speaking aloud, his voice carried an odd tone.

'The soul is truly the gateway to emotion, but the knowledge that transformation back to the white is possible is as important a discovery as I have made today... In human terms, Mr Rialto has become *born again*. I quote from the great man himself.

Reality is merely an illusion, albeit a very persistent one... Albert Einstein...!

To fight evil with violence fuels both sides with negativity, which then spreads, causing other malevolent issues to manifest.'

Five long minutes passed in an uneasy silence as Bran searched the depths of his study. Then his expression gave notice of an eureka moment.

'The Maharishi effect! Back in 1978, a group of seven thousand people meditated continually for three weeks. They predicted this would instigate a measurable positive effect on the surrounding cities. After the event, they produced a statistical analysis. Ensuring to account for extraneous effects and seasonal influences, the results showed that their group meditation accounted for a global average of 16% fall in violence, casualties, and crime rates during that time. They also documented that during this period, terrorism dropped by 72%. In summary, the entire world literally changed because a group of seven thousand meditators transcended into a higher state of consciousness, a state of love and peace over a period. Imagine if the five hundred million that practice Buddhism did the same! The soul is the most powerful force on earth and the tool to effect the changes I seek. I now have the key to tipping the battle of good versus evil.'

Bran stood up and appeared surprised that he was amongst people.

'Mr Rialto, judging by the lack of security, it would seem you have tidied up our turbulent issues efficiently.'

Rialto looked puzzled.

'Well, yes, especially since you erased the memories of anyone who had knowledge.'

Bran's turn to look confused.

'Please explain?'

The president interrupted.

'Except for those of the Columnae. It's as though you never existed.'

I can only assume that my sub-conscious has acted during sleep.

'I'm as shocked as you, as I don't recall this being processed. However, if I can implant memories, it's logical to accept I can also remove them.'

Rialto spoke.

'We still had several deaths to weave into the plot despite this miracle, but thankfully, all is well.'

Bran's expression did not waver. 'And the men of the Columnae?'

'They continue to be passive.'

'Beneventi?'

'A mystery man who conveys compliance, but I sense he is a danger.'

Bran frowned. 'He has thoughts that require calming. I must meet him alone as soon as possible, and no, I do not intend to harm.'

Rialto looked at the president, who nodded before speaking.

'Then I will arrange the meeting shortly, but for now, speak with your family. Shall we say an hour?'

'Thank you, and I suggest you explain our situation to Mr Rialto?'

The president was relieved at Rialto's inclusion and almost applauded. Rialto suppressed his delight at being included at the top table.

Perhaps now I'll understand this boy, hopefully to my advantage.

Bran exhaled. 'I'll stay a few more days, then return home via London as I wish to travel back to Scarth with Christie... time spent together is now paramount.'

The president nodded acceptance. After which, Bran heaved a sigh.

'And may I thank you once again for saving my life?'

'Well, actually you have Duke to thank for that?'

'Really?' asked Bran curiously.

'Absolutely!'

The president explained to which Bran, once again, appeared dumbfounded.

'This day is full of surprises, for sure.'

'May I ask you a question?' said the president.

'Of course?'

'How on earth did you recuperate so effectively?'

Bran shrugged. 'Again, I can only assume that after the initial collapse, my sub-conscious must have taken full control. I'm as baffled as you.'

The president scratched his brow. 'I can one hundred percent guarantee you're not.'

Handshakes followed. Moments later, Bran was alone.

My mortality has finally reared its ugly head, and for that I am thankful, for I was feeling untouchable. The complications of evolution have revealed my fault. A brain unable to cope with a growing pineal gland. On a positive note, we now understand the mystery of the Paragon.

With thoughts paused, he rolled his head clockwise several times to ease a slight twitch that had developed.

Oddly, I have neither fear nor remorse over these developments.

Bran dialled. The joy of speaking with his family was a massive tonic. Again, he played down the operation as much as one could to anxious parents. The discussion regarding Arlo was a difficult one, compounded as he had so many questions to answer.

'Oh, I'll bring Christie home, if that's okay?'

Isla smiled and nudged Ross's knee. 'Well, it would be nice to meet the lady who has captured my son's heart!'

Bran coughed. 'Don't get over excited, and you dare mention dating!'

All laughed, which felt good.

'Mum, Dad, I can't pretend this trip has been easy. It hasn't, especially with Arlo's passing. I'm just happy to have faced a large hurdle and cleared it, albeit just. However, how long the status-quo will last is anyone's guess.'

Ross swallowed a little.

'Son, we just want you home, back in Scarth, safe. The rest we'll deal with.'

'I'll be home in a few more days. That's a promise.'

Reluctantly, he closed the call, leaving a yearning for home. To break his solemn mood, he rang Christie. After his reassurances over their safety, she then blanked his suggestion of hooking up in London, producing an awkward silence.

Mortified, Bran felt himself redden as he spoke.

'I have so much to explain.'

Christie's turn to flush.

So do I, my love.

'Sorry... of course, I guess I'm still a little overawed...'

As the awkwardness eased, they chatted about anything other than the meeting. Twenty minutes later, after exchanging blown kisses, they closed the call.

With her eyes still staring at her mobile, Christie suffered an uncomfortable relief, having dodged questions about her evasive manner.

I just hope my eventual confessional does not push him over the top.

Bran had remained in thought.

Christie is holding something back. I could look into her mind, but it wouldn't be ethical. Therefore, I must await her explanation.

Fifty-one

With Scarth just a few days away, Bran relaxed as he lay on his bed to digress.

The period I dreaded is over, but sadly, I fear further violence is inevitable. By remaining in the physical world, I learned the human doesn't hold a monopoly on the aura. And absolutely, the final sequence of our death and the existence of the soul is unnerving. But how does the soul enter the physical being, be it human, animal, or plant?

Interrupting his thoughts, a light knock at the door preceded Walt entering the room. They embraced for a few moments before Walt initiated the conversation.

'His behaviour was typical... a mixture of sadness and discovery, exactly as he lived his life. Regrettably, he never recovered from the pain of his wife's death!'

Bran frowned.

I owe Walter the truth.

'Please relax, so I may bring you up to date. This will take but a second, but your mind will process the information as a genuine memory.'

Before Walt could reply, Bran transferred parts of his discoveries into his mind. Moments passed before Walt wept openly, before he gathered himself sufficiently to talk.

'You have solved questions that have sat on every human's lip since we evolved.' Firmly clasping his head with both hands, his expression was almost pleading. 'Are you convinced the mass of Nemkis is the same as the soul?'

Bran's thoughts recalled the interaction between Josh and Duke, then to the fact that Nemkis harvests the dreaming mind. In that moment, he became steely eyed.

'The soul *is* the Nemkis, and every living organism connects to it.'

Walt sensed an uncomfortable excitement rise in his gut as he spoke.

'But again, the question raises its head! In death, does the soul remain singular, or is it absorbed to become part of the Nemkis?'

Bran's expression remained concentrated as his mind flipped into overdrive, recalling the exact moment Arlo's soul released from its surrounding aura to merge into Nemkis.

'Arlo's euphoric expression depicted a realisation he was to become unshackled from the restraints of his physical existence.' He paused as his thoughts formed a sentence that would affect both. 'The returning soul appears to gain comfort, on the realisation of being absorbed back into Nemkis. Of course, having experienced this contentment, I understand why. But I speak with caution, for we cannot truly understand until death itself reveals the definitive answer.'

Walt shivered.

'My god, we sleep to process energy for Nemkis.'

Both gave thought to the statement before Bran replied.

'My first reaction upon discovering that Nemkis farmed us was that it reduced our value in this world. I am now of the opinion that the importance of our existence is magnified by the fact that the soul shapes the structure of the Nemkis.'

Walt was in such disbelief that he involuntarily shook his head.

'This implies a creator and immortality, its incomprehensible that this is now fact.'

Bran pondered. 'A god? Unlikely, as that infers a physical shape or being. I prefer *supreme intelligence* of which its composition or presence we cannot yet comprehend.'

'Your *worm theory* comes to mind.'

'True... However, there is, without question, a form of immortality gained on the soul's return. What that form is, again, I feel only death can produce the definite answer?'

Walt turned to look directly at Bran.

'I'm bloody scared, almost too scared to believe this is now fact?'

Before replying, Bran offered Walt a tumbler of water, which was gratefully excepted.

'When my psyche is based on my human reaction, I too become edgy, but as a Paragon, I hold no fear, as the soul is remarkable.'

Bran now expanded on the soul and aura, from Loki, Duke and again the connection he witnessed between the family and the consultant. Walt felt like a little boy who had just discovered wizards existed.

'I have always believed that animals may have a more profound relationship with nature than humans do, and now we can explain the reasoning behind it.' He paused briefly. 'It was the Apache belief that when two people fell in love, their souls would entwine, and each person would receive a tiny part of the other person's soul. Sadly, when your love dies, a piece of you dies also, and that is why the loss is so painful. They also believe that a fragment of them stays with you and so they can still see the world through your eyes. God damn, how close is that to the reality we now understand?'

Emotionally warmed by the statement, Bran sighed. 'Beautiful explanation.'

Both spent a moment's reflection before Walt changed the subject.

'With being able to see the aura, do you react to the person's mood?'

'Definitely, although this information can be a negative.'

'Then perhaps that's why we don't possess this sense?'

'Possibly. Arlo and I discussed a similar topic which formed the opinion that intelligence was the apex of the sensory world. It has definitely cemented our grip on this planet.'

'But at what cost?' replied Walt solemnly.

'An accurate statement, for sure!'

Walt's expression turned serious. 'How do you react when you see a *Grey?*'

Bran, yet again, thought for a moment.

'My abilities to process this information has become natural. For instance, when encountering aggression, my sub-conscious dictates the outcome, leaving me emotionally dormant. Normal encounters pass without judgement or incident. For certain, the darker the tone, the more intense the evil, as is my reaction.'

'When will your sensory development end?'

'Of that I am uncertain, especially if my pineal gland continues its growth.'

'And yes, another mystery solved, something so simple. Ah, my apologies for being a little insensitive.'

Bran chuckled. 'No need. Knowledge often claims sacrifice.'

'I just don't know how you cope.'

'I was born to cope... Would it help if you experienced the Nemkis in a dream?'

Walt shivered. 'I think not at this point. I'm no coward but...'

Bran placed his hands on Walt's shoulders. 'I understand.'

'Thank you. Now our conversation must return to the normal world.' He paused before blurting out a sentence few would ever hear. 'Arlo has bequeathed your family five hundred million sterling!'

For a Paragon, the subconscious world holds more importance than material possessions. However, I will display the gratitude that should match such generosity.

'Really? Half a billion pounds? Astounding.' A smile warmed his expression as he pictured his parents. 'Mum will pamper our house in a manner suited for a Royal visit and dad – well he will finally get his jetty and boat to match!'

Walt laughed aloud. 'You don't think they will up-sticks?'

'No, not a chance, holidays perhaps, treating family and friends, yes, but Scarth is where we belong – especially now.'

The ring tone of a mobile interrupted Bran. The screen gave the name *Pres.* Bran smiled.

Even with all that's happened, having the president's personal number on my mobile is surreal.

'Mr President...' he said as he placed the phone on loudspeaker.

The president took a moment before speaking, leaving Bran expecting a problem.

'Our intelligence is reporting activity by a breakaway cell from the so-called Columnae. Their *younger level* has become fractious over the incarceration of their senior board members. I am arranging for you to be moved to safe quarters whilst we monitor the issue.'

Bran closed his eyes for a moment before speaking.

Will they never learn?

'With respect – my safety is not your concern, but please, may I ask since your dream, do you still hold a clear memory regarding your experience of Nemkis?'

The president, surprised by the side-tracked question, baulked.

'I cannot stop thinking about the emotional plane I experienced. Nothing on this planet can come close to that level of serenity.'

'Then, for now, I ask you to hold all retaliation until I have spoken to Beneventi.'

The president's tone highlighted his concern.

'This escalation is a major threat to which we must retaliate before they act.'

Bran's voice changed to a firmness that unsettled all.

'With respect, history dictates that even with preventative measures, at some stage a persistent aggressor will eventually process a successful attack. This being true, my subsequent retaliation will cause the instantaneous death of all involved. And if within the public domain, explaining that event would, without doubt, be beyond even this government's manipulation! Please, I intend to draw Beneventi into a dream in the hope I can affect his persona for the better. Which is why I asked you the question regarding how you are affected. I could force his change, but that won't work long term. So, if I can motivate Beneventi naturally to our cause, we take the first step forward...'

Bran's words bit deep. As a result, within two hours, he was alone in a room inside Langley, seated opposite a decidedly edgy Beneventi. His first thought was how dark his aura appeared.

'Mr Beneventi, please relax, I mean you no harm...'

Beneventi shrugged. 'Unless I attempt any level of violence towards you.'

Bran ignored the terse reply. 'May I call you Antonio?'

Another shrug from Beneventi.

'Thank you. Now... historically your family's interaction against the ¥ dates back centuries, resulting in deaths on either side. Your hatred is obvious and has fuelled your own violent *forays* against the ¥. My point being, rooted deep in your mind, I am your enemy, and you wish me dead. Fair assessment?'

'Your people eliminated us with the same hatred?'

'No... we responded out of necessity, nothing more. I have no desire for active violence – none. Even my human experiences of physical combat were born from retaliation.'

Beneventi's expression revealed an absolute distaste for Bran's comment.

'I witnessed your *lack of desire* in that meeting...' Shaking slightly, he barked out his next sentence. 'What do you want from me?'

Bran remained calmed. 'Hope! I hope you will realise I am not your enemy. I hope you understand we are the only people that can end this historical bloodshed peacefully.'

'Peacefully!' Beneventi laughed aloud. 'You mean if I don't comply, you'll erase me from the planet like the others?'

Bran quelled his rising frustration. 'Money and power are your veritable god. I'm correct that you asked for financial reward to kill me.'

'Reward for destroying your sworn enemy is not a sin.'

'Then tell me, do you worry about your wife and family? Are you concerned when your young daughters venture beyond the protective bubble you provide?'

'Irrelevant. Every father holds concerns regarding his family?'

'Then if you had a choice of unlimited wealth or an absolute guarantee that your family's entire life enjoyed unbridled happiness in complete safety... your pick?'

'No one can guarantee that.'

'The path would become easier if we eliminated evil.'

'By killing those who stand against you...'

'By understanding the *true* meaning of life.'

'True being what you promote?' snapped Beneventi.

'No – true being the truth! Look, all religions claim they worship the one *true* god, based on historical writings and faith. What if I could *show* you the facts behind death?'

Beneventi's expression showed concern.

'I've witnessed your mind control. Signor Russo's death, as an example, proves you can concoct to suit... it was hideous! How can I be certain your objectives are not to mislead?'

Bran acknowledged the fact with a compassionate nod.

'Antonio, I have no intentions of deceit. I just need you to understand why I am attempting to forge a peaceful solution. How can I gain your trust?'

Beneventi then raised the question many would have asked.

'You say you now understand death itself?'

'Unequivocally, yes.'

'Then Paragon, are you afraid to die?'

Slightly ruffled by the question, Bran stalled before answering.

'As a Paragon... I am compelled to say no...! As humans, we all have an innate fear of the unknown, and I'm not an exception to that. Incidentally, this fear has been the foundation of religion throughout history.

'Are you confirming that the Christian God is fact?'

Bran stepped towards the only window in the room which, despite having a heavy metal grill in place, allowed an external view. Beneventi tensed slightly at his sudden silence. Moments later, Bran began a recital from the depths of his memory, which acted like a redemption.

'When Einstein gave lectures at U.S. universities, the recurring question that students asked most was: Do you believe in God? And he always answered: I believe in the God of Spinoza. Baruch de Spinoza was a Dutch philosopher considered one of the great rationalists of 17th century philosophy, along with Descartes. This is my adaption of the words of Spinoza.'

A God would say. Stop praying. I want you to go out and enjoy your life. I want you to sing, have fun and enjoy everything I have made for you. Stop entering those dark, cold temples that you built yourself, pronouncing they are my house. My house is the mountains, the woods, rivers, lakes, and beaches. That is where I live and where I express my love for you. Stop blaming me for your miserable life; I never told you that you were sinners. So do not blame me for everything they made you believe. Stop reading alleged sacred scriptures that have nothing to do with me. If you cannot read me in a sunrise, in a landscape, in the look of your friends, in your children's eyes... you will most definitely not find me in a book! Stop being so scared of me. I do not judge or criticise, nor get angry or bothered. I am pure love. I filled you with passions, limitations, pleasures, feelings, needs, inconsistencies... free will. Do not hold fear, for I cannot punish you for being pure in the way I made you. All I ask is that you enjoy your life, and that absolute purity is your guide. Your life is the only thing here and now, and it is all you need. I will not tell you if there is anything after this life, but I can give you a tip. Live life as if there is nothing thereafter. Live it as if this is your only chance to enjoy, to love, to exist. So, if there is nothing after, then you will have enjoyed the opportunity. Stop believing in me; believing is assuming, guessing, imagining. I do not want you to believe in me. I want you to believe in you. I want you to feel purity when you kiss your beloved, when you tuck in your little child, when you stroke your dog, when you bathe in the sea. Stop praising me. What kind of egomaniac God do you think I am? I am bored being praised. I am tired of being thanked. If you are feeling grateful, prove it by taking care of yourself, your health, your relationships, and nature. Express your joy! That is the way to praise me. Stop complicating things and repeating as a parakeet what you have been taught about me. What do you need more miracles for? The only thing for sure is that you are here, that you are alive, that this world is full of wonders.

His mind surmised.

Every religion has similarities when explaining our existence. Afterlife, the soul, heaven, each providing hope and faith. Therefore, instead of denouncing religion, I must attempt to integrate belief with fact and eradicate the influence of the evil.

Bran clapped, causing Beneventi to flinch. With an expression of sheer joy, he turned to Beneventi, who appeared almost hypnotised.

'Antonio!'

Beneventi remained silent as Bran spoke.

'I do not promote a God. But I seek to cleanse religion to where it serves people, not dominate them.'

'How?' said Beneventi, confused.

'Words are not enough. Please, allow me to show you?'

Beneventi sighed heavily. 'What choice do I have?' he said in a tone that depicted compliance, relaxing Bran.

'A choice made from the heart; a choice born from the love of your family.'

Gently kissing the silver cross hung around his neck, Beneventi spoke aloud in Italian.

My God, if this boy is to kill me, please, as a reward for my sacrifice, keep my family safe.

'Very well, do what you have to.'

Not revealing his fluency in Italian, Bran replied softly.

'Thank you for your trust. Now, in the following moments, the visions will appear as real as life itself, causing confusion and panic in your brain. You must stay focused on my words as I guide you.'

Beneventi, fearless during violent confrontation, looked petrified.

'Just do it and be quick.'

With closed eyes, Bran pulled Beneventi into a dream set at the edge of a Sentinel. Now staring at his grey spectre, the sheer horror caused him to lapse into shock. Bran spoke softly.

'Antonio, your mind is now in trauma, for we are inside my dream. I will awaken you for a moment, enough for you to regain your composure before we return.'

Once awake, Beneventi looked around frantically, and spoke with a terror in his voice.

'I don't wish to die in that place. Kill me now.'

'Antonio, trust me – no harm will befall you and when we next return, I will have blessed you with an experience you'll never forget.'

Jolted back in front of the Sentinel, Beneventi screamed.

'No, you're the Devil... I...'

His journey through the tunnel began, as did his expected hysteria. As Bran needed to hammer home the fate of evil, Beneventi would endure the extinction of the grey souls for an extended period. On passing through the lightfall, he experienced death's call, right to the very edge, bringing his mind to the fringe of insanity before being drawn into Nemkis. At that moment, Beneventi experienced insanity, then purity, within an incalculable time scale. With his soul succumbing to the majesty and splendour, a stream of joyous tears flowed.

Minutes later, hopeful about the outcome, Bran set to close the dream.

Now we shall see if the wonder of the Nemkis can truly inspire.

Upon waking, Beneventi spoke incoherently and began pacing about the room, slapping his face. Moments later, he charged at the wall with a sickening thud.

Concerned, Bran called out.

'Antonio, you have experienced a vision of what death brings, nothing more.'

Sobbing and dribbling from his mouth, Beneventi slipped down the wall and began crawling on his hands and knees towards Bran.

Bran's reaction was to call out the name of Beneventi's youngest daughter.

'Gianna needs you!'

Beneventi froze.

'GIANNA needs her father back home... NOW!'

The acid tone cut through Beneventi's scrambled mind, releasing him from the confusion.

'Desperately fighting his mental chaos, he stuttered an answer.'

'Is my daughter safe?'

Surprised at the intensity of his own relief, Bran answered passively.

'Yes, Antonio, perfectly, I just needed to deflect your confusion. Please look at your watch.'

With a body language depicting absolute bewilderment at the command, Beneventi glanced at his watch.

Bran waited.

Completely mystified, Beneventi raised from his knees to look at his surroundings.

'Nine hours, impossible? Madness, it was just minutes... How can this be?' Beneventi's confusion continued. 'That was no dream. No, it's simply not possible.'

Bran moved closer and whispered. 'Take your time to recall everything you experienced.'

Involuntary shaking, Beneventi closed his eyes. Thoughts turned to fear, then joy as the experience re-played.

'That world, its vibrant spectacle. How can it evoke such euphoria? Please tell me that is heaven?'

Bran blew out his cheeks. 'Only the pure soul can experience this utopia, to which I named Nemkis.'

Beneventi wanted to ask a thousand questions, but he settled back to recall his memory. Bran waited.

Five minutes passed before Beneventi spoke. 'The death tunnel that extinguished those dark spirits. Is that hell?'

'No, hell, as you understand, does not exist. You witnessed grey souls attempting entry to the purity of the Nemkis; they cannot. Total extinction is the end for those who choose an evil life. Nothing, no forgiveness, no trace.'

Beneventi paused for a few seconds.

'Paragon, what do I have to do to ensure my family becomes accepted into this *heaven,* your Nemkis?'

Bran looked deep into the eyes of Beneventi and recognised his word was true. Fully understanding this was the first step for peace between the ¥ and the church, Bran spoke honestly.

'Trust me!'

Beneventi moved to face Bran directly, who did not flinch.

'I've never trusted a living soul since I can remember. Tell me to my face, the heaven is real.'

'Even if you cannot access it?'

'I do not care about my fate, just my family. Is it reality?'

'Yes, Antonio, a place of true harmony. The responsibility of our existence is to maintain the purity of the soul as those that choose an evil life prevent its return.'

With tears in his eyes, Beneventi spoke.

'Those men you *erased*, were their ghosts real or a manipulation of our minds?'

'What you saw was a fact. The Poltergeist exists!'

After swallowing, Beneventi took a few deep breaths to calm a racing mind.

'I believe in this heaven because nothing on this planet could invoke the unrivalled serenity I experienced. Paragon, you watched me dribble and weep like a baby after I witnessed a wonderment that surpasses everything I have coveted. Do not betray my trust.'

No question, Beneventi's character had become affected, but that his aura remained grey, disappointed Bran.

The darkness within this man must have distorted his soul beyond forgiveness... then there is a line drawn!

'Antonio, betrayal is not part of my character; you have my word.'

'Then for my family. How can I help?'

Electrified with emotion, Bran cut to the chase.

'The younger element of the Columnae is instigating an attack in response to the incarceration of your board. I do not seek conflict and death, so I would appreciate your influence. Once nullified, we can share my experiences in the hope of alignment with the same cause.'

Beneventi paused for a few moments before his reply.

'My influence over the Columnae has to be passive... would be my understanding?'

Nodding, Bran replied softly.

'Of course, fighting violence with violence has been mankind's solution since time began preventing any possibilities of peace – this continued escalation must change.'

Beneventi clutched his head, sighed, then looked at Bran with an expression that appeared docile.

'This... *power* you hold. Are you not tempted to use it and force your issues?'

'I could link to every white soul, then erase the evil in the blink of an eye. However, this would be a false, temporary gain, for evil would rise again. I require people who believe, for it is those willing who secure triumphs – without honesty and truth, I will fail.'

'Have you all the answers to our existence?'

'Some, but as yet, not all.'

Beneventi closed his eyes and again spoke in Italian.

'Then, for the future of my family, I will stand with my sworn enemy to find this utopia.'

Bran replied in the exact dialect.

'Antonio, your inner love for your family is the key to our success. Thank you for this sacrifice.'

Beneventi shook his head in astonishment, then held out his hand.

'Then shake my Paragon brother. I trust you with my family's future... do not let me down, for then I will happily die trying to find a solution to erase you!'

Bran held off the shake.

'Antonio, had you been aware of the Nemkis from a young age? What path would you have chosen?'

Beneventi paused in thought before exhaling.

'I'm extremely wealthy, indulged in many types of vice, drugs, women, violence and, of course, power. But Paragon, nothing compares to the intensity I felt in your Nemkis.' Pausing again for a few seconds, he continued. 'I would, without question, devote my life to attaining the purity required to return to that *heaven*!'

Bran felt a shiver pass through his body at Beneventi's statement.

'Your words inspire Antonio. Truly, there is hope. I am honoured to shake your hand.'

Neither man had expected to feel such comfort from the outcome. For Bran, he had taken a gigantic step, whereas Beneventi, for the first time in his life, experienced an unbridled calm.

Within the hour, he had restored order within the youthful ranks of the Columnae. One glitch caused him concern.

'A small section remains against the alliance; at this moment they have gone offline. I have people tasked to find them.'

Bran frowned. 'Thank you for your honesty. This issue will not devalue our trust.'

An obvious relief flushed over Beneventi. 'May we speak with the detained members? Perhaps then I can lay the seeds to this pact.'

'Yes, of course, our first step.'

The arrangements would be prompt.

Now alongside Beneventi and Walt, Bran talked openly to the Columnae in which some wept, whilst others prayed. All favoured the prospect of a new beginning, and a lasting peace with the Paragon. Furthermore, no one would break the code of silence requested, fear being the major contribution. A historic meeting between Bran, the ¥ and various religions had now become a possibility.

With the meeting completed, a convoy drove Bran, Walt and Beneventi from Langley to a ranch set in over one thousand acres, for discussions with the president. During their journey, Beneventi broke the silence.

'We must address the problem of the *initiate* and their Awakening.'

Walt's sharp intake of air showed genuine concern, causing Bran to recall Arlo's leather-bound book.

I would know when to read his chapters.

'Tomorrow we will address this issue.'

Bran's tone was firm enough to close the conversation.

On arrival at the ranch, Bran walked directly to his room, leaving Walt and Beneventi to greet the president, who, although unsettled by Bran's discourteous retirement, did not suggest they disturb him.

After unpacking his case, Bran placed the leather-bound book on the bed. Oddly, it appeared to taunt him. With gritted teeth, he thumbed his way to the last chapters.

Fifty-two

Truth comes with a price.
Nature produced you without sensory loss, and the ability to adapt to the advances gifted. To ensure you trod your own path, I withheld certain information, but now I must address the issues of the Awakening.

During the Paragon's evolution, thousands of humans, known to us as the "initiate" possessed a singular level of sensory advancement. Thankfully, they have zero awareness or control over the sub-conscious actions required to awaken its power. This, we now understand, as the fault in nature as she progressed towards perfection. If I may make a comparison, there are thousands of people who, given the opportunity, would become an elite professional, but their life path does not provide the key to unlocking their natural talent. Wide scale understanding of the Paragon would instigate an Awakening of those who unknowingly inhibit their gift. Imagine if one of the "grey" held the Paragon's destructive capabilities?

Of course, those of the white will also unlock their inner sense and so will align against the grey, creating a conflict set within the sub-conscious world currently not accessible. This will have a catastrophic effect on normal humanity, unable to defend itself against a growing army of sub-conscious manipulators.

With two pages remaining, Bran slammed the book closed. Sighing deeply, he shut his eyes to find himself on the Nemkis facing the vision of a smiling William Cranson! Unperturbed, Bran relaxed as William began the dialogue!

"Our ancestors bow to your achievements; may it continue, but never forget the suffering our kind have endured to reach this point. To succeed you need just one thought, the dimensions of time."

The image filtered away, leaving Bran extremely agitated. Several hours passed before he summarised.

Every living organism possesses a soul that is extracted from the Nemkis and housed within a physical form, thus producing what we perceive as life. These life forms, whose creation is attributed to a superior intelligence, have a significant impact on the continuation and survival of the Nemkis. It appears that this intelligence is developing a fix to address the shortcomings in its human physical blueprint. Our preference for the conscious dimension with its material temptations, rather than the sub-conscious state, is a defect of our evolution. Consequently, the gradual destruction of nature and the entire system of life would be the end result.

Bran took a breath.

But this is where it gets intriguing! Evolution requires one element above all others... time. In terms of human timescale, the process of fixing this has taken centuries to complete. While this moment may seem significant to us, for Nemkis, it is nothing more than a passing moment. Life is progressing towards the purity it was meant to have. It may take a hundred or several hundred years in human terms, but eventually, Nemkis will cleanse all organisms. Questions about the existence of time variants in different life spans have always been present.

Taking the Ephemeral Mayflies as a case study, one could question whether their perception of time is slower than ours, given that their entire life cycle lasts only twenty-four hours in the human calendar. In light of this, humans may have overestimated their value to some extent. The resolution is progressing efficiently in Nemkis' timescale, but from our perspective, it appears to be an endless process.

Another deep breath.

We are just a microscopic component of something remarkable. But perhaps, as with the worker ant, without their contribution, the queen cannot survive. Timescale is the major barrier to our understanding of life, as we cannot operate within the same time dimension as Nemkis.

Now quivering at his next thought, he continued.

Perhaps the end game is a move to a sub-conscious existence? Material gain in the physical world stimulates evil... therefore, defaulting to a sub-conscious existence eliminates that trait, enhancing the production of the pure soul!

Another pause.

Are we simply operating in the wrong dimension?

Once again Bran mused over the possibility, to which he found difficult to conclude.

I hope to evolve to understand this hypothesis, but as I once considered, the worm effect may come into play. This revelation changes my thinking. It isn't about answers, it's about a contribution, my contribution! The Nemkis, do I believe it is a deity? It may well be, but most definitely not in a humanoid form.

The enormity of the revelations sunk in.

The message regarding the dimensions of time has affected all theories. This entire experience has never been about my questions and answers. It is simply the inevitability of evolution. As for the Awakening, my sub-conscious will eliminate any who threaten the pure advancement of mankind. Thus, I am the avenging angel sent by Nemkis.

Finally, recognising his true meaning forged a feeling of acceptance.

'Thank you William, for guiding my path. I will not let our ancestor's brave sacrifices be for nothing.'

He sighed.

I need to dream with my parents.

Bran closed his eyes.

Fifty-three

Inside Bran's created dream, based in the family home, both Ross and Isla took a moment before accepting the state of their situation.

Ross, smiling, spoke.

'Even though I know this is a dream, I still can't comprehend it.'

Isla did not care. The family had reunited, and it felt real.

'Please tell me that the problems with that gland have cleared.'

'Well, the drain has ended my headaches and so far all seems good.'

'Just promise you will abide by what those doctors advise.'

'I will. Now for a change, some good news.' Grinning, he continued. 'According to Walter, Arlo has left our family enough money to fix the jetty and buy dad a new boat.'

Both parents looked shocked. 'Really? That's so thoughtful, but Arlo was always of that nature,' said Isla. 'My word, we will miss him.'

That his parents did not ask how much made him smile.

Ah well in for a penny!

'Yes, he left us half a billion sterling!'

Both Isla and Ross baulked.

'Say again,' stuttered Ross.

'Arlo has bequeathed five hundred million pounds to our family.'

As the shock of the statement washed over his parents, he laughed.

Isla moved directly to the scotch, sank a full glass, then passed one to Ross. Still laughing, Bran held his hand up.

'This is a dream; therefore, we can get drunk and wake up sober.'

Sometime later, Ross and Isla woke, and for a few moments dealt with the confusion before the sat phone rang out.

'Dad – yes, all that happened in the dream is true... your millionaires... enjoy, and I'll see you soon. Love you both.'

Bran placed the phone down.

Mum, dad, enjoy the moment, for the future is about to get decidedly rocky.

Ross looked to Isla. 'That was our Bran, last night's dream was true, meaning he has recovered, and we have become millionaires.'

Both sank back into their pillows.

After a Skype call with his wife and family, Antonio Beneventi lay in his room, deep in thought. His wife had broken down in tears as he announced to changing his way of life. Her instinct suggested that something had happened, but she wouldn't ask why. The call ended on an emotional high that neither had experienced before.

Beneventi poured a wine.

I never wish to erase the memory of this Nemkis. No matter what it takes, I will fight hard to ensure my family remains pure and so when time dictates, they will succumb to the wonder.

Fifty-four

Bran's thoughts had fixated on the soul, and, albeit randomly, he wished to travel to the nearest town, where he would study people going about their day. After tapping Google on his mobile, he hit maps, then typed in *McDonalds*. As the screen processed his search, he laughed aloud as it listed an address of 601 Aberdeen Road.

The time was now 8 A.M. After several calls and various attempts to dissuade him; he was sitting in a Ford pickup truck with Josh at the wheel.

'Maccies breakie is my fancy – yours?'

A broad smile spread across Josh's face. 'I've eaten thanks, diet in place... but I'll take a coffee.'

'I've no cash.' shrugged Bran.

Josh chuckled. 'I'll bang it on the expense account.' In his rear mirror, several black Chevrolets were in close follow. 'We have a protection team in place.'

Bran winked. 'Truthfully, it makes sense, as all my life I've jumped into situations to save others. Just now, my bravado may generate complications we do not require.'

Josh gave an emphatic shake of his head. 'That's for sure!'

Twenty minutes later, they found themselves seated on a bench and eating food. Joss's nostrils had betrayed his diet in the guise of a whopper.

'My apologies if I say little - I'm just observing people,' said Bran.

'Hell, that's what my wife does.' Josh replied, blowing at his steaming coffee.

Bran failed to reply, having become engrained in his study.

A slight breeze gave chase to drivers rushing their day. Pedestrians strode with earphones plugged tightly, or eyes focused on their mobile. The sound of birds, whilst relaxing, differed in tone to the normal chirp of his winged chums. A dog barked at another, delivering a sound that twisted the knife on home thoughts.

Remaining quiet while observing a family eating their meal on a wooden bench in the forecourt, he relaxed.

The laughter shared between the father and his children is pure and radiates, even in this morning sunlight, wonderful.

Two courting teenagers sharing a burger caught his gaze as their aura entwined. Bran turned to Josh.

'Without a care in the world.'

After wiping his mouth with a serviette, Josh mocked. 'It won't last.'

'That's a little harsh.'

'Sure, but hell man women are...'

The piercing metallic impact of a collision shattered the conversation as a Buick van jumped a red light, then slammed into the driver's side of an aging Toyota Corolla. The sickening sound of the crash froze everybody nearby as their brains processed the violent impact. Not so for Josh, who reacted and ran towards the scene. On his arrival, the female driver of the Toyota, trapped in the mangled wreckage, had drifted into unconsciousness. Josh's stomach churned over as she showed to be pregnant. The Buick's driver's voice, muffled by the air bag, gave notice that he had minimal injuries but appeared intoxicated. Bran and others now reached the carnage. One lady, claiming to be a nurse, stirred through the broken front windshield of the Toyota.

'My god, this woman has a femoral bleed from her leg. We need to get her out quickly.'

Attempting to open the passenger side door, Josh grunted as it held tight. Two other men joined the effort; moments later, all fell back as the door released. Josh grimaced, seeing the impact had folded part of the seat over her leg, causing a compound fracture. No question, without heavy equipment, it would be impossible to release her. In vain hope, Josh took off his belt and attempted to attach a tourniquet. Frustratingly, he could not wrap the belt above the gaping wound, which continued to bleed profusely.

'Bran, get the crowbar from my truck!'

As Bran bolted, he was relieved to hear sirens in the distance. After searching feverously, he found the bar, dashed back, and handed it to Josh, at which point the woman regained consciousness. With eyes struggling to focus, she mouthed the words *save my baby* before passing out.

Carefully forcing the bar into a gap in the metal carnage, Josh heaved.

Nothing moved.

With time passing, the blood loss was draining her life force. Moral raised as an ambulance screeched to a halt, dispatching rushing paramedics. Josh called out the information regarding the bleed.

Bran, for all his sensory advancement, felt inadequate. Now motionless, he shuddered as he heard the female medic say they were losing her. Quickly moving to the bench, he sat, then closed his eyes. Although still concerned for the woman, Josh moved alongside him without speaking a word.

The female paramedic shook her head. 'How is this lady showing life signs despite pumping out?'

Her male colleague replied in an uneasy tone. 'No idea, just get the IV in!'

Moments earlier, facing the woman directly in front of the light-fall portal, Bran shuddered as he realised her spectre had enwrapped her child. Guided by his sub-conscious, his hands eased forward, showing for her to link hands. As they connected, three became one...

The fire service arrived, deployed the hydraulic cutting equipment, and released the woman within minutes. With the intravenous, now in place, a batch of O negative began its flow.

'This cannot work?' said the first paramedic.

'Be a miracle.' replied the second.

Inside the Sentinel, Bran's emotional wave peaked as the female's spectre withdrew from their embrace to return mother and child to their physical form. At that moment, her frantic gasp for air shocked the paramedic team, who were preparing a second batch of blood.

The complications of life. Her waters broke! Blue lights were in order.

Seventy minutes later, a six-pound, four-ounce healthy baby girl arrived by a caesarean section. The medical team clapped the unconscious mother, who had actually *died* back in the wrecked vehicle.

On Bran's insistence, they had followed the ambulance whilst he made calls to ensure they placed the lady in private care. Josh was certain that something extraordinary had happened, but stalled his questions.

Emotionally charged, Bran recalled the encounter.

To save a life is beyond all expectations. I feel cleansed! Now I have to find the answer I have been seeking.

On their arrival, he dialled the president and asked for *all level access* to the hospital, which was arranged without question.

Call closed; Bran turned to Josh.

'Thank you for your silence. Today I have experienced a genuine wonder, a wonder that requires investigation.'

Josh's chest raised as he took a deep breath. 'Somehow you saved that lady's life.'

After nodding his acceptance, Bran's reply became tinged with emotion. 'It's a far nicer feeling than killing. I promise an explanation when I have one.'

Josh's face radiated respect.

Ten minutes later, a well-dressed man named Collins approached the two and escorted them to a private room. After discussions, Collins issued "*greens*" to Bran and agreed to accompany him as required.

Some six hours later, he escorted Bran to witness a birth. As they entered the theatre, not one person spoke or acknowledged their presence, to which he was grateful. Almost trancelike, Bran watched a natural delivery by a mother of the white aura. The mother, sucking on gas and air, was most definitely oblivious to his concentrated gaze.

Thirty minutes passed before the baby's head appeared. Halfway out, Bran's heart rate climbed as the child appeared to be encased in a white aura. With one final push, a baby girl entered the world to be placed into mother's arms. Like the female he witnessed in the Sentinel; the mother's aura enshrouded the baby. Once the midwife set to cut the umbilical cord, Bran tensed in anticipation. With a firm snip, the steel scissors cut the cord, causing the bright shroud surrounding the two to split, leaving a six-pound, ten-ounce baby girl encased inside her own aura. Bran, bewildered, stared in absolute awe. The mother, recovering from the effort, now hugged her child as only a new mother can, resulting in an intermingling of the brightest aura he had ever witnessed.

Bran stepped back.

The power of a mother's bond explained, but does the mother gift the soul...?

A fearful thought prompted him to leave the room, resulting in him dashing along the corridor, frantically looking through windows, closely tagged by Collins. Within a few minutes, he lay sight to a pregnant female of the grey. Visibly anxious, he spoke to Collins.

'Sir, I must push your patience; I need to stay until this female gives birth.'

The wait would be three hours.

Logically, the separation makes absolute sense and reinforces the fact that all souls connect. But now I must wait to see if grey gives birth to grey...

Next to Bran's room, a Mrs Boyd, aged eighty-three, having had an *open and shut* operation for stomach cancer, was being consoled by her husband. As Bran passed by the open door, he noticed a bright aura had enveloped both. Turning to Collins, he spoke.

'Was her operation a success?'

'Sadly not, two days ago, they opened her up to find the cancer was widespread and inoperable. I'm afraid her passing will be within the week. Mr Boyd had not left her side since she returned from theatre, bless him.'

Yet the couple are displaying so much comfort from being together, such is the power of love and devotion.

Bran smiled at the gentleman as he glanced over. Smiling back, he then returned to his vigil of holding his wife's hand. Bran stepped into his own room, feeling quite solemn.

They are soon to be apart; knowing they will both return to a harmony beyond their imagination offers a comfort to my own feelings over their current predicament. At such an old age and still of the white, they have truly earned that journey.

Josh had checked on the female involved in the crash several times. With having seen blood loss in its severest form, and that she claimed to be saved by a guardian angel, the miracle became verified.

The impossible keeps happening around this boy, but this is different. My god, I am blessed to be part of this evolution.

Josh's thoughts ended as Bran entered their room. Standing, he spoke.

'Mother and baby daughter are fine... she's awake and claiming an angel saved her life in heaven.'

'Then I need to visit her,' said Bran.

Josh, nodding a smiling acceptance, sat back down as Bran walked from the room. Another glance at Mr Boyd gave him heart.

Five minutes later Bran knocked, then entered the private room of Mrs Chloe Shane and her daughter Joey.

Shane, with one hand draped on her daughter's side cot, and her right leg in traction, squinted in faint recognition. Neither spoke as Bran, smiling passively, approached her side. Still attempting to recollect if she had previously met this young stranger, Shane broke the silence.

'Why do I believe I know you?'

With a gentle shush, Bran placed his hand on her forearm, resulting in both becoming overwhelmed by the memory of their contact within the Sentinel. Shane clasped Bran's hand and wept.

'It was you... you in heaven? But – but, how?'

Still holding her hand, Bran replied in a whisper. 'Perhaps a miracle as we understand, but in reality, a sequence of possibilities I could manipulate. Please, you need to focus on the wellbeing of your baby and yourself, not on explanations. Forgive me, but I would like to cover your medical costs and deposit monies into your account for baby Joey's future.'

Shane, looking shocked, painfully eased herself upright.

'I don't understand...? Why would you do this?'

Bran moved for a chair and placed it close to Shane's side.

'As the father has withdrawn his support, this is my way of thanking you, for without knowing how, you have helped this miracle occur. Now I promise that once you are fit again and settled, we will meet, and I'll explain today's happenings. But may I ask you not to disclose anything other than you already have?' Bran smiled warmly. 'Do we have a deal?'

Shane blinked several times to check if she was awake.

'Am I going mad?'

'No.' smiled Bran. 'Definitely not. It's just as crazy for me, I promise.'

Shane looked lovingly at her baby. 'My daughter has her own guardian angel... so yes; I will keep our secret – Mr?'

'Boyle – Anthony Boyle.' Turning to baby Joey, he exhaled.

'She's beautiful and yes, you both now have a guardian Angel.' Bran stood up. 'Once I leave, you will question your own sanity. Please trust me – there is an explanation.'

Shane sighed. 'Your visit has saved my sanity, for when I told of my experience to the medical team... they insisted it resulted from the anaesthetic. Mr Boyle, I truly believe in what happened, but may I ask you one question?'

'Of course.'

'Are you God?'

Bran clasped her hand. 'I'm just a man with a gift. A gift that is extremely unique.'

'Ok Mr *not God,* then promise me an explanation sooner rather than later...'

'You have my word.'

Shane looked at baby Joey and pulled the contented smile of a new mother. 'Thank you, from the both of us.'

A hearty bellow from Joey brought reality back into the room. Bran's face crinkled with joy.

'You have mother's work to do.'

Shane had already pulled the cord for help and eased herself closer to the cot. As Bran turned to leave, each nodded at the trust they would both keep.

Fifty-five

Several hours later, walking to the maternity ward induced a surreal moment.

I am about to unravel the definitive answer to the creation of the soul... Bran Cranson from the Isle of Scarth. My word.

As the door opened, a nurse gestured for him to enter. Now gazing at the grey aura surrounding the female about to give birth, he shook his head to defuse the influx of human emotion.

This isn't the time to judge.

Within ten minutes, the birth began, causing Bran to grind his teeth in anticipation. Moments later, a baby boy emerged into the world encased inside his mother's grey soul.

The vision repulsed Bran.

The grey in this form looks truly malevolent. Is a child aligned from birth to become evil?

As the mid wife cut the cord, everything appeared to lapse into slow motion. With his heartbeat rapidly escalating, he watched on as the child separated from mother's life blood. In that instant, the child's grey aura changed to white. A surge of human emotion caused him to rush from the room, then for the first time in many years, he broke down in floods of tears.

I actually witnessed the white aura enter the child.

He froze.

The cleansing of the soul at birth creates hope! But how does this happen?

An overwhelming urge to sleep flushed over him, and so he trudged wearily back to the private room. As he half fell through the door, Josh reacted sharply to prevent him falling.

'I desperately need sleep,' Bran said before passing into unconsciousness.

Josh, calling for help, issued strict orders. Within minutes, two male nurses wheeled a trolly into the room and with Bran asleep laid him carefully on top.

The president, on his way to the ranch, took a call from Josh, who reported his concerns. After lengthy discussions, they decided all they could do was wait.

Fifty-six

What prompted me to fall into Darkvoid? That question is for another day. Regardless, whatever is about to be revealed will be another piece of the jigsaw that is the soul.

Thoughts ended with a gasp as a *sea-mist* formed in the distance. Watching intensely, his heart rate increased as his understanding of the event became clear.

The fourth pillar!

Beneventi gazed out of his window at the view of the ornate grounds, spoilt by an overload of security operatives.

I've spent a lifetime entangled with violent conflict and in doing so, my family has had to endure untold agonies along the way. My sworn enemy could have taken my life at any point, but he sought my help to build a world of peace for future generations. The image I keep of Nemkis does not diminish. Effectively, it has become my ever-burning candle of light. I no longer feel hatred or a desire for violence. Is this God at work or is it as the Paragon claims? Either way, I will spend the rest of my days assisting the boy in whatever way I can.

The sound of a helicopter interrupted his thoughts. As he watched the president and Tess disembark from the flight, a message, together with an image of his family tethered on seats in his own kitchen, would test his new belief.

You are suckling on the devil's teat. Fulfil your pledge or your family will suffer. Any attempts to approach the house and they die. Beneventi – kill the Paragon.

The new Columnae.

The image invoked a hatred from deep within.

My family, I have no choice but to take this step, forgive me...

He wasted no time and immediately searched the suite. When he made his way into the kitchenette, he found a steak knife. Having secured it in his belt, he then took a seat and composed a response.

The Paragon is currently not in situ. On his return, I will complete my promise. The consequences of my family being hurt will be long-reaching, brutal and final.

He delivered the message with a sharp stab at the keyboard. Seconds later, came a reply.

Kill the boy!

Beneventi placed down the phone, felt for the steak knife, then settled down.

Time would drag painfully.

Bran had waited patiently for the bright light to arrive at its predictable destination. He found it captivating that the orb was, in fact, another Sentinel. Moments later, the Sentinel ground to a halt.

Could this be a guard protecting another dimension?

After a few moments, rather like the gearings of a Swiss watch striking twelve, the orbs manoeuvred into four equidistant corner positions, burning precise exits from Darkvoid.

Now gazing vehemently at the *set of four,* the exhilaration became overwhelming.

I wonder about the intelligence behind my journey as this moment has been coming. There appears to have been a sequential order conceived to enhance my ability as a Paragon. And so, the fourth pillar, as my mother foretold, is now in play.

Without fear, he moved into the Sentinel to become puzzled as the grey force failed to appear.

That's rather odd. Perhaps this Sentinel does not 'guard' Nemkis?

Upon nearing the lightfall portal, he noticed a diminutive white sphere about the size of a tennis ball, which seemed to follow him closely. The mere presence of it had a profound impact on him, arousing an unrestrained purity within his own soul. The globe then shimmered before leaving a wispy trail as it disappeared into Darkvoid, leaving Brann overwhelmed. Moments later, other globes formed. As a result, a steady stream of light spread out into the darkness.

When I pass through this portal, I will understand.

After steadying himself, he eased through the lightfall to be confronted by a Nemkis dispersing millions of white globes through an uncountable amount of *Sentinels.* The vision snatched his breath away. Although trying to settle, an intense euphoria flooded his system. The emotion was justified, considering he was witnessing the dispersal of the soul into newly formed organisms on earth. Now forcing himself to rationalise the event, he breathed slowly.

The soul exits via a Sentinel, to become encased within the aura from the light-fall portal before being dispersed into a life form.

The statement instigated an urge to scream, and so he did.

Moments passed before he calmed.

The light-fall portal encases the soul within an aura for its period within a living organism.

The implications of what he had witnessed prompted a shocking explanation to form.

Fact, the soul cannot survive beyond the Nemkis without being encased within the aura.

Once again, Bran paused before finalising his summary.

Nemkis is... alive, a living organism? And that being true, our soul is truly immortal in the spiritual sense.

After forcing his reactions to remain within the Paragon state, he settled to digest the reality of his conclusion.

Even processing this as a Paragon, the word "immortality" has stimulated my nervous system to a feeling of giddiness. Mankind's desire for eternity is now answered. Yet still, I cannot confirm if the soul keeps a physical memory of its earthly life. Mind blowing. That Nemkis is a living organism. Where the hell does this take us?

Feeling truly euphoric, he summarised aloud.

'I'm witnessing an incalculable number of souls exiting Nemkis to disperse into new organisms born on earth. The very essence of Nemkis, enclosed inside a protective aura, forms the soul within this living organism. This organism, during its physical existence, reproduces the *soul* for the growth and continuation of the Nemkis. That life begins pure confirms that evil is a defect in the physical being.' Pausing for a moment, he sighed. 'I am the first to uncover this phenomenon.'

But again, as I reach a pinnacle, it then presents more questions, questions that delve deeper. My human instinct has a desire, no, a demand, to understand if the returning soul keeps a blueprint of its physical life.

Another flash of inspiration flickered across his mind.

Reincarnation often suggests a historical memory lodged into the soul. Questions, ever questions, but for now I must take time and simply gaze into the wonderment.

Watching millions of emissions releasing into unknown life forms cemented his theory that all are of the same soul.

Discovery since my passing through Mortis Lux has been easier than I expected, but clearly, this is down to my sensory ability. Looking ahead, as suggested, the issues linked to disclosure will become problematic, along with a fear of the existence of the Paragon. Time, as always, will become the controlling factor in our success. With a return to consciousness, I need to experience my human reaction to completing the circle of life for the soul.

Sometime later, he returned to his conscious self. Hardly daring to open his eyes, he gasped heavily as his human emotions reacted, producing an adrenaline rush above anything else he had experienced. Then, as he looked down at his form, everything slowed before he recited a rather damning statement.

The body is a vessel, nothing more, nothing less! In fact, the entire planet contains a complex system of vessels, all with one aim. To host and generate the soul. Over time, this system has ticked along nicely until introducing the human vessel. This vessel, with its leaning to the conscious world, is heading for self-destruction and so, as I have already surmised, evolution is fine-tuning it to co-exist with the planet and continue on its intended purpose.

The emotions of depression consumed him and so he returned to his Paragon state, leading to a sense of serenity.

I never expected this outcome. The task at hand is to show that a life without evil leads to a tranquil immortality beyond all imagination. This undertaking is not straightforward. However, because the cleansing is unpreventable and Nemkis perfectly fits the heavenly blueprint, promoting purity is a logical choice.

A knock on the door broke his thoughts. Carefully easing himself up, he realised they had moved him from the hospital.

'Come in.'

Josh tentatively entered the room and held an expression that showed relief over Bran's waking.

'Josh – I'm fine. May I have a moment?'

After a silent nod, Josh left the room.

Drinking from a jug of water brought the fourth pillar back to Bran's mind, stirring up his emotions. Within a few minutes, he composed himself.

This emotional lark has got to stop.

'Josh I'm good now.'

Confused about how to respond, Josh stepped into the room and took a chair. Bran broke the ice.

'I'm grateful you stayed with me. How long did I sleep for...?'

'Four days. Your parents are in the loop. I'll leave you to call them.'

'I appreciate your thoughtfulness.' He paused. 'It's all a wonderment Josh, a sheer wonderment.'

His words relaxed Josh visibly. 'We are all in your hands...'

As Josh prepared to leave, the two of them acknowledged each other with a brief nod.

Bran felt a wave of anxiety as he stared nervously at his mobile phone, letting out a deep sigh.

'My first discussion will be with my parents, then Christie. But I cannot disclose my findings regarding immortality – no, not over the phone. Then I must travel – today!'

As the ringing of the mobile filled the air, he felt a wave of elation at the sound of his mother's voice.

'Mum, you were right, a fourth pillar exists.'

'Never mind that. How are you?'

Bran smiled inwardly.

A mother's love overrides all.

'I'm fine honestly, is dad with you?'

Flushed with emotion, Isla held back her tears to speak.

'He's just gone to the jetty to measure up. Love, I can't tell you how much we have missed you. Bloody come home.'

'Bloody good idea. You're getting thrashed at Cluedo.'

Both bathed in an emotional goodbye.

Call closed; hunger made its presence known. As he climbed out of bed, the sound of bedlam caught his ear. Upon opening the door, he noticed Josh had joined the security team grouped outside Mr and Mrs Boyd's room. As he moved towards the scene, a nurse asked him to stop, only to be overridden by Josh, who called him over. Now, peering inside, he felt sickened. As Mrs Boyd lay unconscious, Mr Boyd, sat on her bed, had inserted syringes into both of their arms. With tears running down his face, he begged to be left alone so they may leave the earth together. Bran looked at Josh, who whispered.

'She will pass within days.'

A consultant cautiously eased inside the room and spoke in a calmed voice.

'Mr Boyd, please, may I sit with you?'

Boyd steadied himself, then replied. 'Are you married?'

'No sir, engaged.'

'We've been together sixty-two years tomorrow, and you're about to give me advice on what's best for us both. Son, you will only understand when you reach our age.'

With an expression depicting relief, Boyd pushed both syringes simultaneously, injecting a lethal concoction through their veins. The consultant and others moved quickly, but death would call in moments.

Bran closed his eyes...

Inside a sentinel, he watched on as the souls of the couple reached the entrance, then to his absolute horror he realised the man's aura had turned grey. At that moment, Bran wanted to scream. As expected, termination of the grey occurred, leaving the white soul to drift elegantly towards the lightfall. Bran's sadness turned to admiration as the now youthful spirit of Mrs Boyd graciously dissipated into the body of Nemkis.

The mercy killing of his dear wife did not harbour evil intent, therefore I have to believe suicide turned his soul to the grey side. My god, without knowing, the husband sacrificed his own soul, as has many others have when suffering from emotional instability.

Bran opened his eyes to find that Josh had walked him back to their room and sat him down. After stamping his feet in anger, he recalled the extinction of the grey soul.

'That is just so wrong.'

As Bran appeared to be in thought, Josh waited

That poor man has spent his entire life living honest and pure. Because of that one act, his soul was kept from returning to its starting point. I was correct. There is a line drawn to which there is no empathy should we cross it at any stage. As mother nature has shown us many times, life can be exceptionally cruel and tragic.

Snapping from his thoughts, he sighed, then addressed Josh.

'I have so much to disclose. Kindly arrange a meeting with the president, Tess, Rialto, and Walt. Oh Josh, the explanation will take some time.'

Josh began his calls. Bran would return to finish the final two pages of Arlo's written words regarding the Awakening.

Two hours later, Bran closed the book, drew a breath, and immediately changed his mind about how he would present his latest experiences.

The initiates... damn you!

The *team* had assembled. To say the mood felt anxious would be correct. With everyone seated comfortably, Bran entered the room. Sitting down, he sighed, then began.

'What I have to explain is extraordinary, and judging by your aura, you all appear as I would expect... to be crapping yourselves.' His words broke the tension as each eased into a nervous chuckle. 'Such is the immensity of my discoveries I feel I must talk our way through the facts one stage at a time. Now... if Arlo was present, he would suggest a drink.' He smiled as the memory of the *Thistle Gold* square carafe flashed through his mind. 'And I agree, for you will struggle to cope with my disclosures.'

No one argued.

Moments later, with drinks to hand, they made a toast in the memory of Arlo. Once finished, Bran began.

'I have gained full knowledge of all that is the soul. It exists and is within all living organisms on the planet...'

Their expression exacted his expectations. The disclosures would take over five hours, step-by-step, stage by stage, to allow the emotional ride to progress cautiously.

Tears, shock, and absolute wonder flowed and ebbed during the conversation, with each reacting differently throughout the various stages. With unfolding the story in the exact time sequence he had experienced, he closed with the deaths of the elderly couple. The room fell silent. Throughout, Bran had monitored their aura and wondered how he ever coped without it.

Emotionally, they have become drained. Questions will be forthcoming, but I must turn the tide on their current mindset, as with nature... cruel to be kind!

'The death of Mr Boyd hit me hard, as it seemed to be unjust. The fairy-tale of their souls returning together became a nightmare caused by a compassionate act in a desperate ploy to remain together. Had Mr and Mrs Boyd been aware of the knowledge we now possess; their fairy-tale ending would have been complete. I questioned myself... would mainstream benefit from this knowledge? And now I am fully behind that people deserve the right to live out their life, making decisions that ensure their soul returns to Nemkis to accept immortality in whatever guise that may be.' Everyone nodded approval, pleasing Bran immensely. 'And so we now have a monumental task ahead and must not allow our own emotions to take precedence. Therefore, from now, accept the facts, digest them, and move on. No more wallowing in self-pity or fear. I have opened the truth, so deal with it! If you cannot, I will erase your memory bank, enabling you to return to a normal life.'

Bran's words bit hard. Josh was the first to respond.

'Message understood. I can't speak for the rest, but all my life I have required a purpose. And now I have the chance to deal with the most important purpose ever tasked. So yes, I'll keep my emotions in check and will give you everything I have.'

The *soldier's* attitude set the perfect example, resulting in the president clapping to be joined by all. As the aura around each brightened, Bran felt contented. Tess, with tears rolling down both cheeks, spoke.

'Josh has nailed this for us, so Mr Bran Cranson, you have your team?' Turning to the president, she bowed. 'Sir, we won't fail that's my promise.'

'Count me in, Mr President, but can we open another carafe?' laughed Walt.

Rialto, looking rather forlorn, remained silent.

The president moved to pour. With each holding a tumbler, he proposed a toast.

'To a pure soul and the promise of immortality!'

'To a pure soul,' came back the retort, including Bran, who was now grinning broadly.

'Your support, trust and saving my life have bonded my quest with you all. I hope you believe me when I say you are now my extended family. We are part of a phenomenon that, in its entirety, is far and beyond our intellect. However, we forge on to ensure our efforts succeed for the good of future generations. I now have full knowledge of the *Awakening and the initiates*, and so will complete a written dossier, which will enable your team to plan a structure to begin research that can integrate any historical incidents that may match an initiate. Initiates, be it, consciously or subconsciously, could be the main instigators of spirits or ghosts. Therefore, sort facts from fiction! We cannot close our minds to any phenomena, no matter how implausible, as a complete understanding of the initiates will be required before we can make any disclosures public. I am correct in saying that all have tried looking through closed eyes?' Each nodded shy confirmation. 'Then imagine the entire world looking through closed eyes!'

The penny dropped!

'The primary search has to be the apocalyptic sense I possess. With understanding its creation, we can at least separate fact from fiction. I suggest we collate a dossier on every suspected instant of the poltergeist and see if we can link it to a missing person. Those we believe are fact, have to be examined in depth. Not to cause panic, but I believe that most occurrences are from initiates who are unaware of what they have done or understand the sense they can evoke. Finally, the sensory attributes of the initiates vary dramatically along the evolutionary path leading to myself. In short, never say never to anything irregular in your findings. Questions?'

A brief silence ended as Walt spoke.

'If I may ask one question, it has to be... is there a divine presence?'

Bran closed his eyes for a moment then replied. 'At this point I can say for certain there is an intelligence, but I feel we can no longer promote supposition regarding a celestial god. We now have factual knowledge of other dimensions, something that has been impossible for our entire existence until this day. Therefore, we must never again invent a belief. No, we now continue forward for who knows how many other dimensions exist.' Noticing Rialto had been muted and that his aura had dimmed, he spoke.

'Tom, are you feeling unwell?'

Rialto's forehead furrowed as he looked directly at Bran.

'I'm finding this all very difficult. I need a break alone if that's okay.'

'Understood. If you need a chat before I leave, let me know.'

Nodding bluntly, Rialto left the room with no acknowledgements, something Tess found peculiar. As she caught the eye of the president, he shrugged, acknowledging both shared a concern.

Bran continued.

'Before I set off, I must look at any personnel that you bring onboard.'

The president spoke.

'As soon as you have cleared our staff, we will begin. And plans for your travel; shall we say six hours? This will give Tess time to present the candidates.'

'Excellent. As I mentioned, I wish to travel home to Scarth with Christie via London on the train?' He smiled... 'Much to discuss...!'

'Not a problem. One more thing, Antonio Beneventi has requested to speak with you!'

'Give me ten minutes.'

'Of course. Oh, and security for you and your family is now in place.' He frowned. 'We cannot afford for you to respond to any confrontational situation.'

'Accepted and appreciated. One more favour. Would you supply a new John Deer six-seater and four new generators to the Isle? Our credit is good?' he asked, smiling.

'They will be in position before you arrive you have my word.'

'Excellent and regarding Tom, let me know if he needs a chat. Perhaps he needs to experience the Nemkis.'

'Tom will be fine he has always been a brooder. He has an uncanny knack of convincing people to take his view, so I'm sure he will sort himself out.'

'Very well,' said Bran.

Emotional handshakes were in order. It would take several hours for Tom to sort his feelings to which a private discussion with the president would be required.

Whilst Bran walked to his room, an image of his father receiving the JD and generators made him smile.

A Paragon I may be, but I need my family.

He dialled Christie.

They would chat incessantly, understanding that upon their reunion, each had confessions to air. After the call, Bran set to recall his encounters from day one. Closing his eyes, he began.

As for the president and his team, each would have to fight their own individual battle to remain on an even keel with the knowledge they now possessed.

Fifty-seven

Beneventi heard every footstep he made during the walk to Bran's room. After knocking, he felt for the steak knife tucked inside the nape of his back.

Bran opened the door.

'Antonio, I hope all is well?'

'I appreciate this meeting. May I step inside for a few moments?'

After acknowledging the accompanying guards, Bran stood to the side to let Beneventi pass. Closing the door, he waited for him to speak.

Beneventi turned, reached into his pocket, pulled out his phone and passed it with a shaking hand.

'I received this message days ago.'

Bran swiped the screen open and took a deep breath on sight of the image. As he looked up, Beneventi had drawn the steak knife.

Bran remained silent.

With tears rolling down his face, Beneventi carefully handed Bran the knife, handle first.

'To save the future of my family, I remain true to my word and will no longer retaliate with violence. This is not an act of cowardice.'

Bran accepted the knife, then closed his eyes for just a moment.

This act of trust has an enlightening energy to it. That this man has sacrificed his instinct and placed his family's welfare into my trust is remarkable.

Bran nodded his acceptance. Beneventi spoke with a dry mouth.

'I do not seek revenge, just the safety of my family.'

The change of mindset appeared as a miracle in the eyes of Bran.

'Antonio, I have no choice over the response taken, but your honesty and trust permit me to embrace your loved ones. In doing so activates the protection of my sub-conscious, and – as of now, your family is safe.'

Beneventi swallowed hard. 'Are you certain?'

'Your family is secure. With no memory of their experience, their life will continue as before capture.'

Beneventi moved to hold Bran's hands.

‘And what of those men?’
Bran coldly shook his head.
‘Please – contact your family.’
Beneventi made the call. A yawning wife answered, only to be mystified by his *overenthusiastic* care during their conversation. The call ended after an uncountable number of blown kisses and a dozen *I love you’s.*
‘Words are not sufficient... how can I thank you?’
‘The very fact you held your word under such extreme circumstances is thanks enough. But I require a favour.’
‘Anything.’
‘Keep the Columnae in line until I have the answers I seek. Once achieved, you have my word that the church and the Columnae will be involved in discussions over how we move forward.’
Beneventi embraced him, then kissed both his cheeks. ‘Then consider this done.’
‘Thank you, Antonio, I will, if I may, over this period, consult with you if needed.’
‘Of course... I have one question.’
Bran nodded. ‘Please...?’
‘Why did you exterminate and not manipulate those renegades?’
‘In war or major disputes, the spilling of innocent blood is a major factor. The kidnap of your family is the blueprint used by the evil to gain leverage. My sub-conscious would never hurt or use innocent people. Menacingly, it will annihilate those that attack myself and those I care for. No compromise, no empathy, no leverage, just absolute extermination.’
After remaining silent for a moment, Beneventi closed his eyes to recap his past. ‘Before we met, I would have hunted every one of them down, plus their immediate family...’ he paused once more. ‘But I feared this would affect my family’s purity.’
The sentence flushed through Bran.
Despite his righteous intentions, a darkness still envelops this man. He crossed the line and there's no turning back.
‘Then we truly have hope, my brother.’ Bran paused for a moment. ‘Antonio, I have a question that you may have the answer?’
‘Please, I will try.’
‘The church stole the last book. Do you know of this tale?’

Beneventi's brow furrowed. 'It is a story of dread.'

'I see. Please explain.'

Beneventi dredged his memory bank and began.

'With knowing he had a copy, our men followed William to a cave on the Isle, convinced it was to be his hiding place. After William left, they discovered it buried under a pile of stones. However, as they shifted them, an evil spirit raised itself from the bowels of the cave and chanted a curse of the most horrific kind. The men bravely fought back with crosses and beads chanting our Lord's name, but failed to disperse the evil spirit and so fled the scene. Apparently, they never recovered mentally from the encounter. Later that week, we sent our most senior priest to perform a full exorcism. After hours of battle against the evil spirit, his brave actions cleansed the area and so he claimed the Last Book! That is the story as I understand it.'

Bran's expression was one of amazement over the fact that his appearance, back in time, had actually taken place.

'The tale is interesting.'

Beneventi looked curious. 'Were you aware of that night?'

'Let's say it's part of my ancestral knowledge.'

'Did our men dispel an evil spirit?'

'My suggestion would be that the men's fear of William brought about an exaggeration of their task. But either way... they took the book.'

'Then your version differs?'

'Perhaps Antonio, but for now, I thank you for your answer. Let's make plans for our return home; Family time will give us both a boost.'

Within two hours, Beneventi was on a flight home. The consequences of kidnapping his family ended the new order and anyone who harboured thoughts of rebellion against Beneventi.

Two hours later, Bran presided over the eighteen people proposed to form the research team. None were told they were under scrutiny. Within minutes, he chose eleven who were of the white aura. Historically, it was a poignant moment, as this was the first official governmental task force formed to investigate the Paragon, alongside validating paranormal anomalies regarding the initiates. Their work, without doubt, would instigate a level of mental trauma that would push their human limit to the edge.

In his last hour, Bran settled to assess the *reality* of the soul from his human perspective. A recap of the sequence resulted in an anxiety attack, forcing him back to his Paragon state.

This reaction was a warning, one I must heed if I am to be successful in my disclosures. Without doubt, when processing the truth to my family, I must give an explanation by word and not with a memory implant.

Fifty-eight

Fourteen hours later, seated at Euston Station, Bran awaited his rendezvous with Christie. A natural sleep had helped, but his emotions were off scale with the knowledge the fourth pillar had provided. He wanted to stand and shout out that the soul holds the key to immortality. Quickly dismissing such an impossible notion, he gazed anxiously towards Christie's pending arrival, as nervous, if not more than his first entry into Darkvoid.

He found leaving the USA had been an emotional wretch and surmised that during such trauma, strong bonds had formed, therefore excessive sentiments were to be expected. Losing Arlo, whilst devastating, became eased by the experience of witnessing his soul returning to the body of Nemkis. He gave no thought to his pineal gland.

I could not have envisaged this trip would open my sensory advancement to such a point of discovery. Was it fate, or something else? Now, amongst a crowd of people, observing the aura is becoming increasingly natural. That the vast majority of people are of the white gives hope.

A shout of "*heel*" caught his attention. As he looked to his left, a black Labrador was pulling his anxious female owner at pace towards him. Standing to greet the canine's enthusiasm, the dog bounded into him, followed by an apologetic burst from the baffled owner.

'No worries, I'm a dog lover. He's a beauty. What's his name?'

'Mack. I'm so sorry, he normally doesn't run to strangers.'

Bran smiled and sat down as the dog ceased his burst of excitement, only to lean into his leg and gently wag his tail. After warming strokes and a few whispered words, the dog yapped, then moved closer to his owner.

'Are you a dog trainer?'

Bran smiled. 'Of a sort.'

Now tugging at Mack to leave, the female shrugged. 'Well, you certainly have a link with dogs. Nice to meet you, and again my apologies.'

'I enjoyed the moment, thank you.'

As he watched the woman walk away, Mack kept turning his head towards Bran, only to receive a sharp tug on the lead. Undeterred, he continued until they left the station.

A link to dogs, plus every living soul on this planet...

Thoughts came to a halt as Christie strode into Bran's vision. Standing, his entire body shivered as his mind questioned the view his eyes presented. As Christie drew ever closer, no matter how many times he blinked, his vision confirmed the sight.

Christie was pregnant!

As her eyes fell upon Bran, she also stared in shocked bewilderment.

How is that possible?

As the two closed the distance, Bran began a nervy attempt to cradle her lightly.

'I'm pregnant, not broken!' she uttered with a false confidence.

Bran's *black and white thought process* instantly accepted that Christie had kept the secret for his benefit. Therefore, arguing would diminish her sacrifice. A question regarding the paternity wasn't required. Now speaking at almost twice his normal speed, he began.

'Are you both well? Do you know the sex? Have you thought of names? My god I'm going to be a dad – hell is your family okay with this?'

Her expression exuded a certain coyness.

'Yes, my family is comfortable becoming grandparents, and before you say I look fat... we're having twins... a boy and a girl!'

The shocked expression on Bran's face made Christie giggle. Bran was indeed... bamboozled.

Twins! I'm ecstatic. The woman I love is going to become a mother, yet the problems could be far-reaching.

Quickly dismissing the thoughts that bombarded his mind, he hugged Christie as firm as he dare.

'Twins – get us, this is wonderful...!' Dropping to one knee, he swallowed, then coughed to stabilise his composure. 'Christie McCall, will you marry me?'

'On one condition.' she said, causing Bran to shuffle nervously.

'Of course, anything!'

'Life or death, whichever is to be my fate, always trust my word forever.'

Bran's head sank a little. 'I've much to explain, but that's for the journey – erm, will you marry me?'

Christie repeated the words.

'Life or death, whichever is to be my fate, always trust my word forever. I have knowledge of your journey as a Paragon.'

The sentence completely dumbfounded Bran, and for the second time, his expression asked the question. Christie pulled at his hand, bringing him back to standing.

'Obviously, the fact I became pregnant had implications beyond the normal. Professor Watkins, as requested by Arlo, brought me on-line.'

A monotone voice announced the pending departure of their train. Bran moved to assist Christie, only to receive a sharp dismissal, as was a pregnant woman's entitlement.

'Before anything else, how are your headaches?'

'Nothing, so far, but please let's stay off that topic for now.'

'But..'

'Please, I'm fine. I just don't want to give it any thought.'

'Okay, providing you tell me if there is a change. Now, will our children become Paragons?'

Bran took a moment before replying.

'Truth... I don't know, but as centuries are required to implement the evolutionary changes, it's highly unlikely.'

Christie's face dropped. Bran responded.

'Does that upset you?'

'A little, but only because as Paragons they could certainly look after themselves.'

'Comes at a price...'

'I know.'

Bran paused, then looked quizzingly at Christie's face.

'You're not wearing sunglasses?'

'Correct.'

'But why?'

Christie's eyes sparkled. 'Bran Cranson, my status as a new mum was undoubtedly a shock to your system... now standby for another.'

Bran's forehead wrinkled. Christie began.

'Shortly after my ninth birthday, my vision became blurred. After a visit to the doctors, they sent me for tests with several specialists, none of which pinpointed the problem. By the age of eleven, the abnormality had evolved, producing a blurred sheen around every living thing.' Bran felt the hairs on his arm raise as Christie continued. 'By this time, they had prescribed sunglasses, and being exhausted with test after test, I agreed that this corrected my vision. It hadn't! But as I learned to live with the issue, I noticed that if someone had a darker sheen, I would take an immediate dislike to them.' She held Bran's hand tightly. 'When we met, I had never witnessed such a dazzling sheen. At that moment, I fell in love with the *bright boy* from Scarth.'

Bran, yet again, became lost for words...

With a smile, Christie leaned close and kissed his cheek. 'When Professor Watkins explained your life story, I became both intrigued and sceptical, as expected. This altered when he told me of the change to your vision after the death sleep. Imagine how I reacted when finding an answer to my lifelong issue. I see both the white and grey Aura...' Pausing for a deep breath, she closed her eyes. 'I am your first encounter with an *Initiate.*'

The silence lasted for several seconds before Bran replied.

'Since I left uni, every day has contained startling revelations. Today has not failed! And now I find my fiancé...'

'To be,' interrupted Christie, smiling.

Bran sucked on his teeth. '*To be...* is having twins and informs me she has the *vision* – incredible.'

Christie leaned closer.

'Astonishingly, the entire phenomenon surrounding you is now sharper, and one hundred percent brighter than I remember.'

Bran placed his hands on top of his head in astonishment. That another person could clarify that aura existed exacted a relief that showed.

Christie picked up on his emotions. 'Yes, I really can see the aura.' Turning to look at fellow passengers, she then whispered, 'I see two grey, the rest are white!'

As Bran scanned the immediate area, his eyes cast quickly to Christie and then back to those of the white. My love, I cannot say that your aura has increased, but it is distinctly brighter than others on this train.

Christie looked shocked. 'Has mine advanced being I am the mother of your children?'

Bran thought for a moment before replying. 'Sounds workable... Or perhaps an initiate's aura is brighter, that being we would benefit from being able to distinguish them.'

'The grey may be darker.'

'Absolutely!'

Changing the subject, Bran's expression depicted relief. 'Being the only person with this vision always created doubt, but now all concerns... vanquished.' He paused and looked a little impish. 'You look just as cool without sunglasses.'

Christie shrugged.

'Of course.'

'Have you confided in anyone?'

'No, I wanted to talk with you first... Having lived with this all my life, then understanding what it means, well... it's raised the bar somewhat!'

Sighing, Bran replied. 'I understand completely. Well, we have around eighteen hours' travel, so to ensure we're on the same footing, I'll begin from day one. Much of which is truly wonderful, but I warn, some issues are disturbing. Then, once settled at Scarth, I want you to experience a vision of the journey into Nemkis. Without doubt, this will change your perception of all you currently understand.' Pausing, he clasped Christie's hands. 'But before I begin, are you certain you wish to become part of this? You are soon to be a mother, and are financially secure, and so you can limit your involvement should you wish.'

Christie gave a dismissive wave of her hand. 'And what if our twins are Paragons? Do you believe I should sit by an open fire knitting matching cardigans? I am an Initiate and crave to learn.'

Bran took a deep breath. 'Very well.' Beaming, he continued. 'Your other answer?'

Christie flushed, kissed his cheek, then whispered into his ear.

'Yes, my love, I will marry you, but only because you're a millionaire.'

The two giggled like young love birds should. Christie spoke.

'I understand the need to learn, but please – I would like to meet your family as your expectant fiancé.' Gently tapping his hand, she continued. 'We've plenty of time to deal with the future of mankind – so the full update can wait. Agreed?'

A warmth flushed through Bran, a human warmth that he allowed to override his Paragon senses.

'Is it any wonder I love you? Now that I've come to a complete understanding of the soul's existence, I need to talk to someone to relieve the stress. Seeing the Aura is amazing, so let me open your thoughts to this wonderment.'

Christie snuggled closer to Bran. 'Then yes, please begin.'

Ten minutes later, with the two settled in first class seating, the train whined into movement.

Christie took the lead.

'The soul and all its secrets, please...'

Fifty-nine

The president, Tess, and Tom Rialto, seated inside the oval office, looked serious after an emergency meeting with his senior staff, who had become concerned by the president's lack of interest in his day-to-day business. Questions about his commitment and mental state had been increasing. Now standing, the president spoke.

'Tess, do you ever stop thinking about the Nemkis and all Bran has explained?'

Tess took no time in replying.

'Ever since we took the dream, my mind has become consumed by the events.'

Aggressively throwing his arms up in anger, the president's tone raised an octave. 'I am not capable of running the country in this mindset.'

Rialto reacted first. 'Sir, we need you at the helm, so to steady the ship, perhaps replace myself and Tess, giving notice that you are still in control. Of course, we can retire gracefully into the background to focus entirely on the *project*?'

The president looked at Tess, who shrugged.

'The move will certainly quell the rising tide!'

'But I still have to cope with my own issues, as just now everything else has become insignificant.'

Rialto spoke again. 'That may be, but you must remain in power, for without your influence, well, I fear for Brans' future.'

The president, close to tears, replied.

'I've been wallowing in my own personal trauma and you're correct, my lethargy is no help.' Settling, he continued. 'Then you're both sacked.' Laughter broke the tension.

'Once we draw up a short list of your replacements, kick the task force into operation.'

Normally, the action of halting senior political careers would take its toll on those involved. However, all understood that they were now entangled in decisions that ultimately would shape the future of mankind.

Rialto spoke.

'Sir, I was rude yesterday and I apologise. Truth being, I had a full wobble about all things Nemkis, especially the *Awakening* event. Hell, I even questioned my sanity.'

'I understand Tom,' he looked at Tess, 'we both do. Take time out if you must?'

Rialto nodded his thanks. 'Sir, I've concluded that I need to see this Nemkis, so with your permission, I'll travel over to Scarth once we have set this team in motion.'

'That's an excellent idea Tom, but be prepared for it to change your focus.'

Absolutely, it already has...

'I will Sir. Oh, I'll sort my own arrangements, thank you.'

Rialto left the room promptly. Tess immediately spoke out.

'Tom is definitely not himself. Have we made the correct decision regarding his inclusion?'

'As Bran gave the last nod, yes. Look, I'm sure that once he has experienced the Nemkis, he'll be back online.'

'I guess so. Well, we best push on with this team.'

'And I've a country to placate...'

Sixty

Three hours into their journey, Christie had asked questions to which Bran explained and expanded upon. Confirmation that the soul existed had pushed her emotions off the scale. With her head in her hands, she asked Bran the question he expected. 'Do we preserve knowledge of our life after death?'

Bran paused just a little.

I need to be honest and open the possibility of immortality.

'Upon its return to Nemkis, Arlo's soul attained a level of tranquillity that was truly inspiring. It was clear from his expression that he was experiencing a sense of pure elation. Being back in the body of Nemkis means becoming part of an experience that is incomparable to anything we have ever known on Earth. This undoubtedly signifies a form of immortality! Just to clarify, I have no understanding of what this form represents. However, my thoughts on reincarnation have led me to believe that we may hold memories of past lives. Fact is only death will reveal the absolute truth.'

'Immortality... my god! Does this make death a coveted choice? I mean... as in suicide?'

Bran expanded over the incident with Mr Boyd, leaving her completely shocked.

'That is so sad, and horribly unjust... then, I agree, people deserve the truth, especially those suffering from suicidal thoughts.'

'My feelings concur, at least Mr Boyds sacrifice will now no longer be in vain.'

Christie nodded in agreement. 'I can appreciate that.'

'Are your emotions holding?' said Bran.

'I'm good, yes. Perhaps it is easier for an Initiate to stay level-headed. The knowledge that the soul exists and all that it encompasses, is difficult to process, however the promise of immortality is truly exhilarating.'

Bran's eyes glinted. 'The answers have always existed, but without the requisite senses, they are impossible for the human to decipher.'

'Makes perfect sense. However, proving everything as fact, as you know, will be extremely difficult.'

Their chatter stalled as two drunken yobs crashed into first class service and begun screaming at the attendant for alcohol. Christie spoke first.

'I see the greys.'

Her words flushed around Bran like a cleansing potion.

'You do not know how happy that makes me.'

At that point, a middle-aged, overweight carriage attendant brushed past Bran, who then felt Christie's breath close to his ear.

'Do not get involved!'

Clasping her hand, he whispered. 'I dare not.'

The guard, trying to recall the self-defence measures learnt on his recent S.I.A. refresher course, stopped short of the men, took a breath, then asked to see their tickets. As the yobs mocked his command, the fear in the attendant's expression was clear to see.

'Fatty, do one! Or you'll get hurt.' Now turning to the service attendant, the yob poked the man's chest aggressively. 'Two beers, on the house before this gets messy.'

As the nervous attendant began his reply, four large men in dark suits descended on the youths like a dust storm. Within seconds, the men had them handcuffed and removed from the carriage. Firmly holding Bran's hand, Christie's look questioned.

Bran gave her a wink.

'The president suggested my intolerance for bullies could be catastrophic, so now we have full-time company!'

'Now that is a comforting thought.'

'I have to agree,' shrugged Bran.

After a moment's silence, the confused attendant, hiding his inner relief, spoke out.

'Ladies and gentlemen, our apologies for any foul language. Please enjoy the rest of your trip.'

The journey continued, as did their conversation regarding the soul.

'I honestly did not know my aura had changed. I can only assume this is because of my sensory advancement,' said Bran.

'Do you remember Charlie Diaz from Uni?'

Bran's expression revealed a slight sarcasm.

'How could I forget him being my first major brawl on your behalf?'

She shrugged. 'I know, but his aura was so dark, I feared him. Anyway, last month he stood charged with murder.'

'Who?'

'His ex's new fella. Hit and run, causing multiple fractures and internal bleeding. Four days in intensive care before he died.'

'He always seemed destined to commit an evil act. It also confirms that the darker the grey, the closer to pure evil the person becomes.'

'Agreed.' said Christie, before moving her hand close enough to connect their Auras.

'Without touching you, I can sense your emotions.'

Bran smiled warmly. 'Yes, I first experienced this with Loki.' Pausing, he then fed off a notion sourced from deep within his mind's research database.

'Reiki...!'

Christie questioned the sheer randomness of his statement.

'Pardon?'

'Reiki is a form of complementary therapy relating to energy healing. Proponents say that it works with the energy fields around the body and involves the transfer of universal energy from the practitioner's palms to the client.'

'Another stage of an Initiate?'

'Certainly something to ponder over...'

Christie mused for a moment. 'I wonder if science could create a machine that could see the aura.'

Excited by the suggestion, Bran jumped at it. 'And with our understanding of the aura increases the possibility... The project needs to become a priority.'

Christie touched his hand. 'Is the purity and connection of the soul between loved ones the reason it is so painful in the eventuality of their death?'

'Without question.'

The two sat back in hushed thought. Their silence would offend neither, understanding both had to evaluate the implications of their discussions. Bran composed a text intended for the president.

Random, I know, but have a muse over a project to develop a machine for detecting the surrounding aura that shrouds all physical life. If we can see infra-red etc... perhaps?

P.S. Sir, I am to become a father of twins... Blush.

The president, having an absolute yearning to gaze upon his own aura, would reply with a positive answer... Followed by honest congratulations and a heads up over Rialto.

Bran mused over the information.

Rialto, once a grey, now struggling... interesting. We shall see!

Some seventeen hours later, yawning, the two disembarked from the train and stepped into the nip of a spring evening. Bran sucked in the air like a tonic before offering Christie his coat.

'As I'm a typical southerner, I won't say no.' she smiled wearily.

Ross and Isla came bounding down the platform, to which Bran choked back on his emotions. Immediately noticing Christie's condition, Isla held her hand to her mouth in stunned excitement. As the four met, a group hug ensued, to which happy tears flowed in abundance.

In a decidedly nervous tone, Christie opened the conversation.

'Mr and Mrs Cranson, I'm so sorry to have kept this secret from you – but...'

Isla held her hand up. 'Please, Ross and Isla, and apologies are not a necessity. Welcome to the family – I'm guessing you're aware of everything that has happened?'

Christie, experiencing a warmth from the aura exuded by both, nodded. 'Yes and please, I'm at ease with the scenario.'

Ross interjected. 'Then that conversation can wait. Becoming grandparents takes precedence. Welcome to the mad family.'

With a beaming grin, Christie added. 'Oh, we might include, we're having twins... boy and a girl!'

Both Ross and Isla, shaking their heads in delirious excitement, moved to hug Christie, which ended in another group bonding. Ross broke off.

'And you, my boy, only this morning, four state-of-the-art generators and a new JD... delivered by a Chinook helicopter. The president himself called us about your request.'

Bran laughed. 'Well, he promised to make delivery before I returned, and our credit is sound.'

'That is a point, I suppose,' laughed Ross.

'Wait till I tell you of my other plans, but that can keep. Let's go home.'

'We've made up Cliff Cottage for you both. Looks like we will have to arrange for an extension,' smiled Isla.

Within the hour, they were back at the main house on Scarth, taking supper. Isla looked on caringly as she chatted to Christie like a long-lost daughter. With Loki sound asleep, resting his head on Christie's feet, and Bran discussing plans for the Isle with Ross, her contentment felt complete.

My family! Just now I wish that all was normal and that our future was without complications. But looking at my loved ones enjoying a harmony so natural, one fact is true. Once evil is cleansed, mankind will become blessed.

With a broad smile, she moved over to Christie and gave her a hug before addressing all.

'I understand the importance of what is happening, but please may we, for just tomorrow, enjoy a simple family day, without referral to Nemkis or anything connected.'

Ross clapped. "Nothing would please me more.'

'Nor I.' replied Christie.

A moment's silence passed as everyone looked at Bran, who leaned back in his chair.

A rest! My word, suddenly I feel exhausted, but thinking logically my mind has been on overload since I left college. Certainly, won't do my pineal gland any harm. So be it!

'Agreed. It's exactly what we all need. One tiny issue... security about the Isle has become beefed up a tad, including satellite surveillance. Our *au-natural* cottage is to be given a makeover, courtesy of a covert section of the CIA for their operators who will remain on the Isle. Of course, in a major threat...' He shrugged. 'Well, let's hope that's a false concern. So, let the fun begin?'

Christie responded. 'Then let's toast the twins, in Scottish tradition, and please, I'm comfortable remaining tee total, whilst you all drink till ye wobble.'

Isla stood up and looked directly at Bran.

'Just one question. Do you believe the twins are Paragons?'

Bran exhaled.

'As I explained to Christie. I cannot say, but as history dictates that centuries are required to implement evolutionary changes, I would have to say no. And to be honest, it's a burden I do not wish on them.'

Christie rubbed her stomach. 'I'll take healthy in any guise.'

'Seconded,' said Isla.

Motion carried.

The next day, Bran and Ross set about various requisite tasks, which helped take the edge of the withdrawal from all things Nemkis. First, they announced on their website that they were no longer offering holiday lets. After which they informed Jim McTay that the Professor had bequeathed them some money, and that he was to receive ten million pounds. It was some time before Jim calmed.

They then set the generators in three properties, putting an end to midnight fixes by torch light! However, their most exciting plan was to form a partnership with the National Trust for Scotland to further develop the Isle with the creation of natural habitats for rare species and plant life.

Ross would take his time to choose a fishing vessel, to which he regularly pinched himself as he perused the internet. Isla's choice... new furnishings and an aga cooker for each property.

Bran concluded that helping others was definitely the only way he gained satisfaction from wealth. He also took time out to contact Chloe Shane and her daughter, Joey, who were both doing fine. The conversation lasted over thirty minutes, to which he enjoyed immensely, especially as Chloe accepted Bran's invitation to the Isle once she became fit to travel. A return to normality had been the recharge all required.

Sixty-one

The following morning.

Seated around the breakfast table, Isla opened discussions.

'My word that break was enjoyable that but hey, time ticks and so we must turn our attention to the future.' Looking at Bran, she smiled. 'We are aware of your concealment of the full circumstances, so I'm calling for the unconditional truth, warts and all.'

'Seconded.' added Ross.

Christie raised her arm. 'I vote with my in-laws.'

After calling Loki to his side, Bran stroked his muzzle.

'Well, fasten your safety belts, as... oh I forgot to mention Tom Rialto is calling over to talk with me, not sure when, but he's a decent chap for a chief of staff.' Grinning at the family's shocked reactions, he set to begin his explanation. Seconds later, his expression glazed over, resulting in an uneasiness from the family. Moving to the door, he stepped out and closed his eyes...

One hour earlier

A young male, of standard height and build, set off rowing aboard a kayak from Wick headed for Scarth. He wasn't ignoring shouts of concern from close by. No, being deaf since birth was his justification. Just now, he was ten minutes from reaching the Isle.

Stepping inside the cottage, Bran snatched a coat.

'A visitor will arrive at the Isle shortly. Fear not, he has the white aura.'

The explanation calmed anxious faces, but the question of how he knew loomed heavy. He continued. 'I have said many times that every day poses yet another situation beyond natural parameters. Today is no different. We must leave promptly to collect him.'

The traveller, having just climbed from the kayak, gazed blankly as the shiny JD rolled to a standstill. The words *Mortis Lux,* emblazoned across the bow, sent a shiver through the family. Tired, dishevelled, and confused, the traveller walked from the jetty and spoke in a tone that highlighted his disability. 'My name is Vilhelm, from Denmark, and unsure of the purpose of this journey. I can lip read.'

As he stepped from the vehicle, Bran recited the last words from the message written by Gregor.

'And let no generation forget the sign speak...'

The family, dumfounded, looked on, as Bran stuck up a conversation using sign language.

'Welcome to Scarth, Vilhelm.'

'Have we met before?' asked Vilhelm cautiously.

'Bran Cranson. Your recall of our friendship is vague?'

'As is my journey.'

Ross, also using sign language, interacted.

'How about we secure that boat, get you home for a bath, dry clothes, and a hearty meal?'

'I have no money,' responded Vilhelm.

'You are our guest. Jump in, the clouds are gathering, Ross Cranson is the name.'

As handshakes began, Bran secured the kayak before turning to Christie, whose face portrayed a nervous understanding that something paranormal was developing.

Stress is having a deliberating effect on her aura.

Throughout the ride back, Vilhelm remained mute, whilst appearing to be searching for a lost memory.

A theory chilled Bran's soul.

Vilhelm, have we been in contact since the beginning?

One hour later, bathed and provided with fresh clothing, Vilhelm seated at the table, straightened his posture, then spoke.

'I am a stranger, and yet you have opened your home and for that, I'm extremely grateful. Please continue to talk amongst yourselves. And Isla, this lunch looks splendid.'

'Tuck in... Wine?' she asked.

'I'll pass. Regrettably, I fall over with alcohol, but thank you.'

Hilarity ensued.

Thirty minutes later, Vilhelm dabbed his mouth with a napkin before standing.

'That was exquisite. I'm pretty tired. May I excuse myself to the guest room?'

'Of course, and sleep through the afternoon if you must,' said Ross.

'Thank you.' Vilhelm smiled. 'Forgive me Christie! You're tired, stressed perhaps, therefore may I suggest you think of the twins! Rest easy and chill through the months until the birth.' Turning to Bran, he opened his arms. 'You have accumulated many words. Take time out to build the sentence you seek.'

Bowing, he retired, leaving an uncertain silence within the room. Before anyone spoke, Loki, ignoring Bran's commands to stay, moved to the guest room door and whimpered several times.

Slightly perturbed, Bran walked to the room and knocked. With no answer, he gingerly peered inside.

The room was empty.

Bran closed his eyes for a second, exhaled, then turned to the family.

'Do not concern, however, Vilhelm was a visitation!'

The expression *you look like you've seen a ghost* suited.

Ross moved to search the bedroom. Tipping the bed on its side proved fruitless.

'Are you suggesting Vilhelm was an actual ghost?' he asked, slightly unsettled.

'A visitation yes.'

Christie asked a glaring question.

'How did he know we're having twins?'

Before Bran answered, she squealed, causing everyone to twitch. 'A kick.'

Excited, Bran moved to touch her abdomen. Thirty seconds later, another kick, which drew smiles and soothed nerves.

Isla hesitated for a second before speaking.

'Mortis Lux printed on the kayak, Vilhelm, a ghost? Capped off by a couple of kicks from the twins my word, when will our world default to normal?'

Ross interrupted. 'I'll check if the kayak still exists?'

'No need. Vilhelm's purpose was to ensure that Christie and the twins experience a safe and stress-free pregnancy. His specific message, *You have enough letters...* also suggests that I have to ease down for the sake of my health. As for Vilhelm, whilst he represents the *unexplained,* he was of the white aura, and therefore is no threat.'

Isla held up her palms. 'I've just witnessed a ghost whose sole purpose was to ensure the health of my family becomes paramount. Aside from the obvious questions and our stress levels, I see no fault in his plan.'

All made a shrugged approval as Ross rummaged for the remote.

'No time like the present. This Netflix? Let's see what all the fuss is about.'

Isla clapped. 'Christie, put your feet up. You're going to be treated like a queen.'

A smiling Christie replied. 'This clan... my word, dull moments... never.' Laughing, she offered Bran a high five, who reciprocated.

Observing her aura recover its dazzling sheen, Bran had one thought.

Thank you Vilhelm!

He grinned.

That Vilhelm translates to William in Scandinavian is possibly a hint.

The lure of streaming television began. Not so for Bran, as Vilhelm's words had made its mark.

What sentence?

Loki, having moved inside the guest room, sat beside the bed, tail wagging. Arlo had been correct. The animal kingdom's sensory abilities were above and beyond that of a human.

Netflix and its abundance of violence had not impressed. After watching the beginning of five films, the family decided that time was best used in other ways.

Bran suggested they visit the Major to which all agreed until the sound of a helicopter interrupted discussions.

'Ah Tom Rialto, mused Bran.'

Sixty-two

The helicopter's landing prompted everyone to rush outside. Despite experiencing everything Nemkis offered, having the Chief of Staff land in your garden was still surreal. Gleaming faces greeted Rialto as he stepped out of the chopper and waved. When a single armed guard pushed out a hooded and handcuffed Jim McTay, everyone did a double take. The parents immediately glanced at Bran and Christie, who had both noticed that Rialto's aura had returned to grey. Upon hearing Loki growl, Bran promptly ushered him inside, closed the door, then whispered to the family.

'Say nothing. Let me handle this.'

Rialto approached to within four feet before speaking with a blatant arrogance.

'Cast your mind back to that first meeting inside Langley.'

Bran took a step closer.

'Remove the hood and cuffs before we continue.'

'Just the hood,' spouted Rialto to the guard holding Jim.

After a sharp nod, the guard complied immediately.

With the hood removed, the family gasped in horror, being Jim had suffered a broken jaw and cheek bone.

Ross, sickened, moved forward only for Bran to stop him with his arm.

'Inside Langley you said.'

'Yes, just after you murdered the assets holding Christie.'

'And.'

'In the following moments, I fired a Glock mounted under the table aimed directly at you. The round misfired, but as everyone was fucking vanishing, I bottled a second shot. Never gave it a moment's thought until you mentioned the Initiates! Now, I'm certain that your *special powers* could not have predicted a misfire. Therefore, my Paragon friend, I do not know what sensory shit I possess, but are you getting where this is going?'

Time appeared to stand still for all, except for a smiling Rialto.

Bran shrugged. 'And the point of this façade.'

'Ah, the point... Revenge? A little, as many of the agents you murdered were close friends. However, as the honourable senator Finney had speculated, you're one hell of an asset. Whereas the president believes in peace and harmony, I'm a realist. As history proves, the biggest armies and the best weapons dictate the world. Therefore, providing I'm in control, your family remains alive.'

'I see. You believe you can injure or kill me without repercussions?'

'One hundred percent. I never understood how, but throughout my life, no one could *read* me. Add to that, I always knew I could sway minds, hence the nickname, *Persuader*. However, learning about the Initiate gave me a train of thought. Wasn't too long before I put two and two together.' Truth... I don't know how I convinced you I was of the white, but I did!

'Well, if you're that confident, go ahead, shoot me!' taunted Bran.

Rialto laughed.

'No need. I was the man who broke Uncle Jim's face and lived.' Rialto pulled out a bloodied knuckle duster and tossed it to the floor. 'Three decent hits... no repercussions.'

Carefully hiding his reaction, Bran took a step towards Rialto. 'Then I'm going to break your jaw using the conventional method.'

Rialto grinned and stepped back. 'Soldier, shoot the prisoner.'

Isla shouted in terror. With no hesitation, Ross charged forward, yet as the soldier pointed his firearm... gone!

A silent lull hit for a few seconds, heightened by the engine and blades of the chopper coming to a halt. In that moment, Rialto drew his firearm and jabbed it into the back of Jim's head, causing him to grimace.

Rialto shrugged. 'Expected, but let's see what transpires when I pull the trigger, oh mighty Paragon.'

A single gunshot echoed around the courtyard, and for a moment, all stood in shock as Jim slumped to the floor to leave Rialto, aiming his firearm at Christie. Bran closed his eyes for a second.

Rialto laughed.

'Oops, no misfire...! Okay, do I take the shot that would kill three, or are we now compliant?'

Isla hurried to hold her brother. Trembling with rage, Ross moved to cover Jim's shattered head with his jacket.

Rialto mocked.

'Paragon, your invincibility is in tatters, but I need to hammer my point. Perhaps I'll pop a round into either your mother's or father's leg... Your choice.'

Without replying, Bran appeared to lapse into a trance before he turned towards Christie, who had doubled over, with both hands holding her stomach.

'Am I correct, my love?'

After taking several deep breaths, Christie stood.

'Absolutely.'

Now side by side, holding hands, the couple stared ominously at Rialto, who for the first time looked agitated.

Using sign language, Bran conveyed to the parents that everything would be fine. With a return of his unnatural demeanour, both nodded their acceptance.

With Bran's turn of expression igniting memories of the fateful day at Langley, Rialto settled into a combat stance.

'Changed my mind. I choose your mother.'

Isla did not flinch as Rialto turned his aim to her right knee. Bran responded.

'You have choices. Lay down your weapon and face the legal consequences for murder. Or attempt to pull that trigger, and cease life.'

Rialto grinned. 'You uncle lies dead, so I have no fear of your threat.'

'Then pull the trigger and when you are gone, I will sit and watch your soul in torment. A torment you will suffer for eternity.'

With a nervous grin, Rialto replied. 'Paragon, I have to call your bluff. '

'Then do so...'

At that moment, Rialto was gone, resulting in an unbridled relief to flood through the family as they moved to a huddle. Now looking at the sky, Bran spoke.

The disappearance was caused by the subconscious mind of our twins. Their transformation into Paragons occurred because of their mother's fear following Jim's death.

Through tear-filled eyes, Christie shared her feelings.

'It's a fact. The twins eliminated him...! When that bastard killed your uncle, I felt a tingling inside, and then a frenetic kicking. I put it down to stress, so I massaged my stomach, which seemed to have a calming effect on both. But when he tried to fire his gun again, the sensation returned with an intensity that made me double over. It was at that moment I understood that our twins had become Paragons and that they had connected with their father.'

After a pecked kiss to Christie, Bran spoke

'Rialto was correct. I couldn't stop him from acting violently. However, the stress felt by Christie over Jim's murder initiated the twins' defensive capabilities. That said, evolution has eradicated the fault I appeared to have. So from that point, Rialto faced the evolutionary conclusion of the Paragon. Our twins! I literally sensed the moment and now I have a sub-conscious connection to both babies. Such an amazing event at a time we are saddened by Jim's murder. Life is a cruel pastime for sure!'

As his words flushed around the family, the grey spectre of Rialto appeared in a state of agonised terror. Showing zero empathy, Bran ignored the spiralling grey form trapped on a figure-of-eight path around the edge of the bosk.

Oblivious to the poltergeist, the family held a moment of silence around Jim's body. Isla began weeping, then slumped down to cradle his hand.

Loki's barking at the grey spectre interrupted, prompting Bran moving to placate him. Once inside the house, he quickly grabbed the last blister of Ibuprofen, and Paracetamol, took two of each, then returned outside.

Exiting the helicopter, the pilot kneeled and raised both hands in surrender.

Bran stepped forward to speak to him.

'Relax, you are in no danger, providing you remain passive. Shortly I will make a call to the president, who will decide your outcome. Understood?'

The pilot, looking relieved, nodded his compliance.

'I'm sure you have body bags packed. Pass one and wait. Do not leave!'

The pilot obliged.

Walking back, Bran spoke compassionately.

'We should move Jim inside, then gather ourselves.'

Without speaking, the family gently and carefully eased Jim into the bag. Their silence was interrupted by Loki scratching at the window, then barking at the ever-spinning spectre.

Bran closed his eyes

I want you to suffer, but my dog's welfare is more important.

The grey spectre was gone.

Twenty minutes later, after laying Jim to rest in the spare room, the family moved to the breakfast table. Shock had affected everyone, Isla the worst.

'How on earth are we going to explain Jim's death to Mary?'

The question hit hard.

Now staring at the sat phone, Bran sighed. 'We have to conceal the truth for now.' Prodding hard at the keypad, he dialled the president. After a long conversation, he moved out to the chopper, handed the pilot the phone, then returned to the family.

'They will capsize Jim's boat ten miles out. We will then lay him to rest on Scarth. Sadly, Mary will have to live without closure, until the day we can explain all. That Jim has gone is utterly devastating.' He paused. 'Please, may we all go to *his room* for a moment?'

Isla stood.

'Yes, of course.'

In humble silence, the family moved to the guest room and respectfully stood around the body bag shrouded with a quilt. With being the last inside, Bran gently closed the door. A light breeze and a beam of sunlight from the half-open window gave the room a natural feeling. Bran spoke.

'In the instant of his death, I observed him entering the Nemkis as a white soul, in total harmony, to take immortality in whatever guise it presents. The soldier who murdered him – I committed to a sentinel.'

After asking all to hold hands, he implanted a true vision of Jim's passing into their minds. Moments later, a serene calm enveloped the family, having witnessed the pure tranquillity in his expression.

'What lies before us is merely the physical organism that Jim's soul entered at the moment of birth.' Bran ceased to speak as a butterfly fluttered through the window and chose the bedside lamp as its resting place. 'My word a Speckled Wood, I believe the first ever on our Isle.' Bran glowed with delight at the timing. 'It is my understanding that the selection by the soul of the physical entity it occupies is purely random. For instance, if Jim's soul had released a micro second earlier... or later from Nemkis, it could have been to a butterfly, or any other lifeform created in that moment.' After looking at each of his family, he continued. 'During Jim's final transition to Nemkis, I realised the human should celebrate both life and death equally, as our soul continues its existence, albeit in another dimension. Yes, we mourn the loss of the physical presence of a loved one, however we can now celebrate the passing into immortality by those of the white. This fact above all else, validates that everyone deserves this knowledge in order to make a choice on how they live out their physical life.'

For a few seconds, a silence descended, as all eyes fell on the butterfly. As the breeze stiffened, the open window called and so the Speckled Wood took flight around the room on an exit path only a butterfly could plot and was gone.

Showing a depth of emotion rarely seen from Ross, he spoke

'In some circles, butterflies are symbols of change, transformation, and rebirth. Some say they are omens of luck and bring messages of light, hailing new beginnings. They are beautiful creatures and will rarely enter a building, so finding one in your home is a positive that means good things are coming for you.' His words triggered an emotional release, effecting the family to bathe in a combined aura that glowed ever bright. Now, as they looked at the body, the pain of Jim's physical death eased.

Christie welled up. 'My father is soon to pass, but this changes everything... everything! My god!'

A respectful knock on the door broke the mood.

'Sir, all arrangements are in place. With your permission, I will leave.'

Bran gave a nod, his voice unwavering. 'When you leave, your memory of this entire event will be erased completely.'

The pilot exhaled deeply as he turned to leave.

'Truth? I'm relieved, as what I experienced would have haunted me forever.'

With the door closing, Isla looked at the family.

'But it's not our Jim's goodbye, is it?' She paused. 'I once doubted that *knowing* was a positive... not now!'

The warmth of the moment prompted a family embrace, ending in all touching Christie's stomach. Moments later, they watched the flight disappear over the horizon. Each would now find their own way of dealing with Jim's passing. Christie settled on the sofa with Isla. Both holding her stomach. Ross stacked a night's worth of wood, and with a tumbler of scotch to hand, gazed deeply into the flames. Bran set off for a run with Loki.

Upon reaching the Bosk, he vomited. Wiping his mouth, he set off in search of the Major, giving no thought to the demise of Rialto.

Within twenty minutes he reached Scraghill. With no sign of the herd, he sat down on a flat rock to gaze over the harsh landscape, in which, for once, vegetation was winning the battle against granite. Memories of his childhood with Jim swirled inside his mind until Loki picked up a scent on the breeze. The Major, having made his way up to the hill, was now just eighty yards away. With Loki remaining passive, Bran turned to gaze on the stag who snorted, stamped his foot, then closed the distance.

Standing, Bran spoke gently.

'Thank you for this moment.'

The Major snorted again then raised his antlers to allow Bran to hold his head. The touch became electric.

'My friend, I wanted to see you before my life changes. For when we next meet, it will be as a human and not a Paragon. I truly hope we can keep our bond, but either way, I will cherish the moments shared.'

The Major backed off, gave a bellow that echoed around the hillside, then turned to amble back to his herd. As Bran sat down on the rock, Loki huddled close and, with their aura entwined, Bran spoke aloud.

'My Loki, the headaches and vomiting have returned, therefore, I will have the operation to remove the pineal gland.' Grimacing, he continued. 'Of course I will no longer be a Paragon, but losing my sensory gifts is not as painful as leaving my family in death. Make no mistake, I will recover to remain a son, become a husband, then a father. Vilhelm's suggestion, "*you have accumulated many words. Take time out to build the sentence you seek,*" make sense. For everything I have learned has to be opened and expanded upon, especially reincarnation. That people can exist in a world without evil, then return to Nemkis and its offer of immortality is now in the hands of our twins. Crucially, I've witnessed first-hand the consequences of the Awakening, with Rialto killing for his own gains. No question, my experience and guidance will become vital to the twins as evil will put up one hell of a fight!'

A memory of Arlo filtered into his mind.

Ah, my friend, you advised me to learn was the easy bit. I did not accept that statement. However, as always, you were correct.

Taking a deep breath, he hugged Loki, then wept unashamedly. Five minutes later, he stood, stretched for the run home, then formed a thought.

And so begins the final chapter of the Cranson lineage...

'Nothing is mysterious – it either exists or it doesn't.'
Woodrow McKane.

Acknowledgements.

Writing a novel is not a singular action, as every author has an unpaid, devoted and patient team behind them. Without them we would struggle – absolutely!
During Beyond the Light, my team, once again, has risen to the challenge. Therefore, I tip my hat to the following sufferers.

Alison McDowell
Keith Hutchison
Dave Owen
Guy Keen
Billy Green
Loki Dokey
Ernie Doodles
Logan Berry

Team Woodrow - I love you all!